Never Trust a Sorcerer

Authored and Illustrated By:
L R Barrett-Durham

Never Trust a Sorcerer

All characters in this book are fictitious. Any resemblance to actual persons, living or dead, is purely coincidental.

Cover and Interior Art by L R Barrett-Durham
Published by L R Barrett-Durham

ISBN-13: 978-1463791483
ISBN-10: 1463791488

http://www.facebook.com/LRBarrettDurham

Dedication

For James and Patrick, the loves of my life

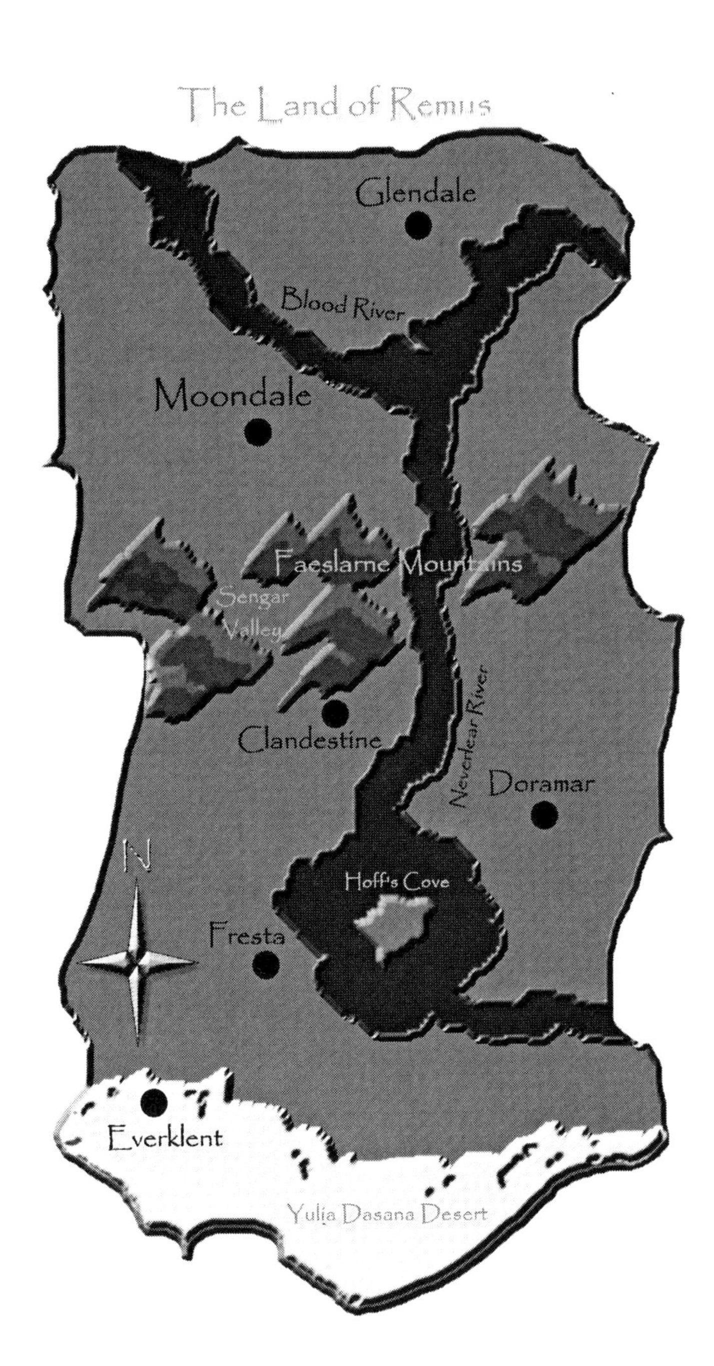

The Land of Remus
Glendale
Blood River
Moondale
Faeslarne Mountains
Sengar
Valley
Clandestine
Neverlear River
Doramar
N
Hoff's Cove
Fresta
Everklent
Yulia Dasana Desert

Prelude

Serra Bloodmoon sat straight up in bed, clutching her blanket as if it were her sword hilt. Her soaked, fiery hair flew wildly, and sweat and tears streamed down her ashen face. Her breath came in ragged gasps as she looked around her chamber, trying to gain her bearings.

It was a horrid nightmare, possibly the worst she had ever experienced. A dark figure had been haunting her dreams for a long time now, and it seemed that it drew closer every night.

She arose from her bed, perspiration pulling her already tight fitting nightgown closer to her slender figure.

"How long have I been having these dreams?" she asked herself as she walked across her dark chamber to the small wooden table close to the door. It had been at least a year, she knew. But recently the nightmares had grown more intense and real.

She picked up a white porcelain pitcher that had once been her mother's and poured some water into a crystal goblet. Taking a long drink, she walked slowly and quietly to her door. She cracked it slightly and peered into the torch lit hallway to see if she had disturbed anyone. All seemed quiet in the castle.

She lowered her goblet back to the table and ambled over to her bed. Still dazed from her restless night, she didn't notice the wetness of her blankets. As she laid in it again, she jumped from the now cold perspiration that soaked through to the goose-down mattress.

Her grogginess disappeared and she knew, no matter how hard she tried, sleep would not return this night. Judging by the pitch-black darkness out her window, it was still hours before dawn.

In a silent cry of defeat, she walked slowly to her chest, picked up her robe, and slid it on. The silky fibers of the cloth only intensified the chill that refused to go away.

She retrieved the candle on her bedside table and walked to her chamber door. Trying to be as quiet as possible, she stealthily wandered down the corridor to the staircase, stopping only to light her candle along the way. She made her way to the first floor, careful not to slip on the rug that descended the staircase.

As she came upon the water room door, she saw a guard turn the corner, and quickly went into the room before he could see her. The guard's identity was obvious to her just by the broadness of his chest and his tremendous height. Hildvar of the Elkhorn Tribe was been one of the most recent additions to Bloodmoon Castle. The outcast barbarian with the strength of ten had been granted asylum in the house when he had been injured in battle and left to die by his own people. He had shown his loyalty and fighting prowess right off, and had been granted officer status in the notorious Bloodmoon Brigade in only a few short months.

The barbarian, seeming to read her thoughts, opened the door just as Serra began pouring some water into a large bath basin.

"Oh, pardon me, my Lady. I did not mean to..." he stumbled in embarrassment, turning his back to her quickly, "I did not expect anyone was about at this time of night."

"It is quite alright, Hildvar. I am dressed. You may come in," Serra replied, pulling her robe more tightly around her.

Hildvar turned around apprehensively, staring at the floor. He was a great bit of a man, standing almost eight feet tall with a chest the width of two average men. Blonde locks of hair hung from his helm and he had eyes the shade of the ocean that seemed to brighten his tanned features.

"Did you have another nightmare, my Lady?" he asked nervously.

Hildvar never was much for leading up to anything, and he was rarely ever wrong. He had been increasing his passes by her bedroom door each night, knowing full well that the shuffling that always came from within was the girl being tormented by her dreams. He feared for her sanity.

"Nothing gets by you, does it Hildy?" she replied, as she picked up a bucket of bath water. She had adopted this nickname for him shortly after he had formally joined the Bloodmoon Brigade. It had been mainly to tease him. Barbarians normally would kill a woman for forsaking their name, but Hildvar had always been kindhearted to her.

"I worry about you, my Lady. These dreams have been coming more often in these past few months. Should I awaken your brother?" he asked in genuine concern, finally looking up at her.

"No!" she replied too loudly, nearly dropping the bucket. "I am sorry, no, please. I do not wish to worry my brother. Since our parent's death he has had enough on his shoulders than to worry with the likes of me."

Guilda and Frendar Bloodmoon had also died the day Moondale had been attacked by the barbarian army. It had broken the hearts of every member of the castle when they had been found murdered in the library directly after the battle had begun, thus infuriating the brigade and increasing their adrenaline by ten fold. Her brother, Renfar, had become Lord directly after, assuming a great deal of responsibility for one of only twenty-three years.

"You always have been the strong one, my Lady, but let me know if there's anything I can do," he said humbly, breaking her from the dreadful memories.

"They are dreams, and only dreams, but I do appreciate your concern. You may continue your duties," she replied, forcing a smile on her weary face and gesturing toward the door.

"Yes, my Lady," he replied, turning his broad form, walking out the door, and closing it behind him.

Serra bolted the door to prevent further intrusion and walked back over to her basin. She removed her robe and her nightgown and began to bathe away the memories of her dream and of the past. Washing away her fear, sadness, and wonder of what was to come the next night.

Chapter One
The Dark Dreams

Keifer stared out his window at the upcoming glory of another dawn. He watched in earnest as the two suns peaked over Denbar's Rise, a small part of the Faeslarne Mountains that stretched across the land. The sky suddenly brightened from the darkest black to beautiful shades of purple and blue, and he welcomed the rush of warm air that filled his chamber.

Bringing his glass of red wine to his lips, reflected in satisfaction over another long night of manipulation. The open mind of the young lass had been easy prey for many months now, and he could feel her beginning to resist his game. He had no worries; however, this only made it more challenging.

His hostility toward the young beauty had begun with her absolute revolt at his proposal of marriage a year before. When his master had made an offer he couldn't refuse, he began tormenting the girl with images of unworldly beings.

"Sir?" Fenlin Karling inquired. He had been looming in the doorway, watching his master welcome the dawn, and making note of his odd expressions as he consumed his wine.

Infuriated by the sudden intrusion, Keifer turned on his heels intent on scolding his servant. But his green eyes brightened considerably when he saw what lay in the man's hands.

"I beg you pardon the disturbance, but I knew that you had been waiting for this for some time."

Sight of the book made Keifer's palms sweat with eagerness. It was the spell book of Gyndless the Almighty, a spell book that any sorcerer would die to have. Though the runes of many of the spells had been deluded beyond recognition over the centuries, the few spells that remained were powerful indeed.

"Thank you, Fenlin. You have proven your worth to me today," he said with a wicked grin, reaching almost hungrily for the tome.

"Yes, Sir," he replied with an unsure smile, handing the book over, "Would you need anything else?"

"No, leave me, and I'll have no visitors, not even you, Fenlin. I must be alone with my thoughts," he said, caressing the book ever so carefully in his hands with a fanatical expression on his face.

Fenlin left the room without another word, and as soon as Keifer heard his descent, he mage locked the door with a wave of his hand and a muttered incantation.

Sitting cross-legged in front of his altar, he placed the book on a sheet of black velvet in front of him. Knowing his master would burn him alive if he attempted to open the book, he merely stared at it with longing.

He placed a hand on the worn, black cover and closed his eyes. The book's magical vibrations seethed through his hand like an earthquake. He only grinned and continued to connect with the book in the only way he was allowed.

Pleased with herself, Frelia put the pie in the hot oven and latched the door shut. She had been preparing her Lady's favorite dish: mincemeat pie. Hildvar had informed the little plump woman of the night's demons in the strictest of confidence. She, too, had taken the girl under her wing, fearing for her sanity as she heard the continuing tales of the vicious nightmares the girl suffered from.

The clerics in the castle had no answer for the girl, except that it was more than likely recessed feelings about the recent loss of her parents causing bad demons in her soul. Frelia didn't fall for that old trick though, that was just another way of them saying that they had no idea. All she knew to do was to make sure that the girl was taken care of.

Frelia stood erect and stopped what she was doing as the Lord of the castle wandered into the kitchen.

"Do ye need anythin', me Lord?" she asked, brushing back a lock of brown hair that had fallen out of the bun at the base of her neck.

Renfar rarely made it into the kitchen, not because he was too good to wander with the help, but because he was always so busy with other matters. Normally, Frelia would have had to bring his breakfast to his study, but this day he seemed relaxed, without a care in the world.

"Good morning, Frelia, what's in the oven?" he asked cheerily, with a spring in his step that she hadn't seen in months.

"Mincemeat pie, me Lord. Why aren' ye the light o' the day!" she exclaimed, clapping her hands together in excitement.

"Mincemeat pie, I'm glad I got here before Serra ate the whole thing. They are her favorite, you know?" he said, edging toward the oven.

Frelia grew solemn at the mention of Lady Serra.

"Aye, and a good thin' too, she'll be needin' some cheerin' up this morn," she replied before she could realize what she was saying. She made note of her error as soon as she saw the look on her Lord's face. It suddenly turned from the face of a cheery bright-eyed man to the worried face of an elder.

"What are you talking about, Frelia? Do not lie to me or there will be no extra pence for you this season!" he said loudly, with a scowl clearly etched on his face.

"Pardon me, me Lord, but I been sworn not ter say anything ter ye by the girl's wishes 'erself," she answered with fright, hating to disobey her master.

"It's the dreams, isn't it? I swear that something foul is about. She is having them all the time now! I must speak to her at once, Frelia, go fetch her now!" he demanded, his anger engulfing him and turning his face the shade of his fiery red hair.

Renfar loved his sister dearly, but it angered him that she would wish to hide something so important from him. He hated to make Frelia go back on her vow to the girl, but he honestly feared that soon his sister wouldn't wake from one of her dreams. He wasn't sure that he could live through the loss of another family member so soon after their parents' death.

"As ye wish, Lord Renfar," she gave in. She was sure that the barbarian would have her hide when he heard of this, but the fear of an eight-foot barbarian wasn't near the wrath of a Bloodmoon enraged. She left the room immediately and walked up the stairs to the girl's room.

Serra sat in the study pondering over her nightmare from the night before. As always, she could only remember the dark figure that loomed just out of reach and the sheer terror that made her feel like a frightened little girl

She could smell the mincemeat pie cooking at the other end of the castle. Despite the fact that the door was closed and the kitchen was quite a distance from the study, Frelia always had some way of making the aroma reach her nose.

A sudden commotion broke out from down the hall. She could hear the frantic opening and closing of doors, and a woman muttering incomprehensibly. The study door slammed open and Frelia entered, obviously in distress.

"Me Lady! There ye are! We been lookin' all over fer ye! Ye weren' in yer chamber, er the library! This was the last place I was goin' ter look before I notified the guards!" the little woman yelled, wringing her apron into a corkscrew.

"Have no fear, Frelia, I am alive and well. I smell the heavenly pie you have made this morning and can't wait to sink my teeth into it," Serra said with a smile.

She knew she must look awful. Having only slept an hour or two the night before, she could feel the swelling under her eyes from her lack of rest.

"Me Lady, ye do no' look well. Lord Renfar wishes to see ye. He is very worried," Frelia replied, noticing the bags under Serra's eyes and wondering when the girl had last had a good night's rest.

"Where is he now?" Serra asked with a dreading tone.

"Last I saw, he was in the kitchen about ter tear me 'ead off," Frelia said, fearing her next words, "Please, me Lady, do not bear ill will toward Hildvar, 'e did no' mean any harm by tellin' me o' last night's...er....event. It was me blasted tongue that slipped and told the master."

"That's quite all right, Frelia, it's not like he can't see it on my face," she said as she rose out of her overstuffed chair.

She walked over to the stocky little woman and gave her a hug.

"I don't know what I would do if you two didn't care for me so. I bear none of you ill will. So don't be worrying about that," she said and walked out the door without another word.

She made her way down the corridor slowly, not at all looking forward to the meeting with her brother. He would most likely tell her to keep her dreams to the family instead of worrying the staff, as well, but he never failed to surprise her in what he had to say. Their father was a loving man, but never knew how to show it. Her brother had inherited the same trait.

Taking a deep breath before entering the room, she walked in prepared to meet his angry eyes, but she found the kitchen empty. She could smell the pie strongly now, and hoped that Frelia would not let it burn to cinders before she made it back to the kitchen.

Having an idea of where to find him, she made her way to the staircase. She passed a few guards along the way. They just stopped, bowed, and waited for her to pass. Hildvar was really the only guard that she ever spoke to openly. The rest seemed to see her as a master like her brother. She wasn't exactly comfortable with that, but knew that it was a necessary evil.

Climbing one level, she walked to the first door along the vast hall. The door was cracked. She could hear movement in the room. As she peered in, she saw her brother muttering to himself, shuffling papers around on his desk. His short, red hair was disheveled and his forehead was drawn into a tight frown.

"Renfar," she said, walking in, "you wished to see me?"

He turned and gazed at his older sister with a concerned gloom about his face.

"Yes, Serra, please come in," he said, gesturing toward a stool next to his desk, "I wanted to talk to you."

He finished his shuffling and stood watching her every move.

"I feel like I am being interrogated," she said, watching him as well.

"I have no reason to interrogate you, but I do want to ask you something. Serra. How often are you having these nightmares of yours?" He asked with genuine concern.

"They come to me every night now," she replied uncomfortably.

"And what are they now? Still the dark figure and no further details?" He sat down in his chair and leaned back, still not taking his eyes off her.

"Yes. Same as before, but they are more intense now, like he is near, and seeking me out." She glanced at the floor, not wanting to look into her brother's eyes.

"I am worried about you. I feel that bad spirits are playing a role in this," he said as caringly as he could.

"Don't be, you have enough to worry about. They are just dreams Renfar, nothing more, nothing less," she replied, getting up from her stool, wishing to end this line of questioning immediately.

"Serra, you never talk to me anymore. Have these occurrences changed you so?" he asked, crossing his arms over his chest.

"Renfar, I appreciate your concern, but there really is nothing that can be done for these ghastly nightmares. I just have to sort them out myself," she said apprehensively.

"Serra," he said, stopping her as she began to clear the doorway.

"Yes?" she asked, without turning around.

"I think that you need to see Dretho the Mage."

The words her brother spoke struck fear into her heart, perhaps an equal fear to the terror she felt for the dark figure in her dreams. Dretho the Mage was one of the most feared in the land. He was renowned for making his captives quiver at the site of him until their hearts exploded with panic.

He was not an evil man as most mages of the realm were, but he was deadly. He was not kind, but had respect for the Bloodmoon family. A respect her father had won from the elf during the heat of battle. Despite the respect that he held for her, she had no desire to see the man.

"No," she said in a whisper of shock and denial.

Dretho paced patiently in front of one of his finest fighters. The man crouched low to the floor begging his master's forgiveness. The mage had to make a choice: punishment or death.

Praying for his life, the warrior did not dare look up to meet the man's eyes. Though the human towered over the elf normally, he knew the mage could kill him in an instant snap of his fingers. If Julian were to make any false moves, his life would more than likely end that way. He continued his prayer to the God of Drakevin, the deity that the mage worshipped, in hopes that the elf would take some pity on him.

Just as the mage raised his hand to allow the warrior to leave, there was a knock at his door.

"Enter," he said simply, noting that the warrior continued his endless groveling.

"You have a visitor, Your Greatness," Bern Hilda, the fearless, brunette dwarf said as she entered the doorway. "It is the young girl of the Bloodmoon family."

Intrigued, Dretho kicked the warrior and gestured for him to leave. Not making any arguments, Julian scrambled for the door, nearly knocking the woman over in the process.

"Is it Lorna or Serra?" Dretho asked simply.

"Serra, I believe."

"Curious," the elf said with a puzzled expression.

Serra Bloodmoon had been the last person he had ever expected to enter his domain, much less come to him for a visit. The Bloodmoon family had been his only diplomatic ally for all his three hundred years. It seemed like yesterday that the girl's father had saved his life. It was an unexpected chain of events even to the wise mage.

The Battle of Sengar Valley had been a brutal one. The vast elven army nearly wiped out by mountain giants from the east.

At first the mage had thought the Bloodmoon Brigade had come to fight with the giants. When the fearless Lord Bloodmoon took a particularly large giant down in a single stroke of his magical scimitar, just as the creature was about to end the mage's life, he knew otherwise.

Dretho had been so preoccupied in the casting of a spell that he did not notice the huge beast raising a boulder above his head. The fierce Bloodmoon had saved his life, and the mage was forever indebted to him, even in his offspring.

"Send her in immediately and see that we are not bothered during her stay!" he said in such a demanding voice, even the brave Bern Hilda quickened her pace to seek out the girl.

Serra was not enthused about the meeting. Her brother had all but ordered her to see the mage.

Even Serra and her iron will could not escape the fact that the mage would probably be her only hope in finding the source of these nightmares.

Dretho's tower was a tall, black monolith. You could not see any windows from the outside. It just appeared to be as a large black column shooting up from the ground. It had two great double doors at its base, and as far as anyone knew, that was the only entrance, or escape.

Once inside the tower, a staircase spiraled the walls of a great foyer, and it seemed to have no ceiling. It was so dark inside that it seemed the stairs continued forever up the walls.

When she saw the little dwarf descending the staircase in a mad rush, her stomach churned with dread.

"The master wishes to see you immediately," she said, out of breath.

Serra, finding her booted feet heavier than she could ever remember, followed the woman obediently up the stairway. After rising three hundred feet, the stairway flattened out into a long corridor with an enormous, elaborately decorated door at the end. Serra knew that she had not seen any leveling out from the bottom floor. It seemed that there was more magic to the place than met the eye.

Bern Hilda seemed to quicken her pace at the sight of the door, pumping her little, short legs so hard that even Serra had trouble keeping up.

"I will leave you now," she said, and without another word, she departed and headed toward the staircase.

Serra knocked lightly on the enormous door, noticing carvings of beasts and runes unfamiliar to her.

The door opened to reveal an altar room flowing with ornate tapestries and with lush pillows scattered about. The mage stood at the only window in the room, with his back to her. His long black hair met his waist. His black flowing robes seemed to blend so well with it, you could not tell where his hair ended and the robes began.

"Why do you come, young Serra?" he asked, not turning around.

"My brother has sent me to seek your help with a problem that I have," she said reluctantly, moving to the center of the room.

One end of the room held a wall size bookcase with tomes so dusty that even the sight of them would make a person sneeze. On the other end was a statue of a god unknown to her, with offerings of herbs and wine scattered about its base. In the center of the room were an altar with lit candles and an open book dominating its top.

The mage turned to gaze upon the young woman that he hadn't seen in nearly ten years.

Expecting to see a young girl, the beauty before him took him aback. Hair like fire hung to her waist, complimenting the emerald green eyes that were like her father's. She was not dressed in the usual gown décor of royalty, but the studded leather armor of a warrior ready for battle.

"You have grown well, Serra," he said with a slight smile.

Serra wondered if anyone else had ever seen a smile on the elf's face.

"Thank you," she said uncomfortably.

"Please, sit with me and tell me of your woes," he said, gesturing to a small table in the center of the room, surrounded by plush pillows.

The mage walked over and sat down on a large, red cushion, not taking his eyes off of her.

She slowly made her way and sat down in front of him, uncomfortable being so close to the vile man. She did not take off her sword; however, she merely raised it so that she would not sit on it.

"You need not be scared, Serra, your people have been kind to me over the years and your father saved my life," he said, sensing her apprehension.

"My father spoke very highly of you as we were growing up, but I must ask you mage, where were you when my father was brutally killed?" Serra asked, avoiding his gaze. This question had been bothering her for a year and was the main source of her anger and discomfort toward him.

The mage sat silent for a few minutes.

"Is that why you hate me as you do? You think that I could have prevented your father's death?" He was not angry. In fact, he had also asked himself the same question.

Not waiting for an answer, he said, "Serra, the loss of your father took a great toll on me. I have often wondered what I could have done to prevent it. The attack on your castle was so swift and fierce that even the likes of me could not have prevented it. When I first heard of the event, your parents were already dead. An investigation that I took upon myself proved that they were dead before the battle even began. Do not blame yourself, or me. The dealer of fate dealt them an evil hand indeed."

He sat back and watched the girl as his words sunk in.

Serra stared pensively at the elf and felt guilt rise within her chest.

All this time she had blamed him personally for the death of her parents. While in the recesses of her mind, she had always known he was miles away. Though he was renowned as being powerful, she knew he could never have been there in time. His reputation as such a horrible person had played on her emotions and had drawn her to this conclusion.

Though as she looked at him now, she noticed how handsome this ancient elf was. His angular face was stern, yet his golden eyes held a depth that was intriguing. He only seemed in his late thirties by human standards, but she knew he was at least ten times that.

"I have bore you ill will over the past year mage, but your words to me today have shown me that you are not the defiant man I have always thought you to be. Please accept my truest apologies, Dretho, for I have wronged you." Serra admitted softly.

The mage remained quiet for a moment, feeling something that he had not felt in hundreds of years: compassion.

"You are forgiven. Let us not dwell on the past any further, and let us look to the present. Tell me of your problem."

Serra straightened her posture and looked the mage directly in the eye. His skin was a light shade of brown, and his dark hair could not cover the distinct points of his ears, marking clearly his race.

"I have been having nightmares for many months now, dreadful dreams of a dark figure."

After she stated this, the mage noticed the purple bags under the girl's eyes and knew that her words were true.

Chapter Two
The Answer

Serra and Dretho spent many hours together. The mage knew that a sorcerer had to be involved. He tried all the disenchant and remove curse spells he knew, but nothing broke the hold of the sorcerer.

"I only have one other option, Serra," the mage said in defeat.

"What is that?" she asked in exhaustion.

"I need you to sleep in my presence," he said, sensing her exhaustion.

"In your presence?" Serra asked in outrage.

She still barely trusted the mage awake, much less asleep. Though she trusted him now more than ever before, she was a very wary person as a whole and did not like tempting fate.

"Yes, this way I may be able to determine the source of the entity causing your discomfort. If he enters your mind, I will find him," he said simply, "It's our last option."

Serra eyed him for several moments and then sighed in exasperation.

"Very well," she agreed, "Where shall I go?"

"You require sustenance. Stay here and I will fetch Bern Hilda. Rest, dear girl, but pray you don't fall asleep before my return," he warned, rising gracefully from his pillow and heading toward the door.

Left with her thoughts, she realized just how tired and emotionally drained she was. She had never experienced so much magic used on her at one time. Though they were harmless on her part, she felt the depletion of her energy profoundly.

She sat unmoving on the silk pillow that she had been perched upon for hours. At least in the presence of the dark figure in her dreams, she was allowed some sort of rest, but the endeavors of the mage were relentless. As soon as she began to recover from one spell, he would already be chanting another using the dusty books from the bookcase.

The huge door swung open, tearing her from her thoughts. Bern Hilda walked into the room and motioned for her to rise.

"Lady Serra, your dinner awaits you in the dining room," she said, gesturing toward the door.

Serra found it hard to force her aching bones to move. She began to rise slowly and in realizing that her legs had gone numb, quickly plopped back down.

"Bern Hilda, it looks like my dinner may be waiting a few more moments," she said defeatedly.

The dwarf gazed upon her intently, waiting for her to stand.

Serra sat there trying her best to stop the endless tingles in her legs, knowing well that the woman was growing impatient.

"Bern Hilda, I'm sorry, but you are just going to have to wait."

"Begging your pardon, my Lady, but the master is waiting."

"Well, he is just going to have to wait!" she shouted, growing angry.

Bern Hilda remained where she stood and after a few tense minutes, Serra finally rose from her position.

Avoiding the angry gaze of the dwarf, they made their way down the corridor, and descended the staircase. As they reached the bottom floor, Bern Hilda crossed the enormous foyer to a door opposite the staircase that Serra had not noticed before. She opened the door to a lavish dining room lit with hundreds of candles. At the end of a long table sat Dretho, sipping a glass of wine.

"Bern Hilda, leave us," he snapped.

The dwarf left the room and shut the door behind her.

"Please Serra, sit down," he said kindly.

The table was covered with elaborate dishes of various roots and fruit lying in colorful sauces. A wart hog lay in the center with the traditional apple wedged into its maw. She noticed it was not cooked, but lay there with its throat slit and bleeding onto the platter.

Serra sat down at the opposite end of the table, putting as much distance between her and the carcass as possible.

"I hope you aren't growing disheartened," he said as he put his napkin in his lap.

"I am just wondering if all this is worth the effort," she admitted, looking down at her plate.

Keifer stared out his window as he had done many nights before. He had felt odd all afternoon, as if there were a disturbance in the magical bond he kept with Serra. Sipping on his glass of red wine, he pondered the relic that had fallen into his hands that day. The book had stayed with him, even after hiding it behind a large painting in his room. He figured that it could be the only reason for the disturbance. Even now, he felt it's incessant pull.

He turned and walked to a chair in the center of the room and sat down.

Relaxation was the key for what he was about to attempt. He had grown used to the long nights, but knew that this night would be tougher on him. With no rest that day, he worried if he would be able to perform at peak level.

Splaying his long legs over the arm of the overstuffed chair, he leaned back into its lush comfort. It would be at least another hour before the girl slumbered. He patiently awaited the darkness of her dreams.

Though the meal was mostly spent in silence, Serra felt more comfortable with the mage. She appreciated how relentlessly he had pursued her resolution. The meal had renewed her strength a little, but she still felt the weariness in her bones.

Dretho had encouraged her to remain vigilant and that if there were a way to be found, they would find it. She tried to keep her head high, hoping that the mage would not notice her lethargy.

They had returned to the altar chamber directly after dinner, and Serra now sat cross-legged as she had before on her lush floor pillow. The mage sat across from her, meditating to gather his thoughts. She remained silent, eyeing the mage curiously.

Serra had been trained as a fighter and knew little of the ways of magic, though years of living in Bloodmoon Castle had made her more comfortable with it. She was not thrilled at the thought of this next spell. Sleeping in the presence of a man had been something she had never known. She knew that it would not entail the normal aspect of it, but nevertheless, she was uncomfortable.

The mage opened his gaze to her and asked, "Are you ready for sleep?"

"Yes," she said, wondering how she could go about the act while sitting upright on a pillow.

Sensing her thoughts, the mage rose and gestured for her to do the same. Serra obeyed and stood, awaiting further instruction.

The elf waved his hand and muttered under his breath. The bookcase disappeared with a glow of purple sparks, revealing a bedchamber. She hesitantly followed the mage into the room.

The walls were lined with silk tapestries of old, showing various magicians in the act of battle. She took an extra interest in one of them, recognizing her father's face immediately. He was in midair, with his scimitar raised high above his head, obviously about to crash down on a huge giant. Dretho stood in front of the creature oblivious to the danger behind him. Her hand absently went to the hilt of her father's scimitar on her hip.

"That was a day that I will never forget," the mage said from behind her, making her jump in surprise. "Your father was one of the bravest men I have ever known. Human's are not known to aid an elf in such a situation."

He stared at her for a long moment, "Shall we begin?" he asked quietly.

"What shall I do?" she asked, eyeing the bed.

"What you always do, go to bed. Do not worry. I will not be joining you, nor will I rest this night. Would you like more suitable attire, or are you comfortable like that?" he asked, looking at her leather armor and her sword by her side.

Her armor was like a second skin to her, and now she noticed how she must appear to him. She quickly removed her sword belt containing her sheathed daggers and scimitar, along with her pouches containing healing potions and various other items of worth.

The mage muttered under his breath again, and a red nightgown appeared in his hand. He handed the nightgown to Serra, taking her belt. He pointed to a changing screen in the corner of the room.

Serra walked behind the black screen and began undressing when a thunderous knock came from the door in the other room.

Furious, the mage cursed and walked out of the bedchamber. Serra strained her ears to hear what was said, but the unannounced visitor was being very hushed about the news.

Serra redressed herself as she heard Dretho enter the room. She stepped out from the behind the screen still clad in her armor. The look on the mage's face was overwrought with despair.

The flustered mage gestured to a chair and said, "Please sit, I am afraid I have terrible news."

Serra thought she saw moisture in the corners of his golden eyes.

Keifer grew impatient as the night grew longer. The girl must have been asleep by now, but each time he tried to initiate his evil plot, all he felt was a null void.

"I wonder if she has found a way to counter my spells," he muttered to himself.

Knowing that his master would have his head if he didn't follow through, he waited no longer. Keifer went to his window and called upon the God of Justar and sent his message to the girl with a new spell of enchantment. This spell being stronger than any he had dared impose on her before.

Serra sat in earnest as the mage gathered his thoughts and cleared his throat.

"Serra, something terrible has happened," he said, looking into her emerald green eyes.

"Good God, man, tell me before I explode!" she exclaimed, growing impatient.

Dretho merely looked at her for a long moment and said, "Your brother has been murdered, and your sister, kidnapped," he said, feeling the pain of Frendar's death all over again.

Serra stood up and her eyes suddenly glazed over. She screamed in agony, pushing her palms into her temples, and squeezing her eyes shut. Just as her scream faded into a whisper, she fell to the floor, completely unconscious.

Hildvar stood in the immense chamber at the bottom floor of the tower. Still not accustomed to buildings, the barbarian marveled at the height of the ceiling.

Noticing movement out of the corner of his eye, he watched as a robed elf descended the stairs that spiraled along the great walls.

"I come for the rightful master of Moondale," he said, extending his broad chest to intimidate the elf.

"I am afraid that she is in a deep sleep that I can not bring her out of," Dretho said sadly, waiting at any moment for the barbarian to draw his axe.

Hildvar noticed the look of discomfort on the elf's face.

"Is this of your doing?" Hildvar asked, growing nervous.

"No, I am afraid it is a spell from the same creature that has been causing her nightmares."

They stared at each other for a long moment. The mage admired the young man's brute form and his obvious determination to help the girl.

"I wish to see her," he said simply.

Dretho turned without another word and led him upstairs to a long corridor. Hildvar grew more nervous as they closed on a huge carved door. Barbarians, as a rule, did not practice magic, and were very afraid of what they did not understand. He had felt very uneasy the moment he had entered the tower, and this door and the runes carved upon it sent shivers up his spine.

They entered an altar room and turned. As they entered another room with a huge bed in the center, the barbarian gasped. Serra lay on the blankets, still in her armor with her sword belt by her side. A painful expression was bathed over her face, one of sheer torment and distress.

Hildvar went quickly to her side, placing her sweaty hand in his own.

"Serra, awaken!" he thundered, but a hand on his shoulder calmed him instantly.

"There is no point, my friend, she will not awaken," the elf replied as he removed his hand from the extensive shoulder. "I need to be alone with her now, for this may be our only chance to discover the one who is responsible."

Hildvar was reluctant to leave the vulnerable girl, but obeyed and went into the altar room, never taking his eyes off the large bed.

Dretho stood over Serra, awaiting movement. A few minutes passed before she began to toss and turn. She moaned in agony as the mage took her hand. He began a counter spell to deflect the images being sent to her mind.

He concentrated on the signal, sent a blast of power along that thin thread, and felt the hold begin to weaken.

Many miles away Keifer felt the incoming force and increased his concentration. Never before had she put up a fight like this, even with the weaker spells he had performed.

The battle for his hold became almost impossible. Shades of purple and blue formed around his body as he stood trembling beside the window. Keifer used every bit of energy he had just to keep the connection, no longer bothering with the images of the dark figure.

Beads of sweat began to pour from his forehead as he strained to keep his hold. He could see a light coming toward him and tried to push back. It was no use, as the light grew ever closer, he fell to the floor, not moving.

Chapter Three
The Sorrow

Serra and Hildvar mounted their horses to make the long journey home. She was still quite exhausted from the day before, but when Dretho had fended off the sorcerer, she was left to sleep soundly throughout the night. Probably the soundest she had ever slept.

Dretho had advised them that the signal was coming from a city toward the east, but he could not discover the exact source. He had promised to try to find the sorcerer, but the dreams were the least of her worries now.

Hildvar had explained to her that a few hours after she had left the castle a dark figure had emerged, killing her brother, and taking her sister with him. Renfar and Lorna had been in the dining room alone while Hildvar had stood guard at the door.

All had been quiet when suddenly he had heard Lorna scream. By the time he had made it into the room, Renfar lay dead with his head in his plate, and he could make out a fading dark figure holding Lorna in his arms. The figure was gone before he could get to her, vanishing into thin air.

The clerics that resided at Bloodmoon Castle could not make heads or tales of what had caused Renfar's death, but they had not waited before burying him in the garden beside his parents.

Dretho stood beside her horse, "I suggest you go to Clandestine, it is the nearest city to the east. That is the only place this sorcerer could be," he said, handing her a pouch of dried meat and a skin of water.

"I know a magic user that lives in Clandestine," she said with a rush of memories of the year before, when she had been proposed to by a treacherous man in hopes to join their two territories.

"No doubt you should go there and speak with him," he said.

He feared for the young woman's sanity through these trials. She appeared to be fine as she sat upon her mare with her scarlet hair blowing in the wind.

"Thank you for your help, Dretho, surely our next meeting will not be so unpleasant," she said, taking his hand with a smile on her face.

"Go now. May your journey be swift and safe." With that, he patted her horses behind, and they began their long journey.

Hildvar stared at Serra, trying to decipher what she was thinking. He admired her strength. She would make a fine leader to the people of Moondale. Though it were not a custom that a woman be the master of the territory, Serra was the oldest, and the only Bloodmoon left besides her younger sister, Lorna. Lorna was still just a girl of thirteen and was more interested in dressing in fine clothes and playing in the garden. Serra, unlike her sister, had gone through years of training to be a ruler, and warrior.

In the battle for Bloodmoon Castle, Hildvar had witnessed first hand the deadliness of her blade.

"Do you remember when we first laid eyes on each other, my Lady?" he asked, recalling that day well.

Serra thought for a moment and also recalled the memory. The barbarians had taken over the castle, breaking through the main portcullis with a huge battering ram. She had joined in the battle against the wishes of her brother. She had stormed into the courtyard, scimitar in hand, and slashed across the chest of the first barbarian she had seen, which ironically had been Hildvar.

"Yes, I do," she said, gazing at the barbarian with a smirk on her face. "What about it?"

"I still have a scar you know, so you don't have to worry about me ever forgetting that day. The day your people showed me kindness I did not know possible," he said, looking to the horizon. They were trotting along a narrow path between spurts of elms and oaks. The two suns hung high in the sky making the air warm and humid.

"You should be glad that you lived to allow it to heal," she said laughing.

She knew that he was making an attempt to give her courage. By reminding her of the day she had wounded him, he was not trying to remind her of more deaths that day, but of the appreciation he felt for her in not ending his life and instead taking him as a prisoner of war. He had only spent a few days in the dungeons shackled to the wall, but they had healed him with their magic, and they had fed him better than he had eaten in the week it had taken to march to Moondale.

It had been a harsh winter. His clan had had no food and could not hope to survive out until the spring when a sorcerer came to their rescue with herds upon herds of livestock.

In order to receive these gifts, they had agreed to take Bloodmoon Castle and hold it until the sorcerer could arrive. They had readily agreed and had left the women, children and elderly to tend the cattle while they marched for conquest. Along the way they had been granted a half loaf of bread and a goblet of mead a day until they reached Moondale.

"It will make you thirst for their blood more. It will make you fight harder," the sorcerer had said, when they whimpered on edge of starvation. They should've quit while they were ahead and killed the sorcerer in the plains.

"I am truly sorry for what my people did that day, but we were all lead astray by an evil man that had taken over our minds. I actually think that your wound to me was what broke the curse."

Serra thought hard about his words and decided that it was possible.

"Who was the man that misled you, Hildy?"

"Jarmassad Truth was his name," he said.

"Where does he reside?" she asked growing more curious.

Before Hildvar could answer, he saw movement to his right out of the corner or his eye. Serra saw it too.

They barely had enough time to get their weapons drawn when two goblins ran out of the woods at them. Serra watched as the feeble creatures tried to swipe the barbarian from his horse, only to be mortified as his huge axe cut them both down in a swift comfortable motion. The small, green creatures both lay dead on the ground, decapitated.

"We must go," he yelled, "goblins do not usually travel in small numbers, and I have no doubt there are more about." He kicked his horse hard, and as they both rode on, they could see just less than a score of the little creatures running after them, deserting their hiding places in the bushes along the road.

Serra drew her scimitar and donned her rarely used shield and looked to Hildvar for any hint that he would slow to take the attack head on, but he only kicked his horse harder.

Hildvar had no fear that they could take the group by themselves, but with his company being the present ruler of his home, and with the other likely dead, he was taking no chances on her life.

Serra had a different idea. She stopped her horse in mid run and faced the oncoming group. Hildvar abruptly stopped his horse, staring in awe, and quickly rode to her side. They both dismounted simultaneously and stood side by side in front of their horses.

Four of the goblins fled at the sight of the huge man, but the rest came on. Wearing only leather armor and carrying wooden swords, they surrounded them quickly.

Serra displayed her skills immediately to the doubting man as she swung her scimitar with skill, blocking with her small shield. Two goblins ran up to her fast, preferring the weaker foe, and thrust at her quickly with their swords. Before Hildvar could look over his shoulder to check her position, she had already impaled both goblins and seemed to have no injuries.

With renewed vigor, he struck at a close goblin that was unsuccessfully trying to climb up his leg and quickly dispatched it with a wide arc of his axe through the top of its head. It fell limply to the ground, only to have another stand on top of its carcass trying to get closer.

Serra found that they were not formidable foes for they lacked strategy and only swung wildly in hopes that they would hit their target. She dispatched several more with ease.

She raised her scimitar high in the air and sang the Bloodmoon battle cry:

"You should fear our fire and fury,
For know it will seal your doom,
We are the red and mighty,
Fear the wrath of the Bloodmoon's!"

As soon as she finished, her scimitar seemed to gain a mind of its own. It leapt from her hand and began an odd sort of dance, slashing and thrusting at the remaining goblins. The three that faced Serra stood dumbfounded to the spot, watching the sword weave its dance. Within minutes they were dead.

The remaining two turned and ran when their weapons were destroyed and the dancing scimitar attacked them as well. Serra watched as it impaled one goblin, sending him end over end to land in a heap in the road. The scimitar seemed to be struggling to pull out of the beast. Finally it gave in and disappeared in a plume of red smoke. Serra's jaw dropped as she feared she would never see her father's sword again. Then she felt a tug at her left hip. She looked down to see the scimitar had returned to its sheath.

She looked up to see the last remaining goblin running as fast as it's spindly legs would carry it. It was screeching an awful, gut-wrenching wail the whole way. Serra watched it until it disappeared into the brush.

She felt a hand on her shoulder and looked up to see Hildvar staring at her in awe.

"I know not what you did to cause such a thing to happen, but glad I am that you did," he said with a smile.

They only looked at each other and galloped toward Moondale without another word.

Keifer sat upright. As the room spun before him, he began to realize what had happened. He looked down and noticed that he only wore his nightshirt and lay in his own bed. Someone must have carried him there with full knowledge of what had happened.

There was a knock at the door. Keifer struggled to speak, but could not. His normally booming voice came out as just a whisper.

Fenlin walked into the room with a tray of bread and water. He had short blonde hair and eyes that were black as coal. He wore the standard tunic and breeches that were common to servants. He figured his master would still be unconscious from the night before. He looked up expecting to see Keifer lying there and nearly dropped the tray when he saw his master's scowl.

"I beg your pardon, sir!" he exclaimed, stopping in his tracks and standing to attention.

"Who...." Keifer cleared his throat. "Who brought me here?"

"I did, master," Fenlin said, not moving.

Keifer attempted to rise from his bed only to sit down quickly from the nausea taking him over. He put his head between his knees and attempted to fight the bile back down his gullet.

Fenlin walked slowly and quietly to the bedside table and placed the tray in the center.

"Do you need anything, sir?" Fenlin asked, coming to his master's side. He placed his hand on Keifer's shoulder, trying to comfort him.

"Water," he said simply.

Fenlin quickly retrieved the glass of water from the table and brought it over to the weak man. He was careful sitting on the bed, trying his best not to disturb the sorcerer too much.

"Here, sir," he said softly, handing the glass to Keifer.

The man drank hungrily. He gulped the water down, ignoring the vertigo developing around him. He finished the glass and looked up. The room began to turn circles in front of him and he fell back onto the bed, unconscious once again.

The arrival home was not the normal celebration that a Lady would receive. The guards and servants seemed to drag their feet as they continued their duties throughout the castle.

The weather was just as dreary as the mood. The sky threatened bad weather with billowing black clouds covering the two suns and making everything seem a dull blue-gray.

"It's like my parents' death all over again," Serra said, as she sat upon her horse. They passed through the courtyard and made a right, heading for the stables at the southwest corner of the grounds.

"Aye, my Lady, they'll not likely recover any time soon. Nor will the rest of us."

He turned on his mount and eyed her curiously. Hildvar had always thought the woman very strong and brave. But now, as she looked upon her people passing by, she looked like a scared, little girl hiding in a tree.

"I don't know what to do, Hildvar. Lorna must be found, but I know that only I can find her," she said, dismounting her horse and handing her reigns to the stable master.

Leaving her horse and Hildvar behind, she strolled absentmindedly to the southern garden.

As she entered through a trellis and past a few rows of flowers, the site was almost too much to bear. Three tombstones stood in the center of a circular row of stone benches. Flowers and offerings of mourning scattered the still freshly turned earth of one of the graves.

Serra slowly walked into the circle, trying hard to hold her composure. She was careful not to step on any of the precious gifts and found a clear spot, falling down to her knees.

She had not cried like this since her parents' death, but now the tears flowed freely. She jerked and shook as the horror finally sunk in. She was alone in the world without her sister now. And she was now the ruler of the land that was her home.

It was like the whole world was crashing down on her shoulders. She had never before realized the impact of what Renfar had to resume after the death of their parents.

A sudden flash of blue-green lightning made a brilliant display across the sky. Serra winced at the booming sound of thunder. As she looked up, the rain began to pour. Serra didn't make any attempt to get out of the rain. She only sat there drowning in her own sorrow.

Chapter Four
The Quest

Frelia stood in the kitchen staring at the rations she had laid out. Hildvar and Serra would be leaving this morning to see Keifer in Clandestine.

She feared for Serra. Keifer had proposed marriage to her the year before in hopes of combining their domains. Renfar had been all for the wedding, but Serra had refused. In the end, Keifer had admitted to the plan of taking over completely and killing every Bloodmoon in the castle. He was lucky to get away with his life. He had vanished after his confession. It was said that he now lived in Clandestine.

Renfar had sent many groups of the Bloodmoon Brigade in search of the traitor, but none were ever successful in tracking him down. Serra had begged Renfar to let it go. She had told him that it had been his idea in the first place. Serra disliked Keifer, but she knew that he had made the declaration in anger because she would not take his hand. If she were going to marry, it would be for love, not for land.

Hildvar walked into the room just as Frelia began putting the items in a backpack.

"Well met, Frelia," he said with little enthusiasm.

"Why Hildvar, ye look as if a wagon ran o'er ye, have ye had any sleep?" she cried as she saw his exhausted expression. Tremendous bags hung under the barbarian's blue-gray eyes. He tried to smile, but despite his young age, he looked one hundred years old.

"I haven't slept, Frelia," he said, reaching into the cupboard for a small loaf of bread.

"Oh dear, please tell me yer no' havin' dreams like the missus, are ye?" she asked, her brown eyes going wide.

"No, nothing like that. I've been trying my best to keep an eye on Lady Serra. I've just started putting a chair outside her door. I spoke with the Captain. He cleared that it was all right to do so. She has not slept since we arrived. I think she fears she will not wake. She paced her chambers the entire night, crying," he said, cutting a few slices from the bread with a large butcher knife.

"Well, ye need yer health, Hildvar! Ye can't be puttin' yerself out like this, or ye'll be no good to her," she proclaimed, closing the tie on the last backpack and picking them up to take to the stable master.

"I'll rest when I know she's safe," he said, taking a huge mouthful. He watched as Frelia left the room and absently rubbed his eyes with his large fingers. Today would be very hard on him, but he knew it would be harder still on Serra.

Serra slid her leather bracers onto her wrists and clasped her red cloak about her neck. She glanced in her mirror and sighed. She knew that she was doing her people a disservice for abandoning them just after the death of her brother, but if she did not try to find Lorna, she knew she would never forgive herself. She looked at herself once again. She had tied her red hair in a ponytail to keep it away from her eyes and had donned a studded leather scull cap. Her armor fit her well, though it was thick and strong as any, it hugged her curves evenly. It had been tailored this way for freedom of movement.

Her eyes wandered to her scimitar.

Her father's sword had been forged by elves in Sengar Valley. He had always been rather fond of elves, which she could only presume was why Dretho drew his attention those years ago. Elves were not very numerous, but they were loyal and very secretive about their way of life. Not many would dare oppose an elven clan. They were fierce and bred to fight at a very young age.

Along the blade were runes that Serra had never understood. She had claimed the sword after her father's death, as she too had been trained to use a scimitar. She had used the sword several times, but it had never seemed to do anything extraordinary until the day before in the battle with the goblins.

She had begun training at age twelve against the protests of her mother.

"She should be in gowns going to balls and playing with dolls," her mother had said, "not dilly dallying with a sword she'll never use."

How wrong her mother had been. Since the age of sixteen, Serra had always taken her place on the front lines of any skirmish that came against the castle. She had never been afraid to take up arms and had never been fond of dressing in gowns. In fact, the only time she had ever really bothered was when Keifer had made his appearance. Renfar had been insistent that she be dressed like a Lady, even if she wasn't going to act like one.

She tore her gaze away from the mirror and walked over to her bed to the note that lay there.

My Dearest Friends,

It is clear to me now that I must go alone to find Lorna. It is the only way I will find her alive. Please forgive me for my absence. Renfar's scribe, Gallo Suntrestle, is to handle political matters while I am away. Renfar trusted him explicitly, and so shall I.

Captain Gnarl Knottytrunk, your orders are to defend the castle at all costs and to await my return. If I am not back in a month's time, send Hildvar to summon Dretho to take control of the castle. I trust he will rule with an iron fist, but better that than a giant horde. Please show him this letter and ask him to be kind to my people.

Be well and I will return soon,

Serra Bloodmoon
Lady of Moondale

She quietly walked to the end of the corridor, which ended in a wall of stone. She knew that stealth was her ally in this quest. An army of the Bloodmoon Brigade behind her would not likely be very stealthy. She glanced around to make sure no one was about and tapped two stones with her dagger.

The wall of stone swung backward to expose a secret staircase. She walked down the stairs a few steps and pulled the lever to put the wall back into its proper position.

The steps leveled out to a dark corridor lit only by very small openings where stones were intentionally left out for circulation. She walked for a few minutes before coming to another wall as unremarkable as the first.

"*Bloodmoon incentra,*" she chanted softly.

A shimmering golden pinpoint of light immerged from the wall and broadened to an oval portal the size of a man. She gazed into the golden oval and saw the stables on the southern side of the castle. People walked back and forth, going about their business, oblivious that they were being seen. She saw Frelia leave the stables with a distressed look upon her face. She waited for several moments until she could see no one about. Stepping through the portal, she immerged on the other side of the wall, and immediately crouched beside a large shrub. She quickly made her way to the stables.

She checked again for passersby and walked to the second stall where Gypsy, her black mare, awaited. The horse was already saddled and tacked for the road, as were the rest of the horses. She knew the warriors that were to accompany her were in the castle, finalizing procedure.

After making sure she had all her provisions, she climbed into the saddle. Gypsy lovingly nipped her leg as they backed out of the stall and crept to the entrance.

They would have to be quick. There was a dense forest just to the south, which conveniently came out to the main road if you knew the way. There were still no people in sight. Serra kicked Gypsy into a run and they dashed for southern portcullis that led the forest.

Only the two sentries at the portcullis had seen them go out, and they thought nothing of it since it was only Serra. They quickly slowed once they were out of sight of the castle wall and into the forest. The trees were very close together and Serra did not want to risk Gypsy stumbling on a root.

She dismounted fairly quickly as they plodded through the underbrush. Not many people ventured in, and it had been a long time since Serra had mustered the strength to take a leisure walk. However, she had spent much of her childhood in these woods and knew them like the back of her hand.

They traveled for nearly an hour when the woods ended at a dirt road. She mounted Gypsy and they ran along the eastern path toward Clandestine and hopefully, Lorna.

Hildvar arrived at the door to Serra's chambers and knocked softly. He had been in a meeting with the Captain and other Lieutenants of the brigade. They had decided to keep Serra in the middle of their march, to keep her safe, as they walked briskly to Clandestine. Upon arrival, Serra was never to be left alone, and to never have less than four bodyguards at any given time.

No answer came from within, so he knocked more loudly this time. He waited a few more minutes before turning the knob. The room was deserted but a note lay on the bed.

Hildvar hurried over to the bed, praying to Galstat that she had not been kidnapped. After seeing the loopy signature at the bottom of the note, he breathed a sigh of relief. But as he read the contents of the letter, he felt anger rising in his chest. He grunted in protest, ran out of the room, and down the stairs to notify the Captain.

Frelia entered the foyer just as he was running out the doors. Noticing the distressed look on his face, she dropped her basket of bed sheets, and scurried behind him.

"Hildvar, where are ye goin' in such a tizzy? Ye're to be leaving soon with the missus aren' ye?" she asked, quickly running out of breath.

Hildvar did not slow, but instead yelled, "She's gone! The Lady has gone off by herself to find Lady Lorna!"

Frelia stopped in her tracks, wide eyed. She fell to her knees in the dirt.

The Captain slammed his fist down on the table. "How coul' she do such a blasted stupid thin'?" he yelled.

"I know not, Captain," Hildvar replied, still standing to attention.

"I swear, if anyone harms a hair on 'er head, it'll be the hell ter pay!"

Captain Gnarl Knottytrunk looked as if he were ready to burst with rage. He was a dwarf with fire red hair and a mean disposition. Everyone thought that it was fitting he was the Captain of the Bloodmoon Brigade as he had the hair and temperament of the Bloodmoon family.

"What are your orders, Captain?" Hildvar asked rather stiffly.

"Gather twenty men and get on the road now ter Clandestine. She can' have gone far. I realize she's the Lady but she's filled with grief and it is affectin' her judgment. The rest will remain here as she wished. STONEWALL!" he yelled.

A ruddy looking soldier with short brown hair burst in. "Yes, Captain?"

"Gather four groups o' twenty men each and form a line with each group along the northern, southern, eastern, and western edges o' the castle perimeter spaced evenly. We are ter defend the castle at all costs. If ye so much as see a child unknown cross that line, I am ter be informed immediately! Understood?"

"Yes, Captain," the ruddy soldier replied, "But, Captain?"

"Yes, whelp?" Gnarl asked in agitation.

"Are we expecting attack, Captain?" he asked unsurely, hoping Gnarl wouldn't rip his head from his body.

"Are ye questioning me authority?" Gnarl cried out, his piggish face turning scarlet.

"No, Captain!" the soldier shouted back.

"Dismissed!"

The soldier tripped on his way out the door, and made a dead run for the barracks.

"Hildvar, no one is ter know she's gone. No one!"

Hildvar bit his inner cheek thinking of Frelia. By now the whole city of Moondale probably knew.

Serra entered a village just before sunsset. She had been riding for hours to make sure she put as much distance between herself and Moondale as possible, knowing the brigade would be right on her heals.

Gypsy was lathered in sweat from the long run. She had stopped several times to allow the horse some rest. It was obvious Gypsy wasn't used to such exercise, nor was she used to riding at such a quick pace.

They came upon a fountain in the village square with a statue of a long forgotten icon in its center.

Gypsy drank heavily from the fountain as Serra dismounted to get the feeling back in her legs. She removed her ration saddlebags and started rummaging through them. She found a feedbag and a pouch of oats. After Gypsy stopped drinking, Serra strapped it on, and sat on the edge of the fountain. She pulled an apple from her backpack and took a bite while she looked around.

Shops surrounded the cobblestone square. She could see a smithy at his anvil, hammering out a chink in a breastplate. Next to his shop were a general store and a tavern called, The Squire's Den. On the other side of the fountain were a stable and a few other shops.

She sat there until the suns slipped past the horizon. A dark sky full of stars soon ascended.

Another traveler upon a chestnut horse walked to the fountain. Not wanting company, Serra quickly replaced her saddlebags and backpack and started to remove Gypsy's feedbag.

"Don't leave on my account," said the man. He wore a black cloak with his hood up and she couldn't make out what he looked like. He wore leather armor under his cloak and knee-high wool boots.

"I must be on my way. Good evening," Serra said, as she fought Gypsy for the feedbag.

"You may as well let her finish," he laughed, "She doesn't seem to want you to go, now does she?"

It was obvious that Gypsy was not ready to leave. Finally, Serra gave in and put the feedbag bag securely back on the mare's head. She instead grabbed the reins and started to walk away.

The stranger pulled down his hood and Serra took a deep breath.

This was the most handsome man she had ever laid her eyes upon. His hair was black as night and his eyes were so blue they seemed to gleam in the starlight. He had a small, straight nose and a thin mouth curved in a grin that took her breath away.

"I'm Jareth. Please don't leave. I haven't had the company of a human in many days. Old Gallant here doesn't talk much," he said, gesturing toward his horse.

Serra's feet seemed to be glued to the spot.

"The tavern would be a good place for you then. Surely they have a scald and wenches to keep you entertained," she said, finding her voice.

"Aye, that they may," he said, looking into her eyes. "Though none as lovely as you, I'm willing to bet."

Serra blushed despite herself.

"I thank you for your kind words, sir, but regretfully I must be on my way. Good evening."

She led Gypsy east out of the courtyard feeling the eyes of Jareth on her back the whole way. She would have liked to talk with the man, but due to the current status of her sister, she couldn't be too careful. She was currently the only heir to Moondale whose whereabouts were unknown... at least to them.

It had been close to noon by the time the twenty were ready to leave. It had been several hours since Serra had left. They were given strict orders not to divulge her absence to the rest of the brigade. Though by midmorning of course, word had spread quickly, beginning in the kitchens, oddly enough.

Everyone seemed to be in disarray. Gallo Suntrestle paced the library with his eyes the size of galleons. Frelia had burned breakfast in her escapade to tell everyone she saw that Serra had left unprotected.

Hildvar had escorted the twenty, insisting that he go with them. Gnarl had finally given in. Hildvar had been watching after Serra for half a year now. Gnarl figured if anyone knew her thoughts, it would be the barbarian who was like her protector.

The group of soldiers made camp in a clearing next to the road. They had traveled for several hours, but they could find no sign of Serra. There was only one road, and they had run their horses to the brink of exhaustion, hoping to make up for their slow departure from Moondale.

Hildvar continued to be very edgy and snapped at anyone who spoke to him. He was obviously taking this very personally. He put out his bedroll by the fire, right after yelling at some men throwing bones.

"None of that, this is not a pleasure ride you heathens! Walk the perimeter of the camp and report back to me in thirty minutes," he'd yelled. When the young soldiers had just looked at him in mock amusement, the barbarian had pulled his axe, and given them a threatening stare that got them moving.

He stared into the fire now, thinking of Serra. He should have posted a guard outside her door. But in the thick of getting ready to march, he'd overlooked that she was known to defy what was asked of her.

His mind wandered to a time a few months before, when Renfar had ordered her to dress in a gown for a meeting with one of the courtiers of a nearby village. Serra had dressed in a gown all right, with her sword belt around her waist. Renfar had been furious. The courtier, who had known her since her birth, had only laughed goodheartedly and continued with the business at hand.

A small smile came to his lips for a brief moment then he remembered what was at stake. If both Serra and Lorna never came back to Bloodmoon Castle, the people of Moondale would be left to an elven mage who was known to behead his followers for putting a toe out of line.

With this thought in mind, he didn't sleep for the second night.

Chapter Five
The Handsome Stranger

Fenlin had finally managed to rouse Keifer. He had been unconscious for several hours when he sat bolt upright in bed and yelled for Fenlin to get out.

"But sir, you're not well," he protested

"Out!" Keifer screamed.

Fenlin scrambled to get out of the room and closed the door sharply behind him. He stood just outside, listening.

"What in the nine hells is going on?" Keifer muttered. He looked out his window and noted that the suns had gone down already; the stars mocked him from the night sky.

Keifer got out of bed on shaky legs and went to his altar. He sprinkled some silvery powder into a steel brazier.

"*Inflamaray Totalus,*" he muttered as the brazier lit up with blue flames.

He sat on a cushion in front of the brazier and began chanting. Slowly he began to relax and he regained his lost connection.

Serra had found a small clearing just north of the road and made camp. She sat next to a small fire while Gypsy slept on her feet next to a tree not far away.

After she rolled out her blanket, she took her sword belt off. After laying her scimitar not far out of reach, she watched the flames flicker for a few minutes, and was soon fast asleep.

The fog was so thick, she could not see her hand in front of her face. The ground was solid below her feet, but she could not hear her footsteps. She reached up and rubbed her eyes, hoping her vision would clear.

Opening her eyes again, the fog had lifted, but now she saw nothing but blackness. She continued to walk, glancing from side to side, frantically trying to see anything that might give her a clue as to where she might be. She reached for her belt and to her horror, she realized she was only in her nightgown.

She heard someone breathing up ahead. The sound was barely audible, but in the silence, it was deafening.

"Hello?" she asked groggily, "Show yourself."

With no answer forthcoming, she began to walk slowly forward. The breathing was getting louder. After several steps she noticed a small pinprick of light ahead. It slowly grew in size as she walked forward. As it became clearer, she noticed it was an orb of red flame.

She stared at the orb as it grew larger and larger, finally stopping when it became the size of her head. Then it began to rise into the sky and in only a few moments, it had ascended into the heavens. It looked oddly like a moon of fire.

The breathing seemed to be getting louder and Serra lowered her gaze to note she could now make out her surroundings. She was in a vast chamber, the flagstones under her bare feet were made of granite and she could just make out a door in the wall just before her. The fire moon cast an eerie red glow over everything.

She reached the door and noted it was oak with a brass handle. Right after she reached for the handle, the breathing seemed right beside her ear. She turned around and began to scream.

The dark figure loomed before her, only inches away! It was the shape of a hooded, cloaked man, only tattered. Where a face should be, there was only blackness. Sickly gray hands reached for her and grabbed her around her throat.

It's touch was like ice! She reached up, choking, trying futilely to dislodge the firm grip. Just as she began to lose consciousness, she reached up to pull back the hood and heard a voice.

"My Lady! My Lady! Please Wake!"

Serra opened her eyes to see the young man from the fountain half-laying on top of her. His hands were on her shoulders and he looked distraught. His beautiful blue eyes were wrought with concern and fear.

Her shaky hand reached for her sword and raised the sharp tip just to his neck. He sat up slowly and raised his hands in surrender.

"My Lady," he said softly and then gulped, his gaze never leaving her own. "You were screaming. I was traveling on the road and heard you. You were having a nightmare."

She could see she was dripping with sweat. Her hair was wet and matted, and her armor uncomfortably damp. Her hand on the hilt of her scimitar was bone white.

"Stand and move near the fire," she said in a hoarse whisper.

He stood and walked to stand next to the flames with his arms still raised in surrender.

Serra lay there looking at him. He looked like an angel. The flames danced in his eyes and made them seem to glow with an ethereal light. She lowered her sword arm and took a deep breath. As she rose to a sitting position, she began to get dizzy.

The man ran to her side and his knees hit the dirt. He quickly put his arm around her to support her back. Serra started to raise her sword again, but was too weak to lift her arm.

"There, now," he said, gently sliding up next to her. "Take a few deep breaths. Gain your bearings."

"Thank you," she said softly. Her head was pounding and she was covered with goose flesh despite the fire being so near.

"You're welcome. I'm just glad you didn't decide to skewer me," he said with a bright smile.

Serra started to breath normally again. She stood up very slowly, took a few tentative steps, and had to stumble to a tree for support.

It was still night. Gypsy stood grazing in the same spot she was in earlier, except Gallant had been tethered to the tree next to her.

"How long have you been here?" she asked, looking at him still sitting on her blanket.

"A while," he said uncomfortably.

He stood up and brushed off his knees.

"I heard you scream and came at once. You would not wake up. What do you dream that makes you so scared?" His eyes were filled with wonder and puzzlement.

He knew by the look on her face that he had said the wrong thing. Serra scowled at him and advanced a step.

"That is none of your concern. I appreciate your help in waking me. Please do not worry with it again. I will wake when I wake, and not otherwise. You can rest and enjoy the fire for the night."

She reached down and tried to pick up her blanket, but her knees gave way and she dropped to all fours.

He knelt next to her.

"My Lady, I am going to be honest with you. I realize you are stubborn as an old mule and want no company, but if you were attacked at this moment you would be perfectly helpless as you can't stand on your own two feet. I have been traveling long and hard as I told you before, and just wish to remain in the company of another. You do not have to talk to me. You can pretend I don't exist. But for the love of Justar, let me stay if only to make sure you don't fall into your fire while trying to walk around."

He looked into her green eyes and saw that she was defeated. And he also saw that it pained her to admit it.

She turned over and sat down.

"Jareth, was it?" she asked, pointedly not answering him.

"Aye," he said with a smile.

Keifer smiled as the connection was broken. He had never come so close to her before. He had actually managed to touch her this time. His master would be pleased.

"*Inflamaray Finitus,*" he muttered and the blue flame of his brazier went out. He rose slowly to his feet and noted he was still very shaky from the unseen attacker from two nights before.

He walked slowly to his mirror and gazed in to see his green eyes were sullen, his face as white as snow. His brown hair was disheveled and he was still in his nightshirt.

"*Summonus Incentra,*" he said into the mirror.

Its depths swirled with black smoke and within moments a face stared back at him that was not his own. It was the face of an old, wrinkled man with long, white hair and piercing, blue eyes.

"Report," the old man said to Keifer.

"I have reached her, master. She put up a fight two nights hence and I was unable to reach her last night. But I managed to touch her tonight," he said passionately.

"And? Did you kill her?" the man asked coldly.

"No, master," Keifer said, looking down.

"Maybe I should find another to do my bidding. As from your appearance to me tonight, you look as if this simple task is too much."

Keifer's eyes widened.

"No master, I have the book!"

The man grinned evilly.

"Bring it to me at once. Leave the girl be for now, I have something to show you, at any rate."

Keifer retrieved the book from his hidden cubby and walked back to the mirror where the man's face waited. A pale white handed reached out of the mirror and grabbed him by the throat. In moments, he was pulled through the glass into one of the largest libraries he'd ever seen. An unremarkable, oak desk lay before him with a black, leather chair with its back to him, facing a fire in the hearth.

The same pale white hand reached over the armrest as if waiting for Keifer to kiss it. He walked around the desk and knelt, kissing away in desperation.

"The book, you fool!" the man yelled, slapping him across the face sharply.

"Ye... Yes, master," Keifer groveled, pushing the old tome into his master's lap.

The man sat easily in his chair, dressed in robes of black on black. His white hair hung about his shoulders, bone-straight and thinning on top. He fingered the book as if it was a pet and he grinned.

"Do you know how long I have been waiting for this?" he whispered fervently.

"No, master." Keifer stayed on his knees and looked down at the floor, afraid to ask how long.

"Justar has shined upon you this day, you wretched child. The spell book of Gyndless the Almighty has been lost to me for three decades. That pompous Harper Bloodmoon, curse his grave, stole the book right from under my nose. I trust you paid the thieves well for retrieving it." He looked down, finally, at the groveling man.

"Yes, master, one hundred galleons each to the Band of the Yellow Sash. It had been hidden deep in the hills of Glendale, in a labyrinth of tunnels that wound under the mountains. Eight died in the search, which was just as well, as I did not have to pay them," Keifer said with a weak smile.

"While you have been lazing, I have been on a quest of my own," the old man said with a venomous laugh. "Lorna Bloodmoon is currently in attendance at my holding."

Keifer tried hard not to ask him how. He knew he would be flayed to death if he did. He waited patiently for his master to continue.

"Why, Keifer," he said in mock concern, "I thought for sure this would please you."

"Yes, master, most definitely!" he exclaimed with a smile.

"You may go," the old man said and with a wave of his hand, Keifer swirled through more black smoke and landed rump first on his room's cold wooden floor at Fortin Manor.

Serra tried her best not to stare at Jareth across the firelight. He sat on his bedroll across from her, whittling on a piece of wood with a small knife. He hadn't said much since she had agreed to let him share her fire. It was comforting to have someone with her, but the silence was driving her mad.

"I am sorry I was so rude to you before," she said, looking up at him with her emerald eyes.

He stared back and it took a moment before he said anything. They just shared a quiet moment together. Though it heated her blood, it was comforting.

"Do not be sorry. You never can be too careful," he said, looking back down at his knife and chunk of wood.

"Aye." She wished he hadn't looked away. "What is your last name, Jareth?"

He looked up again and smiled.

"Now that would not be fair, would it?"

"What would not be fair?" Serra asked, confused. Since when was giving a surname such a terrible thing?

"It would be unfair, my Lady, for me to give you my second name, when I still do not know your first." He kept smiling at her.

Serra blushed. She hadn't realized she had not given him her name. But should she? Her last name, definitely not, but Serra was not such an uncommon name.

"Yes, I didn't think of that. My name is Serra," she said at last.

Something seemed to move behind his eyes at her statement. Like he knew something he shouldn't. He dropped his items, stood, and bowed low before her.

"It is a pleasure, Lady Serra."

She tried not to flinch at the *Lady* reference as he took her hand, and kissed it. He then walked back to his side of the fire and sat down on his blanket.

"Likewise," she stated plainly.

She had been around men all her life. Training as a warrior tended to do that to you. Although, she had never felt as unsure of herself as she did now. Why did he have such an effect on her? And what was that that had passed over his eyes when she had told him her name?

"And I do not have a surname, Serra, it is only Jareth. Simple... and sweet," he said, smiling as before.

"Aye, and I am Serra, and only Serra. Simple..."

"And sweet," he said, looking into her eyes once again.

Dretho the Mage paced anxiously across his altar room. He had scryed to Moondale that night to check on Serra, only to find that she had taken off alone to find her sister. He knew that the young woman could handle herself in battle. He had heard many tales of her prowess with the sword. However, in her weakened state due to the nightly demons, he thought her move foolhardy.

He continually berated himself for being unable to locate the sorcerer causing her distress. It was unlike him to fail in such matters. He would have liked to try again tonight, but he knew she could not stay in his safety with her homeland in such disarray. And now, she had gone off alone.

He walked through his heavily warded oak doors into the corridor that led to the grand staircase.

"BERN HILDA!" he bellowed.

Something crashed below and he heard thunderous footsteps ascending the staircase.

"Yes, master?" she asked anxiously, as she came into view.

"Prepare my travel attire. I shall be embarking on a journey."

"Yes, master. At once, sir," she said, waiting for dismissal.

"And Bern Hilda, tell no one of this," he said, as an afterthought. "Go now and be quick."

"Yes, sir!" she proclaimed as she hurried down the stairs, making twice as much noise as before.

Dretho walked back into his altar room, mumbled under his breath, and waved his hand toward the bookcase. It dispersed in a flash of purple sparks to reveal an alchemy chamber instead of the bedchamber, like before.

He walked over to his glass cabinets along the eastern side of the room and said, *"Ethinar probladra!"* and the doors disappeared in a haze, to reveal shelves upon shelves of potions and spell components.

Gathering a small empty pouch from one of the shelves, he began filling it with more items than such a bag could possibly hold.

Bern Hilda returned shortly after, carrying two backpacks, a set of heavy, gossamer robes, and a wineskin. Her master was kneeling in front of his altar in prayer so she crept, as quietly as any dwarf could, to his small sitting area next to the window. She placed the items on the small table there and turned to leave.

"Bern Hilda," he said calmly.

"Yes, sir?" she asked in a whisper.

"Go fetch Julian and Isaac and tell them to be ready for the road within the hour."

"Yes, sir."

"You may go."

He never turned to watch her leave, but continued his meditation. He knew he must be fully prepared for what he was about to attempt.

Hildvar began packing his horse an hour before dawn. All the men were still asleep on their bedrolls. He knew they were tired from the long day of riding, but there were more important things than sleep.

In his youth, he had slept only two or three hours a night. Staying up late drinking mead with his kinsmen and waking up before dawn for the hunt. He was only twenty-eight years old, but had been made a man at the age of twelve when he had slain his first deer with one mighty throw of his battle-axe.

He missed the camaraderie of his clan, but continued to feel betrayed by their weakness toward the sorcerer. Barbarians were trained at an early age to never trust magic. They were also trained to never accept anything that Galstat, the God of War, did not provide. However, when they were on the brink of starvation and dying by the score, they had gone against their ways and died anyway.

Since his stay in Moondale, he had grown comfortable with magic. If not for Bergearon's healing spells, he would be long dead. It seemed ironic to him that he mistrusted his people for their succumbing to a sorcerer, when he saw magic of some sort every day. However, this was different. A tyrannical mad man had misled his clansmen, whereas he saw magic in Moondale done only for the good of the populous.

The clan still existed, of this he was sure, but he no longer felt like one of them. One day, perhaps, he might rejoin them. But for now, he owed his life to the Bloodmoon clan, and that he did not take lightly.

He finished with his mount, walked over to the closest warrior, and kicked him in the side.

"Hey! What in the bloody hell," the warrior screamed, as he sat up quickly, favoring his side.

"Get up now, you mangy worm, and wake the rest or you'll be tasting my axe next."

The warrior scratched his red hair and stood up scowling but said nothing.

They were on the road as the suns crested the horizon.

Chapter Six
Unexpected Company

Jareth kicked loose dirt over the fire to put out the few remaining hot embers and rolled up his blanket. He glanced over at Serra who slept peacefully. Her hair had long ago fallen out of its tie and had cascaded down her back and framed her face.

She was easily the most beautiful creature he had ever set his eyes on and he had traveled the country far and wide. *Jareth the Wanderer,* he laughed softly to himself.

He watched as she rolled over onto her back at the sound, and he held his breath for a moment. Her fire red hair had fallen back from her face to reveal her creamy, pale skin. Her lips were full and red. Her nose was small and just thick enough at the end to make it almost childlike. Her eyes were round, but not too large. He remembered how remarkably green they were, like a pear tree leaf in the spring.

Sighing, Jareth realized he should probably wake her, although he hated the idea. The suns had been up for an hour now. The night before when she had left him at the fountain, he had been able to restrain himself from following her for almost a full five minutes. He had crept many yards away as she made her camp and had snuck up to her as she had fallen asleep. Normally he would have waved her off and kept on his merry way, but something about this woman was not what it seemed. The way she walked was regal. She moved with grace. And her voice was like the song of a sparrow. She intrigued him. Jareth had learned long ago that intriguing people were few and far between, especially beautiful ones with fire red hair.

He had watched her sleep for perhaps half an hour when she had started tossing and turning. As he had turned away to leave, she had started screaming. It was the scream of mortal terror in the view of death itself. Throwing caution to the wind, he had run to her side. It had taken him a while to rouse her. After screaming at her at the top of his lungs, he had finally managed to wake her.

When she had at last opened her eyes, she had looked like a frightened child. How he had longed to hold her.

Seeming to sense his thoughts she opened her eyes. As she gained her bearings, she sat straight up, her hair flying wildly.

"I didn't dream!" she exclaimed. "I can't believe it, he..." she paused, looking up to see him staring at her.

"He, my Lady?" he asked in curiosity.

"How long have the suns been up?" she asked, quickly changing the subject.

"Oh, I don't know," he said, gesturing toward Belos and Halos, the two suns of Remus. "An hour, hour and a half, I suppose."

Her eyes widened in shock as she jumped up and started packing her supplies.

"Why didn't you wake me, Jareth?" she asked, as she hastily rolled her blanket.

"I didn't realize you were in such a hurry," he explained in confusion, "I thought after your rough night, you could use some rest."

She stopped packing her tinderbox long enough to look at him.

"Jareth, I know you owe me nothing. But I must ask your word on something important."

He looked at her in puzzlement.

"Yes, my Lady?"

"If anyone were to inquire of you, whether you had seen a woman with red hair that has nightmares, please, tell them you've never met anyone such as that." Her voice was almost pleading.

Jareth continued to stare at her and was very quiet.

"My Lady, are you in trouble with the law?" he asked matter-of-factly.

A look of puzzlement crossed her face and then her eyes lit up.

"Yes! Yes, I am! Now, please, sir, may I have your word?"

"Aye," he said sarcastically, "and my mother's a horseshoe."

Serra put her backpack down on the ground and walked over to him.

"I'll not lie to you," she said, drawing very near.

She smells like a strawberry patch in the middle of summer, Jareth thought.

"But please, know that I am in a hurry and I can not tell you why," she said, looking into his eyes.

Jareth looked into hers and then at her lips. His mouth suddenly went dry and he licked his lips unknowingly.

"I understand, my Lady," he said, stepping closer to her.

"Your word?" she whispered, they're faces barely inches from each other.

Jareth continued to stare at those red lips. "A man would do just about anything," he whispered, "For a kiss."

He reached up and stroked her full lips with the tip of his finger.

She closed her eyes at the touch. It was as if he were trying to bring her heart right out of her chest with his touch. Before she could open her eyes, his lips brushed across hers. She sucked in her breath and ran her fingers through his soft hair.

He had never felt anything as soft as those lips. They were like rose petals on top of fluffy cushions. He felt a twinge of desire flow through him like lightning. He pressed harder and she responded by running her fingers to the back of his head and pressing.

He had just begun to part her lips with his tongue when they heard, *Hmm Hmm Hmm.*

Serra looked up to see none other than Dretho the Mage, standing beside them, flanked by two warriors in full plate mail.

"Hope we aren't interrupting," the elf said with a rare grin.

Hildvar held up his hand for the procession to halt. They had been traveling for nearly an hour at a quick pace, and still had seen neither hide nor hair of Lady Serra. It was still two days march to Clandestine and he had thought they would've caught up to her by now. He had been scouting about three hundred yards before the cavalry and a noise off to the side caught his attention. He had thought he heard a woman's voice.

She stepped away from Jareth as if he were on fire.

"Dretho!" she exclaimed.

"Yes," he said, unable to hide the grin on his normally stern face. Her companion simply stood there as if in a daze.

Who could blame him? he thought with mirth.

"Serra, why have you ventured off alone? Why could you not have summoned me to escort you?" he asked in all seriousness.

Her eyes grew large as Jareth looked at her. She looked back at Dretho whose smile had disappeared as quickly as it had arrived. He wore a stern look that oddly reminded her of her father.

"I needed to go on my own," she said, glancing again at Jareth. He stood staring at her as if she had his full attention. "Stealth is my ally in this... mission. I must be very careful."

Dretho looked from her to her companion and raised an eyebrow.

"And you are?" he asked condescendingly.

Jareth glanced at the elf and then at Serra.

"I am Jareth the Wanderer, at your service," he said with a bow. "And you are?"

"Who I am is of no concern to you," he said, stealing his gaze from the man. "Serra, you are the ruler of Moondale with no readily available heir, and you venture alone consorting with riff raff while your sister is missing and your countrymen are looking for you scared for your safety. Is this how your father raised you?" he asked in a scolding tone.

The hand that slapped his face had the force of a bull running into a wall of stone.

"How dare you!" she screamed.

Dretho was stunned. No one had ever struck him before in such a manner.

"Speak not to me of my father, or of my actions you miserable man. I am not your plaything!"

She stomped off, retrieved her backpack and blanket, and quickly mounted Gypsy. She gave Dretho a venomous glance and then looked to Jareth as if in apology. The two warriors flanking Dretho stared straight ahead as if they hadn't heard a word.

She kicked Gypsy into a run, and they exited the clearing just as Hildvar was entering. Gypsy jumped over a low bush to avoid him and they galloped down the road toward Clandestine.

Cursing under his breath, Hildvar pumped his strong legs to get back to his horse, and they were quickly in pursuit.

Finally overcoming his shock, Dretho shook his head. He had never been a soft nor gentle man in any way. He was used to getting what he demanded, no matter the cost. However, he also knew the temperament of the Bloodmoon family. It seemed, after three hundred years, one could be humbled after all.

He paid no attention to the wanderer, but only raised his head, muttered a spell, and clapped three times. He and his two guards disappeared in a shower of yellow sparks.

Jareth's head was spinning.

Moondale, he thought. Then this fiery woman that had so caught his attention was a Bloodmoon. She had to be. And if she was the last, what had the elf said? Available heir?' then that meant...

Jareth climbed onto Gallant and he reached into one of his belt pouches and took a pinch of white powder. He placed his hand on Gallant's neck and muttered, "*Arcanus traveelus,*" and they both disappeared from the clearing.

She was crying and had never felt so humiliated. Hearing the cavalry behind her, she knew there was no way for her to escape. She would run as far as she could before she was caught.

Why did they have to get involved? This was her sister, not theirs. Could she not have the freedom to rescue her own kin if need be?

Gypsy ran as never before, kicking up rocks and dirt in her wake. The cavalry was less than a half-mile behind her. As Serra glanced back, she could see Hildvar in the lead. When she turned to look straight ahead, she had to blink twice to make sure she wasn't seeing things.

Jareth, atop Gallant, was only twenty paces away.

He turned his horse around and they started to run the same way. He slowed a little to allow her to catch up. He grinned at her as they leveled off. Their horses were running the same speed.

"Take my hand, Serra!" he yelled over the noise of the horses.

She looked into his eyes and saw nothing but good intentions. He reached out his hand, edging closer to her with his horse. She saw him glance to his left side. He let go of the reins and reached into his belt pouch. He raised his hand into a fist and she grabbed his other, tentatively at first. Then he entwined his fingers with hers, gripping tightly.

He looked into her eyes and said something under his breath that she couldn't understand. Something happened that Serra had never felt, or seen before. One moment she was riding beside him and the next everything went very quiet. Serra looked up to see that the road had distorted. Looking behind her, she could see a shadow of the pursuing cavalry and she watched as they disappeared into blackness.

"Don't let go, love," he said, smiling at her.

She gripped his hand more tightly and looked ahead to see peaks of the Faeslarne Mountains pass by her at an alarming rate. Serra would have thought that they were flying if everything hadn't been so hazy and distorted.

As quickly as their ethereal trip began, it ended with the horses landing on the dirt road right outside of the mountains, with a small city visible in the distance.

Gypsy reared and bucked when her hooves hit the ground. Serra landed with a thud in the dirt and the mare took off running full speed back toward the mountains.

Jareth jumped off his horse while Gallant was still running hard and landed in a roll. Gallant, who was obviously used to this type of travel, just cantered to a slow pace and stopped. The wanderer stood up and ran to Serra who lay still on the ground.

A red bruise was beginning to rise on her forehead and she had been knocked out cold. He lay down next to her in the middle of the road and supported her head with his arm and pushed the hair from her face.

"Serra?" he asked softly, but she would not sir.

He slipped his arm under her legs and carried her off the road into a wooded area. There had to be some type of cave close where they could hide. They were just outside Clandestine. He knew it would take her pursuers two days ride to get here, but that elven mage had already proven his worth in finding her.

He whistled and Gallant walked over to him and nuzzled his neck. Touching his palm to the horse's chest, he sent his thoughts, *"Go find the mare and bring her back to me."*

Gallant walked off in the direction of Gypsy's escape route.

After laying her down under a large oak tree, he made a quick circuit about the hillside on foot. Finding a small cave about three hundred paces from where he had left her, he quickly ran back, scooped her up in his arms, and made his way there. He knew Gallant would find him.

Hildvar watched in fear as Serra and a young man on horseback disappeared into thin air. He slowed his horse to a stop and stared in trepidation.

This was not a magic he was accustomed to, not that he was used too much at all. Serra seemed to not want help from her people and that hurt him deeply. He sighed and motioned for the others to come near.

"We're going home," he said plainly, turning his massive steed back in the direction of Moondale.

"But our orders, sir!" the same red headed warrior from that morning proclaimed.

"Our orders were to find her and to bring her home. Am I the only one who saw her vanishing with that man?" he asked in a monotone voice. "We must go back to the castle and get our orders. We have failed here."

They made their way slowly back to their previous camp. They didn't see a need to be in any hurry to be flayed by Gnarl Knottytrunk.

Chapter Seven
Truth

Lorna looked around her cell for what seemed the millionth time. She was shackled to the low wall with iron chains, and her legs were numb from sitting for so long. Her white nightgown was stained with mud and who knew what else from the nasty stone floor.

"HELP!" she yelled hoarsely.

She knew no one would come. The dark figure had brought her here and left her to die, disappearing right after securing her chains. It hadn't said a word. She had only seen one human being since her capture, and that was the young blonde man that had brought her bread and water. Her belly rumbled with hunger and her throat was parched from yelling.

The young man would not talk to her, nor would he look her in the eye. He just came in, gave her bits of bread until the loaf was gone, and slowly let her drink water out of a small glass that he held to her lips.

"*Why are they doing this? I never hurt anyone,*" she thought.

She had been in the middle of her cobbler when Renfar had grunted. Looking up to see him face down in his own cobbler, she had thought he had fallen asleep. When she'd felt a cold hand on her left shoulder, she had thought Serra was playing a trick on her. Well, she wasn't going to fall for it this time, so she slapped the hand and turned around grinning from ear to ear. What she saw was not her older sister, but a man figure in a black tattered cloak. After screaming at the top of her lungs, she had seen Hildvar rush through the door, just as the dark figure grabbed her by the throat. As she began to lose consciousness, she could see nothing but a cloud of smoke and the arm of her captor. She had awoken in this very room, shackled as she was now.

She had tried her best not to cry while she had been there. Serra wouldn't have cried. But she wasn't like her sister. Serra was strong and knew how to take care of herself. Lorna had always been a little lady. She didn't care for weapons and armor. She was too busy dressing up and going to parties with her friends.

A door opened down the hall, casting a far too short moment of light in her dark cell. The young man walked up to her cell door, candelabra in hand. She saw him lie her dinner on the floor, reach to his belt, and unclasp a key ring hanging there. He unlocked the cell door and picked up the plate of bread and cup of water.

"Please, talk to me," she said in a pleading, childlike voice.

The young man walked over to her and placed the candelabra on the floor a few feet away. He pinched off a piece of bread and held it before her. She opened her mouth obediently. She was so hungry, and she wished he would bring something more than this moldy black bread.

He waited patiently for her to chew and then offered her the cup of water.

After she drank a sip, she said, "I know you're not supposed to talk to me."

He didn't respond, but only pinched off another piece of the bread.

"Would you please just tell me your name?" she implored, dipping her head lower to try to catch his gaze.

He looked into her eyes for the first time. His face was expressionless, but his eyes told her that he pitied her.

"They call me Spike," he said in a whisper. "Now eat." He pushed the bread into her mouth and waited again for her to chew.

"Thank you, Spike. I don't know what I would do if you didn't come. I imagine I'd go insane, alone here in the dark." She said before she took another sip of water.

He didn't say anything else throughout the meal. But he grinned at her as he left and relocked her cell, leaving her alone in the dark once again.

Gnarl Knottytrunk paced the planning room floor. It had been only two days and he was already on edge. Nothing had happened other than the normal daily routines at the castle. But it was obvious the people were on edge. The extra soldiers in two shifts guarding the perimeter, and, of course, the absence of their Lady, were unnerving.

He turned to make another row across the room and started in surprise. An elf in a black robe, with two armed soldiers, stood in front of him. He hadn't heard a sound.

"Did ye ever think ter knock ye durned elf?"

Gnarl had been the Captain of the Bloodmoon Brigade for forty years, serving first under Serra's grandfather, Harper. He had met Dretho on that fateful day when Frendar had saved him from a giant's boulder. The gruff dwarf had even been there when they had made their pact to seal their alliance and friendship.

"Hello to you, too, Captain Knottytrunk. The years have not altered your surliness, I see," Dretho said sternly, standing as rigid as ever.

"Aye, that they haven't and a good thin' too er I'd be cryin' in me mead ternight. I expect ye be knowin' the details. Ye always seem ter," Gnarl said, continuing his pacing.

"Yes, I've just met with Serra, actually," the mage replied calmly.

Gnarl stopped dead in his tracks and turned to face the elf once again.

"And?" he asked with a scowl that nearly creased his plump nose into his forehead.

"She apparently does not wish to be found, nor does she want any help. She has gone to find Lorna, and has a most unusual companion with her."

"Companion? Don' ye talk in circles with me, elf," Gnarl warned. "Out with it."

"He calls himself, Jareth the Wanderer. He seemed, from the few minutes I met with him, to try to portray himself as your average rogue. Yet right after my arrival into their camp, I cast a bit of a spell to sense anything unusual. This man glowed with magic," he said, ignoring Gnarl's threatening gaze.

"Did he hurt her? Does he have her under some blasted spell? Is that why she's acting like this?" Gnarl stomped right up to Dretho and nearly spit his questions in his face.

"I know not," Dretho replied, not backing down an inch. "She made it quite clear to me that she did not wish my company." He gestured toward his left jaw, where there was a distinct red handprint.

Gnarl laughed, "Bet that hurt! She's the only human woman I ever met that could almost beat me at arm wrestlin'."

"Indeed," Dretho retorted, not seeming to find it as amusing. "At any rate, I suggest we sit and discuss our options."

"Aye, we'll sit and wait fer two months like she asked us ter begin with, and if she don' come back, then we need ter talk," Gnarl said, reaching into his hauberk and pulling out the crumpled letter Serra had left on her bed two nights before.

Keifer was enjoying a nice port wine in his study. He had been so obsessed with doing his master's bidding. He seemed to have forgotten the finer things in life. It was a relief to give his mind a rest. It had seemed every day it was harder to keep up his unrelenting torment of the woman's dreams.

How he had wanted to marry her those months before. It had seemed the only way to take over Moondale without being obvious. Marrying such a sassy Lady was only a perk. Of course, she had seen right through him, even if her brother hadn't. He had managed to court her for nearly two months before she out right refused.

"I do not love you," she had said plainly.

He remembered how beautiful she had looked that night. She had tied her hair up with pins, so that it looked like a waterfall of fire. She had worn an emerald green dress that fit her snugly at the waist, and accented her curvy figure in all the right places. It had been rather obvious she had been uncomfortable with him and the dress.

"When I do marry, it will be for love. I am sorry but I must ask you to leave my homeland as soon as you have your affairs in order."

She had tried to be civil in her dismissal and diplomatic like her ever-dealing brother. Keifer, however, had taken it personally.

He had scowled at her immediately and spat, "You dare refuse me? Wench! I am the Baron of Fresta! You should thank me that I have not just murdered you all and taken Moondale for my own!"

He had reached for his sword at his side, but before he could draw, she had pulled a dagger from somewhere in the folds of her skirts and pressed it to his throat.

"I do not take kindly to threats, Keifer. Baron or no, you will leave this place now. It is your decision if it will be on your feet or on your back on a stretcher headed for the funeral pyre," she had said coldly with her eyes gleaming in the candlelight.

She had humiliated him. Once the Council of Fresta had been sent word of his actions, his Baron status had been withdrawn, and he had been exiled from the city. They had taken him at sword point to the barren island of Hoff's Cove. It was an odd sort of place, a large island in the center of a lake along the Neverlear River that was nothing but a mosquito infested swamp. It was said that no human could survive on the island as it was completely isolated by the river and no boats ventured too or from it.

He had wandered for days, living off vermin and frogs that he had managed to stun with his mind. He had almost lost all hope, when he'd found a staircase in the middle of the island. This was the first sign of civilization he had seen.

Figuring he had nothing else to lose, he had walked down the staircase into a dungeon. The first level of the dungeon had seemed deserted until he had come to a door with the likeness of his God, Justar, depicted on it.

There had been no knob, but Keifer had been trained as a sorcerer and knew this type of door. He had chanted, "*Justar incentra plamaray,*" and walked through the illusion. After entering a well-lit conservatory, he was surrounded by ten guards. They took him down a long corridor into a dining room. They had waited perhaps an hour, the guards saying nothing, when his savior had arrived.

Jarmassad Truth had surprised him right off. The old man had talked with him instead of killing him. He asked Keifer what had brought him to the island, and seemed particularly interested in what he had to say about Moondale and its royal family.

He had offered him a new life in Clandestine, where Truth ruled the nobility like puppets, if he would only swear allegiance to the old man. He also required that Keifer do his bidding without question. Keifer had readily agreed and now lived in the lap of luxury once again.

Sipping on his wine, he muttered a silent thanks to Justar for his good fortune, and sunk heavily into his overstuffed chair.

Serra woke with the worst headache she had ever had, and felt as if her skull would crack open from the pounding. After opening her eyes, she saw she was in a cave next to a small campfire. It was dark outside and she could smell something rank that reminded her of rotten cabbage.

"Good evening," she heard from behind her.

Jareth sat next to her working a mortar and pestle. He added water to whatever he was crushing, and looked up at her as he worked the stone into the bowl.

"What is that smell?" she asked, pinching her nose. The movements made her head spin, and it took several moments for her eyes to focus once again.

"Ah," he replied in mirth, "that smell, is what is going to make your head better. It seems your horse does not care for teleportation and took it out on you in the form of a lump on your forehead."

Everything came flooding back to her with his words. Dretho, Hildvar, and the other men, and flying over mountains hand in hand with this man that she did not know.

"I never would've taken you for a mage," she admitted hoarsely.

He stopped working his salve and looked down at her curiously. "And why is that?"

His words made her think. She, in all actuality, knew nothing about this man other than his name. "I don't know, you don't seem the type, I suppose," she said, starting to sit up. She changed her mind quickly as the pounding in her head renewed tenfold.

"I wouldn't suggest trying to get up yet," he said, coming closer to her with the bowl. "Now, this won't hurt, but please lie still. I would have given you a healing potion, but I seem to have left my alchemy chamber in my other armor."

Serra laughed and immediately felt nauseated. She closed her eyes to focus, and gritted her teeth against the pain.

"I'm sorry," he whispered in concern, "Lie still."

He pushed the hair back from her forehead. Her bruise had turned a sickly purple-green, and had risen into a large knot. After dipping two fingers into the salve, he gently spread it on the wound.

Serra felt like a child. Images of Frelia tending to her scraped knee, after a fight with Renfar crossed her mind. They had always fought, even after they had grown older. The thought of her dead brother brought tears to her eyes.

Jareth looked at her in concern and asked, "Have I hurt you? I am trying to apply it lightly."

"No," she said with a sniffle, "It's not you, but it is feeling some better." The swelling was going down quickly, and the pounding had slowed to a dull thud right after the salve had touched her skin.

He wiped the tears from her cheeks with his clean hand, and put the bowl aside.

"Well, Lady Serra Bloodmoon. I think it is time we were honest with each other."

Her eyes widened as he spoke her full name, but he only smiled and continued, "Fate seems to have thrown us together for a reason."

She waited for a moment, unable to meet his eyes. After taking a deep breath of defeat, she said, "Go on."

"You are looking for your lost sister, if what that ass of a mage said was true, is that right?" he asked.

"Yes, that is the truth," she admitted, biting her inner cheek.

"I believe I may be destined to help you find her, since you seem to be refusing the rest of the country's assistance," he said with a grin.

She couldn't help it, she grinned and chuckled, "You are very perceptive for a wanderer."

"Aye," he said, looking out at the opening to the cave. "I believe someone is here to see you."

Gypsy stood with Gallant at the entrance to the cave. She neighed in greeting, and then nuzzled Gallant's neck.

Serra rose to a sitting position, and noted her headache was not so bad now. She slowly stood up, and Jareth caught her by her waist as she stumbled. Their eyes met for a brief moment, but after Serra gained her balance she walked away from him.

"How did you find her?" she asked. She walked slowly to Gypsy, rubbing the horse's neck soothingly.

"I have a way with animals. I asked Gallant to go find her while I tended to your wounds," he said, walking over to the chestnut steed.

"Jareth, can you help me find Lorna?" she asked, looking up at him in apprehension.

"I can certainly try."

He retrieved a flat, marble bowl from one of his numerous backpacks. Serra stoked the fire to allow him better light. He poured water into the bowl and reached for his sword belt, which was lying next to Serra's on the cave's stone floor.

He opened a small pouch containing a silver powder and pinched out a small amount. As he slowly sprinkled the powder into the water, he closed his eyes, and began chanting, "*Asseeleeum brachtath tumadra estinar.*"

After chanting perhaps five or six times, the water began to glow a pale blue. After opening his eyes to gaze into the bowl, a shiver went up Serra's spine. His eyes were bright blue to begin with, but the reflection from the bowl made them glow fiercely, not to mention his face was set in a look of intense concentration.

"I see a girl wearing a white nightgown. Her hair is the same color as your own, and she is in a dark cell, shackled to the walls. She is alone.

There are no guards outside her cell, but there is a door down the corridor, guarded by two ogres. They are armed with clubs and are wearing shabby armor that seems to be made of fur. Past that door, there is another corridor, only this one is well lit. Several doors line the walls, but a staircase lies at the end. It opens into an empty conservatory.

Wait, tapestries line the walls and I see feet under them. The guards are in hiding. There is another door that leads to another hallway. There is a large door at the end. It is opening, and someone is walking out. It's..." Jareth gasped, and the bowl stopped glowing.

"What? Whom did you see?" she asked urgently, dropping to her knees in front of him.

Jareth looked as if he had seen a ghost. His face was ashen with his mouth slack in surprise. "I know where she is." he said, looking back down at the bowl. "She is in the holding of Jarmassad Truth. I fear for her life, Serra."

"I know that name. He is the bloody bastard that set those barbarians on my homeland a year ago," she said in anger. She remembered Hildvar telling her of the sorcerer on their ride back from Dretho's tower. "Do you know where he lives?"

"Aye, I've been there," he said, unable to look at her.

Chapter Eight
Thoughts and Defenses

Dretho decided to stay at Bloodmoon Castle that night. He had exhausted his teleportation spells for the day and needed to rest before attempting them again. Taking himself across the expanse of the region was one thing, but taking two others with him was quite a feat indeed. He was possibly as strong a magician as there was in all of Remus, but he still had his limits.

After ordering his two guards to stay in the barracks, a plump little woman had served him dinner at a long table in the dining room. The walls had been painted white with gold leaf etchings and large chandeliers illuminated the vast room.

The woman had almost dropped his soup in his lap as she was serving him. Her face had been wrought with terror and her hands had trembled in fear. Dretho was, of course, used to this reaction. He had woven quite a reputation across the land, and thought it best not to try to comfort the woman, as he did not feel he should ruin that reputation.

"Are ye needin' anythin' else, sir?" the woman had asked shakily.

"No, this will be fine, leave me," he had said, waving her away.

He sampled the soup tentatively. Elves were not overly fond of cooked food. They tended to eat their meat raw. Cooking the meat seamed to make it lose its natural flavor. But it wasn't too bad after all. The vegetables were a bit soggy, but the venison had been marinated in salty mead and tasted fine.

As he pondered the events of the past few days, he couldn't help but shake his head. He understood Serra's wish to be brave and courageous, but there were some things that could not be done alone. Even Dretho had summoned his kin in the Battle of Sengar Valley. The elves were not overly fond of him, but blood was thicker than wine, and he had always come to their aid in their time of need.

He had left his clan right after his one hundred and seventy-fifth birthday. He had decided that he needed to travel abroad to further his study in the craft as he had already learned all there was to know from the elders.

They had not agreed with his decision, but did not openly go against him either. He had traveled from one end of Remus to the other. He found the southern domain of Everklent to be the most rewarding. The dark skinned southerners had not seen many elves and basically told him whatever he wished, just to be in his presence. They had granted him permission to study in their vast libraries, and he had gained a lot of knowledge and had changed his ways of life, as well.

After spending eighty years studying abroad, he had come back to his homeland, and had raised the tallest tower anyone had ever built, a thousand-foot, black monolith for all eyes to see. He had wanted to strike fear into their hearts and make them stare in wonder.

He had adopted the ways of the southern domain. If someone was caught stealing from him, he merely cut off his or her hand. If one of his peasants raped another, they were drawn and quartered naked in front of the populous. His reputation as a heartless cruel man had spread to the reaches of Remus in just a few short decades. Though more often than not, he thought this reputation unfitting. But it did have its perks; nearly everyone who knew his name was afraid of him and that fear made his life less complicated.

Now, here he was sitting in an empty castle, eating soggy vegetables, and worrying about a twenty-year-old human girl who had stolen his eye. He sighed and pushed his soup away, no longer having an appetite. He stood and walked out of the dining room in search of a wine cellar.

They sat around their small campfire, both lost in their own thoughts. Jareth seemed unusually pensive. He hadn't said much since his divination spell. Serra was just as quiet, though she did seem happier than she had been, and more at ease. Lorna was alive. This revelation had given her an incentive she had never put much stock in before; hope.

"Jareth," she said softly.

"Yes, my Lady?" he asked, still staring into the fire.

"Do you remember when you brought us here, from the road in Sengar Valley to this one?" He nodded, looking in her direction. "Could you take us to Lorna? Not on the horses, of course, but just you and I?"

He sighed and rubbed his eyes. "I have been thinking of that. You see, Serra, when a sorcerer or a mage has a holding of some sort, like a dungeon or a castle, they will do everything in their power to protect it.

He'll put up wards to prevent other magic users from entering, and maybe even desecrate certain areas so that magic is of no use. I do not believe we can just waltz in and carry her away without being confronted, but I know I can get us close. After that, who knows what will happen? I only know that Jarmassad Truth is a very powerful sorcerer. He has many men, and will stop at nothing to protect what is dear to him. Even more so, when he is protecting something he has stolen."

He glanced back into the fire, picked up a twig, and absentmindedly started pulling the bark from it, as if he needed something to do with his hands.

"Do you think we can do it alone?" she asked, after his statement sunk in.

"I think it would be easier to go stealthily like you proposed before to the other mage..."

"Dretho," she interrupted.

"I do not think it wise to march up to his door with the infamous Bloodmoon Brigade. She would be dead before we breached the door," he said, throwing his twig into the fire.

"That was my thought as well when I left Moondale in search of her. My people love me, but I fear sometimes they do not understand my reasoning."

She paused for a moment, a far off look on her face.

"My brother, rest his soul, never could understand my logic in certain matters. He would ask me repeatedly to dress up like a Lady whenever the courtiers and other rulers would call. However, I fear that he never understood that clothes do not make the person, actions do. My father raised me in his footsteps. He was ever the warrior. I have known how to use a sword since before my teen years, and whenever my father met with another leader, he would take me, and I would listen. They treated me like an equal, just as they did him. They knew I could carry my own weight and that meant something to me. I never wanted to be the ruler of my homeland. I never wanted to be just something pretty to sit around as a trinket either. Renfar had always been versed in the ways politic, but I... I have just been Serra. The fiery daughter of a Lord of Lords who would follow him around like a pup soaking up everything she could about battle."

"No one ever really knows anything about another until they've fought beside them. Risking your neck to save another is one of the noblest things anyone can ever do in this life. You are a Lady among Ladies, Serra, if you understand that already. I'm sure that was the first lesson your father had in mind the first time he placed a sword in your hand," Jareth said, reaching over and taking her hand, "I am honored to serve you." He kissed her hand and held her gaze.

"I've never met one such as you, Jareth. You are most unusual. You always seem to know what to say to make me feel better about things. I feel as if I've known you for a long time, though we've just met," she said quietly.

"Aye, I feel the same. Time is a strange thing, Serra. Sometimes it takes years for a soul to get to know another, but old souls tend to recognize each other quicker." He let go of her hand and said, "You should get some rest. I need to prepare myself for tomorrow and it may take half the night, I will wake you later on to keep watch. I don't know this forest or its inhabitants. One of us should remain awake to make sure we are safe."

Serra smiled, lay down on her blanket, and closed her eyes. She only hoped that she would not dream, as she didn't fancy screaming at the top of her lungs in the middle of the night, attracting who knew what lurked about.

Lorna had been asleep when Spike had arrived with her evening meal. She had been chewing her bread in increments as normal when something met her tongue that made her feel like a child with a money purse in the marketplace; dried meat.

She opened her eyes wide in surprise to see Spike looking at her with a smirk on his face. He was carefully tearing strips of the jerky and quickly smudging it between the black bread, so it would only appear she was eating the usual if anyone happened by.

He smiled as he brought the cup to her lips. The moment the liquid met her tongue she had to stifle a smile. Honey mead. It tasted wonderful.

"Thank you so much, Spike," she whispered between mouthfuls.

"Shhh, I know it is not what you pictured before, but I'm sure it is an improvement," he said so quietly she had to strain to hear him. "I am taking a great risk in this and may not be able to again. But I will try."

"It is appreciated," she whispered with a grand smile.

They were about halfway through the meal when they heard the door at the end of the corridor open. Spike immediately put the jerky in his pocket and doused the mead onto the floor filling it quickly with his water skin. He had a look of abject terror on his face as he did this.

An old man dressed in black flowing robes stopped before the door. And Spike rose to his feet and bowed his head.

The old man waved his hand and the door opened without a touch. He walked in, muttered something under his breath, and a red ball of light erupted from his hand. It rose to the center of the room, illuminating the chamber.

Lorna closed her eyes against the pain. She had not seen any light, other than Spike's candelabra, in what seemed to her like forever. She blinked repeatedly through the tears until her eyes finally focused. As she looked up at the old man she noticed his hair was white and straight, and hung well past his waist. His beard blended with his hair so that only his eyes, nose, and lips were visible. His eyes were the most remarkable of all. They were bright blue and seemed to shine in the red light, but his expression was grim.

"Well, Miss Bloodmoon, I hope you are enjoying your stay," he said in a booming voice that hurt her ears. But Lorna merely stared back, unable to find her voice.

"Leave us," he said to Spike, who looked back at Lorna apologetically as he shut the cell door, and walked away.

"Now," he said, clasping his hands and bending his knees to look her in the eye. "I suppose you think me a vile man, as I am holding you hostage. However, my dear, please understand that I am granting you a great service by letting you keep your life during your stay. As you've noticed by the absence of noises in this dungeon, you are its only occupant."

"Why... why are you doing this?" she asked shakily. "I have done nothing to you."

"You are correct, you have not. Though your family has and shall pay for it dearly." he said slowly. "You are from a long line of thieves and I intend to stop your bloodline so that no Bloodmoon shall ever interfere with me ever again."

"You'll never be able to do that. My sister and brother are still alive. They will never bow to you," she said defiantly.

The old man shook his head slowly and smiled. "Ah, yes, you wouldn't know what happened would you now. I fear your brother is dead, my dear, and your wretched sister soon to follow. I am holding you now, awaiting her arrival. If I am correct, she will try to rescue you in a few days, and then, I will be able to finish my business with the both of you at once. I only have to keep you alive because she has... friends, who can see you. Though, don't bother to hope they can rescue you, it is quite, impossible."

Tears had come to her eyes at the disclosure of her brother's demise. She tried very hard to hold back her sobs as she asked coldly, "Who are you?"

"Ah, where are my manners?" he stated in mock amusement. "I am Jarmassad Truth."

"What has my family done to you to make you so mad at us?" she asked insolently.

"Ah, young people," he said coldly. "They never seem to know when to hold their tongues." He reached out and grabbed her by the throat. Lorna cried out and closed her eyes tightly.

"You shall pay for your family's deeds you impetuous whelp. You and your sister are the last Bloodmoon's alive. I shall purge you from this land so that no others will have to deal with your larceny," he spat.

He let go of her throat and Lorna, whose face had turned purple, began coughing violently. He waited patiently for her retching to stop and shouted, "Enjoy your last days on Remus. I shall make sure you never see your sister again."

He waved his hand at the cell door and it opened as before, without a touch. He did not turn back as he strode out of the cell. As he ordered Spike to lock her up once again, the light went out, and cast her in total darkness.

Jareth had been pacing the cave as she slept. He knew that what they were about to do would be almost impossible for just the two of them. He also knew that Serra would not agree to bring an army, nor should she. But would she agree to a select few additions?

He knew that he would not have enough power to defeat Jarmassad, but she obviously knew other mages. He had met one of her comrades already. He knew she was a fighter, but how good, he did not know. At the sight of her sister, she would most likely be defenseless simply because of the deep emotional bond between them.

Now that he knew where Lorna was hidden, he was scared. Scared of what Serra might think of him if she knew the truth about him. He had told her he had been to that dungeon before, and he had thanked Justar many times for her lack of questioning thereafter. He knew how the old mage loathed the Bloodmoon family and knew the reason as well. Forty years past, none other than Serra's grandfather had stolen a spell book from the old mage.

The book held spells that could allow one to take over the land if they could interpret the runes. The spell book of Gyndless the Almighty was without equal.

Two hundred years ago, Gyndless Goreseeker had been the ruler of all of Remus. It was a dark time when all humans, dwarves and elves had been enslaved to serve the one-eyed giant.

The monsters of the region were made slave masters and preyed upon what Gyndless had called the lesser races. Giants, as a general rule, were not very intelligent, but were fierce in battle. Their skill of throwing boulders and other large objects was unparalleled. Their sheer strength was unmatched by any other race. That was where Gyndless had his edge. He ruled with an iron fist, as well as an understanding of magic that was unprecedented.

After Gyndless died of old age, the giants, orcs, ogres, and goblins rebelled against each other as they no longer had a figurehead to spur their cooperation. No other giant had ever come close to matching his skill in magic use.

The spell book had been lost. For twenty years, Jarmassad Truth had searched the world over for the book. He had found it in a system of caverns under the Faeslarne Mountains near Sengar Valley. It had seemed that after Gyndless' death, the elves had stolen the book and had given it to a dwarven clan to hide. Many traps had been laid in the underground complex, but dwarves had never been known for their understanding of magic. They had not foreseen another sorcerer using otherworldly ways of finding the book.

Just after the tome was stolen, a Dwarven Lord had traveled to Moondale in search of help. Harper Bloodmoon had taken the quest head on and had managed to steal the book back, in just a matter of months, right from under Jarmassad's large nose.

Harper had sent his infamous Bloodmoon Brigade to Truth's small castle in Doramar and had cleverly sent in thieves of his own to steal the book while Jarmassad was preoccupied with the battle. Truth had been furious to no end. He had, of course, tried to get the book back by magical means, but Harper had hidden it in an undisclosed location heavily warded against prying eyes.

Jareth knelt next to Serra and took a moment to look at her. Why did he care for her so? He had seen many beautiful women before and had passed them by without a second glance. Maybe it was her attitude. She did not act like royalty. She was rebellious and wanted things done her way. Her refusal to fit the mold of a Lady, and be herself, was like a magnet. She was like him in so many ways. He, too, had wanted to be himself. He did not wish to be labeled and expected to follow suit.

"Serra," he whispered, as he lowered his head close to her ear.

She opened her eyes slowly and smiled. Jareth had to hold his breath to keep from sighing.

"Good evening," she said. "Or is it closer to morning?" She did not get up, but just lay there looking into those gorgeous blue eyes of his.

"In between, I would imagine. I see you've slept well," he said.

Once again Serra had not screamed out in her sleep. She thought on this for many moments before responding.

"Tell me, have you placed some type of enchantment upon me so that the dark figure does not stalk me?" she asked in all seriousness.

"Nay, my Lady, I would not do such a thing to you without your permission. I am very dignified in that respect," he said, still so very close to her.

"Well, it appears I have found my good luck charm after all," she said as she leaned into him and kissed him sweetly on the cheek.

Jareth blushed.

"Get some sleep, kind sir. I shall make sure you are protected." She smiled and stood up to allow him to use her blanket.

He watched her walk to the entrance of the cave, and lay down on her blanket, which was still warm from her body. He watched her pick up her sword and rummage in her backpack. She began to sharpen the scimitar with a pocket whetstone, and he felt oddly comforted that she was willing to watch over him.

He had not had anyone in his life in so long, friend or otherwise. Gallant had been his only companion for nearly three years. He fell asleep with a smile on his lips, as he listened to the rhythmic passes on her blade.

Serra spent most of the night gazing at the stars. Bergearon, the High Cleric of Bloodmoon Castle, had once told her that fate was written in the stars. He was an odd sort of priest. Most would say that their God wrote the tale of each of his or her followers, but it seemed that he was looking up more than ahead most of the time.

They had spent many hours on top of the southern tower of the castle, pointing out constellations and individual stars. She had always been interested in what he had had to say, and she was glad now that she had paid attention. It seemed to make the night go faster.

Just before dawn she had heard the crack of a limb somewhere to her right. She had instinctively knelt into a crouch, and looked over at the horses. They had been asleep, but were now wide-eyed with their ears perked to listen.

Serra looked over to Jareth, who slept soundly with his hand behind his head. Another noise from the same direction drew her attention. There was something out there.

As she crept slowly out of the cave, she was careful to walk heal to toe, as her father had taught her, so that she could feel with the balls of her feet through her soft leather boots. She crept for perhaps ten feet, and hid behind a small pine tree.

After waiting perhaps five minutes, a humanoid figure stepped out into the starlight. It stepped on another stick and paused, as if it were intentionally trying to sneak its way through.

She stood up and shouted, "Stand and be counted!"

The figure immediately stiffened and turned in her direction. A cloud uncovered the moon at that moment, and she flinched at the sight before her. It was an orc; gray-skinned, thick around the middle, and with tusks protruding from its mouth. She had not seen one in many years, but she remembered well what they looked like.

"Get away from this place, you are not wanted here!" she shouted, drawing her scimitar.

"Guthuga Usuna!" it screamed as it charged toward her.

Serra ran to meet its charge with a vicious swipe across it's forearm. The orc raised a crude club over it's head and tried futilely to bash her skull in. Serra dodged out of the way and made another pass, this time cutting deep into its right thigh.

The orc screamed in pain and raised the club to make another swipe, this time horizontally aimed again at her head.

Just as the club passed quickly over her head, she bit her cheek as she realized it had only missed her by a few inches. She plunged her scimitar deep into it's belly and the creature doubled over in pain, screaming again.

She could hear movement behind her, and she chanced a glance over her shoulder. Another smaller orc was slowly creeping up behind her. It had no weapon, but was holding out its gnarled hands to try to grab her.

Serra dashed to the side and ran around the wounded orc, confusing them both. She thrust into the creature's back, her scimitar coming out the other side, piercing it's heart along the way. The hideous creature fell to the ground with a thunderous crash.

The other orc seemed not to care in the least, but only stepped on its dying comrade's backside to get closer to her. Serra noted something moving in the bushes to her left, and she suddenly had a revelation. She began her battle cry just as the third orc clamored into view, this one holding a small axe.

"You should fear our fire and fury,
For know it will seal your doom,
We are the red and mighty,
Fear the wrath of the Bloodmoon's!"

As she finished her chant, her sword once again jumped from her hand, and began dancing toward the newest foe. She reached to her belt and pulled out two daggers, one for each hand. She hurled each toward her unarmed attacker, both thudding deeply into it's chest.

It was not going down as easily as it's former friend, however. It made a clumsy grab for her arm, and she once again dashed to the side to get out of it's range.

Her sword reached the axe wielder and slashed it viciously across its face, drawing blood, and putting out one of its eyes. The orc did not understand, and looked at the sword in confusion as it took another swipe across its ugly face.

The creature howled in pain, and swung its axe wildly to clang with the sword. The scimitar shot off in one direction, and came hurling back immediately, gaining momentum. It shifted diagonally, and pierced through the creature's head as its short trip came to an end.

Serra did not see her sword's performance. She was too busy fending off the other orc. She drew her last two daggers and threw them both in rapid succession. They both hit the orc; one in the thigh and the other buried itself deep in its throat. Blood spurted out of its neck and it fell to its knees. Its rugged, fur armor turned from gray to crimson red in just a matter of moments. It looked at her in disbelief and fell backward. Dead.

With the battle ended and no more foes present, the scimitar returned to its sheath at its owner's hip.

She walked over to the carcasses and retrieved her daggers, wiping them clean on the creature's tunics. She dragged all three away from the cave and placed them beside each other. As she glanced over at the horses, she noticed that they were sleeping side by side as they had been an hour before.

Serra smiled. It was nice to know she could defend herself alone. This was the first time she had ever had to.

Chapter Nine
Reunited

Hildvar and the twenty other soldiers of the brigade arrived in Moondale just after sunsrise. All the villagers had greeted them with cheers, until they noted the absence of two certain redheaded ladies. Word had spread quickly that Ladies Serra and Lorna had not returned. The looks of relief turned to looks of fear, and followed the procession every step to the castle.

Captain Gnarl Knottytrunk met them at the main portcullis in the north wall.

"Well met, lads," he said in greeting. He noted the mortified looks on their faces and couldn't help but chuckle. "Don' ye be lookin' so dreary. That elf mage has already come ter tell me what happened."

They all breathed a sigh of relief, except Hildvar, who just looked at him wide-eyed. The others might be glad they weren't going to get a thrashing from Gnarl, but the dwarf was the least of his worries at the moment. Serra was gone and did not want him to help her. She had run away from him.

"I'm thinkin' ye might need ter be comin' with me boy," Gnarl said, gesturing for one of the stable hands to take Hildvar's horse.

He dismounted and followed the Captain into the castle, feeling eyes on his back as he walked obediently behind a dwarf half his height.

They walked into the main foyer and Hildvar heard a high-pitched squeal. He looked up to see Frelia running down the main staircase, a pile of sheets scattered behind her. She nearly knocked Hildvar off his feet as she grabbed him around the middle at full run. She began whimpering as she hugged him tightly.

"Calm yourself, woman!" Hildvar yelled, trying to dislodge himself from her grasp.

"Don' ye be talkin' ter me like that, ye great oaf! Is Serra with ye?" she asked hopefully, with tears in her eyes. But the crestfallen look on his face brought forth more squeals and tears.

"Oh, would ye quit yer whinin' woman. I told ye the elf had talked ter her," Gnarl said in disgust.

"Oh yea!" Frelia yelled defiantly.

She walked over to the dwarf, prodding his chest with her finger with an outraged look on her face.

"That durned elf is goin' ter be the death o' us all! Ye shoulda sent the brigade after her, you shoulda! If she don' come back, that elf is goin' ter kill us!"

"Indeed."

They all looked up at the main staircase to see Dretho dressed in his usual black robes, with a confident look upon his face.

Frelia squealed again and ran behind Hildvar, peeking out from under his elbow.

Jareth stood scratching the back of his head. The three ugly orcs lay dead at his feet. Serra stood next to him, grinning from ear to ear in triumph. She had awoken him just before sunsrise to tell him he needed to see something. This was not what he had anticipated.

"Well, I see you've been busy," he said, turning to her. He looked her over and noted she didn't have a scratch on her.

"Aye," she said, smiling, and snickered as she said, "I told you I would protect you."

He walked over to her and wrapped her in a great hug.

"Serra," he said, enjoying the feel of her in his arms.

"Yes?" she asked, doing the same.

"I think we need to go back to Moondale," he said hesitantly.

She pulled from his grasp immediately with an angered expression. "What?" she asked sternly.

"Do not misunderstand me," he said, taking a step toward her. "I don't mean for us to stay, but you and I will not be able to do this alone."

She looked at the orcs and then back at him, shaking her head.

"Wait, I do not mean to say you cannot handle yourself in battle. You obviously can. But I am not worried about guards and monsters." He said, gesturing toward the orcs. "Jarmassad Truth is a very powerful man, as I have told you. I only think we need a few more to help, including your elf friend."

She turned her back on him and hung her head. It was several minutes before either of them spoke.

"If you promise me two things, Jareth," she offered quietly.

"Anything," he said, placing his hands on her shoulders.

"One, promise that we will leave as soon as possible to go to Lorna," she whispered

"And two?" he asked, stroking her long hair.

"Two, you must promise me that you will not let them make me stay in Moondale while you all rescue her without me," she turned to face him. Her eyes were watering.

"Oh, Serra," he said, wrapping her in another embrace. "I would never do that! I promise you, I will be by your side the whole time, and we will leave as soon as we've drawn our plans."

She returned his embrace and they walked back to their cave arm in arm to gather their gear, leaving the dead orcs behind.

Dretho walked the rest of the way down the staircase. He was about to speak to the plump woman when there was commotion in the courtyard.

The four of them ran out the great double-doors to see a black mare rearing and bucking. She ran full out toward the stables, whinnying the whole way.

After the horse was out of sight, they saw the real cause of commotion. On a chestnut horse, in the middle of the courtyard, sat Lady Serra, with a handsome young man sitting behind her.

Frelia fainted on the spot and Hildvar ran up to the horse.

Jareth had dismounted, and was offering Serra his hand when he saw the barbarian. He quickly drew his rapier, and stood at the ready. But the barbarian paid him no heed. Hildvar walked right past the armed man and plucked Serra right from the saddle, wrapping her in a great bear hug.

"Hildy! I can't breathe!" Serra gasped, laughing at the unusual display of emotion from the big man.

He let go of her and sniffed. His eyes were glazed with tears and he cleared his throat.

"Welcome back, Lady Serra."

Jareth sheathed his rapier and tried very hard not to let his jealousy show on his face.

Serra waved to the gathering crowd of onlookers, and walked quickly over to Gnarl, who had an unconscious Frelia slung over his left shoulder.

"What happened to her?" she asked in concern.

"Bah, she's fine darlin', glad ter see ye home be'd my guess. Just like the rest of us." He smiled and punched Serra in the shoulder.

Serra turned her attention to Dretho who had been standing idly by. His face was expressionless.

"I'm sorry I hit you," she whispered softly.

He looked casually at Gnarl and a small grin came across his handsome, angular face.

"Welcome home, Lady Serra," he said. She wrapped him in a hug that he was reluctant to return. After the brief show of emotion, he stood straighter and cleared his throat, pointedly staring at her companion.

Serra turned around to see Jareth still standing by Gallant. A look of discomfort splayed across his face. She smiled, walked over to him, and took his hand.

"Gnarl, will you have the stable hands take wonderful care of this steed? See he is put next to Gypsy's stall please. Meet me in the planning room with Hildvar and Dretho in an hour. I must show our honored guest around."

Jareth grinned widely and followed her into the castle. His jealousy, which had increased three fold, melted away into nothingness.

After a brief tour of the castles vast bottom floor, Serra had shown him to the planning room and excused herself. "I will be back shortly," she said with a great grin. "Make yourself at home."

She left him and then walked up the main staircase to her chambers. He watched her leave and turned back to the planning room, which was right off the main foyer. It was enormous. Grand tapestries adorned the walls, depicting battles and long lost heroes. Some were very old and others seemed more recent.

In the center of the room was a vast rectangular table surrounded by heavily lacquered high-backed chairs. There was a grand map of Remus in the middle.

He walked over to a cabinet along one wall and peaked in the first door. It was filled with miniature castles and soldier figures. There were even miniature trebuchets and catapults. In the next door, he found what he was looking for. A crystal bottle and six goblets sat on one shelf, with various bottles on the shelf below. He took one of the goblets and chose a bottle of elven brandy.

After pouring half a glass, he downed it in one gulp. He was very nervous being here, especially in this room, without Serra. He refilled his glass and put the bottle back on the shelf. Walking back over to the table, he sat in one of the chairs, directly to the right of the head of the table.

Just as he sat down, the door burst open and three men walked in: the dwarf and barbarian from the courtyard and the elven mage Jareth had already had the unpleasantness of meeting.

They paused when they saw him sitting there. And he found it amusing that they seemed to be just as uncomfortable in his presence as he was in theirs.

"Well," the dwarf said, clearing his throat and looking at his companions. "Everyone 'ave a seat, I'm sure Lady Serra will join us momentarily." He walked over to the cabinet and retrieved four more goblets and the crystal bottle filled with amber liquid.

The barbarian and elf took their seats across the table from Jareth, leaving the seat directly opposite him empty. The dwarf took that seat and began filling three of the goblets, and passing two down the table.

"I'm Captain Gnarl Knottytrunk," the dwarf said, offering Jareth his rough hand. "And this here is Hildvar and that elf is called Dretho the Mage."

"Jareth the Wanderer," he said, giving Gnarl's hand a firm shake. Hildvar and Dretho did not offer their hands, but merely nodded their heads in greeting.

"Nice ter me ye, Mr. Wanderer, glad we are that ye've been keeping our girl safe," Gnarl said with a smile. Hildvar and Dretho both shifted in their seats at his statement.

"She's quite capable of handling herself actually," Jareth said, before taking another sip to wash down his jealousy at the *our girl* comment. He could not resist a glance at Dretho, hiding his smile with the cup of his glass.

But Dretho noted the implication and scowled.

Gnarl gave a great booming laugh. "Don' ye be such a prune, elf! I'd've done the same meself if I weren' afraid ye'd turn me inter a toad or somethin'."

Dretho directed his scowl at Gnarl, just as the door opened once again.

Lady Serra entered the room at a brisk walk, buttoning the left cuff of her billowing white blouse. She was wearing tight, black, leather trousers and knee-high boots that accentuated her lengthy legs.

Chairs scraped the floor as each man stood. Lady Serra waved them to their seats as she sat at the head of the table.

She looked at them each in turn, and then glanced down at the chair, rubbing the armrest fondly.

"Renfar should be sitting here," she said remorsefully. She stood there a long moment merely looking at the chair, and then stood straight and said, "I am relying on each of you to help me formulate our next move."

"He would be proud of you, my Lady," Hildvar said in a deep baritone voice.

"Aye," Gnarl and Dretho answered in unison.

She nodded to them in thanks.

"Well, shall we get down to business? Gnarl, Hildvar, Dretho, this is Jareth. He has been most helpful in my quest to find Lorna. With his help, we have discerned her location."

The three men looked wide-eyed at Jareth across the table, which merely sipped his brandy once again, and looked back up to Serra.

"Who's got her, lad?" Gnarl asked, pouring Serra a drink.

Jareth looked to her, and she nodded with a reassuring smile.

"Jarmassad Truth has her hidden in his secret underground fortress on the island of Hoff's Cove," he said matter-of-factly, looking directly at Gnarl.

Hildvar took in a sharp breath and clinched his teeth in anger.

Serra looked at the barbarian in sympathy and said, "Hildvar, I think you should recount your tale of the day my parents died."

Hildvar told them of how his people had suffered, and how they had gone against their ways to follow the evil sorcerer. He explained to them their orders to march on Moondale in return for the care of their feeble clan members. He said all this in a very hushed voice, looking down at the table. The barbarian was ashamed and it was obvious.

They all listened in silence and it was many minutes before anyone spoke, after he had finished. To everyone's surprise, it was Jareth who spoke.

"Jarmassad Truth has a vendetta against the Bloodmoon family. That is why, I believe, he sent Hildvar's clan against you, and," He looked directly at Serra. "Why he kidnapped your sister and murdered your brother."

This statement took Serra aback. As far as she was concerned, the domain of Moondale had no enemies, except perhaps Keifer, who was no longer in noble standing, as far as she knew.

"Why does he bare us ill will, Jareth?" she asked with wide-eyes.

"I think a better question would be, how do you know all of this, Sir Wanderer?" Dretho interrupted.

His gaze shot daggers into Jareth's soul. But to his dismay, everyone looked to Jareth in anticipation. He felt like the whole of the world was bearing down on him at that moment. He looked straight in Serra's emerald eyes and sighed.

"I used to work for him," he said plainly.

Serra gasped and the rest stiffened. Hildvar's hand went to the head of his axe, and he fixed Jareth with a scowl of hatred.

"Go on," she said after a moment of silence. The blood in her veins seemed to have turned to ice water. She had a nagging feeling in the pit of her stomach, but she would wait to hear what he had to say before drawing any conclusions.

"I worked as his apprentice for two years learning the craft," he continued. "I knew he was a vile sort, but my father had insisted that I learn from him. Three years ago, I completed my study and he asked me to hire on as his second. He then told me of his plans to go against the Bloodmoon family. I felt repulsed and betrayed. I never wanted to practice the black arts. I never wanted to become a magic user at all, but my father had insisted. And that was when I left. My father disowned me and told me to never show my face again. That is why I have no surname, Serra. I have no father... anymore. I have wandered the land for three years and have used more magic in the last two days than I have since I left the holding."

Jareth looked at each of them in turn to gauge their reactions. Dretho was as sullen as ever, but seemed satisfied. Hildvar nodded to him, as if in understanding, and placed his hands back on the table. Gnarl simply stared back showing no emotion at all. But it was Serra, lovely Serra, who looked at him in pity.

"I am sorry if you felt judged just now," she said lovingly. "I know how hard it must be for you to relive your past, but I must ask you one more thing."

"You may ask anything of me, my Lady," he said, feeling the weight on him lessen a bit.

"Why does he bear us ill will?" she asked again.

Jareth turned from her to Dretho.

"I believe you are familiar with the book of Gyndless the Almighty?" he asked.

Dretho's eyes widened and fear splayed across his face. This was the first time any of them had seen him look afraid of anything.

"Aye," he said in a dreading tone.

"Oh, not that durned book again!" Gnarl shouted, slamming his fist down on the table. They each turned to the dwarf in surprise. He turned to Serra and took her delicate hand in his own. "Girl, ye know I've served yer family since yer da' was a pup."

She nodded, a look of surprise still plainly etched upon her face.

"Back before I came to Moondale, I worked in the mines below Sengar Valley with me clan. The elves had entrusted that blasted book ter us ter keep hidden. That old bastard, Jarmassad Truth, stole it from righ' under our noses, and I came ter yer grandfather, Harper, fer help. He sent the Brigade ter attack his castle while a group o' thieves stole the book back. He didn' know it was gone 'til we retreated and headed back home. Yer grandfather hid the book and didn' tell no one where it was. That ol' bastard must be holding one hell of a grudge."

After they had finalized their plans, it was already past noon. They had decided to leave at first light.

Frelia, who had regained consciousness, had gone straight to the kitchens to prepare a grand feast. All of Bloodmoon Castle had been invited, even the servants. Her small kitchen staff, which consisted of two other aging women, and a boy about the age of ten, worked tirelessly.

"I can no' believe they are leavin' again in the morn," Frelia muttered, stuffing a turkey with breadcrumbs and sage.

The others merely ignored her. They had already heard this speech six times in the last hour alone.

Hildvar walked in, stopping next to the young boy who was cutting lettuce.

"And you! Yer lettin' her go!" Frelia yelled.

The boy cut his finger as she shouted, and started to cry fervently. Frelia grabbed him by the arm and walked him over to a bucket of water.

"Never in me life have I been so confused!" she continued to rant, as she began cleaning the wound, and wrapping the boy's finger in a tight cotton bandage.

"Frelia," Hildvar said simply, trying to draw her from her constant ranting.

"Can' believe ye would let her go..."

"Frelia!" he shouted, slamming his fist on the counter.

Frelia stopped her whining as she finished with the boy, and looked at Hildvar with frustration.

"Lady Serra wishes your assistance in her chambers. She asked me to help with the feast while you were away," he said uncomfortably. He didn't know the first thing about cooking.

Frelia pulled off her apron and threw it at him.

"Ye put that turkey there in the oven and don' ye be thinkin' o' lettin' it burn!" she said rashly. She left through the kitchens double doors.

Hildvar stared down at the apron, then at the raw stuffed turkey, and sighed in defeat. The sooner they were on the road, the better.

Serra stood before her floor length mirror dressed in an emerald gown of the finest silk. She had applied some rouge to her already apple red lips and had pinched her cheeks so they blushed.

There was a knock at the door and she ran behind her changing screen.

"Enter."

Frelia walked into the room and looked around, seeing no one. Her expression instantly turned frantic.

"Oh my! She's gone!" she gasped, bringing her hands to her face in fear.

Serra walked from behind the screen, and Frelia grinned from ear to ear.

"Oh, missus, ye look absolutely divine," she said, walking over to her.

Serra blushed and watched as the woman walked all the way around her to get a full look.

"Frelia, I need your help," she said, pulling at the strands of her damp hair.

"Ah, I see, ye'll be wantin' ter look yer best if yer ter impress that handsome stud," she said with a knowing look and a wink.

Serra had never blushed so fiercely.

Frelia grabbed a high-backed chair from the corner of the chamber and motioned for her to sit.

Jareth was looking into a mirror, as well. He had just finished shaving his light beard, and was drying his face when there was a knock at his door.

"Come in," he said, wiping the rest of the cream from his face.

The same servant, who had shown him to his quarters earlier in the afternoon, walked in carrying some folded clothing.

"I've taken the liberty of bringing you some suitable attire for tonight's feast," the man said, looking at Jareth's dirty tunic and breeches.

The man was in his mid-thirties with salt and pepper hair and a small nose.

"Thank you," Jareth said, accepting the clothing. "What was your name again?"

"Justin, sir, Justin Wolfsbane. Will you need anything else, sir?"

"Aye, Justin," he said, looking down at the clothing. "Would you mind finding me a comb and a hair tie? I seem to have left my belongings on my horse."

"Of course, sir," Justin replied before bowing and leaving the room.

A few hours later, Jareth entered the formal dining room to be once again in the company of strangers. He was dressed in a sky blue tunic with black trousers. A yellow sash was tied around his slender waist. He had combed his long, straight, black hair and tied it into a ponytail.

He looked up to see Gnarl motioning to him. He let out a sigh of relief and walked over to him. Gnarl motioned for him to sit opposite him at the end of the table, right next to the throne-like chair at the end.

There were perhaps fifty people sitting at the table. He recognized Hildvar, who had a bandaged hand and Dretho the Mage, sitting uncomfortably between two women talking excitedly to one another. The only person not present was the one he most wanted to see, Serra.

"Ye clean up good boy, though ye coulda kept yer beard," Gnarl said, pulling his own red beard that nearly reached his waist.

Jareth laughed and raised his glass to him. The table was covered with every food he could imagine. Pies of every sort, brightly colored vegetables in various sauces, and a slightly burned turkey were but a few.

The double-doors at the end of the room opened, and everyone at the table fell silent and looked up expectantly.

Justin Wolfsbane walked into the room dressed in a red tunic and brown breeches with his chest puffed out importantly.

"I give to you," he said regally, as soon as he had everyone's attention, "Lady Serra Bloodmoon, Ruler of Moondale."

Serra walked around the corner and entered the room. Everyone at the table rose to their feet, unable to tear their eyes from her. Her emerald green gown made her eyes sparkle like jewels. Her fire red hair had been swept up in the back so that the smooth contours of her face were visible. Everyone at Bloodmoon Castle was so used to seeing her running around in armor or clothing more suitable for a man, sometimes they took her beauty for granted. They all stared in awe and wonder, as she walked gracefully to her seat at the head of the table.

Jareth felt as if his heart would burst with longing. He realized at that moment that he loved this young woman.

She was everything he had ever wanted. She was fierce in battle, spoke her mind, was rebellious by nature, and the most gorgeous woman he had ever set his eyes on. He silently thanked Justar when she motioned for them all to sit. He was beginning to feel his knees weaken.

He glanced over the table at Gnarl, who was obviously trying hard not to snicker at him. He looked back to Serra who was still standing

"People of Bloodmoon Castle, we have gathered here today as equals and I wish to thank each and every one of you for taking such good care of things while I was away," she began, "Tomorrow, a specially selected group and I will leave to rescue our other Lady of the house."

She motioned to the chair next to Jareth, which he had only now noticed was empty of a person. Peace lilies rested in the seat, bound by golden twine.

Everyone at the table, save very few, gasped at the proclamation and began talking excitedly. Scribe Gallo Suntrestle turned positively green with the thought that he would have to continue to handle Moondale's trade.

"I assure you," she continued, as the noise died down. "We will be back as soon as time permits. Before we partake of this grand feast that our own Frelia has overseen," she gestured toward the plump woman toward the end of the table, "I have a few announcements.

"While we are away, Castille Thornberry will be temporarily assuming the post of Captain of the Bloodmoon Brigade," she said, motioning to a surly looking dwarf with hair as black as coal. "Captain Gnarl Knottytrunk will be accompanying me and my companions. Silvera Sunstone shall be also assuming the temporary post of High Cleric while Beargeron is away." A silver haired woman in gray robes nodded to Serra. "And last, but certainly not least, I am sure you have noted a stranger at our table this night," she said, looking down at Jareth and taking his hand. "I would like to introduce you to Jareth the Wanderer, the person responsible for the discovery of my dear sister's whereabouts, and my own safe return home."

Thunderous applause broke out. Jareth grinned appreciatively up at Serra and kissed her hand.

"Now, the food is getting cold and as my father always said to me, *clean your plate*." Everyone laughed as they dug in and Serra finally took her seat.

"Well done, girl," Gnarl said, slapping her on the arm.

She grinned at the dwarf and looked to Jareth who was still holding her hand.

"You are the most remarkable woman I have ever met," he said, bringing her hand to his lips again.

Chapter Ten
Search and Rescue

They all gathered in the courtyard at first light; each prepared for the road and waiting in anticipation. All of them were as different as night and day; an elven mage and his two personal guards, a dwarven Captain, the Lady of Moondale, a barbarian outcast made Lieutenant, a balding high cleric, and a magic wielding wanderer. They were the most unlikely group of travelers Bloodmoon Castle had ever seen.

"Are we ready?" Serra asked, once again adorned in her studded leather armor.

"Aye, my Lady," they all agreed in unison.

"Well, before Dretho and Jareth weave their spells, I would like to say something to each of you. You have been chosen to embark on this quest because I trust each of you with my life, and more importantly, Lorna's life.

You are each my closest friends and allies save Julian and Isaac," she said, looking to Dretho's bodyguards. "And I trust you, because Dretho trusts you."

The two warriors nodded to her in response.

"And finally, if something happens to me," she continued, "your orders are to rescue Lorna at all costs and protect her until she is old enough to don the mantle of Lady of Moondale."

They were silent, but nodded their heads in agreement.

"Jareth, Dretho, we are ready."

The two mages stepped forward. As they both closed their eyes in meditation, the courtyard grew quiet. Not one of the others drew breath, for fear of breaking their concentration.

"Form a circle and join hands," Dretho said, startling most of them. As the other six formed a ring, they took their places opposite one another in the circle.

They had discussed this method of travel many times the day before, but none could anticipate what would happen. Hildvar and Gnarl had outright refused to travel through teleportation until Jareth had explained that it would take nearly a week to arrive to the banks of the Neverlear, and even then most of a day to cross the lake.

Serra's persistent pleading that Lorna's life was on the line was the key to their changing their minds. The barbarian and dwarf fidgeted nervously. Their strong, scarred hands were sweaty and their faces ashen.

Dretho closed his eyes and each person gripped their comrades' hand more tightly.

"*Espin Sanctus Tormenus Zee,*" he chanted. A blue light shot out from his chest, illuminating Jareth first, and slowly began to spread around the circle. Onlookers gasped and pointed, fearing what they did not understand.

Jareth watched closely to make sure that the magical transfer of power made the circle, and ended back at Dretho. "*Arcanus Traveelus Occuli,*" he chanted, and Bloodmoon Castle disappeared.

They soared over the plains, passing farms and villages in the blink of an eye. They flew over the Faeslarne Mountains, and came in view of the great Neverlear River. A lake appeared with an island at its center

They touched down abruptly, and all but a few stumbled to the ground. Bergearon stumbled to a bush and retched. Hildvar and Gnarl were positively green, but managed to hold their breakfast and stand back up with dignity.

Just beyond the small beach loomed the thick forest that was feared and lamented by all. The island of Hoff's Cove had been named after Ripamus Hoff, the vilest ogre to have ever walked Remus. He had lived almost a hundred years ago, and was said to have eaten every human who had ever set foot on his island. Bones littering the sand under their feet reminded them of the tale.

They looked about to make sure they hadn't been seen, but all they saw were towering trees and a mile of sandy beach.

Jareth walked up to the edge of the wood and waited for everyone to join him.

"There is no path. So please, no one wander off, and keep your wits about you," he said in an authoritative voice.

They formed a single file line with Jareth and Gnarl in the lead, Serra and Isaac in the middle, and Julian and Dretho in the rear.

Serra noted immediately the absence of sounds among the trees. No birds sang. No crickets chirped. All they could hear were their footfalls and the breathing of the person next to them.

They wound their way through the thick trees slowly, taking care to stay close to the person in front of them. The two suns were bright, without a cloud in the sky, but the trees were so dense that it seemed a dark and dreary day.

After perhaps an hour of miserable trudging, they came to the edge of a marsh. No one had said a word the whole time, and they all flinched as Jareth spoke.

"We must be careful through this marsh. It is not vast, but there are pockets of quicksand everywhere," he whispered, pulling a length of rope from his backpack.

He tied one end of the rope to his belt and handed the coil to Gnarl, who looked at him in confusion.

"Hook this rope to your belts, giving the person in front and behind about six feet of slack. This way if someone sinks, the others can pull him or her out."

"Damn fine thinkin', boy," Gnarl said in a hushed voice. He worked the rope between his hauberk and sword belt, handing the rope to Serra when he was finished.

It took about five minutes for them to secure the rope. Jareth gave them a firm nod and set off at a slow pace. They were careful to prevent the rope from getting snagged.

After wading in knee-deep water for about an hour, Jareth finally stepped up onto dry land again. The group had walked about thirty paces when Jareth and Gnarl sunk into the sand.

Serra took up the slack immediately and ordered the rest to fall back and pull.

In seconds, Gnarl was chest deep in the sand, thrashing violently in his feeble attempt to gain footing.

"Stop," Jareth yelled to the dwarf, "If you thrash, it will only consume you faster."

Gnarl looked at him in disbelief, but stopped moving. After a few tense moments, he noticed he didn't seem to be sinking as fast.

They pulled hand over hand and the heavy dwarf slumped onto solid ground before the quicksand reached his neck.

Serra grabbed the rope on Gnarl's waist and began to tug harder. The sand was up to Jareth's chest now. They tugged fiercely and with every movement he sunk lower. Jareth did not pull against them because he knew it would make it harder in the long run. He was three feet away from her when he sunk completely under the sand.

Serra cried out and began pulling faster. In less than a minute, Jareth's head emerged and he gasped for air, sputtering and coughing. They pulled him completely out and Serra ran over to him wiping off his face with her hands. She retrieved her water skin and washed the sand from his eyes, and then offered the water, so he could clear his throat.

They stayed there for ten minutes while they calmed down. Gnarl and Jareth both looked as if they had escaped a sand storm. Everyone else was just wide-eyed and thoughtful.

"Damn fine idea, boy," Gnarl said again in a husky voice.

"I have a better one," Serra said, picking up a long limb. She tore the braches and leaves off, leaving about four feet of walking stick.

"Before each step, put this on the ground before you, so that you may gauge the density of what you are about to walk on." She handed the walking stick to Jareth and retook her place in line.

"Now why didn' you think o' that?" Gnarl asked Jareth, punching him in the arm.

"She's not a ruler for nothing," he replied with a smile, rubbing his arm.

They walked around the sand pit while Jareth used the stick and managed to avoid three more pits before they exited the marshland into more dense forest.

"We are getting close," Jareth said, stopping suddenly and breaking the silence.

"How do you know?" Dretho asked from the back of the line, genuinely curious.

The mage had been silent throughout their trek. He was still very untrusting of Jareth and feared they were walking into a trap. There was still more to this story than Jareth was telling, he knew. He did not want to ruffle feathers in the middle of enemy lands, so he remained silent of his fears.

Jareth pointed to a tree beside him. The bark had been stripped in the shape of a J next to the bottom of the trunk. The J was only about three inches long, and one would have to have been looking for it to see it.

"The mark," he said. "There will be thirteen trees marked this way before we find our destination. I say we prepare now."

Each nodded their understanding. They unstrung themselves from the rope. Gnarl and Jareth tried their best to wipe the dry sand from their armor and belongings. Jareth made a quick inventory of his spell components, making sure none had been damaged. Dretho produced his small belt pouch and began unloading some of its contents into the many pockets of his black robes.

After they all seemed prepared, they drew their weapons and reformed their line.

Lorna was the most miserable she had ever been. She was sitting in her own feces, and was covered in filth. Her red hair was matted to her head, and her face was streaked where her tears had dried.

Spike had not come back after her meeting with the old mage. Her stomach rumbled, and her lips were cracked from dehydration.

She could hear the rats scurrying around her, but she was past the point of caring. She was going to die here. This revelation had hit home a few hours before when Spike had not come to feed her. They were going to leave her there to rot.

Where was Serra? Did she no longer care? Did she think her dead already and had given up her search?

The only thing that had given her hope, oddly enough, was what the old mage had unknowingly admitted. Serra had friends who could see her. She could only hope they would not be too late.

They reached the thirteenth tree early in the afternoon. Beyond the trunk lay a stairwell leading into the ground, camouflaged by branches and shrubs. They knew that they would have passed right by it, had Jareth not pointed it out.

Jareth turned to face them.

"This is it," he said, pointing to the hole in the ground. "We make final preparations here."

Bergearon stepped forward. His holy symbol, the great white star of Mialkin, in hand. "Everyone stand together," he said, presenting his holy symbol. "I call forth the awesome power that is Mialkin. Lady of the Stars, grant us with your blessing so that each of us may perform to the greatest of our abilities. Grant us the wisdom to finish this most noble quest and leave healthy to serve your glory again." As he finished his prayer, an odd golden aura appeared around each of them, disappearing in seconds.

Bergearon nodded his bald head to Jareth, and stepped back to take up the rear. He was a very tall man, second only to Hildvar's eight-foot frame.

"Serra, I need you in the back with Bergearon and Dretho. Julian, Isaac, Hildvar, and Gnarl stay behind me. And also, whatever I might say when we enter; please take with a grain of salt. I will try to get us in without bloodshed, though I doubt it will work," Jareth said.

He glanced up at Serra who smiled at him reassuringly. He took a deep breath, lit a torch, and took the first step down the stairwell.

Keifer had been meditating when Jarmassad Truth walked into his room. The old man had never come unannounced before. Even though he treated Keifer like vermin on a regular basis, he usually had the decency to use the mirror.

"The time has come for you to repay my kindness," the old mage said, staring down at him.

Keifer stood and nodded.

"She has come then?" he asked, wringing his hands in nervousness. He was not looking forward to this, despite his anger toward Serra.

"Soon. Gather your things, we must go prepare." Jarmassad said impatiently. Of course, she had come, why else would he have bothered to visit the fool.

"Yes, master," he replied obediently and ran to grab his spell book and components.

The staircase leveled out to a great dusty room. It had obviously once been a dungeon. Rusty shackles adorned the walls of stone, and some were still holding the skeletons of their former occupants.

They moved through the room to a deteriorated door on the other side.

Dretho stepped up to the door and muttered, "*Inseena forenza.*" Nothing happened, but Jareth seemed to understand the incantation and took hold of the knob. He turned it slowly, and the door opened with a great groan of protest.

They walked through the door into a room nearly identical to the first; however, his room was littered with old torture equipment. A rack lay beside one wall, while a table of cat-o-nine-tails and other tools of torment lay beside another. The skeletons in the previous room had been whole, but these were broken and mangled.

After continuing on to another door, Dretho repeated his spell and they moved along. Room after room, they followed the same pattern while the rooms grew more and more grotesque as their purposes were revealed.

Finally walking though one room, they were greeted by a grand, oak door carved into the likeness of the god Justar. Jareth looked to each confirming they were ready, and turned toward the door.

"*Justar Incentra Plamaray,*" he chanted. After he had muttered this, Dretho's eyes narrowed in suspicion, but he continued to say nothing.

Jareth turned back to the others and said, "All you have to do is walk through the door now. Remember, there are guards inside. Just remain silent, and let me do the talking." With that, they each walked through the illusion of the door into the conservatory beyond.

The room was about thirty feet square. Tapestries lined the walls and a small fountain surrounded by plants of various species surrounded it. No one was in sight, but Serra glanced below the tapestries and saw feet. Jareth had warned her before that the guards hid behind them.

A guard dressed in full plate walked into the room from a door to the left of the entrance.

"Halt!" he said in surprise, drawing his broadsword and advancing.

Jareth showed him his hands, palms up, as a sign of peace.

"We come to see a friend," he said, hoping the guard would not feel affronted that the rest were armed and ready.

"Who might that be? Wait, don't I know you," he said, raising his visor to get a closer look at Jareth.

"Aye, Caster. It is I, Jareth." Jareth lowered his hands and held his breath.

"Come out here boys, we got ourselves some visitors," he said, pulling off his helm. A score of guards, all dressed as the first, appeared from behind the tapestries. Some even pulled off their helms, thinking the danger passed.

"Well met, Jareth, how long has it been now? Two, three years?" the guard asked, walking over to Jareth, and offering him his hand.

"Aye, we can't stay long, Caster. We'll get on with our business, and leave you to your hiding," Jareth said, shaking the man's armored hand. He thought the ploy had worked until he saw one of the guards point at Serra. She had her hair pulled back in a ponytail and was wearing her studded skullcap, but the resemblance was unmistakable.

"It's a trap, Caster!" he screamed, resetting his helm, and drawing his pole arm from a loop on the back of his armor.

Jareth, who was still gripping Caster's hand, muttered, "*Insenata Lightnay Forcitha.*" The man began to convulse as lightning raced through his hand and over his body, his armor being a perfect conductor.

He let go just as the other guards advanced. Serra, Bergearon and Dretho stepped back, while the rest formed a line abreast of each other. Jareth did not draw his rapier, but touched his thumbs together.

"*Insenata Flamaray Forcitha!*" he chanted, and a fan of flames burst from his outstretched fingers. Three of the guards took the brunt of the flames through their visors, and fell back screeching that they could not see. However, six guards stepped up to take their place.

Hildvar advanced on one, swinging his large axe down on the guard's right shoulder. It cracked his armor, and blood seeped from the indention. The guard tried futilely to lift his mace and take a swat at the barbarian, but there was no strength behind it. He might as well have been trying to swat a fly.

Sensing his weakness, Hildvar took his advantage and cleaved the guard in the same indention. The sharp axe nearly split the man in two. The barbarian kicked the man off his weapon and turned to face another.

Julian and Isaac advanced on the guard who carried the pole arm. He took a lunge at Julian, catching him in his left thigh, but the long weapon glanced off his armor, and swung wide.

Taking the guard's brief opening, Isaac swung his broadsword in a wide arc. The sword glanced off the man's helm with a loud clang. The guard fell to the side, and Julian jumped on top of him, running his broadsword through the opening between his helm and breastplate, severing his minimally exposed neck.

Gnarl held his morning star at the ready, it was a small weapon for a dwarf, but he wielded it with authority. As another guard advanced on him with a rusty claymore, Gnarl reached back and slammed the spiked ball into the man's chest. An inch-deep depression was left behind, and a crack was visible in the guard's breastplate.

The guard stiffened his resolve and thrust his sword at the dwarf, drawing a deep gash in his forearm. Gnarl bellowed in rage, and struck the man again in the same spot, the crack widening extensively. The guard fell back to let another take his place, and began running down the same corridor Caster had come from.

Gnarl began to take up the chase, but Jareth grabbed his shoulder, and put him back in line. It wasn't often that the dwarf would take orders from a human, but this one had proven his worth already in the marshland.

Jareth had not been attacked yet, the other guards had seen what he had done to poor Caster, and wasn't about to jump into another fan of flame from his hands. He pulled out something out of his belt pouch, and bellowed, "*Insenata Boltinsa Forcitha.*"

He pointed his index finger at the retreating guard before eight bolts of light emerged from it, hitting the guard in the back. The armoured man went down in a heap, convulsing as Caster had done only moments before.

While Gnarl and Jareth had been dealing with the other guard, Julian and Isaac had taken down two others, suffering only minor injuries. Hildvar had downed the last of the six with his axe, cleaving the man through his unprotected skull.

As five more guards advanced, Jareth looked around anxiously to find the three he had hit with the fan of flame. They were lying on the floor at the back of the room, smoldering and unmoving, apparently cooked in their own armor.

Dretho, Bergearon, and Serra could only sit back and watch. All three of them were pinned against the wall by the half circle formed by their comrades.

But Bergearon had different ideas. "I call upon you now, most magnificent Lady of the Stars, grant me the power now to make these evil men stop in their tracks!" he said boomingly, holding out his holy symbol in the direction of the five advancing guards.

They stopped immediately and remained motionless. One guard with a small war hammer was actually standing with one foot about three inches from the floor, as gravity seemed to have forgotten about him.

Bergearon turned to Serra and grinned. "That ought to buy them some time, my Lady," he said, folding his arms over his chest in triumph.

Serra patted him on the shoulder and looked back to her comrades on the front line.

Jareth turned back and nodded his thanks to Bergearon, and they ran around the immobile guards to face the remaining five, who were looking to each other in fear while inching slowly forward.

Keifer walked down the hall toward the conservatory and heard the telltale clang of swords. He knew that twenty guards would keep Serra busy for a while, if not kill her outright. He looked to the wall on his left and pressed one loose stone with his hand. The wall opened to reveal a secret stairwell.

He walked down the stairs with a lit torch in his hand and reached the foot of the stairs before running down the one hundred foot hallway that ended in another short staircase. He walked up the stairs quickly and pulled a lever that opened a secret door in the wall opposite of Lorna's cell.

After closing the door quickly, he looked at the pitiful little girl in hatred. She looked up at him, squinting painfully in the light of his torch.

"Spike?" she asked drearily, "Is that you Spike?"

Slowly her eyes began to focus and as the man reached her cell door, she gasped. "Keifer! What are you doing here? Where is Serra?" she asked, trying pointlessly to stand up. Her legs had been numb for three days, and her hands were chained so close to the wall, she couldn't stand if she wanted to.

Keifer smiled. "Hello there, Lorna. Enjoying your stay?"

"You are behind this aren't you? You're in league with that old man!" she said with as much venom as her debilitated frame could muster.

"You always were a smart, little girl," he said condescendingly, "Your sister is here now, actually. She'll be joining your brother soon, of that I am sure."

Lorna beamed at the proclamation, despite his attempt at callousness. Serra had come for her. Her heart swelled with love for her sister. All this time she had thought that she had forgotten about her.

"She'll shred the hide from your bones, you stupid oaf," she replied with renewed energy.

"Nay, I shall kill her before your very eyes, so that you can feel the ultimate loss before you lose your own life," he spat, waving his hand. The cell door opened and he walked in, shutting it behind him.

"Get out of here, you slow-witted slog!" she yelled in defiance.

Keifer didn't bother to respond to her petty insults, he only said "*Incentra visatar estinar*", disappearing before her eyes.

Julian dispatched the last of the mobile guards just as Bergearon's spell wore off. As soon as they saw they could move again, they ran straight toward Serra, who drew her scimitar, and bellowed the Bloodmoon battle cry,

"You should fear our fire and fury,
For know it will seal your doom,
We are the red and mighty,
Fear the wrath of the Bloodmoon's!"

Her sword leapt from her hand and stabbed at the first guard it danced to. Jareth, Julian, and Isaac did a double take as they watched the sword weave its dance.

"It's her father's sword, lads, its supposed ter do that!" Gnarl yelled at them as he clocked one guard in the back with his morning star. He had seen Frendar Bloodmoon cry those very words before in battle, and was accustomed to seeing the dancing scimitar do its magic.

Hildvar brought his battleaxe over his head at a dead run just as the guard in front of him turned, and extended his sword. The barbarian impaled himself, unable to stop the sword from going through his left side, crushing two ribs in the process.

The other three guards were advancing quickly on Serra when Dretho stepped in front of her and threw a potion at the one in the middle. The green bottle shattered onto the man's helm and the metal began to melt in a sulfurous cloud of smoke. The guard screamed in pain. The liquid had splashed into his eyes upon impact, and they were melting as well. He fell, writhing in agony, until he lay motionless on the floor.

Serra's scimitar lunged at one of the guards, stabbing him through a chink in his armor. The sword sunk deeply into his armpit, and pierced his lung. It retracted immediately, and the man fell to the floor gasping for air.

Dretho drew another potion from his robes and threw it at the last guard. It exploded upon contact with his left thigh, and the man burst into green flames. He began running in circles screaming for someone to put him out. But this fire was magical and did not go out until all it touched was consumed. Serra watched in horror as her sword impaled the frantic man right through his unprotected neck.

Hildvar watched as the guard retracted his sword. He went down on his knees, pressing his hand over his wound while watching his lifeblood spill out onto the floor.

The man had raised the sword to finish the barbarian off when Jareth jumped over in front of him, and stabbed the man through his breastplate with his rapier. He backpedaled in shock, taking Jareth's sword with him. Jareth advanced, retrieved a dagger from his belt, and let fly. The dagger hit home in the man's elbow, severing the muscle, so that his arm hung loosely immediately, and his sword clanged to the floor.

Jareth walked up to the man and grabbed the hilt of his rapier, putting his foot on the man's chest as he pulled. He lunged at him again, and sent his thin blade through the guard's right eye and out the back of his skull with a sickening crack.

Gnarl's opponent had turned around after stumbling from the blow. Serra's sword whistled inches from the dwarf's head and plunged deep into the man's neck. As the fresh corpse lay dead on the floor, the scimitar disappeared in a plume of red smoke.

Lorna looked around her cell, trying to see where Keifer had gone. She felt a sharp pain to the top of her head, saw a brilliant white light, and knew no more.

Keifer, invisible right beside her, smiled. He knew she was not dead, but he didn't need her giving him away should Serra survive the legion in the conservatory.

He walked over to a corner and waited patiently.

Hildvar was feeling weak. He didn't know how much blood he had lost, but he was beginning to slip into darkness.

Bergearon ran over just as the barbarian's eyes closed. He grabbed a clear potion from the pocket of his robes, propped the man's mouth open, and poured the potion in while holding his nose so that he would swallow. He followed that by four more of the same color.

After only a few minutes, Hildvar opened his eyes. Bergearon examined his grievous wound, which was fast closing. The healing potions he had concocted the night before were doing their job well.

Serra ran over to Jareth and started looking him over. He had a nasty cut on his leg, but was otherwise unhurt.

Bergearon moved from Hildvar over to Gnarl and began rubbing herbs on his forearm and bandaging his wounds.

The conservatory was littered with bodies. The man Hildvar had cleaved through the head lay half in the fountain, turning its water a bloody red. The smell of charred bodies and the sulfurous smoke from Dretho's potions burned their noses.

"Ok, let's go," Jareth said, moving toward the staircase that went down to a lower level. The others followed closely behind.

The stairwell ended after fifteen feet and met a long corridor. Two doors adorned each side and one familiar door lay at the end.

"Julian, Isaac, take the doors on the left. Gnarl and I will take the doors on the right. The rest of you stay in the hall, and alert us of anyone coming." Jareth ordered.

Julian stood by while Isaac turned the handle of the first door. It opened easily to a small barracks with empty beds. They moved into the room and checked under each to make sure no one was in hiding.

The surly dwarf was not so careful. He merely kicked the wooden door in, revealing a small kitchen, also empty

They moved back out to the hall where Dretho, Hildvar, Serra, and Bergearon stood. Hildvar was standing tall, but it was obvious he was weak from the loss of blood. His face was ashen and expressionless.

Jareth pointed to the next set of doors, and nodded to Julian and Isaac. But the next two rooms revealed an abandoned dining hall and a weapon room.

They moved out into the hall again and progressed toward the door at the end of the hall.

"I know that two ogres were here two nights ago, so be prepared," Jareth said, motioning toward the door. "Lorna is in that room, unless they have moved her."

Jareth reached down to the knob and slowly turned it, but it didn't budge. He reached down to his belt pouch and took out a set of lock picks.

Gnarl laughed quietly, "Jack o' all trades, that one."

Jareth smiled as he picked the lock. It took a minute, but it was a simple mechanism that he was accustomed to.

As he stood back up, he nodded to them all, and turned the knob. When he pulled the door open, a foul stench filled their noses. They heard guttural noises from down a short stairway. They all stepped back as two fur-clothed ogres came into view. Their hair was orange and matted. Their faces were gray and contorted into a natural snarl. Their teeth were green and broken, dripping with saliva. They ambled up the stairs with a look of madness in their eyes.

"Man flesh!" one said, raising its club, ready to strike.

Gnarl stepped up to it, making a rude gesture before taking a swipe at it with his morning star. The spiked ball glanced across its temple, but it did not phase it in the least as it continued to move forward.

"Uh oh," the dwarf said, stepping back.

Dretho stepped past Serra and advanced on the monster. He pulled out yet another potion from his robes and popped the cork. The ogre opened his mouth to bellow at the elf. Silently thanking Drakevin for the opportunity, Dretho poured the red liquid down its gullet.

The mage stepped back and smiled as the ogre's eyes bulged and contracted. The flesh on the ogre's body began convulsing as it shrunk smaller and smaller, taking on a green hue. Its legs popped at the knees and folded backward.

Its comrade looked on in horror as the ogre turned slowly into a frog. In seconds, the transformation was complete and the ogre-turned-frog leapt down the steps, and disappeared from view.

The remaining ogre looked at Dretho, who was grinning at Gnarl, and whimpered. It raised its club weakly then dropped it as it ran down the hall toward the conservatory.

Jareth shined his torch tentatively down the stairwell looking for any other signs of enemies. He turned to Serra, who was still watching the ogre's escape.

"Serra," he said, drawing her attention, "I don't think I need to remind you that when we find her, she may not be well."

She visibly stiffened, but nodded for him to move on.

They slowly descended the staircase. A lit torch lay in the floor of the second cell. A girl sat next to it, unconscious, held up only by her shackled hands.

Serra gasped and ran to the cell door, futilely trying to open it. Lorna looked awful. She was so frail and dirty. There were scabs on her wrists where the manacles had rubbed them, and a large knot was visible on the top of her head.

Jareth laid his hand gently on Serra's shoulder. "Let me unlock the cell, so you may go to her," he whispered. She backed tentatively away, and Jareth put his lock picks to use again.

None of the others said a word. They merely stared at the poor young girl lying there so helplessly.

Jareth finally unlocked the door and barely had it open when Serra slipped past him and ran to her sister. She knelt next to Lorna and took her into her arms.

"Oh, baby," she mumbled as the tears flowed freely. "We're going to get you out of here and you'll be fine." She absently stroked Lorna's dirty hair while laying the girl's head on her breast.

Bergearon knelt beside her and began examining the girl. He took out his holy symbol and touched it to her chest.

"Mialkin," he started in a cracked voice, "Oh, Lady of the Stars, heal this young soul for she is worthy of your mercy."

After a brief flash of white light, Lorna's eyes fluttered open slowly. She gazed up at Serra groggily.

"Hi, sis," Serra said, wiping away her tears.

"Trap," Lorna said weakly. Her voice was barely above a whisper, but Serra understood and stiffened.

Jareth had managed to unlock the manacles and Lorna's arms fell limply to her sides.

Serra stood up after Gnarl scooped the girl into his arms. She looked around the cell trying to discern what Lorna was talking about, and had just begun to speak when a dagger appeared out of thin air at her throat and an arm wrapped around her waist.

Jareth was the first to notice the man holding her. He yelled, "Serra!" and everyone looked up in alarm.

Keifer smiled evilly at the man, bringing his lips close to Serra's ear.

"Ah, my dear, I see you've brought friends. Here I thought you would be stupid enough to come by yourself."

Serra recognized that voice, and a rage welled within her like nothing she had ever felt before. She clinched her teeth and growled in anger. "You bloody bastard!"

The dagger pressed closer to her throat.

"Ah ah ah, temper temper. Seems fitting doesn't it, love, that last we met you held a dagger to my own throat. Oh, how the tables have turned," Keifer said mockingly before licking her earlobe.

"I should have killed you that day!" she screamed in disgust.

Jareth reached into his belt pouch, and then thought better of it. He knew the moment he began an incantation, the man would slit her throat. "Let her go," he said sternly.

Keifer looked up to Jareth as if it was the first time he had noticed him.

"No, I don't believe I will," Keifer said with a smile, putting pressure on the dagger and drawing a thin line of blood.

"Ye rotten maggot!" Gnarl yelled, "I always knew ye were no good! Serra's ne'er been anythin' but kind ter ye 'til ye insulted 'er clan and ye know it!"

"Shut up, you stupid dwarf!" Keifer bellowed, "Now, lay the girl back down and move into the hall slowly."

"No!" Serra yelled, "Get her out of here, you have your orders!"

As they stared into her eyes, it was not a look of fear, but of loathing. She abhorred the thought of them giving in after coming all this way. She was determined to get Lorna to safety, even if it meant her death.

Suddenly, Keifer convulsed wildly. The dagger fell from his hand, but not before drawing a deep gash in Serra's throat. Her lifeblood began to pour, and she could not draw breath.

Dretho had materialized right behind Keifer and had slit the man's throat with a dagger he had taken from Julian's sword belt while invisible.

Bergearon and Jareth rushed over to Serra. She saw Jareth's worried expression right before she slipped into darkness.

Bergearon pressed his hand over her neck immediately and began to pray. The blood slowed, but did not stop. He reached into his pocket and pulled out a small clear vile. Pouring the liquid over the wound, the blood flow finally stopped.

He pressed his ear to her chest and cried out, "She's not breathing." But then he looked down at Serra's sword belt and saw the three potions he had given her earlier in the day. He uncorked each in turn and poured them down her throat.

They all waited with baited breath and after what seemed a lifetime, Serra gasped for air. Jareth ran over to her and scooped her up in his arms, knocking the bald cleric over in the process. Serra had not opened her eyes, but at least she was breathing.

"Let's get out of here! To the corridor!" Jareth yelled, leading the way.

They stopped in the corridor and he laid her down on the floor. He pulled out his own three potions, and poured them down her throat, as well. Everyone was staring at him, hoping that he would somehow awaken her.

She had just opened her eyes when Jareth heard a familiar voice.

"Hello, son."

Chapter Eleven
Revelations

An old man with a long, white beard stood in the corridor blocking their path. He was wearing black robes and carrying a tall, black, gnarled staff. His face was old and wrinkled, but his blue eyes told the tale. They were identical to Jareth's.

Dretho and Gnarl merely looked at each other, an alarmed look on their faces. Lorna had passed out once again. Bergearon, Isaac, and Julian had just entered the hallway and noticed the man. Hildvar, who had been standing motionless just past the doorway, drew his axe and scowled at Jareth in hatred.

Serra was very weak, but she turned her head to see the speaker, and then looked back to Jareth. He was still holding her in his arms, but he was frozen to the spot. A look of abject terror was splayed across his face, as if he were seeing a ghost.

"Once again, Jareth, you stand in my way. It is bad enough you choose to be a thief by trade, but to fraternize with the very people who have stolen from your own father, is unforgivable," the man said, taking a step toward them.

Jareth's face contorted into fury.

"You are not my father. You killed my mother and disowned me after I found out what you really are; a shell of a man only out for his own glory, never thinking of anyone, but himself. The Bloodmoon's did not steal anything from you that you did not steal first, you bastard!" he yelled in defiance.

The old man shook his head.

"What are you to gain by going against me now? Do you think these people will stay with you now that they know you are Jarmassad Truth's son?" the old man offered with a sardonic grin.

Serra's eyes widened and Jareth looked at her. His scowl turned to a stare of the deepest regret. He had hoped she would never know. He had hoped that he could just be Jareth, as he had been for three years. But now she knew. Oh, how he had wanted to love her, to be with her.

She was in shock. This old man in the hallway was responsible for the deaths of nearly everyone she loved. And Jareth was his son. He had helped her in so many ways. He had given her hope when there was none. He had convinced her to seek help, when no one else could. He had brought them here at his own mortal peril so they could rescue Lorna. This man, unlike the one a few paces away, was not a murderer. This man had honor.

She reached for his face and stroked his cheek. "A man without honor is no man at all. You are honorable," she whispered hoarsely, and then she closed her eyes again and descended into blackness.

Her words had set him free. She understood. He didn't know how, but this woman knew his heart. He laid her carefully on the floor and stood up to face the unknown.

"They, unlike you, see past power and greed. They understand what it is to be a family. You never have and never will," he said gruffly. "Dretho, get them out of here."

Dretho, who had been watching all this develop, nodded.

"You will not be going anywhere!" Truth said in fury.

Jareth took a few steps forward and raised his hands.

"Go!" he yelled to the group behind him. He knew that if he kept his father busy with magic, the ward over the dungeon would lift for teleportation.

"*Insenata Lightnay Forcitha!*"

A bolt of lightning sprung from his hands toward his father, but unlike before, this bolt continued in a bright blue-white stream. As the lightning reached Jarmassad, it crackled against a red globe shield that emanated from his gnarled staff.

Jareth did not waver, but continued his magical assault. His lighting crackled against the red sphere steadily, but did not penetrate.

Jarmassad muttered continuously to keep his shield intact.

Bergearon rushed over to Serra and scooped her up just as Dretho was herding them in a circle once again. The persons on either side of Bergearon and Gnarl, who were carrying the two unconscious Bloodmoon ladies, grabbed hold of their shoulders to complete the ring.

"*Espin Sanctus Tormenus Zee,*" Dretho chanted and watched the group glow with blue magic.

"*Arcanus Traveelus Heptali!*" he thundered and the group disappeared, leaving only Truth and Jareth in their seemingly endless battle of wills.

They all arrived in the courtyard of Bloodmoon Castle within moments. Gnarl and Bergearon ran immediately into the castle to seek help in healing the women.

"We must go help him," Hildvar said, turning to talk to Dretho, but the elf was gone.

Jareth was weakening. He could tell that his father was much stronger. Thinking he could not keep his lightning spell up for much longer, something happened that was wholly unexpected.

Just as fast as the rest had left, Dretho reappeared by his side.

"*Amaretus Forcitha Blasatha!*" the elf yelled and Truth's shield dissipated instantly, sending him flying up against the wall with Jareth's bolt of lightning.

Jareth slumped to the floor exhausted.

"*Insenata Acida Forcitha!*" Dretho chanted with a snarl, advancing on Truth, who was struggling to get to his feet. A purple liquid burst from the elf's hands and covered the sorcerer. Everywhere the acid touched, small plumes of smoke began to rise. Jarmassad screamed in agony as the acid began to eat him alive.

"You will pay for this you mettlesome elf!" he screamed, his lip folding and dripping. He muttered under his breath and disappeared into thin air.

Dretho walked back over to Jareth who had tears streaming down his face. He could not help but realize he had just attacked his own father. An evil man, yes, but his father all the same.

"Thank you for that," he said, looking up to the elf, "I did not expect to see any of you again."

Dretho offered Jareth his hand.

"I'll not pretend that I like you much, human, but Serra's father once saved my life and became my closest friend. If you had any intention of killing Serra or Lorna, you could have, many times, but you didn't. A man is judged by his actions, not his relatives."

Serra awoke with a start three days later. Her throat was very sore, but she had slept well. She turned her head and saw Jareth sitting in a chair at her bedside. His head lay on his arms propped on the back of the chair, and he was asleep.

"Jareth," she tried to say, but it just came out as a wheeze.

Jareth raised his head immediately, looking at her with wide eyes. He jumped out of the chair and sat on her bed, taking her pale hand in his.

"Don't try to speak," he said excitedly, "Bergearon said it would be a few days before you're able to talk again. Your vocal chords were severed. The healing potions held them together for a short time, but only time will heal them now."

Serra nodded her head painfully.

Jareth cleared a lump in his throat and fought back the tears welling in his eyes.

"Oh, Serra, there is so much I need to tell you. When that man slit your throat, I thought you were dead."

Serra looked at him and smiled weakly.

"I should have told you the truth, but I did not know what you would think of me if I had. I have been cast out so many times by the discovery of my parentage. I wanted you to know me for who I am."

Serra gripped his hand tightly and raised her other hand. After posing her hand as if holding a quill, she began making writing motions.

Jareth looked to her hand and said, "Of course, I will be right back, let me get some parchment."

He jumped from the bed and ran out her bedroom door.

She understood the uncertainty he had been feeling. She had felt the same when she had left Bloodmoon Castle, not knowing if she would find Lorna alive or dead. Especially knowing she may have inadvertently caused it by her actions with Keifer.

He sat on her bed again, inked up the quill, and handed her the thick paper.

She tried to rise, only to lie back down quickly as the muscles in her neck contracted and burned like fire.

Jareth reached behind her with his palm on her spine, lifting her into a sitting position, and quickly propped big, fluffy pillows at her back.

She nodded her head in thanks and picked up the quill,

Lorna?

Jareth read the word and smiled.

"Oh, she is well, Serra. It has been three days since we left Hoff's Cove and she has been up walking around. She was very thin and dehydrated but your maid, Frelia, has her plumping back up as we speak."

Serra smiled and began to write again,

What happened in the hall after I passed out?

Jareth read these words and it was a moment before he spoke.

"After you passed out, I worked a spell to fend off my... Jarmassad Truth. While I was fighting him, they brought you home, leaving me to fight him. Dretho came back and saved my life. He brought me back here."

Serra's smile widened at the proclamation that Dretho had not abandoned him.

He is a good man, just misunderstood. I have made the mistake of hating him for a year, when he did nothing wrong. You must not judge him for his demeanour. He is of a different culture and does not think or act like the norm. I wish to see him.

Serra frowned and wrote,

Is Truth dead?

Jareth thought on this a moment.

"No, I do not believe he is dead, he is much too powerful for that now. I believe he is alive, but only just."

I meant what I said about honor. I have never thought that you would harm me, nor do I think that now. Do not berate yourself for something you have no control over.

Jareth smiled and kissed Serra on her forehead.

"Rest now, I will ask Dretho to come see you soon. I imagine Lorna will want to see you, as well. She's quite the little character."

He left her then. Serra put her parchment, quill, and ink aside and closed her eyes. The past week had been the hardest of her twenty years. She allowed her exhaustion to take her and fell fast asleep.

"Ye better eat girl. Ye're skin and bones, well, ye always were skin and bones, but ye need ter eat." Gnarl said impatiently to Lorna.

They were in the dining room at the evening meal. Lorna was still very pale, but some color was returning to her face. When she had been well enough to stand on her own, Frelia had scrubbed her raw to clean off the filth. They had been trying to get her to eat every waking moment of the day ever since.

"Gnarl, I just ate an hour ago! Leave me alone will you!" the young girl shouted. She was dressed in a long, lilac-colored dress and had her red hair pulled up into a bun.

Dretho grinned at Lorna. She had regained her fiery temper shortly after their arrival at the castle three days before. The mage had not seen her much since then. He had taken it upon himself to cast enchantments around the castle grounds to prevent offensive spells. He knew that it would be a while before Jarmassad tried to attack the Bloodmoon's again. If he did, indeed, have the book of Gyndless the Almighty, it was a definite possibility it would be sooner than later.

"Dwarf, leave the girl alone, that woman has been shoveling everything down her throat from the moment we walked in the door. Let the girl breath or she'll be looking like you soon," Dretho said with amusement.

Lorna blanched at the thought. She did not know this elf very well. All she really knew was that he had been a friend of her dad's and had saved Serra in that dungeon. But she had to admit; it was funny watching him argue with Gnarl all the time.

"Hmrph," Gnarl grunted, gnawing on his turkey leg again.

Jareth walked into the dining room and everyone froze, looking up at him expectantly. He looked awful. His hair was in disarray and his clothes were rumpled. However, he had the biggest smile on his face any of them had ever seen.

"She's awake!" he said excitedly.

Jareth had been at Serra's bedside day and night since his return with Dretho. He had refused to leave her side, except to go to the water room. Frelia had even brought his meals to him in Serra's chamber.

Lorna grinned from ear to ear and jumped from her seat.

"No," Jareth said, motioning for her to sit back down, "I told her to go back to sleep and rest, but she did write to me a bit. She can't talk."

Lorna sat back in her chair and crossed her arms. Her red lips were drawn into a great pout.

"What'd she say, boy?" Gnarl asked through half a mouthful of turkey.

"She asked about Lorna first, and I told her she was fine." Lorna's pout disappeared, but she was still upset she wouldn't be able to see Serra. "She asked what happened after she had passed out and I gave her a summary. She said she wanted to see Dretho later on also."

Dretho remained expressionless, but noted everyone gazed up at him.

"That all?" the dwarf asked.

Jareth looked a little crestfallen.

"Yes, I guess I was just in a hurry to make sure you all knew," he said, sitting down in what was now his customary seat between Lorna and Serra's.

Lorna, who had only seen Jareth in passing, frowned at him.

"That is not your chair!" she shouted and Jareth jumped. "That is Serra's chair."

Jareth looked to Gnarl, who put down his turkey leg, and looked at the girl in pity.

"No darlin', that, is Serra's chair," he said, pointing to the empty throne at the head of the table.

Lorna did not waiver. "Then I should be sitting where he is sitting, since I'm the other Lady of the house."

Gnarl looked from her to Dretho then down to the table, and shook his head.

"Explain it ter her, elf," he said, nudging Dretho with his elbow.

Dretho shifted in his seat and then fixed Lorna with a patient stare.

"It is customary, Lady Lorna, for the companion of the ruler of the house, to take the seat to her right, with her Captain on her left."

Lorna looked to Jareth then, finally understanding.

"Oh," she replied, blushing.

Jareth, who had never heard himself put in that light, grinned stupidly.

"Don' ye be getting' yer hopes up either boy, she ain' committed ter nothin' yet!" Gnarl shouted, throwing his turkey bone at Jareth across the table.

They all shared the first laugh the castle had heard in days.

Dretho entered Serra's bedchamber just after the meal. He carried a lit candle, and was trying not to make much noise. He walked up to the bed and sat down in the chair next to it.

When she had come to his tower, she had been pale and fatigued to the point of exhaustion, but she now looked peaceful in her slumber. The cut on her neck was healing nicely. The cleric had said that it should not scar thanks to the salve Jareth had concocted.

Her eyes fluttered open and she looked up at him. She reached for him and he tentatively took her soft, pale hand.

"Good evening, Lady Serra," he whispered, "I was told you wished to see me."

Using Dretho's hand for leverage, she pulled herself up to a sitting position. It was painful, but was nothing like it had been a few hours before. She was actually able to support herself without the pillows long enough to prop them behind her. She took a deep breath and reached for the parchment and quill.

Thank you for helping Jareth in his time of need. I did not know how he would be treated after his identity was realized.

Dretho read the note and sighed.

"Serra, I know what it is to be misjudged. I am still wary of him, but I believe his intentions are good. It is as I told him, if he had wanted you or Lorna dead, it would have only been too easy."

He said you saved his life.

"Aye," he said softly, "After we teleported back to the castle, I went directly back to the dungeon, unsure if I would be too late. He was growing weak, but he was holding his own. He is no beginner by any means. When he said he finished his apprenticeship, he was being honest."

Do you trust him?

Dretho was surprised by this question.

"I would be lying if I said I trusted him fully. Though we cast the same enchantments and use the same components, there is a difference between a sorcerer and a mage. Jarmassad Truth is a sorcerer. They are only out for their own personal gain and will do anything within their power to do so. Mages use magic to further their own ends, but not to the expense of other's lives unless they are defending themselves. I am a mage and I believe Jareth is as well, but he was trained as a sorcerer despite what he says. Mages are trustworthy, but you should never trust a sorcerer."

Chapter Twelve
Competitions

Light poured into the bedchamber where a very weary and disfigured Jarmassad Truth slept. He opened his one good eye and cursed as the memories of the events in Hoff's Cove came flooding back. The elf's acid had eaten away his right hand and a portion of his left leg.

His face, which was now missing some of its beard, looked as if the right side had been melted away, like candle wax. His eyelid and the surrounding skin were smooth, shiny, and joined together to cover the orb that was useless to him now.

After teleporting to Fortin Manor, Keifer's former house in Clandestine, Fenlin Karling, who had worked for Truth for a number of years, though he had never met the man, had immediately summoned a cleric to stop the acid and heal the sorcerer. The cleric had been successful in halting the acid, but since the scars were of a magical nature, there was no way to heal them.

The sorcerer had laid in this very bed since then, wallowing in his own misery. The pain was virtually gone, though it was his pride that hurt the most. He had been so close. They had both been only a few feet away, but his own son had stolen his chance to reach his goal to rid Remus of the Bloodmoon line.

Jareth had surprised him in the ferocity of his attack. The boy had never attacked him before. Even when Jarmassad had killed Rowena, Jareth's mother, he had not put up a fight. Rowena, who had found out about his evil ways, had threatened to leave him and take Jareth with her. Jarmassad had told her he intended to apprentice the boy, but she had replied that she did not wish for him to turn out like his father.

One night while they both lay in bed, she had died in her sleep of poison. Poison that Jarmassad had placed in her water right before they had turned in. Jarmassad had tried his best not to let the boy know who had done it, but he knew he suspected. He had only been fourteen at the time. It was right after his second year of training, that he had he found out for sure.

Jarmassad had sat down with Jareth, to convince him to join him in his plans for the death of the Bloodmoon family.

Jareth had outright refused. He had said that they had done nothing to him and that he was not the one with the grudge. He had struck the boy and told him about his mother's demise in anger, threatening to do the same to him, if he did not cooperate. Jareth had left that very night.

He had waited nearly a year to contact him, knowing he needed time. Jareth had been traveling the country, trying to find a place for himself. He was in the northern city proper of Glendale, stealing food, and living on the streets, when they had met again. Jareth had refused him and had told him to leave him alone. That was when Jarmassad had disowned him, telling him he would die in his own feces one day, poor and alone.

Though his son would not yield to his wishes, his trip had proved fruitful after all. While in Glendale he had felt a magical connection that he hadn't felt in twenty years. It was the book. The spell book of Gyndless the Almighty was almost sentient, for any who had cast its runes would feel it's connection the rest of his days.

He had sent many to find the book, but none had prevailed, except Keifer. Keifer, who had been the Baron of Fresta, had had connections to a thieves' guild in Glendale called the Band of the Yellow Sash. It had only taken the guild a year to find it.

With renewed energy, Jarmassad slowly sat up in bed. If he couldn't get rid of the Bloodmoon line, he would have to take their land. He would once again call upon the book and unite the tribes of creatures that roamed Remus. He would send an assault on Moondale of which the likes had never been seen. He intended to rival Gyndless Goreseeker, and would succeed, even if he had to kill his own son.

Four days had passed before Serra was strong enough to rise out of bed. Jareth had walked in carrying a tray of food and had nearly dropped it at the sight of her. She was dressed in a thin, white, silk nightgown and was holding herself upright by way of one of the posts of her canopied bed.

She looked up to him as he entered the room and motioned for him to help her. He ran over to her, after quickly setting the tray on her dresser.

"I should have waited for you to come," she whispered and then her eyes brightened. Those were the first words she had uttered since their return to the castle a week ago.

Jareth laughed, picked her up, and spun her around. He quickly stopped as he noticed the faint expression upon her face. As he stopped and held her close, he realized how sheer her nightgown was. He could see the swell of her breasts under the garment. He hurriedly turned his eyes to the ceiling.

"I'm sorry," he laughed, "I'm just so happy to hear your voice again."

"Could you hand me my robe, please?" she asked with a smile, pointing to a green, silk robe on a peg on her wall.

After he helped her back to the bedpost and grabbed the robe, he turned back to her and had to fight the desire swelling in him. She was standing there scantily clad, right next to a huge bed. He adverted his eyes back to the ceiling and held the robe out to her, carefully helping her into it.

"Will you go fetch Frelia, Jareth? I am in sore need of a bath," she whispered.

He looked at her and laughed heartily. He realized she had been in this bed for a week.

"I honestly hadn't noticed, love, you look just as beautiful as the day we first met," he said, stroking her cheek.

She blushed and sat on the edge of her bed.

"I'll go get her for you at once, do you think you will be strong enough to join us for lunch?" he asked excitedly, walking toward the door.

"One step at a time," she replied, amused at his anxiousness.

Word had spread quickly through Moondale that Lady Serra was able to speak once again and was up and around.

Hildvar, who had been confining himself to the barracks, came into the castle in a rush to see her. She was sitting in an overstuffed chair, reading a small book when he entered. She wore a simple green dress, but looked every bit the Lady to him.

"My Lady?" he inquired as he walked over to her chair.

Serra looked up at him and smiled.

"Hi Hildy, where have you been?" she whispered, motioning to the chair next to her.

Hildvar sat uncomfortably in the lush armchair. He was barely able to fit in the seat and his legs were so long they bent nearly to his chest.

"I have been in the barracks, I did not wish to bother you while you recovered," he said uncomfortably. He had not wanted to see Jareth mainly. He just did not want to admit it openly.

Serra cocked her head and gave him a questioning look. "Something is bothering you, tell me," she whispered.

Hildvar looked down at his hands and sighed.

"What is it? Did something happen that I am not aware of?" she whispered in concern.

"No, my Lady, it is your friend. He is the son of the man who led my clan to ruin," he said, unable to look into her eyes.

Serra was not surprised. Barbarians were proud of their heritage and took pride in the feats of their ancestors before them. Hildvar was obviously distressed that such a man was so close to her.

"Hildvar," she whispered, closing her book, "If it were not for Jareth, we would all probably be dead. Do you realize that?"

"Aye," he answered, still looking at his hands.

"Jareth is not his father. You've heard yourself that he left as soon as he realized how his father was. You've seen that he is most willing to battle him to protect those he cares for."

"Aye," he answered again, shifting uneasily in his seat.

"Then why do you despise him so?" she asked in all seriousness.

"I know not, my Lady, it is not something I can control. I have a bad feeling when he is around. I do not know why."

"Hildvar, you are familiar with the story of Dretho the Mage and my father, correct?"

"No, not other than your father saved his life," he answered, finally looking into her eyes.

"Aye, that is the gist. However, there is more to the tale. You know how Dretho is feared across the land. His reputation is so dreadful only because he has different methods of punishment for his people. He does not do this because he is evil. He does it because it is his way. But my father was able to look beyond that and save his life, because he was just a man in need," she whispered.

Hildvar merely stared at her.

"Dretho had been attacked by an army of giants and the Bloodmoon Brigade arrived in time to turn the battle. My father took down a giant that was about to crush Dretho to death. I do not believe Dretho had understood the power of a good deed until that fateful day. That is why you must try your best to understand where Jareth is coming from. His father is evil, yes, but he is not. He has helped me find my sister. If not for him she would be dead. I also, would be dead, Hildvar, if it were not for this man you so despise." He visibly flinched at her last statement. "I must ask you to let go of anger toward him for the suffering of your people. In controlling our emotions and forgiving our peers, we grow stronger and are bound by something stronger than any spell or weapon; friendship."

Hildvar understood what she was saying. Though he knew it would not be easy, he would try simply because she had asked him to. Moondale had become his home and the Bloodmoon's, his clan. He had come to this city to conquer it and take it for the sorcerer, but ended up finding friends in his enemies. He saw the irony in that and decided he would try, he would try very hard.

Jareth had been wandering the castle grounds. It had been days since he had been out in the sunslight and he found that he had missed it. He wandered the south garden, with its many flowers and shrubs. A statue graced the middle of the grounds. A man on horseback with a scimitar held high. He walked over to the statue and read the plaque at its base.

Lord Frendar Agradan Bloodmoon
Who turned the tide of the
Battle of Sengar Valley
Accompanied by the Bloodmoon Brigade
The Elves of Sengar Valley Thank You

Jareth looked up at the man. His face was contorted in fury, his hair flying wildly as if blowing in the wind.

So, this was Serra's father.

He was continuing his stroll through the garden when he heard someone crying. He rounded one large shrub to see Lorna sitting on a bench in front of three tombstones. Two of the graves looked as if they had been there for a while. The other, looked very recent.

Lord Renfar Agradan Bloodmoon
Beloved Son and Brother
Rest in Peace

Jareth had turned to quietly walk away and leave the girl in her mourning, when she spoke.

"Please, don't leave," she said with a small squeak.

Jareth turned to her and she looked up at him with her big, green eyes streaked with tears. He walked over to the bench, sat down beside her, and put a reassuring arm around her shoulder.

"Renfar was your brother?" he asked quietly.

Her shoulders wracked with sobs and she nodded.

"Serra has told me little about him. However, I have heard he was a great man," he said reassuringly.

"Yes," she said softly. "He was mean to me sometimes, but it was because he had so much to do. I never got to say goodbye. I was there... when he died. I didn't even know he had died until that old man told me."

Jareth was instantly flooded with guilt. Did his father not understand how his single-mindedness affected people?

"I am sorry that my father did this," he said.

She cried on his shoulder for many minutes before either of them spoke.

"I am glad you are not like him, Jareth. I am glad you have come here and that you helped save me from him. I couldn't fight him. I couldn't do anything," she said with a renewed wave of tears.

"I had not seen him in years, Lorna. If I had known what he had planned, I would have done everything I could have to stop him," he said, rubbing her back.

"I don't think anyone could have. It was so sudden and Serra was gone. If she had been at the castle, she would probably be dead too," she said, finally clearing her eyes with her fingers.

"Where was Serra?" he asked. He knew Serra had not been in the room, but he did not know she had been gone from the grounds entirely.

"Renfar made her go see Dretho, because she kept having those dreams. I don't think she is having them now."

"The night I met her was the last one she had, I believe. They stopped after that. I do not know why," he said.

"Maybe your dad was doing it and saw you were with her. Maybe he thought you would know," she said hopefully.

"Perhaps," Jareth said, though he wasn't sure. He doubted he would ever know.

"Me Lady, ye shouldn' be worryin' yerself with dressin' up. We all know ye're pretty. Ye're too weak," Frelia said, fussing over Serra, helping her into a dark-blue, silk gown.

"Frelia, please just help me. Everyone in the castle will be there, not to mention some of the folk of Moondale. I do not want them to see me in a nightgown," she said, holding onto the post of her bed, while Frelia held the skirt for her to step into.

"Bah, ye'd prolly draw more o' a crowd that way," Frelia said snickering.

Serra blanched. She had not told anyone of her moments with Jareth earlier that day. She had been trying to get out of bed on her own when she was stuck in this same spot, without the strength to sit down. Of course, he had seen her in her nightgown before, but she had been covered in blankets and not standing in the middle of the room.

They managed to slip the dress on.

"Don't tighten it very much," she gasped as Frelia began to clasp the silver buttons on the back of her bodice.

"Aye, ye need ter breath."

After Serra had the dress completely on, she was near exhaustion. She had pushed herself hard this day, but she was growing restless. Nervous energy had tricked her into thinking she was ready. She sat down on the edge of her bed, rubbing her neck where she had been slashed. There was no scar. It had healed completely. But Bergearon had said that the muscles would take more time to heal and to not over do it.

"Is yer neck hurtin', missus?" Frelia asked in concern.

"A bit," she said, smiling weakly at the maid.

"I swear I nearly died o' fright when they tol' me ye was hurt. Gnarl had brought ye straight in, didn' even stop 'til he got ye ter Silvera. They worked fer hours on ye. Wouldn' let me see ye til they'd already brought ye in here," Frelia said as she walked over to Serra's dressing table to grab an ivory comb.

"I don't know what would've happened if I had went there alone," Serra said thoughtfully.

"Well, if ye ask me, yer lucky that fine hunk o' a man came ter talk some sense inter ye," she said, laughing as she began to comb Serra's long tresses.

Justin Wolfsbane knocked on Jareth's chamber door.

"Enter," he heard Jareth say.

He walked into the room and closed it behind him. He turned to the room, but Jareth was nowhere to be seen.

"Sir?" Justin asked loudly.

Jareth peaked around the changing screen in the corner of the room. He walked out from behind it clad only in a towel. His muscular chest glistened with water droplets and his black hair hung limply to his shoulders.

Justin turned to face the door and said, "I have brought your clothing, sir. I am sorry I could not be sooner, but Captain Knottytrunk asked me to comb his beard, sir. It seems there is a certain dwarven lady attending the feast tonight that he wished to impress, sir."

Jareth laughed and took the clothing from Justin. "That will be a sight for sore eyes."

"Indeed, sir, I don't believe he had combed it himself in over a year either," Justin said, stifling a laugh.

Jareth quickly put on the tan breeches and said, "I am semi-decent, I suppose."

Justin turned around and said, "Would there be anything else, sir?"

"Actually," Jareth replied sheepishly, "I would like to ask you a question on a matter, if you would be so kind as to keep it between us."

"Of course, sir," Justin said, straightening his back.

Jareth paused for a long moment and asked, "Is Serra destined to marry anyone? What I mean to ask is, did her father promise her hand to anyone before he died?"

He was very uncomfortable asking such a personal question from one of her servants, but the question had been plaguing him all day.

Justin grinned and stifled another laugh. He cleared his throat and said, "No, sir. Lord Bloodmoon was not fond of prearranged marriages. He said that was for the man or woman to decide. I believe Lady Guilda and he met on a pleasure cruise down the Neverlear. Several young candidates have courted Lady Serra. Though, all of them left the castle in less than three months, one of them at the point of Lady Serra's dagger, I believe."

Jareth blanched, but then began to laugh.

Justin tried futilely to keep his composure, but soon joined in and helped Jareth finish getting ready.

Jareth took his seat across from Gnarl in the dining room. The dwarf looked oddly like a sheep. His red hair was thick and bushy. The dwarf kept glancing down the table to a blonde dwarven woman with a short beard.

Jareth stifled a laugh and the dwarf scowled at him. "You look different Gnarl, did you wander too close to one of Dretho's lightning enchantments?"

"Ye best be shuttin' yer mouth, boy," Gnarl said and then laughed at himself. He cocked his head a few times to the side and jerked.

They were laughing even harder when the doors opened and the room grew silent. They were all anxious to see Lady Serra. Everyone looked up expectantly, but it was Hildvar who entered.

Gnarl raised his mug of mead to the barbarian, who raised his hand in greeting. But instead of sitting down, the barbarian walked over to Jareth and placed a large hand on his shoulder.

"I wish to speak with you after the meal. Will you meet me in the courtyard?" the large man asked, his face expressionless.

Jareth looked to Gnarl who shrugged. "Of course, Hildvar, I would be honored," Jareth said, smiling up at the man.

Hildvar nodded his head in acceptance and took his seat along the table.

"What do you think that was all about?" he asked the dwarf.

"Ye got me there, boy. I haven' seen much o' Hildvar lately. He been holed up in the barracks with the other men. Only comin' out ter do his rounds."

"I didn't think he cared for me much," Jareth mused.

"Bah, boy, if he didn' like ye, he woulda killed ye," the dwarf said, emptying his mug and stealing another glance at the dwarven woman.

Jareth was going to laugh, but then realized the dwarf was serious. He was about to ask Gnarl more when Justin Wolfsbane entered the dining room, puffing out his chest importantly.

"I give to you, Lady Lorna Bloodmoon, Heir of Moondale, and Lady Serra Bloodmoon, Ruler of Moondale."

Lorna and Serra turned the corner and walked in, arm in arm. They were dressed in identical blue silk gowns. Lorna looked frail as ever, but she was obviously supporting Serra who was walking very slowly.

Everyone stood in respect. Jareth, however, left his seat and walked over to the women. A few people muttered disapprovingly, but Jareth did not care. Serra looked as beautiful as ever, but he knew she was on the verge of collapse.

He walked over and took her hand, and Lorna walked ahead to her seat.

Dretho, who was sitting between two women, put on a scowl as he watched Jareth.

"What are you doing?" Serra asked through clinched teeth and a fake smile.

Jareth put on a fake smile, as well, and whispered, "Do you remember our stubborn mule conversation?"

Serra smiled genuinely and whispered, "Understood."

He helped her to her seat and instead of standing in front to greet her guests; she sat down unable to stand anymore. More muttering started around the table.

Serra picked up her spoon and tapped it a few times on her crystal goblet. The room grew silent as she waved her hand to Justin, who was only a few feet away. She whispered something in his ear and Justin stood tall and proud.

"Lady Serra regrets that due to her recent injury, she can not address you as she normally would. She has asked me to thank you all for your prayers and kind words throughout these trials," he stated and then leaned back in to hear more.

"She would also like to give a personal thank you to Captain Gnarl Knottytrunk, Dretho the Mage, Hildvar of the Elkhorn Tribe, Bergearon Nightseer, Julian and Isaac of Sengar Valley, and Jareth the Wanderer for their great success in bringing Lady Lorna and herself safely home."

Serra raised her glass and whispered once more in Justin's ear.

"Lady Serra would like to have a toast. To the saviors of Moondale!" he said with much emotion, lifting his own glass high.

Everyone repeated the toast and they began their meal.

"Fine words, me Lady," Gnarl said quietly, "Though I think ye shoulda stayed in yer bed a few more days."

"Even a mole must come into the light sometimes, Captain," Serra whispered, drinking some of her wine.

Gnarl snorted and began tearing into his venison.

Serra looked to Jareth who had yet to begin eating. He had just been staring at her in wonder.

"Jareth, you should eat before your food gets cold. Frelia's mincemeat pie is most wonderful," she whispered.

He realized he must have been staring and looked down blushing fiercely. "Yes, my Lady," he said, helping himself to a serving.

"He can' help it, girl, he's quite taken with ye," the dwarf said, laughing.

Jareth looked up in alarm, but Serra only smiled.

Jareth left the dining room, made his way through the double-doors, and walked out to the courtyard.

A few torches were lit in sconces on long, wooden poles on one end, and he saw Hildvar working with his axe in the firelight. He was clad only in his breeches, a large, blue tattoo of an elk horn graced the center of his back.

He sat on a bench and watched in awe as the man moved gracefully through his offensive routines. His large muscles bulged with the effort, though he did not look out of breath.

Hildvar went on for ten more minutes, swinging his axe over his head in great cleaves, only to stop the head from hitting the ground by inches. He would turn a circuit, make a great swipe, and then stop the blade an inch from his broad back, only to swing again, as if parrying a blow.

When the barbarian was finally done, Jareth cleared his throat.

Hildvar looked up in surprise and straightened.

"I apologize for not announcing my presence sooner, great Hildvar, but I thought it best not to disturb you during your Angestar," Jareth said with a great grin.

Hildvar's eyes widened. How could this small man know what an Angestar was?

An Angestar was an ancient barbarian tradition. It was a practice routine that allowed the participant to master their weapon.

Generally it was done alone and completely naked, but Hildvar did not consider it decent to practice his Angestar in the courtyard that way. One must make small sacrifices for living in civilization.

"I was not aware that you knew of our traditions," the large man said, walking over to him with his axe hanging limply in his hand. His face was expressionless, but Jareth knew he was in wonder.

"I spent a few months with the Tribe of the Last Horizon. I saved their leader from a falling tree and was asked to stay on for a while. It was unnerving at times when the women were twice my size, not to mention the men, but it was educational," Jareth admitted with a smile.

Hildvar was not familiar with the tribe he spoke of, but was impressed all the same. It was very rare that an outsider was invited into a clan's trust. Especially trust enough to tell that outsider of their secret traditions.

"I will not say I am not surprised, Jareth. You seem to have a lot of talents, knowledge being one of them apparently."

"Aye, so tell me great Hildvar, why have you asked me here this night?" Jareth asked in genuine curiosity.

When he had first asked, Jareth thought that the man wished to battle him. When he saw him practicing Angestar, he thought his suspicions confirmed. However, the barbarian was not raising his large axe in any threatening manner.

Hildvar drew in his breath and puffed out his large chest. "Olegareten," he said in a powerful voice.

Jareth's eyes widened. An Olegareten was a competition for honor, and usually a fight to the death.

Hildvar noted the look on the man's face and stifled a chuckle at his expense. "Not Olegareten in the usual sense, Jareth, but a battle for honor still."

"I do not wish to battle you, Hildvar," Jareth stated plainly. He was not afraid of the big man, but he still did not wish to see that great axe coming toward his head. The barbarian seemed to prefer splitting someone's head open to the general hack and slash method.

Hildvar laughed. "You still do not understand," he said, pointing across the courtyard, "We are not fighting for my honor... we are fighting for yours."

Across the courtyard lay a large bale of hay with a red bullseye painted in the center.

Jareth looked back to the barbarian in confusion. "My honor?" he asked.

"Aye," Hildvar said, putting on a stern face, "I have been asked to trust you by Lady Serra, herself. My clan was nearly wiped from Remus by the actions of your father, and I am not so easy to trust. In my land, the actions of those who have come before you make you who you are. I have changed many of my beliefs when I came here, that... has not been one of them. If I am to trust you, Jareth, you must prove to me you are honorable enough for the attempt."

"I see," Jareth said with a sigh. "Well, if that is what it takes, then that is what I must do. Explain our task this night and I will be more than willing to try."

Hildvar smiled and led the way to the center of the courtyard, about thirty feet away from the bullseye.

"We each throw five times, Jareth. After each throw, we back up ten feet. You may miss once. Any more than that, and I will kill you."

Jareth gulped. He knew better than to believe the man was joking.

"That is all well and good Hildvar, but I have nothing to throw," he said with a shrug.

Hildvar walked over to a shrub and picked up something hidden there. He turned and tossed Jareth's sword belt to him. "I took the liberty of retrieving your weapon belt from your chamber before dinner."

"It hardly seems fair that I may use my daggers when you have to throw that huge axe," he said with an uncomfortable laugh, eyeing the large man's weapon.

"Aye, it may seem like that now, but once we are forty feet away from our present position, it won't seem such an easy task. My weapon is heavier and I am able to throw it greater distances. That puny, little blade you call a dagger will be hard pressed at that distance," the barbarian said with a knowing smile.

In truth, Hildvar did not wish to hurt the man, but oddly at the same time; he did not want Jareth to succeed at Olegareten. He wanted to hate the man for how his father had wronged his people, but out of respect for Lady Serra's personal request, he would give him a chance... one chance... his way.

Jareth unsheathed one of his daggers, a gold one with a blue stone in the hilt.

"I must ask you, Hildvar, because I am an honorable man, are magical weapons forbidden in the Olegareten?" he asked, dreading the answer.

Hildvar stood there a moment, seeming deep in thought.

"Only because you asked, you will be allowed to use your magic weapon, but no spells to strike the target. Only weapons imbued with magic," he said finally.

"I thank you for the consideration, I am ready when you are," Jareth said with a firm nod.

Gnarl helped Serra to the edge of her bed. "I'll go get Frelia ter help ye outta that blasted dress," the dwarf said, turning from her and walking toward the door.

"No rush, Gnarl. I thank you for your assistance this night," Serra whispered drearily.

Gnarl nodded and walked from the room, closing the door behind him.

Serra sat on her bed, trying her best to summon enough energy to lie down. She had pushed herself too far tonight.

"Stubborn mule," she muttered to herself with a weak laugh.

After sitting there in silence for a few moments, she heard voices coming from below her window. She mustered what little strength she had left and walked slowly to the window to peer into the courtyard. What she saw weakened her more. Jareth and Hildvar stood in the courtyard, both holding weapons and talking. She was about to cry out when she saw the large hay bale with the bullseye.

She sighed. They were competing. Well, it was a start.

Jareth stood at the ready and tightly gripped the handle of his magical dagger. He bent his elbow and looked down the blade, trying to get a feel for the distance. He drew back his arm and let fly.

The dagger spiraled through the air at alarming speed and sank to the hilt about five inches above the center of the target.

"Well done," Hildvar offered, taking up his axe.

He did not bother to gauge the distance, but only drew his axe far behind his head. With a grunt, he threw it end over end and it hit the center of the target with a great thud.

Jareth looked to the big man and shook his head. This was going to be interesting.

"Well done, very well done, indeed," Jareth congratulated and they both walked over to the target to retrieve their weapons.

"Ten feet more," the barbarian said as he pulled his axe roughly from the hay.

"Aye," Jareth said as he dislodged his little dagger, barely disturbing the stack.

After walking forty feet, they turned to throw again.

"You go first this time great man," Jareth said, wanting to spend more time studying the target.

"As you wish," Hildvar said, and with a great grunt like before, he threw the axe end over end and it landed a few inches to the left of the center.

Beads of sweat broke out on Jareth's forehead. It was cool night and he knew it was not because he had been exerting himself.

Jareth drew back his arm and let fly again. The dagger sunk into the hilt right in the center of the target.

Hildvar looked at him skeptically.

Jareth noted the look and said, "Fear not, I have not used its magic yet. Would you rather I use another?"

Hildvar shook his head and they walked to the target again.

Frelia entered Serra's room and walked up behind her. She was staring out the window in intense concentration.

"Missus?" she asked in concern.

"Shh, they will hear us," Serra whispered and then motioned to the chair in the corner, "Fetch me that chair, I want to see this."

Frelia wandered to the chair in puzzlement and brought it back over to her Lady.

"If ye don' mind me askin', missus, what is it we're lookin' at?" she asked in a whisper, craning her neck to see.

"Hildvar and Jareth are throwing their weapons into a target in the courtyard," Serra whispered, unable to tear her eyes from them.

Serra sat in the chair and Frelia was finally able to see what was going on below.

"Oh missus, Hildvar's got his shirt off, we should no' be lookin'," the maid said in alarm, but Serra noticed that she didn't turn away.

Jareth was visibly sweating as they walked to the new throwing point. He looked up at the great, muscled man and asked uncomfortably, "I would ask you a favor great Hildvar, as you are not constrained by your hauberk, may I..."

"If you think that taking off your tunic will help you throw, by all means," Hildvar interrupted.

Jareth noticed that the mirth had long ago left the barbarian's demeanor. He pulled off his blue tunic and threw it to the bench he had been perched on earlier.

Serra absently put her hand to her mouth to hide from Frelia that it was gaping open. Hildvar was a heavily muscled man with a chest as broad as two men, but Jareth was by far the more handsome. His lean muscles tightened at every movement and his skin was tanned and unmarred by scars, unlike the barbarian.

"Missus, that be a fine lookin' man, but we should no' be lookin', tis unladylike," she confessed, again not turning away.

"Oh, Frelia, I've been a warrior all my life, I've seen men without their shirts," she said, trying to make some excuse so she could continue to look at Jareth's trim form.

Hildvar let his axe fly again, this time at fifty feet. It hit home about six inches below the bullseye. Hildvar stiffened visibly. It had only been two feet from the ground.

Jareth reached back and threw his jeweled dagger. It buried into the hay about three inches above the axe.

"Very nice, only two to go, yes?" Jareth asked.

"Aye," Hildvar replied as they walked back to the target.

Jareth was trying very hard not to activate the levitation jewel in his daggers hilt. He wasn't sure how it would help him here, but he hoped he would not have to use it at all.

They walked sixty feet from the target and turned. The hay seemed a mile away to Jareth.

Hildvar took a few deep breaths and threw his axe. It buried into the hay about three inches from the ground, right below the bullseye.

"You are remarkable," he said to the barbarian in honesty as he pumped his arm in mock throw.

Jareth let go of his dagger, but this time instead of sinking into the hay, it glanced off the right edge and fell to the ground. His eyes grew large and he looked up to the large man.

"That would be your one chance to miss. You will not have to throw again at this distance, but if you miss the next, you lose," Hildvar said.

Jareth silently thanked him for not reminding him of what would happen if he did miss next time. He was under enough stress.

"He missed, missus, Hildvar's winnin'," she squealed in delight, clapping her hands.

Serra frowned at her and then looked back out the window. She had a knot in the pit of her stomach, and thought it odd that she should be so nervous for Jareth when this only seemed like a friendly competition.

Hildvar placed his axe between his knees and spit on both of his hands. He took up the handle and let fly. It not only missed the target, but also thudded into a torch pole three feet behind it, nearly toppling it.

"Nice to know that you miss sometimes, I only hope that when you aim for my head, you'll decide to miss then too," Jareth said with a weak laugh.

"No pressure," the man said, eyeing Jareth closely.

Jareth closed his eyes tightly and visualized the target. He ran his thumb over the blue topaz in the hilt of the dagger, mentally calling forth its power. He summoned the dagger to levitate itself, but kept his hand on it. He allowed it to rise just at even height with the middle of the target and tapped the end of the dagger. He kept his eyes closed, unable to bring himself look.

The dagger glowed blue in the firelight and made its slow progression across the courtyard. It took nearly a full minute to hit the target dead center. It stuck in with just enough force not to fall to the ground.

Hildvar watched in amazement as the Olegareten ended. A tie. He vowed at that moment to no longer hold a grudge against the young man.

Jareth slowly peaked out one eye and saw the blue light dissipate from the weapon. He opened them fully and looked up at the barbarian.

"A fine show," he said, slapping Jareth on the back and nearly knocking him down. "Let us go to Moondale and celebrate your honor, brother."

Jareth's smile nearly took in his ears.

"So, who won missus, who had struck the target when I wasn' here?" Frelia asked as they watched the men don their clothing, retrieve their weapons, and walk out the castle gates.

"No one, Frelia, they threw five times. Both of them missed once. It was a tie," she said, looking up at the maid beside her.

"Oh rotten luck tha', tie's no good, got ter have a winner," she said gruffly. "Now let's get ye outta them clothes."

They strolled down a cobblestone street and stopped in front of a shabby pub called Bloodmoon's Brew.

"This is where the Brigade comes to lighten the mood," Hildvar said as he opened the door.

Sounds of rowdy people and smells of smoke and mead billowed out as they walked in. Several men raised their mugs to Hildvar as they made their way to the bar.

The tavern was dark and packed with patrons. A bard stood on the small stage getting ready for her next number. She tuned her lute as the crowd cat-called to her rudely.

"Who's your friend, Hildvar?" the barkeep asked as he wiped the ebony bar with a dirty rag. He was stocky with balding, brown hair. His nose bulged as if it had been broken a few times.

"Waylin, this is Jareth the Wanderer," Hildvar said, sitting on a stool.

The barkeep's eyes lit up.

"Are you now?" he asked, pulling out two mugs and filling them with amber liquid. "I've been hearing all about you, Mr. Wanderer. Glad we are that you saved us from that elf."

Jareth looked at Hildvar questioningly.

"Lady Serra left a letter before she left on her own. She said that if her and Lady Lorna did not come home, Dretho the Mage was to take her place as ruler of Moondale," Hildvar explained, taking a mighty swig of his mead.

Jareth was a bit surprised by this news.

"Dretho is not all that bad once you get to know him," he said, taking a few sips of his own drink.

Waylin stopped his cleaning and raised an eyebrow. "You know him well, do you?" he asked in disbelief.

"He saved my life a week ago. He can't be as bad as they say or he wouldn't have bothered with me," Jareth admitted matter-of-factly.

"Aye, Jareth here is mostly responsible for Serra and Lorna's return. I'd be a little more respectful if I were you, Waylin," Hildvar said threateningly. He had known Waylin for months now and knew that he would start an argument at the drop of a hat, if prompted.

Waylin poured them another drink and looked skeptically at them both.

"A strange time, too many damn mages around, makes my skin crawl. No offense, Mr. Wanderer," the barkeep muttered quietly.

"None taken."

Jareth had to admit the man was right. In the three years after leaving his father's holding, he had not met one magic user on the road. And now, he had been in the company of three others in the past week.

Mages and sorcerers had dwindled since the days of Gyndless the Almighty, but they seemed to be making a come back. Jareth hoped that this was true. If his father did indeed have the tome, they would be hard pressed to take it back.

Chapter Thirteen
Calling Out to the Masses

Fenlin Karling helped his master to a chair in the study of Fortin Manor. He had not asked where Keifer had gone or how he faired; to do so was to die.

The old man could not walk without assistance. Fenlin had to half carry him to and from his quarters, all the while trying his best to hold his disgust in check at his master's disfigurement.

"Leave me," the sorcerer demanded, once he was comfortable.

He saw the book in his hand, but did not ask any questions. He felt a sense of dread every time he was around that book. The person he had delivered it to originally had already disappeared.

After the servant was gone, Jarmassad breathed a sigh of exhaustion. He had never been a very fit man, but his new debilitations had shown him just how out of shape he really was. It was an embarrassment that the greatest sorcerer in all the land had to have assistance to rid his body of waste.

Looking down at the sacred book, he opened it to where a ribbon marked a page in the center. He closed his one good eye and envisioned the giants. They all resided in the great mountain range across the very heart of Remus.

Opening his eye to the ancient page of scraggly runes, he began chanting. Each archaic symbol glowed with a green light as it was called out to dominate the will of its wielder's choice.

When he finished he closed his eye again, preparing for the next of his manipulations.

Horace Hangoon stood at the entrance to his cave. He had been watching for game all morning. He hoped it would be a human today. He was growing tired of eating goblins. They tasted all right, but there wasn't much meat on their spindly limbs.

"Horace! Get yer arse in here and hel' me!"

He grimaced at his wife's voice. Horalda Hangoon was actually Horace's half-sister. They resembled each other, both with olive-green skin and hair as black as night. They even had matching hairy moles on their large, bulbous noses.

"What de ye want, wench?" he yelled over his shoulder, continuing to look over the valley.

But Horalda didn't answer.

Cursing, he turned to walk into the cave and saw her standing straight as a board, with an odd look on her face. She seemed as if she were staring at the most amazing nothingness she had ever seen.

As he walked toward her, intending to thrash her upside her ugly head, he felt the most calming sensation come over him. He stood there a moment, as mesmerized as his wife, and then they both felt a most appealing call to the east. The two giants turned toward the entrance of the cave and walked slowly down the mountain.

If anyone had passed by the valley, they would have seen four score of giants walking slowly in one direction. Their legs moving in unison with their eyes fixed and glazed.

They were walking toward Clandestine.

Dretho the Mage prepared his things. The small bedchamber he had claimed at Bloodmoon Castle had been comfortable, though he missed his tower. He felt nearly naked without his alchemy chamber at arms reach.

He walked out into the corridor, down the two flights of stairs, and entered the main foyer.

The little plump woman he'd seen so many times wandered across his path. She looked at him and squeaked in fear.

"Go fetch my bodyguards, woman," he said to her condescendingly.

"Y... Yes, sir," Frelia muttered and ran out the great front doors into the daylight.

He laid his backpacks on the foyer floor and walked over to the planning room and rapped lightly. A grumbling came from inside and the door opened to reveal Gnarl Knottytrunk.

"Oh, ye leavin' are ye, elf?" he asked, crossing his arms and leaning against the door jam, noting the bags.

"Yes, dwarf, my time here has ended," he said stiffly.

"Did ye say goodbye ter the Lady?" Gnarl asked, giving him a stern fatherly look.

"Nay," Dretho said calmly, "I thought it best not to bother her. She knows where to find me, should she need me."

"I think ye should at least say goodbye. She's quite fond of ye, though I don' know why," Gnarl said with a laugh.

The mage tried very hard for that statement not to draw any hope within him. Every time he was near Serra, he felt a pang of longing that he pushed away like hot mead. Though he knew Gnarl was suggesting he see her out of courtesy, he could not fight his longing to see her, even if this would be the very last time.

"Indeed, I suppose it wouldn't hurt," Dretho said, turning back to the main staircase.

Gnarl nodded and watched him ascend the staircase, before turning back to his work in the planning room.

Truth gathered his strength and cleared his throat. He envisioned the goblins that roamed all of Remus in small packs.

He opened his eye and called the runes again, their green auras glowing more fiercely than before.

Goblins from Glendale to Everklent stopped what they were doing and walked slowly toward Clandestine.

The small creatures walked in plain sight of villages on their trek, and some were struck down without putting up a fight.

The people who saw them were confused and afraid. Some had seen this behavior twenty years before, when an evil sorcerer had tried to take over the land.

Dretho reached Serra's door just as Jareth passed him in the corridor. The human looked at him questioningly, but only nodded and kept walking.

The elf knocked lightly on the door.

"Come in," he heard her say from inside.

Serra was propped up in bed reading a thick book. She wore a simple, purple dress and her long, red hair hung loosely down her back to pool on her pillow. She looked up and smiled widely. Dretho's heart skipped a beat.

"Dretho, what a surprise," she said, closing her book and laying it beside her.

"I was about to leave, the dwarf told me you might want to know. I wasn't going to bother you," he said, feeling a little unsure if he should come closer.

"I'm glad you did. Why are you going home so soon?" she asked, patting the covers next to her.

He hesitantly walked over to her bed and sat down. He sat stiffly with hands clasped in his lap.

"I have finished my work warding the castle. No offensive spells may be cast against its walls, but know that once a mage passes the gate, they will be able to cast at will," he said matter-of-factly.

Serra reached for his hand and smiled.

"I thank you for all your hard work, Dretho. You have proved invaluable to me this past week," she said warmly, squeezing his hand.

Dretho noted that her voice was no longer a whisper. It seemed almost normal now.

"I see you are able to speak better. I am glad the human, Bergearon, is so versed in healing. It would be a pity to have to have that servant speak for you all the time."

"Aye, but Justin has served my family well for years. He has been most kind in helping Jareth during his stay, as well."

A short silence passed between them and Dretho continued to grow more uncomfortable. He was developing feelings for this young human that he had not felt in years. He knew that he did not actually wish to leave; however, he knew he must for fear of these feelings he did not understand.

"I am glad all is well in your domain, my Lady, though regretfully I must attend mine," he said as he kissed her soft hand and stood to leave.

"Dretho," she said as he started for the door.

"Yes, my Lady?" he asked, turning back to her.

"Have a safe trip and know that you are always welcome here," she said with a large smile.

The elf stood transfixed for a moment. He swallowed a lump in his throat and bowed. Walking out her door was one of the hardest things he had ever had to do.

Jareth loomed in the corridor after Dretho had walked into Serra's room.

He felt a surge of jealousy.

He had not been able to see Serra, except at meals, because he was told that it was not proper to have audience with the Lady of the house in her bedchamber. He, of course, understood this reasoning, but could not help but fume that Dretho had been granted admittance.

Hildvar had invited him to the barracks to meet the other men of the Bloodmoon Brigade. They had stayed in Bloodmoon's Brew until early in the morning, swapping tales and drinking way too much. Jareth had a dull headache to remind him not to do so again.

He sighed and continued his way to the foyer, where Julian and Isaac stood next to a few backpacks. After nodding to them in greeting, he stepped out the great double-doors and entered the courtyard.

It was a dreary day. Dark clouds hung low in the sky and the humidity in the air promised rain.

He made his way to the western wall where many long, stone buildings housed the famed Bloodmoon Brigade. Hildvar had told him the night before that the common room was in the first building after the rose bushes. He walked up to the door and walked in without knocking.

"I don' 'are who 'e is! 'e ain' o' the Brigade and 'e don' need ter be in 'ere!" a black bearded dwarf yelled from the back of the room.

Jareth looked up to see Hildvar looming over the dwarf, a furious look upon his face.

"He is honorable, Castille, you should give him a chance!" Hildvar retorted.

"A mag' don' belon' in 'ere!" the dwarf shouted again, this time pumping his fist at Hildvar's waist. The dwarf was half the barbarian's height, but he wasn't backing down an inch.

Jareth cleared his throat awkwardly.

Castille Thornberry looked up at him and snarled. He turned about and walked out a door in the back of the common room.

Hildvar looked up at Jareth and shook his head sadly.

"He doesn't trust mages," he said simply.

"I can understand," Jareth replied. It bothered him that the man would not give him a chance, but you couldn't please everyone. He had learned that very early on, with his own father.

"Come sit," the barbarian said, gesturing to a few chairs around a table next to them.

"Does he trust Dretho?" Jareth asked, taking a seat.

"No one trusts Dretho, Jareth, which is probably why Waylin was so leery of you last night. The elf treats his people like vermin and does horrible things to his prisoners," the barbarian said.

Jareth was silent for a few minutes, mulling over this new information.

"Then why does Serra trust him?" he asked, trying his best to keep all emotion from his gaze.

"Serra's father saved his life. It seems that his bond with Frendar Bloodmoon has passed along to the Lord's daughter. Serra was not very trusting of him until right before Lorna was taken. When we left his tower to come back to the castle, she was very polite and civil with him," Hildvar said absentmindedly.

Jareth's jealousy consumed him then. He scowled and looked away.

"Why does this trouble you so?" Hildvar asked curiously.

Jareth was unable to answer. He shook his head, and stood up.

"I must go, Hildvar. I thank you for your invitation."

Hildvar looked on in puzzlement as Jareth made his way to the door and left the barracks.

Jarmassad Truth finished his last spell and slumped in his chair. He had summoned the giants, goblins, orcs, and ogres. He knew it would take some of them days to arrive, but soon he would be able to finish what he had started.

He picked up a bell on his side table and jingled it impatiently.

Fenlin ran into the room and knelt at his master's side.

"Take me to my room," the sorcerer said gruffly.

As they made their way down the corridor, Truth could not help but sigh. If his son had followed in his footsteps, he would not have to do this alone.

Chapter Fourteen
Contemplations

Serra finished dressing and walked out of her room. She had abandoned her gowns and dresses once again. Wearing black pants and a white shirt, she walked briskly down the corridor and the stairs.

She was surprised to see no one about, but thought she was lucky in that respect. She didn't want to see anyone but Gypsy at that moment. It had been far too long since she had taken a ride and she knew Gypsy would probably still be upset about the teleportation spell.

As she walked, she waved at a few guards replacing torches. It was a beautiful day. It had rained all night and the air felt clean and fresh that morning.

Gordo Flasslet met her as she entered the stable. He was carrying a saddle on his shoulder and nearly dropped it trying to bow.

"Good morning, Gordo! Could you saddle up my horse, please?" she asked with a grand smile.

The smile was infectious. Gordo grinned widely and bellowed, "Of course!"

She nodded and walked out to the garden. The rose bushes were in full bloom. She picked a few white ones for Gypsy and wandered back to the stables. The black mare stood just outside the stable door where Gordo was brushing her coat.

"Hi there, darling," Serra said, walking up to the horse.

Gypsy raised her head and pulled back. Serra showed her the roses and the horse changed her attitude. She walked up to the Lady and began eating the flowers.

Serra rubbed her nose and took the reigns.

"Thank you, Gordo, you do such a wonderful job," she said as she hopped in the saddle.

Gordo flushed red and bowed.

"Ready?" Serra asked, leaning toward the mare's head.

She kicked her flanks and they were off. She rode out into the courtyard, passing Gnarl and Hildvar. The two fighters looked up in surprise as horse and rider made their way past the portcullis and into the city proper.

Serra felt like she was flying. She had been cooped up in the castle for so long. She had forgotten how good it had felt to feel the breeze in her fiery, red hair.

They rode outside the city and into the pastures and farmland outside of Moondale.

Bern Hilda was scrubbing the foyer floor when Dretho walked in the great front doors. She stood to attention quickly, only to slip in the suds and fall on her rear.

Dretho scowled at her and put his hands on his hips.

She rolled over onto her knees and bowed humbly.

"Welcome home, master!" she exclaimed.

Dretho shook his head and made his way up the stairs to his altar room. He closed the door and mage locked it. He glanced around the room and a certain silk cushion met his gaze, the cushion Serra had perched on during her visit. He walked over and picked it up.

Why did she affect him so?

He had been avoiding thinking about these feelings until now. Knowing full well that they would keep him occupied, he wanted to be alone to contemplate.

He muttered and waved his hand at his bookcase to reveal his bedchamber in a shower of purple sparks.

Still carrying the cushion, he threw it onto his bed and stared.

It angered him that he felt so strongly for a human. He had loved once before. After two hundred twenty years, he did not think that he was capable of the feeling again.

When Serra and Gypsy arrived back to the castle, the suns were fast descending the horizon. They had ridden for hours and it had felt wonderful. Serra felt freer than she ever had. It also appeared that Gypsy had forgiven her.

They passed under the main portcullis and she saw that Gnarl was waiting for her in the courtyard. He walked up and took Gypsy's reigns.

Serra dismounted and said, "We had a lovely ride. Were you waiting for me, Gnarl?"

"Aye," he said gruffly, "I think ye need ter talk ter that boy."

"Boy?" Serra asked, already knowing whom the dwarf spoke of.

"Jareth. Seems Hildvar and him were talkin' yesterda' morn'. Hildvar seems ter think he's upset about somethin'," Gnarl stated, his face expressionless.

Serra was a bit taken aback. What could Hildvar have possibly said to upset him?

"Where is Jareth now?"

"Las' I 'eard he was in the southern garden, alone. Ye want me ter come with ye?" he asked protectively.

She shook her head no and walked toward the garden, leaving Gnarl behind with Gypsy.

Soon after entering the gate, she saw Jareth leaning against a stone bench with a book in his hands. His back was to her.

"Am I disturbing you?" she asked.

He jumped and turned around. He didn't seem as happy to see her as he usually did.

"Serra, what a surprise," he said, putting his book away and standing up.

"I just got back from a ride. I needed to get some air," she said, walking over to him and wrapping him in a hug.

He returned the hug, but it was by no means with the feeling she was accustomed to.

"Is something wrong?" she asked, looking up into his eyes.

He turned his head and mumbled, "No."

She backed away and stared at him.

"Jareth, there is something wrong. Have I done something that has angered you?"

He looked at her with tight lips.

"I wish you would have told me that Dretho was your lover before you ever kissed me," he blurt out with a pained expression.

Serra's eyes widened.

"Excuse me? What ever led you to that conclusion?" She was growing angry quickly. She could feel her cheeks burning.

"Dretho came into your room yesterday. Hildvar told me that you went to his tower to see him before we met," he said, crossing his arms.

"I suppose that makes me his lover then?" she asked harshly.

Jareth stood there a moment and then sighed.

"No, I am sorry," he said resignedly.

"Jareth, I do not understand why you drew this conclusion without consulting me. What I do is no one's business but my own. For your information, I have never had a lover. Does that make you feel better?" she scolded.

Jareth's eyes widened. How could he have done something so stupid? He had no reason to doubt her. She had always been honest.

"Serra, may I explain?" he asked pleadingly.

"You may, though I am not sure it will help," she said, clenching her fists.

"When we were alone on the road, I fell in love with you. I know that we have not known each other long, but does that matter? Then we came back here and men who love you too suddenly surround you. I have felt like just another visitor," he said quickly. He hoped so much that his confession would calm her.

"Jareth, we were here a day before we left to find Lorna. That day was spent doing nothing but planning. When we came back, I was bedridden and only today have I left my chamber for more than a meal. You expect too much from me if you think that I must be at your beck and call. I have feelings for you, as well, but your jealousy has taken over your mind. I never promised you anything. Love is something that cannot be rushed. I am not going to make any hasty decisions simply because we get along." Her anger was on the wane, but she was still very irritated.

Jareth slumped down on the bench and looked at his feet.

"It has been so long since I had companionship of any kind, Serra. I spent three long years with no one but my horse. My mother died years ago. You obviously know that my father was not a loving man. I cannot resist holding onto your love so tightly. I am sorry."

His words made sense and her irritation turned to pity.

"I accept your apology, but please will you talk to me before jumping to conclusions next time," she replied, wrapping him in another embrace.

This time, he returned it. It felt good to be in his arms but she knew now that she needed to be wary of his jealous side.

Gnarl Knottytrunk was in his small office just off the barracks. He had been taking a nap when there was a knock on his door.

He snorted and nearly fell from his chair. "Come in," he shouted hatefully.

Hildvar opened the door and ducked through the doorway.

"What is it? I was busy!" Gnarl snarled.

"We've received reports of goblin activity in the farmland on the outskirts of Moondale," the barbarian answered. He knew full well that Gnarl had been asleep. Anyone within a half-mile could hear his snores.

"Are they attackin' the farmers?" Gnarl asked, coming fully awake.

"No, Captain, that's the odd thing. They are just walking south. They aren't attacking anyone. The messenger said that old man Borderu Gusentine even hit one with his cane. The goblin just kept walking like he didn't know he was there," Hildvar explained with a puzzled expression.

"What in the bloody hell are they doin' walkin' south?" Gnarl asked, just as puzzled.

"I don't know, sir. Do you think we should ride out?"

"I think we should ride out and see what's goin' on!" Gnarl ordered and grabbed his morning star. He was still half-asleep, but wouldn't let Hildvar make the decisions.

Hildvar tried to hide his grin. He only hoped Gnarl would come to his senses before they were attacked.

Gnarl, Hildvar, and three other soldiers of the brigade sat on their horses and stared in wonder. They had ridden out to Borderu Gustentine's farm and what they saw amazed them. Half a score of goblins walked slowly across the cotton fields. They were not organized into a group. They were all just walking in the same direction.

They knew the goblins could see them. It just seemed that none of them cared to look. In fact, several of the goblins walked right through large mud puddles without bothering to step around them.

"Hildvar, ride back ter the castle and get Lady Serra down 'ere. Bring that boy too, this ain' normal," Gnarl ordered with a stunned expression.

"Yes, sir," Hildvar answered as he turned his horse and rode back.

Gnarl dismounted and walked up to a goblin that was walking in their direction. The little green creature stared blankly ahead and did not acknowledge his existence. Gnarl stepped to the side as the creature passed him by, walking right under his pony and out the other side.

"Hey!" the dwarf shouted, running in front of the creature.

But the goblin kept walking. It ran right into Gnarl, but tried futilely to keep walking.

"Hey! Yer mother was an ogre's patoot!" Gnarl yelled, knocking the goblin on the top of the head with his fist.

The goblin fell down in a heap. It waited a moment and then stood back up and started walking again to the south.

Gnarl stepped aside and let it walk away. He looked up to the other three soldiers who merely shrugged and remained on their horses.

Gallo Suntrestle handed Serra another roll of parchment to sign.

"This is from Courtier Widowmaker in Everklent. He wishes to make a trade agreement for a thousand pounds of cotton for five hundred pounds of silk," the man said.

Serra looked at the parchment and then up at the man.

"Is that fair, Gallo? A trade for half a trade?" she asked puzzled.

"Yes, Lady Serra. Silk is worth three times that of cotton, though trading has been hard of the people of Everklent for years. They have to travel so far to sell their wares that they offer them at good prices to ensure someone else does not outbid them," he replied patiently.

"Do we have a thousand pounds of cotton?"

"Yes, my Lady. We will purchase it from the farmers outside of Moondale when they reap harvest in a few weeks," he said.

"You have the patience of a Saint and the memory of a God, Gallo. How much was Renfar paying you?" she asked, rubbing her temples and unable to keep her gaze from the window, displaying a brilliant morning.

"Twenty galleons a season, my Lady," he responded simply.

"I'll make you a deal. I will pay you thirty galleons a season to handle these affairs."

Gallo's eyes bulged at her statement.

"You have worked for our family for twenty years and I know you know what you are doing. So, call it a promotion. If you wish for me to sign something, that is fine. However, my head is about to explode thinking about this."

Serra knew she was putting the economy of her land in the man's hands. She also knew now why Renfar was always so upset. This would drive anyone insane.

"You can count on me, my Lady!" Gallo shouted, grinning from ear to ear.

Serra signed the parchment and stood up.

"Arrange these affairs and let me know if I need to sign anything tomorrow," she said, walking toward the door.

Gallo collected the parchment and rolled it up, unable to stifle his grin.

Serra opened the door to see Hildvar with his fist raised to knock.

"My Lady, Captain Knottytrunk has requested your presence at the Gustentine Farm," Hildvar said, standing to attention.

"Is something wrong, Hildy?" Serra asked, walking out into the corridor.

"Yes, my Lady, goblins are acting strangely."

"Lead the way," she offered. She followed the great man down the hall to the stairway.

"My Lady, Captain Knottytrunk has requested that Jareth come with us," he said as they walked.

"Go prepare the horses, Hildvar. I'll go find Jareth."

Serra walked up the stairs to the third floor and walked down the corridor to the second door and knocked loudly.

Jareth opened the door, wearing only his trousers. His eyes widened and he slipped behind the door so his head was only visible.

"Get your tunic on, we need to go investigate odd goblin activity in the area," she said, trying hard not to grin at his modesty.

"Goblin activity?" he asked, opening the door wide and running to his dresser.

Serra walked into his room and watched him put on his tunic.

"Aye, that is all I know. Gnarl sent Hildvar to get me. Hildvar also said that Gnarl requested your attendance."

Jareth finished with his tunic and grabbed his sword belt. They walked quickly down the hall and down the stairs.

They were on their horses and past the main portcullis in minutes.

Dretho had just finished the enchantments on the bloodstone when there was a knock at his door. He cursed and moved into his altar room.

"This better be a life and death matter," he mumbled as he waved his hand and the door opened.

Who he saw was not Bern Hilda, but Eseriant Flamarien, the Elf King. Bern Hilda hopped up and down behind him.

"He would not be announced, my Lord, he ran straight in!" she shouted.

"Leave us, Bern Hilda!" Dretho yelled and the dwarf ran down the stairs, nearly shaking the walls.

Dretho bowed and said, "What a surprise, King Flamarien. You were the last person I expected to see. Please accept my apologies."

The Elf King walked into the altar room without a word. At eight hundred and thirty, he was the oldest living elf. His long, black hair was graying at the temples, but his yellow eyes held the fire of youth. He was clad in a simple leather vest and breeches, but the gold circlet on his head declared his royalty.

"Dretholzar Derathliona, I have come to call upon your services. It seems that the monsters of our realm are acting strangely," the King said, looking around the room.

"Strangely, my Lord?" Dretho asked, walking over to his bookcase and retrieving his scrying bowl.

"Yes. Giants, goblins, orcs, and ogres are sweeping the land. They are all walking in one direction to the east. I presume you know what this means," the King said calmly.

Dretho nearly dropped his marble bowl. He had been alive during the time of Gyndless the Almighty. This was exactly what had happened two hundred and fifty years ago. Gyndless had called the masses of monsters to his mountain home. Shortly thereafter, every village and city had been attacked brutally. Nearly half the population of elves, dwarves and humans had perished. The rest had been enslaved.

The elves called it *Letuminus Munduni*, which the humans simply called The Death of the World. For fifty years, they were all enslaved to serve unthinking creatures led by a tyrannical giant sorcerer.

"Then the book has been found," he stated pensively.

"It appears that it has. We need to find it before the attacks begin anew. I know you remember what it was like. We will not be able to hide this time," the King said solemnly.

"I shall scry the land, my Lord. Do what you will while I pray."

Dretho grabbed a bottle and a small pouch from his bookcase. He carried these items and the bowl to the small table in the middle of the room.

"Blessed Drakevin, lend me your power this day. If it is so that the book of Gyndless the Almighty has been found, help me to retrieve it in your name," he said kneeling.

He poured water into the bowl and opened the pouch. He pinched a white powder between his fingers and muttered, "*Asseeleeum brachtath tumadra estinar,*" several times.

The water glowed with a blue light, turning his golden eyes a hazel color.

"I see the horde crossing the land. They are everywhere. I do not see any attacking. They are all moving toward the east as you said.

The ogres and goblins of Everklent are moving north. The giants in the Glendale territory are moving southwest. The goblins and orcs in Dormar are moving north as well. And in Moondale they are traveling southeast. It looks as if they are moving toward the river. Hoff's Cove, perhaps? No, they are moving across the river. Some are drowning in the Neverlear. They are all going toward Clandestine. I am moving over the city. It is swarming with them. They are moving in from every direction," Dretho explained, finally looking up from the bowl.

King Flamarien stared at the mage.

"Dretholzar, do you know any sorcerers in Clandestine?"

He thought for a moment and shook his head.

"No, my Lord. However, I may be able to find out." He would have to speak to Jareth. If anyone knew of the sorcerers in the land, he would. "Would you accompany me to Moondale?"

Chapter Fifteen
The Horde and the Master

Jarmassad Truth had been asleep when the monsters first began assembling outside his manor. He had been having a wonderful dream of having Serra Bloodmoon's head on a pike outside his manor and he was most upset when Fenlin Karling knocked sharply on his door.

"Master! Master! Awaken, we are being attacked!" the servant bellowed as he barged into the room.

Truth opened his one good eye, but did not rise. "Have you been hurt?" the sorcerer asked calmly.

"No, master!" Fenlin said out of breath.

"Has anyone else been attacked?"

"No, master!" he said again.

"Then why are you waking me up!" the sorcerer shouted, throwing his pillow at the servant.

Fenlin stood straight and tall and said, "I fear for your life, master!"

"I summoned them, you fool!" he yelled, still lying on his side, "Now leave me be!"

Fenlin bowed and ran out the door, slamming it behind him.

Jarmassad smiled and slipped back into a restful sleep, the book of Gyndless the Almighty tucked in the blankets underneath him.

Fortin Manor was only two stories high but its grounds where vast. The well-manicured lawns were stomped to mud as the creatures walked slowly to the house. They stopped only a few feet from the walls to form a line, each stopping in its tracks systematically a foot from the creature in front, behind and to its sides.

The suns were bright in the sky, but not a person was out on the streets of Clandestine. They were shut in their hovels, peering fearfully out their windows.

Serra, Jareth, and Hildvar arrived at Gustentine Farm to see the last remaining goblins cross the field.

"Why are they just walking onward? They are not even stopping when they run up to a tree," Serra stated, watching the procession in confusion.

"I don' know, me Lady. Gustentine said they been doin' that since yesterda'," Gnarl answered, shaking his head. "It ain' good, whatever the reason."

"Gnarl, double the guard around the castle and send out patrols in Moondale and the outskirts. Assemble the Bloodmoon Brigade and have them prepared to march at a moment's notice. If these creatures decide to attack us, we will be ready," Serra ordered sternly.

"Yes, me Lady," Gnarl answered with a nod.

"Jareth, let us go back to the castle to work your magic. I'm sure you'll be able to figure out what is causing this."

Jareth, who had said nothing up to this point, simply looked at her in fear. "I already know."

Everyone looked at him in surprise.

"He's got the book, my father. He's assembling his army to come against us."

"Are ye meanin' the book I'm thinkin' yer meanin'?" Gnarl asked, dreading the answer and closing his eyes tightly.

"The very same."

Dretho and his escorts had teleported in just as Gnarl and Serra entered the courtyard.

"Dretho, who're yer friends," Gnarl asked warily. He knew one of the other elves looked familiar but he could not place him.

"Captain Gnarl Knottytrunk, may I introduce..."

"Take me to Lady Serra Bloodmoon this instant!" the elf next to Dretho shouted.

"And what business do you have with her?" Serra asked disdainfully. She thought this elf very rude, ruder than even Dretho had been at times.

"That is my business, woman, hold your tongue," the elf said hatefully.

Gnarl drew his morning star and scowled.

"Ye best be mindin' yer manners when speaking ter the Lady o' Moondale!" he shouted. "Now answer 'er question."

King Flamarien's face turned from a scowl to one of surprise. He had expected to be formally announced to an old woman dressed in a gown. Not a young girl dressed in a shirt and breeches like a commoner.

"Please understand that you are not what I expected," the elf said directly at Serra, ignoring the dwarf entirely.

"Is that an apology? You still have not answered me. Who are you and what business do you have with me?" She asked, standing tall and proud.

"I am Eseriant Flamarien, King of the Elves. I have come to discuss the odd behavior of the creatures that so plague our everyday lives. Dretholzar has informed me that a friend of yours named Jareth would be able to enlighten me on a course of action."

Serra's eyes grew wide and she looked at Dretho.

He was looking from her to the King, biting his lip.

"Gnarl, take King Flamarien to my study. I will join you shortly. Dretho, I would like to speak with you in private, if you please."

The Elf King's face turned scarlet. He was not accustomed to being ordered to go from place to place. Nor was he used to waiting. And most of all, he was not used to being ordered to wait by a human woman.

The surly dwarf stepped forward and gestured toward the castle. The King said nothing. He only turned to walk into the great double-doors. The King's three personal escorts followed closely behind.

Serra waited until they had gone inside and turned to Dretho.

"Did you tell him of Jareth's father?" She asked with a hurt expression.

Her gaze sent daggers into his heart.

"No. I only told him that Jareth knew more of sorcerers than I. I would not betray your confidence in that manner," he replied apologetically.

She waited a moment, simply staring at him.

"Dretho, that elf was not kind to me. You know how I feel about ostentatious people. You should inform him to watch his words," she said sternly.

"Serra, he is the King of all Elves. He is not accustomed to humans or dwarves. Even you must admit, you are not the typical ruler," he said crossing his arms in an unthreatening manner.

He would defend his King to the death. He only hoped that Serra would understand that this wasn't personal.

"Go find Jareth and take him to the library. I believe he is at the stables with Hildvar. Do not bring him to the study. I have to find out this elf's intentions before exposing my friend."

"Yes, my Lady," he responded and turned to walk to the stables.

Serra ran into the castle and rushed up the stairs to the study.

Jareth was tending to a rock in one of Gallant's hooves when Hildvar tapped him on the shoulder. He turned his head awkwardly, still holding onto the hoof.

Dretho the Mage stood next to Hildvar with a blank expression.

"Dretho," he said in greeting, finally dislodging the rock. He let go of Gallant's leg and patted him on the rump, dusted off his breeches, and walked out of the stall.

"I thought you went back home," Jareth said, picking up a grooming brush.

"I did, though I had to return sooner than I had anticipated. King Flamarien wishes to speak with you," the elf said patiently.

"The Elf King?" he asked in surprise, dropping the brush in the dirt.

"Yes. Serra has sent me to summon you to the library to await an audience," Dretho replied, gesturing toward the castle.

"What does he want with me?" Jareth asked, not moving.

Hildvar cleared his throat and nudged Jareth in the shoulder.

"Well, don't I have a right to know?" he asked angrily.

"If you want to remain in Moondale, you must do as the Lady asks," the barbarian retorted calmly.

Jareth nodded and walked toward the castle, not bothering to look back.

"He is upset. It is understandable. Serra was upset as well. Of course, King Flamarien all but called her a commoner," Dretho said, watching Jareth make his way to the doors.

"You should probably go with him. If he lashes out at the King, he will probably be killed," Hildvar said calmly.

"Good point." He nodded to the barbarian and followed Jareth into the castle.

Serra entered the study and everyone stood except the King. She walked over to her desk and sat behind it.

"King Flamarien, we have recently been out in the field to observe goblins walking southeast. They do not acknowledge our presence. In fact, they do not appear to see anything. They are walking in unison to one destination."

The King nodded. "That was what Dretholzar and I have observed as well. He also observed that they are all gathering in Clandestine. An army of giants, goblins, orcs, and ogres flocking to their master awaiting orders, I presume."

"I once knew a mage in Clandestine, though he is dead now. Do you have any thoughts on why this is happening?" Serra did not want to mention the book of Gyndless the Almighty unless she had to. She wanted to know once and for all what this King wanted with Jareth.

"I believe I do. Though, I know you are far too young to know of the *Letuminus Munduni.*"

His statement angered her. She was growing very tired of this elf assuming she was nothing.

"Before we say anything more, let us make one thing perfectly clear. You may be the King of the Elves, Flamarien, but you are in my domain now. You will either begin answering me straightly without the snide comments to my age and gender, or you will leave here now," she said harshly.

Flamarien took her measure. She sat with confidence and he noted that her sword was ready at her hip. She was young, yes, but obviously a fighter. She wore common attire like he did probably for the same reason, to not be noticed. He may have mistaken her for a commoner before, but it was obvious that she was not to be reckoned with. He respected her for that. He leaned forward and looked her directly in the eyes.

"Very well, Lady Bloodmoon, I have come to believe a sorcerer has found the book of Gyndless the Almighty, which caused the *Letuminus Munduni* over two hundred years ago. This was when all the goodly races of Remus were enslaved. I was the King then as well, young woman, and I remember well what happened before the onslaught against us. What we have seen today is a repeat of history," he said plainly, noticing immediately that what he said did not seem to faze her.

"Aye, that is what we feared as well," she bluntly replied.

The Elf King was surprised by this revelation.

"Leave your escorts here and let us go meet with Jareth in the library."

The three elven guards visibly stiffened. Two were men who had black hair and green eyes and the other was a woman with blonde hair that looked barely older than Lorna.

"Do as she asks," the King offered, standing up and walking to the door.

Serra followed in behind him.

The King looked at her once again and then opened the door to let her pass. Serra could not have known that he had never done such a thing before for anyone, much less a human.

Jarmassad woke from his nap and rung his little bell incessantly.

Fenlin Karling entered the chamber and said nothing.

"Help me to the terrace," Jarmassad demanded impatiently. He rose to a sitting position and swung his good, right leg over the side.

Fenlin walked over to him and took his right arm. The stump on the end was black and mangled. It smelled horrible, but the servant merely held his breath and lifted the sorcerer up. He allowed the old man to lean on him as he unclasped the terrace doors and helped him out into the afternoon air.

Jarmassad hobbled over to the rail and looked across the grounds.

On his front lawn were mindless monsters awaiting command. Giants stood next to goblins less than a tenth of their size and did not move. They only stared up at him waiting.

Fenlin stood idly by and could not help but shudder.

The look on his master's face was fanatical.

Jareth had taken a seat on a leather couch when Dretho walked into the library. He pointedly looked away from the elf and crossed his arms.

"You look like a child when you do that. Sit up straight and do not be so smug. I've already explained to Serra that I did not reveal your parentage. If the King senses any weakness in you, he will not trust you. He wishes to ask you about the book of Gyndless the Almighty," Dretho said sternly.

Jareth sat up and uncrossed his arms.

"I don't know anything about it. I am sure he knows more than any of us," he said harshly.

Despite his conversation with Serra the day before, he still had a grudge against Dretho. He did not know why, but it would not go away.

"Of course he does. However, you know more about the sorcerers of the realm than we do. It may be your father that has the book," Dretho stated condescendingly.

"I know nothing of the sorcerers of the realm. I only knew my father and his lackeys. None of who were sorcerers. He didn't want any competition. I figure the only reason he let me live is because he knew I despised magic."

The door opened and Serra entered with another elf. She closed the door behind her and gestured toward an overstuffed chair next to Dretho.

The Elf King looked up at Jareth and searched the human's face for a few moments before taking a seat.

"Jareth, this is King Flamarien. He wishes to speak with you," Serra said, leaning against the couch where Jareth sat.

It was as if they were segregated. The Elf King sat on one side of the room, with Dretho standing next to him as if protecting him, and Serra stood next to Jareth, who eyed the King warily.

"What is it you wish to say, King?" he asked matter-of-factly.

Flamarien leaned back in his chair, amused that the man was defiant before he had even said a word to him.

"Do you know any sorcerers that reside in Clandestine?" he asked calmly.

Jareth tried to keep his face expressionless, but dread filled his heart. "I know a sorcerer who keeps a manor in Clandestine," he stated, not willing to give up too much, too quickly.

"And who would that be?" the King asked patiently.

"Why Clandestine?" he asked with genuine interest.

The King looked to Dretho.

"I scryed the realm for odd activity, all the monsters of the realm are congregating there," Dretho informed.

"Jarmassad Truth has a house in southern Clandestine called Fortin Manor. Though, I know that he has never even been to the place," he admitted.

The Elf King cursed and stood up.

"He is the very one who stole the book from the dwarven mines," he said to Dretho, abandoning his calm facade.

"Do you know this sorcerer personally, Jareth?" the King demanded.

Jareth's eyes widened and he looked to Serra.

But she would not influence him in any way with her expression. It was his decision to divulge information.

"I do." He answered plainly.

She was surprised that he admitted it. She put her hand on his shoulder and looked directly at the King.

"Know this, King Flamarien, I trust Jareth. No matter what is said after this moment, I want that noted," Serra said to reassure herself just as much as Jareth.

Jareth looked up to her and smiled.

Dretho grew jealous, but held his expression.

The King nodded, "Go on, how do you know him."

"He was my father."

The normally unshakable Elf King visibly flinched. "Was your father?" he asked with a shaky voice, looking from him to Dretho and back again.

"Yes. He disowned me three years ago after I refused to help him in his conquest for realm domination." It pained Jareth to admit this to a complete stranger, but he knew it was necessary. He now had no doubt in his mind that his father had the book.

The King nodded in acceptance.

"Lady Bloodmoon, I believe we may need to stay in Moondale for a few days."

"I can no' believe the King is 'ere," Frelia exclaimed, stirring a large pot of stew.

"He's not our King, he's the Elf King," Hildvar said, taking a large bite out of a loaf of black bread.

"Do ye know if 'e's stayin' fer dinner?" she asked, sipping the stew from a large ladle.

"I don't know. I'd make more to be sure."

"Aye, do ye know what them elves eat? That other elf scared me ter death, I ne'er found out what 'e liked."

"Oh, he is back too," Hildvar said absentmindedly.

The ladle fell to the floor with a clang.

Hildvar looked up to see Frelia with a mortified expression on her face.

Hildvar's eyes widened and he stood up.

"I think I'll take my leave, I'll let you know if I find out anything." He didn't look back. He walked out the kitchen door, leaving poor Frelia behind.

Jarmassad Truth nearly drooled as the creatures continued to mass on the grounds. They were now beginning to line up on the streets of Clandestine.

"It will take a week for them all to assemble," he said to no one in particular, "Then I will have Moondale, and the Bloodmoon family will be wiped from the face of Remus."

Fenlin backed slowly into the bedroom and rushed out the door.

He knew Spike had tended the Bloodmoon girl in Hoff's Cove. He had relocated to Fortin Manor shortly after Truth had arrived.

He had to find Spike.

Spike Forsiad roughly scrubbed a chamber pot in the water room. His sandy blonde hair was disheveled and his brown tunic was filthy. He knew now how Lorna had felt in the dungeon. That job had been by far better than this one. At least the girl had appreciated that he had fed her.

He had hired on for Jarmassad Truth when he was only thirteen. Four years later, he was beginning to wonder what he had been thinking.

With a resigned sigh, he placed the last chamber pot on the shelf, walked to the window, and looked out. Creatures of every shape and size met his view. He knew he should be afraid, but he also knew this was the work of his master, though the notion did not comfort him in the least.

Hearing the door open behind him, he turned to see Fenlin, the Head Servant of the house.

"Mister Karling, how may I assist you, sir?" he asked, trying to act presentable even if his appearance was not.

"Forsiad, do you not see what is happening around us?" he asked with an insane expression. The normally unshakable man's eyes were wide with disbelief and he was trembling.

"Aye, I see that the master has called the masses. I don't know what it means, but I don't think it concerns us," he said, glancing back out the window.

"Doesn't concern us? Are you mad? He's brought the bloody monster garrison to our doors!" Fenlin shouted.

Spike looked back at the man in surprise. It wasn't like Fenlin to speak ill of the master. He knew he had served in this house for years, and though Spike had only been serving at the manor for a number of days, the man had never shown any emotion, good nor bad.

"You don't agree, I take it," Spike stated as he walked over to a bucket of soapy water and started cleaning up.

"You can bet your life, I don't. You knew the Bloodmoon girl, didn't you?"

Spike froze. He couldn't possibly know he had talked to her.

"Yes, I fed her. That was my job," he said simply.

"Does it not bother you that he stole a thirteen year old girl and locked her up in a dungeon?"

"Are you mad, Fenlin? If the master hears you, he'll kill you," Spike whispered incredulously.

"Bloody hell, man, look out the window! We're already dead." Fenlin screamed, pointing at the deadly mass out the window.

Spike looked back out the window and sighed. He was right. If the master died or lost control of the horde, they would be savaged by them.

"What would you have me do?" he asked in a whisper.

"Ride to Moondale, tell them that he is going to attack them," Fenlin pleaded.

"Do you even know that is where he is going to send them?" Spike asked growing scared.

He liked Lorna. He knew he should never have talked to her. He had been informed not to speak, so that he would not feel pity for the girl. The master had said she was already dead. And that it was only a matter of time.

"Yes. He's said it in my very presence," Fenlin admitted, stepping right up to the young man.

Spike was on a horse, weaving his way through the horde, within the hour.

Chapter Sixteen
Decisions

Serra walked into the kitchen to see Frelia sitting on the stone floor crying. She knelt beside the woman and put her arm around her.

"What's wrong?" she asked gently.

"Tha'... tha' elf, me Lady. He... he scares me somethin' fierce!" she muttered in between sniffles.

"Dretho?" Serra asked, turning the maid's face to look in her bloodshot eyes.

"Ye... yes, me Lady."

Serra tried not to laugh. She had known that Dretho had bothered the maid, but she hadn't known it was this bad.

"Frelia, listen to me," she begged, sitting down next to her.

"Elves will treat you like vermin if you let them know you are afraid of them. You have to stand up for yourself. I know you can do that. You've scolded me so many times for sneaking food, I have a permanent imprint of a spoon on my rear," Serra said with a grand smile.

Frelia laughed and snorted. "Oh, me Lady. I don't know what I'd do without ye. I feel like yer me own daughter. I watched ye grow up strong. Ye're so pretty." She stroked a lock of hair away from Serra's face. "Ye look so much like yer mother. I just can' help it. That mage makes me feel like a mouse wi' a cat on its tail," the woman said, wiping her snotty nose on her apron.

"Do you want me to call Hildvar to help you?"

"Ha! Last time ye did that, he burned the turkey. He ain' comin' inter me kitchen ter help again fer that!"

Frelia felt a little better. She stood up and gave Serra a great hug.

"Good, that turkey was horrible," Serra admitted, grinning wider.

They both shared a good laugh.

"Will ye do one thing fer me, me Lady? Will ye ask tha' elf what he likes ter eat?" She pleaded almost childlike.

Serra laughed.

"Of course, I will let you know soon."

Justin Wolfsbane showed the men to the planning room. Gnarl, Hildvar, and Jareth had already been there for a few minutes. King Flamarien, Dretho, and the King's escorts took their seats down the table.

"Lady Serra will be with you shortly," Justin said, closing the doors.

They sat in dead silence. No one made eye contact. Each sat with their own thoughts about the doom that was spreading across the land.

Just as soon as he had left, Justin walked back into the room. He walked up to Dretho and whispered in his ear. Dretho thought for a moment and mumbled something back to the man.

Justin left without another word.

King Flamarien looked to Dretho expectantly.

"The kitchen mistress was asking what elves eat," he said simply.

The blonde, elven woman snickered, but was immediately hushed with a glare from her King.

They sat again in silence for several minutes before Justin returned to the room.

"I give to you, Lady Lorna Bloodmoon, Heir of Moondale, and Lady Serra Bloodmoon, Ruler of Moondale," he announced, stepping aside.

Lorna walked in the room dressed in a regal, yellow gown. Serra, however, walked in wearing a green blouse and black leather pants with her sword at her side.

King Flamarien again took note that this woman seemed to be trying to be inconspicuous like him. Either that or she just did not like dressing up. He hoped that it was the former and not the latter.

Everyone stood, except Flamarien, until the Ladies took their seats.

Gnarl looked from Serra to Lorna and back to Serra again.

Serra noted the look and leaned to whisper in his ear.

"If she is to one day be ruler of this territory, then she must learn somehow," she responded, right before taking her seat.

Gnarl nodded his understanding.

"I have been informed that the evening meal will be ready in about two hours. I thought we could get a head start on this. There is no sense in delaying the inevitable," she began, looking to each of them.

"I think introductions are in order, the gentleman next to Lorna, is Jareth the Wanderer. This is Gnarl Knottytrunk, Captain of the Bloodmoon Brigade, and this is Lieutenant Hildvar of the Elkhorn Tribe," she finished, looking directly at the King.

"I am King Flamarien, King of the Elves," he said, pointing to himself, "This is Dretholzar Derathliona, the Mage of Sengar Valley. These are Gillianthesp and Fillianthesp Hiralderon, my personal attendants, and Florianna Flamarien, my daughter and Captain of my own army."

Each nodded in turn. Serra thought it a good thing that Florianna was a captain. It showed that the King was not as chauvinistic as she had first thought.

"Now that we are all acquainted, I am open to any ideas you may have. King Flamarien, we will begin with you," she offered. She was putting the situation into his hands and rightly so. He had been alive before the book had even been written. He had also dealt with it before and knew what to expect.

"I suggest that we have the mages scry for more information before we make any plans in stone," the King said, looking directly at Serra.

"I agree," she said, looking from Jareth to Dretho, "We do not have a castle mage, but we used to. I'm sure that you may find what you need in the old alchemy chamber. Bergearon will be able to give you directions from his tower."

They both nodded and left the room.

"Captain Knottytrunk, how many of the brigade stand at the ready?" she asked.

"We have three hunnerd aroun' the castle and on patrols. A hunnerd more are in the barracks waitin'. I've sent messengers ter the Brigade that lives in Moondale and in the outskirts. By a day or two we should be two thousand strong," he stated.

"And you, King? Have you alerted your people of the horde?" she asked, turning once again to King Flamarien.

"Yes. They have been aware since the moment it started. We do not live in cities as do humans. Sengar Valley is our home. Quisp, how many?" he asked, looking at the woman who had snickered before.

"I thought you said her name was Florianna?" Lorna interrupted. She had been quiet up to this point. She thought this moment was best to enter the conversation, as she had no idea what was going on, but still wanted to be included.

King Flamarien nodded, trying very hard not to lash out at the girl for interrupting him.

"I did, Lady Bloodmoon. Quisp is a name we have called her since her youth," he said patiently.

"Eight hundred are alerted and ready to march. Four thousand are aware and waiting for instructions," she stated to the King.

Lorna couldn't believe this girl was a captain. She looked barely older than her. She would have asked about that, but she knew the tension in the room was thick and thought it best not to push it.

Serra smiled at Lorna and nodded to Quisp.

Dretho and Jareth were silent as they made their way to the southern tower.

Bergearon was sitting at his desk in front of a window, looking over a star chart. A telescope was perched in front of him, pointing out the small window.

"Bergearon," Jareth stated after walking up behind him.

The bald man nearly jumped out of his skin. He turned around in surprise, but then grinned widely at his visitors.

"Jareth, Dretho. What a surprise!" he exclaimed, getting up from his chair. He leaned backwards and they heard his back crackle in a few places. "I've been at it for hours, needed to get up and stretch my bones anyway."

"Serra told us that there used to be a castle mage. Do you still have his things?" Jareth asked, stepping back to give the man room to stretch.

"Oh? Sure. Poor old Ghulga, she died a few years ago. I left her alchemy chamber exactly as she left it. She used to sit in there for hours, always trying to make a potion to get rid of this big wart she had on her forehead. Ha! We used to call her Three-Eyed Ghulga..."

"Bergearon, we are in a hurry. King Flamarien and Lady Serra are waiting downstairs for us," Dretho said impatiently, interrupting the man's ranting.

Bergearon's mouth went slack. "The Elf King, here?" he asked in earnest.

"Yes, please, show us the chamber," Jareth said, growing just as impatient.

"Of course," the cleric muttered, walking toward the door.

They walked from the room, down a long corridor, and stopped at a door with cobwebs streaming from one corner of the facing to the other.

The bald cleric reached into a pocket of his voluminous gray robes and pulled out a key ring. He fiddled with many keys for a few moments and finally found the right one.

He unlocked the door and pushed it in.

The cobwebs on the door were nothing compared to the interior of this room. They streamed from the ceiling to everything lying about. An inch of dust covered everything from books to antechambers and potions.

"As I said, she did die three years ago. You're welcome to anything and everything you can use. Good luck," Bergearon said with a nod and walked back toward his tower.

Dretho looked at Jareth, whose eyes were wide as galleons. "How are we supposed to find anything in here?" he asked the elf.

"Where's your sense of adventure, boy?" Dretho asked, pushing him inside. He closed his eyes and mutter incomprehensively, waving his hands in a fanlike motion.

Jareth watched as the cobwebs folded back like a curtain and the dust flew to the floor. He looked to Dretho in amazement and said, "You are going to have to teach me that."

They began rummaging around and within minutes found a scrying bowl.

"I guess I could have gone and gotten my own," Jareth said quietly.

Dretho gazed at him in exasperation, but said nothing. He shook his head and wiped the bowl off with the sleeve of his black robe.

"Well, do you have any moon wind salts?" the elf asked in annoyance.

Jareth nodded and they walked out of the room.

They were all seated in the dining room when Jareth and Dretho returned from upstairs. It was not a grand feast like before. The main members of the house sat close with their visitors, being dwarfed by the enormous table. It was set with large pots of different stews and raw venison cut into cubes. Serra thought this was odd at first and only understood when Gnarl told her about Justin's hushed conversation with Dretho.

"Well, what did you find out?" Serra asked, helping herself to some stew.

"It is as we feared. The minions are standing stationary surrounding Fortin Manor in Clandestine. We saw Truth perched on a terrace watching the arrival of the new forces.

They are filling up the streets and any empty space they might find. The people are weaving their way out of the city in a hurry. They are not being attacked, however," Dretho reported, taking his seat next to King Flamarien.

Jareth took his seat next to Serra. She could not help but notice his grave expression.

"What are you thinking?" she asked him quietly so no one else could hear.

"I fear he is coming here, Serra. He will come against Moondale with that horde and it will be wiped from the map," he said in a hushed, but shaky voice.

Serra nodded and suddenly had no appetite. She'd known all along this was a possibility. Jarmassad would not give up until all the Bloodmoon's were dead.

"This venison is wonderful," Dretho said with a mouthful, "My compliments to the chef."

Frelia, who had been sitting toward the end of the table, positively beamed.

Spike made camp in a clearing just past the Faeslarne Mountains. He had not had to worry about being attacked on the road, which was the norm, and had made good time. All the monsters were in full view, walking toward Fortin Manor, paying him no mind at all.

He made a small campfire and settled back onto his blanket. He hoped Lorna would remember his kindness. He knew it was likely he was walking to his death. After Fenlin had explained again, however, he knew that this was the right thing to do. He would most likely die in Fortin Manor anyway, whenever the offenses of the goodly races would appear. He would rather die trying to help than die being helpless.

His parents had died in a house fire when he was very young. He had lived on the streets for six years before Jareth Truth had met him in Clandestine's marketplace. They had become good friends quickly. Jareth had invited him to stay on at Fortin Manor to get off the streets.

They had spent a lot of time together during Jareth's apprenticeship. Spike had even let Jareth turn him into an owl once.

A noise beside him drew him from his contemplations. A goblin walked through his camp, coming to within five feet of Spike. He heard other creatures walking in the woods around him, but for once he was not afraid. He was more afraid of the sorcerer controlling them than the creatures themselves.

He fell into a light sleep and hoped he would be in Moondale by the next night.

They retired to the planning room after meal; all helping themselves to a well needed drink before settling in at the long table.

Serra was scared. She was more scared than she had ever been in her entire life. Her father should be here to handle these matters. Or even Renfar, if only to assist her. It was up to the Ladies of the house to make the decisions now. And one of those Ladies was barely more than a child.

Gnarl was on edge. He remembered the days of Truth's last try at domination. He had not gotten as far with it last time. The creatures had only begun to assemble when Harper Bloodmoon had stolen the book back. This time, it seemed, he may get his wishes.

King Flamarien felt very, very old. He was growing tired of this spell book. After Gyndless the Almighty had died, he had taken the book himself and had summoned every goodly mage in the land to try to destroy it. None had prevailed. They tried dousing it in water to smudge the ink, but the pages did not smear or wrinkle. Fire had proven pointless as well, the book hadn't singed at all. So he had hidden it in the dwarven mines hoping that the numerous traps would keep the thieves at bay and that time would dull the pages to nothingness. At the time, Gyndless had been the only sorcerer Remus had ever seen. Who knew that another, nearly as powerful, would come to know of the tome hundreds of years later? Yes, he felt very old indeed.

Dretho wracked his mind to come up with a plan. He had known that Truth would have to be weak from his acid spell, if not disabled. The man had been supporting himself on the terrace wall when they had scryed for him earlier. He had not thought to examine him. Most people would have melted in seconds, but this man, apparently, was stronger than anyone the elf had ever met.

He wondered if perhaps Jareth was hiding something. Did he have a brother that was just as strong in the arts as his father?

And what of Serra? The tumult of emotions was nearly overwhelming to the elf. Why had she had to come to him that day? He could have stayed in his tower for the rest of his days, alone, and in peace. Peace... had he really been in peace all these years? If he had been so at peace, why did he feel so odd when she was with him? The feelings she drew from his cold heart, felt better than his peace ever had.

"I think we need to get a map of this building's layout," Serra said, breaking the silence.

They all looked up at her expectantly.

"Jareth, have you ever been to this manor?" she asked.

"Aye, I lived there most of my life," he said uncomfortably. He did not look up at her. He only continued to stare into space, deep in contemplation.

"Is it warded in any way?" Dretho asked.

"Yes, no mages or sorcerers can teleport into the house," he answered. There was a collective sigh around the table. "However, the stables directly behind the house are not warded at all. That was where we would come and go."

"Are there any soldiers in attendance on a regular basis at the house?" Quisp asked. She was wary of this man who had lived in the home of their enemy, but she would hide her disdain and try to gather as much information as possible.

"There were just two guards at the front doors when I lived there and several house servants. Keep in mind I have not been there in three years. If Truth is there, he would most likely protect himself," he said, looking up at the elven woman.

Quisp nodded and turned to Dretho.

"Dretholzar, when you looked in on the manor, did you see any soldiers?"

"No, unless you count the thousands of creatures covering the city and grounds that are at the beck and call of the sorcerer," he answered sarcastically. He could not believe the simplemindedness of this conversation. They were worried about human guards when they were the least of their troubles. "We must go and kill the sorcerer before he can order them to attack," Dretho said sternly.

"And then? When the creatures come to their senses, they will attack the town, and everyone will die, including us if we cannot escape. It will be pandemonium," Serra stated, looking directly at Dretho.

Dretho was glad that he wasn't the only one thinking of something other than a few humans.

"You said that the townsfolk left did you not?" the elven twins asked in unison. This was the first time they had spoken.

"Aye, we did. That still does not fix the problem of the ones who have stayed or will be slaughtered when they try to reenter the city," Jareth speculated.

"King Flamarien, Clandestine is on the border of Sengar Valley. Would there be any way to shelter the townsfolk or move them to a secure location until the coast is clear?" Serra asked hopefully.

"We will not invite humans into our homes. But they may wander the valley at will, if they wish," King Flamarien said coldly.

Serra scowled. "This is about the enslavement of our kind, and you are worried about your valley. I understand that elves as a rule are very reserved in their dealings with humans, but there is a time and place for everything. This is not the time for pigheadedness in the face of adversity," she scolded.

King Flamarien stared back, unblinking. "Watch your words, Lady Bloodmoon. We are going to help you any way we can, because we must, but that does not mean that we have to open our doors to strangers. Sengar Valley covers half the Faeslarne Mountains and we occupy the whole of it. That does not mean that we are numerous, however. We must protect what is ours. There is a place between Denbar's rise and our valley that is flat and defensible. They may gather there. Clandestine is not so large a city. Though, collecting the masses of refugees and getting them there will be more work than you know."

Serra nodded. She knew it was the closest thing to an agreement she would have with the elf.

"What about the creatures? Who shall deal with them?" the King asked, glad she had not pressed the issue.

"We have two of the finest mages in the land. I am sure they will come up with something," she replied, looking to Jareth and Dretho.

They both looked up to her in shock. Neither of them had any idea what to do.

"What you ask will be impossible for two people," Jareth stated with fear in his eyes.

"What I ask is impossible in all aspects. However, we must try for the sake of living," she said matter-of-factly.

Chapter Seventeen
Loyalties

After all the others had retired for the night, Jareth rummaged through the alchemy chamber like a bloodhound digging in a foxhole. There was little organization to the chamber. Potions were scattered in clumps around the room, but none were labeled. He found that most of the spell components in the storage cabinet were ruined.

The only things that made any sense were the scrolls and books on the bookcase. They were sorted into offensive, defensive, metaphysical, and miscellaneous groups.

Jareth looked quickly through the defensive spells. He came across something promising called Temporal Stasis, but after further investigation he noted the spell only affected one creature at a time.

He searched for an hour before finally finding some spells worth putting aside. The Mass Charm spell could charm any creatures within a thirty-foot radius. The Hypnotic Pattern spell could fascinate a group of creatures in a thirty-foot radius, also. Perhaps he could charm some creatures and hypnotize others, but to what end?

Dretho entered the room as he began his search anew.

"I can not believe you are bothering with this pitiful excuse for an alchemy chamber," he stated bluntly, folding his arms over his chest.

Jareth looked up from a Hold Person scroll to regard the elf.

"Well, Dretho. This is all I have at the moment. Though, I am sure your collection far surpasses this, I was not invited to rummage in it," he retorted sarcastically, picking up a dusty spell book.

"And have you found anything useful?"

Jareth showed him the few scrolls he had set aside.

"Parlor tricks," the elf said, walking toward the door.

"Come, we will spend the night searching my library. We must inform Lady Serra that we are leaving."

Dretho left the room and Jareth put down his book and obediently followed.

Serra walked to her dresser and retrieved her nightgown and robe, hoping the bath Frelia had prepared would cure her headache. She made her way to the water room. The water in the large ceramic tub was still warm, but not as hot as she would have liked.

She had taken off all her clothes and put one foot in the water when there was a knock at the door. She closed her eyes and shook her head in disbelief.

Donning her robe quickly, she walked over to the door and unbarred it, peeking out.

"I am sorry to bother ye, missus, but Masters Dretho and Jareth are lookin' fer ye," Frelia announced apologetically.

"Where are they now?"

"We're waiting in the hall," she heard Jareth say.

Serra pulled her robe more tightly around her and tied it at the waist.

"If you will go to my study I will be done in half an hour. If you need anything in the meantime, Frelia will be glad to assist you," she said, stepping out from the door.

Jareth and Dretho adverted their eyes from her shapely form.

"We will be waiting," Dretho stated, walking toward the stairway.

Jareth lingered a moment and then followed.

Once they were out of sight Frelia turned and scowled at Serra.

"What?" she asked in confusion.

"Ye should be ashamed o' yerself comin' ou' in yer robe. Ye might as well have been wearin' a glass dress," the maid scolded, shooing her back into the water room.

Serra shook her head and said, "You knew I was here. Why did you bring them then if you did not think it proper to speak to them?"

"I ain' talkin' abou' speakin', me Lady. They may be honorable men, but they're still men! Ain' ne'er seen one withou' relations on his mind all the day. It's bad enough that ye walk aroun' in breeches like a boy, showin' off yer legs and the like. Yer askin' fer trouble an' trouble's gonna find ye!" Frelia said, wagging a finger an inch from Serra's nose.

"Frelia, stop," Serra replied sternly.

"I did no' raise ye ter ..."

"Frelia! Young I am, but I am also still the Lady of this house. Stop this line of chatter this instant," Serra shouted, slapping Frelia's finger from her nose.

The maid looked at her dumbstruck. She had always viewed Serra as her own, but now she realized that wasn't her place any longer. She was grown. Actually, most women her age would be married with a brood of children already.

"Yer right missus," she admitted, looking to the floor, "I've misjudged ye."

"We are all stressed right now, and what you speak of is the very last thing on my mind to be sure. Please leave me be and let me get a bath before I am late meeting them," Serra said, turning toward the tub.

Frelia left the room without another word.

Dretho and Jareth entered Serra's study and took seats across from each other.

Jareth had watched Dretho's reaction to seeing her scantily clad figure. He had turned his head immediately. Did that mean that he wasn't interested after all?

"Serra is one beautiful woman," Jareth stated, watching the elf closely for any reaction.

Dretho looked to Jareth and said nothing, his expression blank of emotion as usual.

"I guess you probably have a harem? Do elves take more than one wife?" Jareth pushed on.

Dretho rolled his eyes and looked away. "You are foolish, human," he answered, focusing on a tapestry of Serra and Lorna as children, playing in the southern garden.

"Seriously, do you have a wife at home in your tower?" he asked finally. He was determined to get an answer, any answer.

"Not that it is any of your business, human, but no. I have never taken a wife," the elf answered coldly, still not meeting Jareth's stare.

"Would you fancy one?" He knew he was pushing the elf's buttons, but at this point he did not care. He wanted to know once and for all if there was anything between them.

Dretho knew exactly why he was asking.

"Would you?" the elf asked, turning to look at Jareth.

Jareth sat back on his couch and sighed. "Aye, I would."

"If you wish to marry someone, then by all means do. My personal affairs, however, are none of your concern." Dretho answered condescendingly.

Jareth's lips drew a line in frustration. His jealousy was nearly at a breaking point, Dretho was avoiding him.

"Do you fancy Serra?" he finally came out and asked.

Dretho rose from his couch and left the room.

She had brushed her hair, but it was still dripping wet. She had thrown on some brown breeches and a green tunic. As she walked down the hall toward the study, she looked up to see Dretho walking toward her.

"Where is Jareth?" she asked, walking up to stand before him.

Dretho's heart felt as if it would explode. He loved her. As much as he had tried to avoid Jareth's comments and questions, he could not deny it any longer.

"He is in the study, though I felt unable to keep his company any longer," he said, standing straight and gazing into those beautiful green eyes.

Serra sensed Dretho was upset about something he was not telling her. She walked up to him and put her hand to his face. "What did he say to you?" she asked with concern.

Dretho wanted nothing more than to wrap her in his arms at that moment. "He is a prying little rat who wants nothing more than to cause discomfort to those he is with. We were going to tell you that we were going to my tower to search for spells to help in the cause. However, he is no longer welcome in my home, so I am going alone," he said, reveling in the feel of her hand on his face, and trying very hard not to let it show.

"What did he say that bothered you so?" she asked, moving her hand to his shoulder.

"I will not bother you with such foolish things." He reached into a pocket in his black robes and brought out a red stone. He took her hand off his shoulder and placed the stone in her palm. "If you need me, all you need do is hold this stone to your heart and mutter my name. It will take you to wherever I am in an instant. Be well, Lady Serra Bloodmoon, I will be back soon with plans in hand for the horde."

She closed her hand around the stone and nodded. She wrapped him in a quick hug and walked past him to the study.

When she looked back, he was gone.

She opened the door and walked inside to see Jareth pacing back and forth across the room.

"Tell me, Jareth the Wanderer, what did you say to my friend?" she asked matter-of-factly, lingering in the doorway.

Jareth stopped his pacing and fixed her with an expressionless stare. "Did he tell you?" he asked curiously.

"Do not answer a question, with a question. Tell me," she demanded, walking into the room and crossing her arms over her chest.

"Well, it's obvious he loves you," he said plainly, crossing his own arms.

Her eyes widened. She could not believe his words. He was yet again being foolish in his jealousy. "Jareth, we have been over this already."

"No, this is not about you and him being together. This is about him loving you in a way other than a friend. I've told you that I love you, though you have not answered me back. Should I leave Moondale today? So that you may begin your relationship without interference?" he asked with a scowl.

"Jareth, I am weary of your demands, expectations, and assumptions. I may have felt love for you at one point. But your behavior these past few days have shown me the folly in that. You do not know what love is. All you know is possession and jealousy. Leave as you may, but you will receive nothing from me other than a roof over your head and food in your belly," she scolded.

She knew she needed him and his information. She would not, however, compromise her friends and honor to get it.

Jareth's mouth turned up into a snarl. He uttered a few words and disappeared.

Serra stood in the study with her mouth agape. She had never been more confused in all her life. Jareth was such a nice man when he did not feel threatened. He had saved her life under pressure. He had gone against his own father's magic to return her safely home. Now, he felt threatened because there was a chance that he would not be her choice. He was being irrational and childish. She could never be with anyone that was so controlled by jealousy and anger.

She did not blame Dretho for leaving him in Moondale. She no longer wished the man's company either. But was what Jareth said true? Did Dretho love her?

She had known a few elves in her lifetime. There were a few in the brigade and some who lived in the city proper. They were all very straight forward in their dealings and duties. She had never seen one show true emotion for another. Even King Flamarien did not seem to look to Quisp as a daughter, but more as a soldier.

Could it be possible? Why did men have to be so damned confusing?

Dretho walked up the stairs to his altar room as Bern Hilda followed him a foot behind. "Do you need anything, master?" she asked for perhaps the sixth time.

He stopped and looked at her.

"Aye, I need you to bring me any maps you can find of Clandestine and find out anything you can about Fortin Manor. I don't care how you do it, just do it," he answered, walking into the room and slamming the door behind him.

Bern Hilda grinned from ear to ear. Dretho had never asked her to do much other than clean his home. This was the first time he had ever asked her to do something that allowed her to leave the tower.

She ran down the stairs and walked across the great foyer into the kitchen. After knocking five times on the wall, it opened to a stairway. She grabbed a torch along one wall and began her trek to the secret exit. The secret exit was actually a drainage ditch in a valley next to the small village of Felden. She watched to make sure no one was about and jumped from the narrow pipe into the ditch. It was still filled with rain, but Bern Hilda didn't notice. She had a mission. Her master had never given her a mission before.

Walking into the village and down the only narrow street, she came upon a tavern called the Traveler's Inn. It was very late in the night, but the inn was still full of patrons.

She walked up to the small bar and hopped up on a stool. "Gooley, give me mead and tell Dergaz that I want to see him," she demanded, slamming her fist down on the bar.

Gooley, the bartender, looked at her in shock. He was a young dwarf, only one hundred and twenty years, but he had a full blonde beard and scars from many brawls.

"Are ye crazy, Bernie? Dergaz ain't gonna talk to ye!" he exclaimed with a condescending, but caring, tone.

"He'll see me today! Master sent me on a mission!"

The room, which was previously filled with chatter and music, went dead silent.

Bern Hilda looked around proudly to the dwarves and few humans in the room. After a few moments, the noise began anew and she turned back to Gooley.

He slammed a large mug of mead on the bar and threw his towel on the counter. "Ye best watch the til, if a pence is missin', it'll be yer arse," he said, storming to the back and through a door.

Bern Hilda downed her mead and tried to act calm. She had met Dergaz before. He was the most renowned thief in all of Sengar Valley. He was a human about thirty years old, but crafty and deadly.

She waited for about ten minutes before Gooley returned to the bar. He nodded toward the door and held out his hand. She tossed him four pence and walked to the back of the room.

She walked in the door and was instantly met with a cloud of pipe smoke. Dergaz sat at a small desk, surrounded by six standing henchmen, weapons at the ready.

"Dergaz," she greeted with a nod.

"Bern Hilda, what brings you to my bar this night? Won't that elf of yours be worried?" he asked condescendingly, drawing chuckles from the other men.

Bern Hilda was always teased that she served an elf. Dwarves and elves got along fine, but they didn't enslave each other often. No one knew, but Bern Hilda had offered her services to Dretho for saving her brother from death years ago. He was not a friendly sort, but Bern Hilda owed him.

"He's sent me to see you, actually. I need information, Dergaz," she countered, standing straight and tall.

"And what will I get out of the deal?" he asked, picking some dirt from under one of his fingernails. His bodyguards just stared straight ahead and acted as if she wasn't there.

She reached into her pocket and took out a small coin purse filled with twenty galleons and tossed it on his desk.

He sat up, his fingernail forgotten, and opened the bag to peer in. He closed it back and tucked it into his leather jerkin.

"Alright, you've got my attention," he said, leaning back again.

"I need maps of Clandestine and Fortin Manor. I also need any information at all on Fortin Manor that you can gather," she said calmly.

He looked at her questioningly. "That is an odd request. Why come to me? Doesn't that elf have a library?"

"Time is of the essence, I need this as soon as possible," she answered, meeting his gaze, "Can you do it or not?"

He scowled at her. "Of course, I can. Be back here same time tomorrow night and you'll have what you ask and more," he said, waving toward the door.

She left without another word and made her way back to the drainage ditch.

She would not fail her master. She would prove to him that she was worthy of his trust.

As soon as Bern Hilda had left the back room, Dergaz turned to Gydian, his first underling.

"Get Thad," he demanded.

Gydian marched out of the door and returned shortly with a scrawny, old man in faded, gray robes.

"Yes, Dergaz?" the old man asked in a small voice. His glasses were so thick they made his eyes look twice their size. His skin was pale and wrinkled and his hair was white as snow.

"Take me to Truth," Dergaz demanded, standing from his seat and towering over the small man.

Thad's large eyes bulged. He stammered and shook his head in denial.

Dergaz drew his short sword and pressed its tip to the man's throat.

"Do it now, or die," Dergaz spat, pressing harder. Thad could hardly breathe.

"Ye... yes Dergaz, anything you say. Just please, do not hurt me," Thad whimpered.

Dergaz sheathed his sword and stood motionless.

Thad took the thief's hand and cleared his throat to prevent it from quivering. "*Arcanus Traveelus Duoti.*"

Jareth appeared in the stables of Fortin Manor and nearly landed on top of a small goblin female. He was amazed at the sight before him. A monster of some sort stood wherever there was space to stand.

The silence was eerie. He could barely hear the breathing of the goblins and orcs standing in the stables. The horses had long since fled when the creatures had pushed past them to stand in their stalls.

He weaved his way around and made his way toward the house. He arrived at the backdoor and stopped. Everywhere he looked there were hundreds, thousands of creatures standing stationary staring blankly at the manor.

Jareth sat down on the step, right in front of a particularly smelly ogre with purple hair. He sat on the step for nearly an hour before drawing out his lock picks. He had the door unlocked in seconds.

If he went in now, there was no going back. He could barely draw breath from the animosity churning within him. After all he had done for her, she would not love him. She had said that he expected too much of her. Was it too much to ask for love? Was it too much to ask for her to deny Dretho? To the nine hells with her, he was tired of trying.

He now understood why his father despised the Bloodmoon family. They were thieves after all. They had stolen the book from his father and Serra had stolen his very heart. He would help his father. He would rid the world of the wench that had so wounded his pride.

With a firm nod, he walked into the kitchen and into the formal dining room.

The house was quiet and dark. He knew they would most likely be asleep, but he needed to speak to his father now. He walked into the foyer and took the steps two at a time to the floor that housed the bedchambers. He knew his father would most likely be staying in the bedroom with the terrace that loomed over the front door. He opened the door and did not bother knocking.

His father, his mangled father, was lying in bed.

"You were right," he said simply.

Jarmassad Truth opened his eye in shock and turned to look upon his son.

"What do you mean I was right, you meddlesome fool?" he asked in hatred.

"About the Bloodmoon family, they are thieves," Jareth admitted, walking up to the edge of the bed.

"So you are here to help them by ending my life? Do you think I am stupid, whelp?" the old man scolded, rising to a sitting position.

Jareth shook his head and offered his hand.

Jarmassad looked down at the hand questioningly and back up into his only son's eyes.

"*Inseena Forenza trutharay*," he yelled.

An orange aura appeared around Jareth's form, but he did not flinch.

"Are you here to kill me?"

"No," Jareth answered simply.

"Are you here to gain knowledge for the Bloodmoon women?"

"No."

"Are you here to help your father kill the Bloodmoon women?"

Jareth paused. "Yes," he said with a snarl.

Chapter Eighteen
Arrival

The next day Serra awoke with an anger she had to get rid of before seeing anyone. She quickly donned her practice attire; a brown leather short vest and pants that stopped above her knees, grabbed her scimitar and went out into the hall.

The suns had just crested the horizon and most of the castle was still at rest. She walked down the stairs and nearly ran over Hildvar in her anxiousness to get to the practice room.

Hildvar looked at her and his eyes widened in fear.

"My Lady, you aren't leaving again, are you?" he asked in concern.

She bit back her frustration and shook her head. "No, Hildvar, I am going to practice. If anyone asks about my whereabouts, you are to tell them I am sleeping in," she ordered, walking around him and down the last few steps.

She did not look back.

Hildvar watched her until she was out of sight. It was unlike her to not make conversation with him. Something was obviously troubling her.

He walked back down the stairs and made his way to the barracks.

Serra entered the practice room and was relieved to see that it was empty.

A huge mat made of resin dominated the one hundred foot, square room. It was hard, but gave just a bit so that injuries were kept to a minimum. Wooden carvings of men were stacked along the wall. Most looked as if they had been cut thousands of times. Serra walked over to the wall and carried one of the mannequins to the middle of the mat. She laid down her blade and propped the form upright on its stand.

She picked up her scimitar and walked to the front of the room. She went down on her knees and closed her eyes, trying hard to focus through her feelings. She pushed away her fear of the Truth horde, the uncertainty of Dretho's feelings, the frustration with King Flamarien, and most of all, and her anger at Jareth. Taking a deep breath, she envisioned these feelings leaving her body with her exhale. After nearly twenty minutes, she finally opened her eyes and stood.

Raising her arms, she stretched on her toes, bringing her sword as high in the air as she could. She felt her weary muscles tighten.

It had been so long since she had practiced. She had trained every day since her twelfth birthday, except the period when she had been bedridden with her neck wound.

She stayed on the tips of her toes and lowered her arms so they made her look like a human T. She rested her head back and gained her balance.

As she stretched her arms behind her back, she raised her head again. Clasping her hands around the hilt of her sword, she pulled so that her shoulders popped and her biceps stretched.

Bending her knees, she lowered herself to the mat. She put down her sword and lay down flat. She raised her legs into the air, supporting her back with her hands. She stretched and pointed her toes, feeling her back pop in several places.

She turned over onto her belly and pushed up with her arms, keeping her toes pointed and on the floor. In this position, she raised herself up and down several times, feeling the burning sensation in her arms and shoulders.

She stood back up and made wide circles with her arms to relax her back.

Finally feeling loosened up; she picked up her scimitar, and walked over to the mannequin.

Letting out a feral scream, she lunged at the form, shoving her scimitar through the wood with ease. She ripped the sword out and turned a complete circuit, slashing at the form again.

She jumped in the air and flipped over backwards to land on her feet and stab, gaining another hit.

Lifting her arm as if parrying, she kicked the mannequin, and it crashed to the floor. She jumped atop it and stabbed down, burying her sword into the neck of the wooden figure.

She stepped off the form and dropped her sword to the ground.

Walking to one corner of the room, she turned several cartwheels to where her scimitar lay and picked it up as she passed, and continued to tumble across the room.

King Flamarien had been walking around the castle when he had heard Serra's scream. He ran to the practice room and stood in the doorway, watching her savage tumbling. He half-hid behind the wall and peered in the doorway, trying not to alert her to his presence.

The Lady of Moondale was fierce and agile. She moved with a grace he had never seen in a human. This one had surpassed the normal fumbling human ways and reminded him of many of his kin.

She stood the wooden man upright and went at him with an intensity that impressed him. Her stomach muscles rippled with the effort of her parries and lunges. She would perform some type of acrobatic feat before each thrust. Sweat streamed down her chest and her hair was soaked from her efforts, but she did not seem to be tiring.

This one had trained. She had trained hard.

Serra was in the middle of another tumble pass across the room, when she noticed the elf peering in at her. She did not stop, however, but kept up her pace to land beside a stack of wooden practice swords. She knelt down and picked two out of the stack. She jumped into the air and turned several flips to land by the door where the elf stood.

She tossed him a sword.

"If you are going to watch me train, you could at least provide an obstacle," she said with a scowl.

Flamarien nodded and walked to the center of the room. He kicked the mannequin out of the way with ease.

Serra walked up to him and bowed, as was the elven custom. They both went into a crouch and began circling, waiting for the other to make the first move. The Elf King saw the savagery in her eyes and was impressed even more. This Lady was no ordinary human by any means.

He lunged at her with his sword and she jumped into a backhand spring to land a few feet away.

She let out another feral scream and ran at him.

Flamarien nearly smiled at her error. He made as if he was about to parry and instead stuck his foot out to trip her.

Serra, however, saw this move from a mile away. She made her pass and jumped over his leg, making a circuit and smacking the wooden sword against his back.

Flamarien grimaced and turned to face her once again.

"Do not underestimate me. If you wish to stop, then stop, but you committed yourself to blows when you made your way into the room," she said harshly, kneeling into another crouch.

Flamarien nodded and lunged at her again. Serra dodged to the side, but his sword scraped lightly against her thigh.

She turned to him and advanced, making great figure eights with her blade.

"I will admit, I have underestimated you most of my time here," he said right before parrying her vicious assault of a stab, stab, and thrust combination.

"I know," she replied simply, launching another combination, gaining a minor hit against his calf.

"Where did you learn to fight like this?" he asked as he stabbed three times in rapid succession. She tumbled back again, taking no hits.

"You have heard of the Bloodmoon Brigade, have you not?" she asked, coming at him again.

Their swords locked at the hilt and they butted up against each other in a battle of strength.

"Yes," Flamarien replied, his nose an inch from hers, and his whole body shaking with the effort it took to hold his sword steady.

She twisted her hand quickly and his sword thudded to the floor. She pressed the tip of her own against his chest. "Most of our weapons trainers are elves," she said.

Flamarien grinned despite his defeat.

Serra dropped her wooden sword and turned away from him. She picked up her scimitar and left the room without another word.

Dretho had not slept at all. Piles of tomes and scroll cases covered the counters of his alchemy chamber. He knelt over a roll of parchment and hurriedly scribbled out the last phrases of a spell that could help them.

He knew he needed to go back to Moondale soon. However, he wanted to be as prepared as possible when he arrived.

He dreaded facing Serra and Jareth. He knew the obnoxious human probably had told her that Dretho loved her. Butterflies filled his stomach and he felt sick at the thought.

Why did that blasted man have to meddle in what did not concern him?

He stood and rolled the scroll up and carefully placed it in one of the ten scroll cases he had filled over the past night. He grabbed a black backpack and packed it full with them. He refilled his small pouch with the entire contents of his potion cabinet.

He would return to Moondale this morning and then return to his tower tonight only to gather Bern Hilda's information. She had assured him that she would know something tonight.

He walked out of his alchemy chamber and into his altar chamber, placing his belongings by the large, elaborate doors. He looked up to the wall bust of Drakevin, the God of Eternal Power, and fell to his knees.

"Oh, Lord Drakevin, give me the strength to make it through the day. I will do everything within my power to serve you through these trials. Please, I beg of you, give me the insight and strength to serve you well," he begged.

He stood back up and grabbed his belongings, only stopping long enough to transform the alchemy chamber back into a bookcase.

Serra did not bother dressing up after her bath. She put on a pair of leather pants and a white blouse and braided her hair out of her face.

Her work out had helped stifle some of the anger at her situation. She still felt betrayed by Jareth, but after further thought, she realized it did not matter. She had known him less than a fortnight. How could he demand her life and love after such a short time?

She only dreaded the explanation she knew she would not be able to avoid.

As she put on her sword belt, she took a deep, calming breath. She walked out of her chamber and down the stairs to the formal dining room for the morning meal.

Justin Wolfsbane was waiting for her outside the doors.

"My Lady, I will announce you now," he said politely.

Serra shook her head.

"No, Justin, go have Jareth's room cleaned out. He is no longer staying with us," she ordered, trying to remain civil.

Justin's eyes widened.

"Yes, my Lady," he answered, obviously flustered. He began to walk away and then stopped and sighed.

"It may not be my place to say this, Lady Serra, but if ever you need to talk, I am here," he said with genuine care.

Serra's shoulders slumped and she walked over to the man, wrapping him in a great hug.

"Thank you, Justin. I needed that," she replied, fighting the tears welling in her eyes.

Justin returned the hug and pushed her back to arms length.

"Everything will be alright. I know you are about to face possibly the hardest time of your young life, but you are a Bloodmoon; that in itself proves you will not fail."

Serra smiled and walked into the dining room.

Gnarl was sitting next to Hildvar when she entered the room. He knew by the look on her face that something was wrong. She walked in casually, without bothering to greet anyone. This was no ordinary thing, especially considering there was a King at their table this morn.

Serra stopped at her chair at the head of the table and looked up at her guests. "Good morning. I regret to inform you that Jareth the Wanderer is no longer in attendance at this castle, nor do I think he will return. Those of you involved in our planning meetings, please retire to the planning room after your meal," she announced without emotion.

She sat down in her chair as everyone at the table glanced nervously to those sitting next to them.

Gnarl looked upon Serra with concern and put his rough hand over hers.

"What happened, girl?" he asked in a fatherly tone.

Serra looked at him with a blank expression.

"This is not the time or the place, Captain Knottytrunk," she answered, trying her best not to sound callous.

He did not take the comment personally. He only nodded and dug into his eggs.

They had all been eating in silence when Dretho entered the room wearing his customary black robes. He looked immediately at Serra, who just stared back with a blank expression. He looked to her right and noted the empty seat.

He took his customary seat in the middle and began eating, saying nothing at all.

They all filed into the planning room right after the meal. Everyone seemed to have the look of gloom on his or her faces. Jareth was the only one who knew the layout of Fortin Manor, and now he was gone.

King Flamarien looked at Serra with pity. He now understood her ferocity earlier that morning.

"Well, here we are," she began, "Dretho, did you come up with anything in your studies last night?"

Dretho looked up to her and nodded. "I believe I have the beginnings of a plan, though it will entail full cooperation of our forces."

"I have no doubt that can be arranged," she said, looking to Gnarl and to Quisp.

"I have amassed several spells that will dominate the minds of the horde. If I am successful, I will be able to move them all to a defensible area where we may contain them."

"Contain them?" Gnarl asked incredulously, "Then what in the bloody hell are we goin' ter do with 'em?"

Dretho scowled at the dwarf.

"If you would allow me to finish... In my former dealings with Lord Frendar Bloodmoon, battle tactics were one of the many things we discussed. I believe the Bloodmoon Brigade Vice will be in order, only on a large scale with elven troops standing at their sides."

King Flamarien eyed Gnarl closely and felt relief when the dwarf smiled wickedly.

Serra smiled as well.

"Good thinkin', elf. Hildvar, go get the other Lieutenants and tell 'em ter come 'ere in an hour," Gnarl ordered, still grinning.

Hildvar looked to Serra, who nodded her approval, and he left the room in a hurry.

"Do we know if all the creatures have amassed?" Serra asked, looking again to Dretho.

"I believe a great majority of them have. The question is where they will attack."

"Do we have any idea how many we are talking about? The monsters of the countryside amassed in one place would be astounding," Quisp asked.

Dretho sighed uncharacteristically.

"I believe a fair estimate would be eight thousand," he said in defeat.

There was a collective sigh around the table.

"Even if we left our homes defenseless to attack with every available sword, we would not have that many." King Flamarien hoped that Dretho had a good plan. It would have to be regardless.

"Aye, but ye don' understan' the vice, if we can pull it off," Gnarl said reassuringly.

"King Flamarien, if we can pool the horde into one large group, we will surround them completely five soldiers deep. We will then use the wall of our allies to push them in so tightly they cannot move. After we achieve that, we will pepper them with arrows and stab them with pole arms until none are left standing," Serra explained with satisfaction.

King Flamarien leaned back in his chair and felt his tension lessen a bit.

"It is a very good plan, but Dretholzar, Truth has the book. Can you compete with the old man's power?"

Dretho sat up straight in his chair and clasped his hands on the table.

"My King, the only way I can hope to override his control, is to call upon the Feral Five."

King Flamarien scowled.

"The Feral Five?" Serra asked in confusion.

"Before I go on, I must tell you all that what I say to you today does not leave this room. I must have your word that you will not mention the name of the Feral Five to anyone... ever," he began in all seriousness.

They each nodded their agreement apprehensively.

"The Feral Five have lived on Remus since the dawn of the world. They are a race of creatures that very few even know exist. They are called wemics. Wemics have the torso, arms, and head of a human and the body, legs, and tail of a lion. There is only one pride still in existence, which I know quite well," he said, trying to gauge their reactions.

"They are magical creatures by birth, but can possess the mind like nothing you have ever seen. If I can persuade the Feral Five to join us, possessing the minds of the horde will be all too easy."

"Where do they live, Dretho?" Serra asked. She had never heard of these creatures, but she trusted Dretho to understand them for her.

"I can not divulge that to you my Lady, though I believe it would be best that you accompany me to their sacred lair."

Serra's eyes widened and King Flamarien hissed through his teeth.

"I can not believe you are suggesting this," he said in anger.

Everyone at the table was taken aback by his rage, except Dretho.

"Do you know these creatures as well, my King?" Quisp asked in confusion.

"Yes. They are brutal killers," he spat, scowling at Dretho.

Dretho had expected this reaction and did not act as if it bothered him.

"Would you like to tell them the story, Flamarien, or should I?" Dretho asked simply.

King Flamarien stood up from his chair and began pacing the room.

"Dretholzar left Sengar Valley many years ago to further his studies across Remus and came upon these creatures in his travels. He asked that I accompany him to their lair, so that I could speak with creatures older and perhaps wiser than myself," he began heatedly, eyeing Dretho.

"I went, of course, this intrigued me, as did it intrigue my wife, Lelorianna. The three of us went to their lair and met. All was well until Lelorianna challenged them to find out their fighting prowess."

He looked directly at Serra and stopped his pacing.

"My wife was a warrior, like you Lady Serra, only she was obsessed at being the best. She miscalculated and was killed before my very eyes that day."

Quisp and Serra gasped in unison.

"You told me mother died on the road! You said she was killed by a poisonous snake!" Quisp yelled, jumping from her seat.

Flamarien turned to his daughter and looked like he was reliving his sorrow all over again.

"I did, but there was a reason, Florianna. I knew that you would try to avenge your mother's death and I could not bear to lose you as well. I gave my word to the Feral Five that I would not divulge their location or existence and I keep my word. Please do not attempt to find them or attack them. They attack with their claws as well as their swords. Not to mention they can control your mind so you just stand and let them take you willingly," he said in fear, placing his hands on her small shoulders.

Quisp turned her back to him and wiped the tears from her eyes.

"Florianna, I have lost both of my parents and my only brother to Jarmassad Truth. I have felt as you do now, and I have tried to go on my own for revenge. Luckily, some sense was knocked into me and now that I have faced Truth and his lackeys, I know that I would not have survived. Listen closely to your father's words and understand that his reasons for not telling you were not out of spite nor to take away your chance at revenge, but to protect you from the consequences of the anger he knew you would feel," Serra offered softly.

Quisp and King Flamarien looked up to her and nodded, each feeling a little more at ease.

Serra looked at Dretho and saw a hint of a smile cross his face for a moment.

"Serra, if we are to do this, we must leave as soon as tomorrow. Truth should begin his attacks at any moment," Dretho said in all seriousness.

Justin Wolfsbane entered the room and crossed to stand next to Serra. He whispered in her ear and her eyes widened.

"Bring him to me and go get Lorna, now," she said harshly.

Justin ran from the room and everyone looked up at her expectantly.

She stared at the door and said, "It seems we have a visitor. A man from Fortin Manor named Spike."

Gnarl stood up and ran toward the door.

"Stop, Gnarl," she shouted.

He stopped in his tracks and turned to look at her skeptically.

"He is alone," she said, gesturing toward his seat.

Spike sat in the foyer surrounded by six guards. They did not say a word, but eyed him warily with their swords pointed in his direction.

He tried his best to remain calm. He had been questioned thoroughly at the main portcullis and had been taken at sword point into the foyer.

He looked around and was impressed by the grand décor and cleanliness of the castle. Normally the stone structures were cold and drafty and there never seemed to be enough light. But the stone had been painted white and the many windows brought in the summer suns to warm the place.

He had explained to a black haired dwarf four times that he was here to see Lorna, but the man had insisted he speak with Lady Serra.

Noticing Lorna descend the staircase with an older man in a light green tunic, he shouted, "Lorna!"

A guard pressed the point of his broadsword to his neck in warning.

But she stopped at the bottom of the staircase and squinted. "Spike?" she asked in wonder.

The man grabbed her by the elbow and pulled her into another room before he could answer.

Justin drug Lorna into the planning room.

"Let me go, Justin, that was Spike, he's my friend!" she screamed, fighting to get back out the door.

"Lorna Bloodmoon, sit down this instant!" Serra shouted, getting up from her seat.

Lorna turned to Serra and scowled. "You're not my mother, don't try to tell me what to do," she shouted back with venom.

"Gnarl," Serra said simply.

The redheaded dwarf got up and grabbed Lorna around the middle and carried her to her seat.

"Listen here. Ye'll listen ter yer sister, she's tryin' ter protect ye. Now, sit there and don' ye say a word til yer spoken to or ye'll be locked up in yer room til this is o'er!" he spat in the young girl's face.

She straightened in her seat and scowled, but did not move or retort.

Serra shook her head in frustration.

"How do you know this man, Lorna?" she asked civilly.

Lorna did not look at her, but said, "He took care of me when that man locked me up on the island."

"Do you realize that he works for the man who killed mom, dad, and Renfar, and nearly killed you?" she asked harshly.

Lorna looked at Serra and scowled.

"He was nice to me. He went against that man to give me something more than ruined bread and water. He was the only one who came to me while I waited for you all that time," she whined.

Serra sighed and looked down at the table.

"Lorna, Jareth was nice too, but he abandoned us," she said, closing her eyes.

"You probably ran him off," Lorna spat, "You never have been able to find a boyfriend! Now you want me to end up like you!"

Serra's eyes widened and Gnarl stood up from his seat and snarled.

"Don' ye talk ter her like that!"

"Lorna, please, we will discuss this later. We are in the company of guests and they are most likely growing tired of this sibling quarrel," she said, looking up to her guests. "I am sorry you have had to witness this tirade. Justin, bring him in."

Justin nodded and left the room.

"Please, let me speak to him before you say anything, alright?" Serra pleaded with Lorna.

"Fine," the girl replied, crossing her arms over her chest and eyeing Gnarl hatefully.

In a few minutes, Justin walked in with six guards and a boy about the age of seventeen. He looked to Lorna and then to Serra. His face was wrought of sheer terror.

"Lady Serra, I present to you Spike Forsiad, of Fortin Manor," Justin announced before moving behind the guards.

Serra nodded.

"Seat him at the end of the table please. Gnarl will guard him, you other six are dismissed," she stated.

They sat him down and tied a length of rope around his chest, securing him to the back of the chair before they left.

Gnarl walked over, drew his morning star, and loomed over the young man with a fierce glare.

"Why are you here, Spike?" Serra asked calmly.

The boy cleared his throat.

"I came to warn you, Lady Serra. Jarmassad Truth has called all the monsters of the countryside to Fortin Manor and he plans to march on Moondale," he replied as steadily as he could.

Dretho rose from his seat and walked over to Serra and whispered in her ear.

She nodded.

"Mister Forsiad, I am sure you are familiar with magic," he said, walking up to the boy.

Spike nodded.

"Then I am sure you understand why I must now cast a truth spell upon you to assure us that your intentions are good," he asked, stopping next to his chair.

"Yes, please, anything to make you understand," he said anxiously.

"*Inseena Forenza trutharay*," the elf chanted.

An orange aura surrounded Spike and he looked again to Serra.

"Why are you here?" Serra asked, rising from her seat.

"I am here because I was afraid for Lorna's life. Truth has called the monsters to our doors and I left in fear. I needed to leave to warn you about his plans to march on Moondale. He intends to kill all those remaining of the Bloodmoon line," he said calmly, unblinking.

"How did you escape?" Dretho asked.

"Fenlin Karling gave me a horse. I rode and only stopped to rest a few hours."

"Does Truth know you are here?" King Flamarien interjected.

"I do not know."

"Are you here to kill anyone?" Serra asked, looking at Lorna.

"No."

Serra looked at Dretho.

"He is being honest, though I suggest we be careful," he said, answering the question in her gaze.

"Take him to the dungeon. Give him blankets, food, drink, and a change of clothes. He is not to be mistreated in any way. Post four guards at his cell door," Serra said to Gnarl.

Gnarl untied the rope, grabbed the glowing boy by the elbow, and escorted him out of the room.

Serra sat in her chair and rubbed her temples.

"Lorna, you can go back to your room. Do not try to contact Spike. I need to speak with him more before he is allowed to roam freely," she said, not looking at her sister.

Lorna knew this was the closest thing to a compromise as she would get. She left the room without another word.

"Dretho, you said we would need to leave immediately to go to the Feral Five?" she asked.

"Yes and now that we know he is to march on Moondale, we need to finalize our plans tonight," he said solemnly.

Chapter Nineteen
Love and Rage

They did not hesitate in preparing Moondale for the onslaught. The Bloodmoon Brigade began setting up massive tents on the extensive grounds to house the people of the town. People began leaving their homes for the safety of the castle before sunsdown.

Engineers began building catapults in the courtyard and wagons of boulders were hauled in to be stacked next to them. Large cauldrons, to be filled with hot oil later, were lifted to the parapets.

Gnarl Knottytrunk had his hands full with orders. They had decided not to march on Fortin Manor, but to await the horde at home. King Flamarien was to leave in the morning to gather his forces.

Gnarl, Dretho, Quisp, and Hildvar had stayed in the planning room when everyone else had left. They had laid out their plans for the Bloodmoon Brigade Vice and went over the steps and possibilities several times before they were satisfied.

Quisp had asked her father if she could help in preparing the castle. He had agreed wholeheartedly.

Hildvar and Quisp stood on the parapet, staring down at Moondale.

"You should clear those trees next to the walls. They would be too easy for goblins to climb. With one strong rope and grapnel, they would be on the walls in minutes," Quisp suggested.

Hildvar looked at the elm trees and nodded.

"Good observation, we could use the wood for the ballista," he offered.

"Yes, and we could use the leafy branches to cover trenches. We should dig a long trench, deep enough to reach a giant's knees. Then we should fill it with oil, so that the archers along the wall may light it with flaming arrows when the time is right," she said, pointing toward a flat stretch of land far to the south of the castle.

"We will make our stand in those fields, I would assume. But that does not mean that we can't leave them a few surprises when they are surrounded," he said with a laugh.

Quisp smiled at the large man. He was nearly twice her height; her head was just high enough to reach his elbows.

"I must go find my father, good day, Hildvar," she said, turning toward the stairs.

Hildvar nodded stupidly and thought himself a fool for it. Who had ever heard of a barbarian and an elven princess planning battle together? He couldn't help but like the idea anyway.

Serra was in her chamber gathering her battle attire when there was a knock at her door.

"Come in," she said as she put her tinderbox in her backpack.

Dretho walked into her room and shut the door behind him.

"Are you busy?" he asked, standing idly beside the door.

"I am just getting my things together, do you need anything?" she asked, walking over to him.

"I thought we should talk before we go see the Feral Five," he said, looking in her eyes.

Serra met his gaze and nodded.

"Let's go to my study," she said, gesturing toward the door.

They walked down the corridor in silence.

Dretho could not help but notice how stiffly she walked. He wondered if it had anything to do with his company.

Serra tried hard not to let her thoughts turn to last night's conversation with Jareth.

They entered the study and took seats on a long couch.

"What did we need to talk about?" she asked, propping her legs up underneath her.

Dretho sat stiffly and said, "The Feral Five are very perceptive, Serra. They will read your mind and reveal your innermost thoughts, just to prove their abilities. You must go in with a clear mind and conscience before meeting them."

Serra thought on that a moment.

"I have nothing to hide, Dretho. Do you?"

He pointedly did not look at her, as he said, "No, I have nothing to hide from them."

Serra noted the reference.

"Do you have anything to hide from me?"

He gazed into her beautiful green eyes.

"Nothing you do not already know, even if I have not told you," he admitted softly.

Serra gazed into his golden eyes and knew the truth, but she had to know for sure.

"Dretho, it is a very good possibility we will all be dead tomorrow or the next day. Let us be honest, shall we?"

Dretho nodded. The butterflies in his stomach returned tenfold.

"Jareth left last night, right after you did. Do you know why?" she asked.

"Yes. He felt threatened," he answered in all honesty.

"And why did he feel threatened?"

"He acted as if your love was a prize to be won," he said, looking away from her.

"And is it?" she asked with intensity.

He looked into her eyes again and sat back on the couch.

"Serra, I've already told you he was a rat..."

She held up her hand to stop him. "We are being honest, Dretho. Tell me not what you have said before, but what you have left unsaid."

"He thought that you and I..." he stumbled.

"That you and I what?" she asked, holding his gaze.

"He asked me that night if I had a harem. He asked if I had ever taken a wife. Then he made a few accusations that I was after you."

Serra sat up straight and nodded, "Go on."

"That was when I left. I refused to play his little childish game. What he asked was none of his business," he said matter-of-factly.

"Is it mine?"

Dretho closed his eyes and turned his head.

"Does it bother you so to answer a few questions about your personal life?" she asked, touching his chin and turning his head back toward her.

He opened his eyes and a painful look crossed his face.

"I was eighty years old the last time I had a companion, Serra. That was two hundred and twenty years ago. She left me for another elf because I chose to study abroad. She would not leave Sengar Valley to go with me. We were not married, but that did not make it hurt any less," he said with compassion.

"Why have you not found another?" she asked, brushing her thumb across his high cheekbone.

"I did not think there was another for me," he said, closing his eyes as she touched him.

Serra felt a pang of longing in her chest. She had thought him handsome before, but now that she knew he was capable of passion, she longed for him.

"I do not talk of it because I do not wish to be left again. I've dedicated my life to my studies and I like to believe that I have done everything I can to master my craft," he said, reaching up to take her hand in his own.

"Is there a hole in your life?"

Dretho never failed to be amazed at how perceptive this young lady was.

"I did not think so until recently," he said, tracing her forefinger with his thumb.

"What happened to make you realize this?"

Dretho brought her hand to his heart and gazed longingly in her eyes.

She stared back and felt her heartbeat quicken.

"I was visited by a beautiful warrior," he said, bringing her hand to his lips, "Who needed help with nightmares."

Serra closed her eyes.

"Then it is true?" she asked breathlessly.

"That I love you? Yes," he admitted.

Jareth carried his father to the terrace to look upon his army.

"You should pay attention son, when I am gone, you will control these mindless creatures. And then you will be a King," Jarmassad said fanatically.

"When do we march, father?" he asked, gazing hungrily at the mob.

"Patience, son. They have not eaten in three days, so most likely they will come out of their trances in rage. It's best to push the weak ones out before we begin," he explained callously.

Jareth looked around and noted the sunken features of some of the creatures. A few, he noticed had fallen over dead from dehydration or lack of food.

"You are going to starve them to an inch of death, then let them loose so they will fight with hunger. Brilliant," Jareth agreed.

"Tell me of our enemies, son," Jarmassad said, sitting painfully on a low bench next to the wall.

"They have but one mage. An elf named Dretho, do you know of him?"

"The one with the tower? The one who burned me?" Jarmassad asked with a grin.

"Yes, have you been there?" Jareth asked, wondering why that would make his father grin.

"No, but I had a most interesting visit last night before you came. It seems this Dretho's dwarven maid has been digging for information on the manor," he replied nonchalantly.

"The dwarven maid came here?" Jareth asked incredulously.

"No, she contacted an associate of mine to gain information," he said with a laugh.

"And?"

Jarmassad did not answer, he only grinned evilly.

They had sat in silence for several minutes after Dretho's confession.

Serra did not know what to say or do. This elf was so different from anyone she had ever known. He had helped her so much these past weeks. In fact, if he had not killed Keifer, she would be dead right now.

"I owe you my life," she admitted quietly.

"You owe me nothing," he whispered.

"You have been there every time I needed you."

"I owe your family my life. It is my duty to protect you and yours," he confessed.

"Why me?"

Her question stumped him for a few moments.

"That is a hard question to answer without sounding like a fool," he said, entwining his fingers with her own.

"Will you try?" she asked hesitantly.

"You are the epitome of an elf in a human body. You are wise beyond your years. You are strong-willed and passionate about everything I've seen you do. Your attitude toward life is astounding. Everything seems to have a silver lining where you are concerned," he said quietly.

Serra sat in silence, running his words over and over in her mind.

He looked deep into her eyes and sighed. "And every time I look into your eyes, I feel lightheaded. Every time you touch me, I feel my heart swell in my chest. I love you, Serra. I know now that I have loved you since the moment you walked into my altar room those few weeks ago," he said just above a whisper.

"It is such a hard thing for me to give in to love, Dretho," she admitted, looking away.

This time it was he who touched her chin to make her look at him.

"I am not asking you to love me. I am not expecting you to tell me back. You wanted the truth, and now you know. I am not like that childish fool, I expect nothing of you," he said in all honesty.

Serra leaned in and wrapped her arms around him.

He leaned back into the couch and pulled her close.

She raised her head and looked into his eyes. She traced his long, pointy ear with her index finger and shivers ran up his spine.

"You have the most beautiful eyes, Dretho. Has anyone ever told you that?"

He could barely breathe from the love swelling within him. They were so close to each other now.

"No," he whispered.

She smiled sweetly and slid from their embrace, but did not move away.

"Tell me about the Feral Five," she asked, entwining their hands once again.

Dretho smiled and was thankful the tense moments had passed. He had so wanted to kiss her, but he knew that to do so was to cheapen his admission today.

"They are very intelligent and easy to get along with, but they are very proud creatures. It is best to compliment them in some way as often as you can. However, you should take care to make it appear that you are not doing so just to appease them. They will be able to tell if you are insincere," he said casually.

"Sounds exhausting," she replied honestly.

There was a knock at the door and Serra rose from the couch. She opened the door to see Frelia with her cook apron on.

"I am sorry to bother ye, me Lady. I figured ye'd be here as ye weren' in yer room. Have ye seen tha' elf anywhere?" she asked in a hushed voice.

Serra widened the door to expose Dretho sitting casually on the couch.

Frelia cleared her throat loudly.

"Master Dretho, was there anythin' in particular ye wished ter eat this evenin'?" she asked politely with a smile.

Dretho rose from his seat and walked over to the women.

Frelia tensed a little, but managed to temper her fears.

"Well, actually, your venison recipe is quite wonderful. I liked how you rubbed it with sage and rosemary and served it at room temperature. I wouldn't mind having more if you have a deer," he said civilly.

"Aye, tha' we do. Sorry ter bother ye, I'll take me leave," she said with a wide grin. She curtsied and walked down the hall and out of sight.

Serra giggled.

Dretho looked at her questioningly.

"She's so scared of you. She's trying to win you over with her cooking. I wonder what she'll ask you in the morning."

Dretho looked at Serra in seriousness.

"I must return to my tower this evening," he said.

Serra looked crestfallen.

"I will return on the morrow. I have a meeting I have to attend. It is for the cause."

She nodded her understanding.

After the evening meal, King Flamarien waited for Dretho outside the dining room door.

"Take a walk with me, Dretholzar," he said, not bothering to wait for a reply.

Dretho followed obediently. They had wandered past the courtyard and to the garden before either spoke a word.

"Do you think it wise to take her with you?" the King asked simply, continuing his stroll.

"I believe so. She is, after all, the one needing the assistance," Dretho answered casually.

"Do you think they will appreciate you bringing a human into their lair? Does Serra realize they feed on the human sacrifices of the Everklent people?"

"I have not told her. Serra is no ordinary human. She is very akin to our people," Dretho stated, clasping his hands behind his back.

King Flamarien stopped and turned to the mage with a look of intensity.

"She is. She defeated me in mock battle this morning. You know as well as I, that is no small thing," he stated without shame.

Dretho's eyes widened.

"You put yourself in harms way to practice with a human?" he asked incredulously.

"She is, as you just said, no ordinary human. She has been elven trained. It is obvious. I came upon her during her practice session and she noticed I was watching. She told me if I was going to watch, I should at least provide an obstacle. Well, I thought, she's just a human," the King said with a laugh, "I underestimated her and she had me at sword point within minutes."

Dretho was shocked. He had known she was good with a sword, but he had had no idea that she was capable of defeating an elf.

"She is remarkable. You should make note of it," the King said, walking back toward the castle.

Dretho did not follow. The walk was over. Was it so obvious to everyone that he cared for her so?

Dretho knocked on Serra's study door.

"Come in," she said from inside.

He walked into the room and closed the door.

She was sitting at her desk with a large stack of parchments in front of her. He could barely see the top of her head.

"What are you doing, if I may ask?" he asked in curiosity, walking around the desk to face her.

She looked up to him and rolled her eyes.

"Affairs of the territory are never finished. I have hired a man to handle trade for me, but unfortunately, I still have to sign all these. Are you headed home?" she asked while standing and stretching.

"Yes. I will be back tomorrow to stay for the duration. I just have to take care of a few things," he said.

Serra noticed he seemed to not stand as stiffly as he always had.

"You seem more comfortable around me now," she admitted, sitting on the edge of her desk and knocking a few rolls of parchment to the floor.

Dretho smiled. "I suppose, I needed to confide in someone, my Lady. I thank you for that. I do feel as if a great weight has been lifted from my shoulders."

Serra wrapped him in an embrace and he returned it, taking time to smell her hair in the process.

She pushed him back to arms length.

"Return soon and be well," she said, kissing him on the cheek.

Dretho's light-brown skin took on a reddish hue for a few moments and he smiled.

"You, as well," he said and then left her to her work.

Bern Hilda arrived at the Traveler's Inn to find it deserted. The door was unlocked, but even Gooley was missing.

She had a feeling of dread, but passed it off as nerves and walked to the door at the back of the room. She knocked and the door swung in, the feeling of dread intensifying.

After drawing her short sword, she walked into the room.

Dergaz sat in his customary seat, though no guards were in sight. He had his feet propped on his desk and puffed steadily on his cigar.

"Dergaz," she said in greeting.

"Bern Hilda," he replied.

"Where is everyone?" she asked, looking around the room.

"I gave them the night off. The tavern is closed tonight," he said casually.

The hairs on the back of her neck stood on end.

"Do you have the information I paid you for?" she asked, gripping her sword a bit more tightly.

"Join me for a drink first," he said, pulling out a bottle of wine from his bottom drawer, along with two mugs.

"I have to be back at the tower soon, I'd rather get the information and leave if it's all the same to you," she replied.

Dergaz placed the items on the desk and leaned back in his chair again.

"Have it your way. Gydian!"

As soon as he shouted Gydian's name Bern Hilda felt a sharp pain in her back. She cried out and reached around to find a crossbow bolt embedded into her side, inches from her spine.

"You traitorous bastard," she yelled in pain. She ripped the bolt from her back and threw it on the table. She advanced on the thief, but before she could take two strides, she fell to the floor. Dead.

Gydian walked into the room carrying his crossbow at his side.

"Truth sure can whip up a potion. Nice of him to give it to us for free considering he paid us so much to kill the bitch," Dergaz said callously.

Gydian laughed and grabbed the bottle of wine.

They drank to Jarmassad Truth the rest of the night.

Spike Forsiad sat in his large cell. He could not believe how he had been treated. He had been locked up in this dungeon, yes, but his cell was larger than his room at Fortin Manor, and was much more lavishly furnished.

The bed was only large enough to hold one person, but it was trimmed with soft pillows and thick down blankets.

A table next to a small barred window, held a pitcher of water with a basket of black bread and cheese.

The walls were stone, but the floor actually had a small, oval carpet that covered the center of the room. A small wooden desk and a high backed chair covered his other wall. He had found the drawer contained a quill, parchment, and a vial of ink as well.

He felt more at home than he ever had, except that he could not wander freely. He had been lost in his thoughts when Serra walked up to his cell door.

"What are you thinking, Spike Forsiad?" she asked, drawing him from his contemplations.

The resemblance between Lorna and Serra was intriguing. The only difference he had noticed, was where Lorna's form was attractive, Serra's was more so, in the way of her strength and agility. They were built the same, Serra being more mature, of course, but he could tell that each of the old sister's moves were calculated and planned. He had noticed right off that she walked heel to toe, probably unconsciously. She was obviously honed to be a warrior.

"I was thinking how ironic it is that I am here," he said, raising from his bed and walking to the cell door.

Serra tensed visibly and put on a stern expression.

"Yes, it is a bit of irony, isn't it? That you and yours imprisoned my sister and now you are imprisoned yourself. Though, I find it necessary to keep you here for the welfare of my sister," she said matter-of-factly.

Spike gazed into her eyes and nodded in defeat.

"I do understand that, my Lady. Though, you know that I mean her no harm," he said quietly.

"I know no such thing, Forsiad. My mage did cast a truth spell on you, but I have learned that sorcerers are not to be trusted, even those who affiliate themselves with them," she said sternly.

She reached up to the bars and gripped them tightly.

"Your master killed people dear to me. I shall not let that happen again."

Spike noticed that her knuckles were turning white with the force in which she gripped the bars.

"I understand your ire, Lady Bloodmoon. I came here only to warn you. I felt this was the only place I had to go."

Serra gritted her teeth.

"I find it hard to believe that you would come to the very destination of this horde, thinking you would be spared."

She turned from the cell door and walked down the hall. Spike felt his second meeting with the Lady of Moondale had not gone well at all.

Dretho had arrived at the tower that night with a spring in his step. He had hoped Bern Hilda would come with the information soon, so that he might go back to Moondale quicker.

As the hours passed, he began to pace and grow worried.

When Belos and Halos crested the horizon outside his window, he was frantic.

He grabbed his scrying bowl and his moon wind salts.

"Blessed Drakevin, lead me to Bern Hilda's whereabouts, guide my eye so that I may serve you again," he begged.

"*Asseeleeum brachtath tumadra estinar.*"

What he found shocked and appalled him. Just outside his tower door, Bern Hilda hung from a wooden pole by her feet. Her head had been severed and had been propped on the top with a large stake.

He fell to his knees and put his face in his hands.

"How could I have been such a fool," he muttered, fighting to stay calm.

He rose from his altar and ran down the stairs. He paused at the door and then opened it tentatively.

Dretho muttered a small prayer and gained the strength to cut Bern Hilda down. He began with her little, heavy body. It took all the strength he possessed to carry her to the tower. He then took off his soiled robes and donned a pair of breeches.

He walked out into the bright, clear morning, but it was as if the darkest night had fallen on him. He began chopping away at the large stake with an axe he had taken from the woodshed.

He knew that he could have done this by magical means, but he also knew that Bern Hilda deserved his manual labor. After all she had done for him over the years, without an ounce of complaint, he had never thanked her. He had never shown his appreciation in any way. He had adopted the ways of the folk of Everklent because they made sense to him, but he realized now he had turned into an unfeeling shell of a man

The elf hacked at the pole with fury. Sweat glistened on his light-brown chest. His hair dripped with perspiration and flew wildly with every chop.

The pole finally tumbled to the ground and poor Bern Hilda's head dislodged and fell with a sickening thud. He walked over to it and discovered a note written in blood that had been attached to the stake in her head.

You will come to know the Truth

He carried her head inside and put it with her body. He retrieved a cotton sheet from the linen closet and wrapped her carefully.

He walked outside where there was a large row of firewood that Bern Hilda had been chopping to prepare for winter. After dousing the entire stack with oil, he went back inside.

Slinging her body over his shoulder, he made his way slowly to the stack and placed her body carefully onto the pile and lit it with a torch.

After many minutes of watching the flames, he teleported to the last friend he felt he had.

Serra was walking into the foyer on her way to the morning meal when Dretho appeared out of thin air in front of her. He was wearing only a pair of breeches and was covered in blood and sweat.

"Dretho!" she shouted, running over to him.

He glanced up at her with a face wrought with agony. His golden eyes were glazed and his lips were trembling. His shoulders slumped up and down slowly with every breath that he took.

"Are you hurt? What happened?" she asked, turning him this way and that, trying to find an injury.

"She is dead," he replied in barely above a whisper.

Tears streamed out of his eyes and he looked up at her pleadingly. Serra noticed a few people coming into the room, drawn by her shout.

"Come with me," she said, grabbing his hand and leading him to the water room.

She had no idea who this *she* was, but she knew that Dretho needed privacy. She didn't think anyone in the world had ever seen him cry.

Thankfully the water room was empty. She rushed him inside and bolted the door.

Dretho slumped to the floor and began to sob.

Serra rushed to his side and wrapped her arms around him. He grabbed hold of her tightly, put his forehead to her shoulder, and let the tears gush. She began crying herself, simply out of sympathy for her friend.

Several minutes later, he raised his head and looked at her.

"Truth killed Bern Hilda. They cut off her head, strung her body up on a pole, and staked her head to the top like a decoration!" he exclaimed through gritted teeth.

Serra tried her best not to envision the dwarf in that state, but she finally understood why he was so upset. In her time at Dretho's tower, the dwarven woman had been the only other living being Serra had encountered there.

"It is my fault. I asked her to get information on Fortin Manor, and they killed her for it!"

She wiped the tears from his eyes and then from her own. His shoulders began to quiver from the emotions ripping through him. She pulled him closer and began rubbing his back with her hand.

Dretho fought for control, but found that her soothing motions began to calm him almost instantly.

"We will avenge her. We will avenger her, my parents, my brother, and everyone else he has ever murdered," she said compassionately.

Dretho nodded and pulled away from her. He looked down at his bare chest and looked away. He seemed to just now notice he was barely clothed.

The irony of the situation almost made him laugh. Here he was, in the floor of a water room with a twenty-year-old human, baring his soul while baring his chest at the same time. But he had known that Serra would be the only one to understand his grief.

"Let's get you cleaned up," Serra said, watching him closely to make sure he was all right.

He nodded, but remained sitting on the cold, stone floor.

She walked over to the window and grabbed a bucket of water and a few towels that had been placed there to warm them. She sat down next to him and began washing the blood from his chest.

"You don't have to do that, Serra, I can..." he began.

She held her finger to his lips and shook her head.

"Do you know where she went to gather this information?" she asked, wringing out the bloody towel in the water.

"No," he answered sadly.

There was a knock at the door and Serra cursed.

"Go away, I will be out soon," she yelled. This was not the time or the place for visitors.

"Is everything all right, Lady Serra?" they heard Hildvar ask.

"Yes, Hildvar. Go away, please," she replied.

The barbarian standing outside the door gritted his teeth. He had been told that Serra had run into the room with Dretho, both seeming to be upset.

People had gathered in the large foyer, peering at him to see what was going on. He sucked in a large breath and left, knowing the people would not disperse until he did.

They heard him stomp down the hall and Serra finished cleaning Dretho's chest. His muscles tightened with every breath and she had to look away to keep her mind on track.

"What?" he asked, noting the movement. He had seen the look in her eyes when she had gazed at his chest.

She shook her head and began washing his face.

"No, what? Tell me," he asked again, taking the towel from her hand and wiping the rest of the blood from his face.

"Improper thoughts at an improper time," she said simply, washing her hands in the bucket and not looking directly at him.

He sat in silence for a few moments, seeming deep in thought.

"You'll find that improper thoughts at improper times are most often the ones that need to be heard the most," he muttered. He put the towel on the floor beside the bucket, but did not take his eyes off of her.

She wiped her hands off on a clean towel and looked up at him.

"I have never seen you in anything but a mage robe, Dretho. I have never seen you show so much emotion. Sometimes I forget that there is something underneath all that black cloth and that cool, calm, and collected demeanor," she admitted in barely above a whisper.

He reached for her hand and placed it on his chest, pressing it down over his heart.

"Do you feel that?" he asked in a whisper.

She felt his racing heartbeat. She nodded. Her heartbeat quickened at the feeling.

"Serra, Bern Hilda was my only friend until you came along and I never had the heart to tell her thank you. I never felt it was needed until she was taken from me today. "

He paused, looking deep into her eyes.

"I have a heart. I have a heart, which had never before been of any consequence until you walked into my life. I have a heart that races every time I see your beautiful face. I tell you here and now, I will never make the mistake of keeping it hidden again," he said with compassion.

She lifted her hand from his chest and ran her thumb across his high cheekbone. His skin was so smooth. She used to think his angular features made him look stern, but now he looked only handsome. His face was streaked with drying tears, but that made him all the more appealing. He was right. He had a heart. And he seemed to have just now realized what that meant.

"You loved Bern Hilda, but you did not know how to show it. You now understand what it is to have love in your life," she said sweetly.

He nodded and looked at the floor. He had never been so full of emotion in his life. He felt sorrow for his friend who had died, hatred for the man who was responsible for her death, and love for this young human sitting so patiently in front of him.

"In the light of understanding, we will see what we will see," he said softly.

Serra nodded and smiled at the proverb.

"My father used to say that nearly every day," she whispered.

Dretho nodded and looked back up at her. His heart felt as if it would simply explode with love and longing.

"If he could see you now, he would understand exactly what that simple phrase really means. I understand now that I have been a fool most of my life. I have sheltered myself against emotion thinking that I was protecting myself. I played the role of the unfeeling mage so that I would not have to answer to anyone or feel for anyone. I've told you that your father was my only ally. The day he saved my life I realized that I needed someone in it. When Bern Hilda came to my tower to save her kinsman, she offered herself to me as payment. I had been alone up to that point and thought it would do me well to have someone there, if only to clean the place. She came to be just as much a part of that tower as I. Last night as I went home, she was not there to greet me. I waited for her to come back until dawn. I suppose I never thought there would come a day that she wouldn't be there. I don't think I can go back, it will never be the same."

He watched as a single tear dripped from her emerald eye. He reached up and touched the tear, smearing it between his fingers.

"I am sorry if this is upsetting you."

Serra smiled and shook her head.

"Dretho, a friend is someone to share with when you need to. A friend is someone to feel emotion with when no one else can understand. I cry because I felt the same when Renfar was murdered. We were siblings, but as different as night and day. We saw each other every day, but were virtually strangers. I never told him that I loved him. I only avoided him and now I will never be able to tell him."

Dretho nodded and pulled her into another embrace. Serra pushed back his long, black hair and rested her head on his shoulder.

"You are so different from any human I have ever known, Serra. I felt a kinship with your father, but you and I are cut from the same mold. I am fifteen times your age, but you understand exactly why I feel the way I do and act the way I do. I've never even known an elf that could do that," he admitted, running his fingers through her long, silky, red hair.

She lifted her head and looked into his eyes.

They could feel each other's breath.

"You can stay here as long as you want. I will tell Justin to prepare a few chambers for your alchemy, altar, and sleeping quarters. I need you here with me now, Dretho. Not only because of Truth's horde, but because I need someone as much as you do," she whispered.

He searched her eyes and looked at her lips. A feeling of panic washed over him as he considered kissing her.

"Serra, I am finding it very difficult to control myself at this moment," he said shakily, unable to pull his gaze from her lips.

The tips of her voluptuous mouth turned up into a wry grin.

Before he could say anything else, she leaned forward and touched her lips to his.

A sense of love and relief washed over him unlike anything he had ever felt before.

Serra pressed harder and heard him sigh as he pulled her into a tighter embrace.

They kissed slowly, testing the other. But after a few tentative moments each gave in to their passion, as if nothing else mattered in the world.

He ran his fingers through her hair as she wrapped her arms around him, to feel his bare skin. He parted her lips with his tongue and she moaned ever so lightly. As desire arced through him, he pulled away.

They were both out of breath, still entwined in each other's arms.

She opened her eyes to see him staring at her, with lust in his eyes.

"I do not want to dishonor you, and I feel that I will if we do not stop this now," he said in a low, raspy voice.

She closed her eyes and looked to the floor, nodding her head in acceptance.

He placed his fingers under her chin and tilted her head to face him.

"Do not feel rejected, my love. I want you more than life itself at this moment."

She opened her eyes and he saw the passion there.

"I do not feel rejected. I feel relieved," she said softly.

"Relieved?" he asked in confusion.

"I have been in denial about my feelings until this moment. I did not know what I would do, should this ever come to pass. I feel relief that you respect me enough to stop me from making a hasty decision based on the heat of the moment. I feel relief that you respect me enough not to force me into anything and to let me make the first move on my own. Most of all I feel relief that you have shared with me today and exposed your heart to me. That in itself has proved your love to me unlike anything else possibly could."

Jareth scowled and tossed the scrying bowl across his room to shatter against the wall. He had been watching Dretho closely this morning. He had only wanted to see his reaction to his father's little deception.

Dergaz, the leader of the Band of the Yellow Hand, had been allied with the Truth family for a few years. When Keifer had been assigned the task of finding the book of Gyndless the Almighty, Truth had suggested him right off.

Truth had told Jareth the night before that Dergaz had come to him with information of a mage in Sengar Valley who had been inquiring of the manor. Truth had ordered the man to kill whoever had requested the information and to place her body unceremoniously at the mage's door with a note.

Jareth had known who the mage was immediately, and found it rather amusing that he would get his revenge so early. But now, his anger at the elf had grown to rage. He had ran to Serra immediately and played on her emotions to make her pity him.

And she had kissed him. She had kissed him with a passion that she had never offered to him.

He looked at the pieces of the marble scrying bowl and growled with anger.

"Conniving bastard," he muttered.

He would make him pay. He would make sure that the elf died so that Serra would see what her deception had triggered.

He walked out his chamber door and down the long corridor to his father's room.

It was time to make plans.

People were leaving the dining room, as the morning meal was over. Hildvar and Gnarl had been the only ones left seated when Dretho and Serra finally made their way to the room. Gnarl gasped in surprise as Dretho walked in without a tunic.

"Elf, ye best be gettin' some clothes on," he said, standing to his feet.

Hildvar looked past the lack of clothing and noticed the blood on the elf's breeches.

"Do I need to get Bergearon?" he asked, standing as well.

Serra shook her head and sighed.

"Hildvar, go get Justin and bring him here. Gnarl, please, Dretho has been through enough today, do not berate him."

Gnarl scowled and then noticed the blood.

"Who were ye battlin' elf?" he asked, walking around the table and up to the pair.

"My servant was murdered today, dwarf. It was Jarmassad Truth, I am sure of it," Dretho said, reaching into his pocket and bringing out the bloody, crumpled note.

Gnarl grabbed the note from his hand and his face turned scarlet.

"There anybody else at that tower o' yers?" he asked, trying to keep his temper.

"No," Dretho replied.

"Ye stay here, elf. We'll get ye yer revenge. Who was yer servant?"

"Bern Hilda Silversword," he muttered.

Gnarl's eyes grew wide.

"Wither Silversword's sister?" he asked in a shout.

Serra jumped and looked to Dretho in question.

"The very same."

Gnarl handed the note back to Dretho and stormed out of the room.

Hildvar walked over to them and bowed his head.

"I am sorry for your loss, Dretho the Mage. I will go and get Justin now. But I will alert Frelia to serve you first."

Serra nodded and smiled at the large man. She was glad that he had not asked her about her curt manner this morning. He left the room through the wooden side door that led into the kitchens.

"Come, sit with me. Are we still leaving this morning?" she asked, gesturing to two chairs at the table.

Dretho sat down and put his head in his hands. He had nearly forgotten about the trip to Everklent, with all that had happened that morning. His belongings were already at Bloodmoon Castle, but was he ready to face five wemics today?

"We must, though we may take our time in getting there. Have you packed for the road?" he asked, looking at her as she sat gracefully in the common chair next to him.

"Yes. Do you think they will accept me?" she asked.

It was obvious she was nervous. She had worried about the impending meeting all night. What would they think of a young human walking into their lair to request their help in a matter that did not concern them?

Dretho felt a knot well into the pit of his stomach. He reached over and took her hand in his.

"Serra, no matter what happens when we get there, I swear on my life I will not let them harm you," he said, squeezing her hand.

Serra smiled and nodded.

Frelia entered the dining room and squeaked.

Dretho let go of Serra's hand and sat up straight as a board. They both looked away and blushed.

The maid stood dumbfounded, looking from one to the other in shock. There Serra sat, like a commoner at the midsection of the grand table, and she was holding his hand!

"Um... are ye ready fer somethin' ter eat?" she stammered, trying her best to act nonchalant.

Serra nodded and Frelia hurried back into the kitchen and leaned against the door. Maybe it was not what she thought. Maybe they were just talking and Serra was consoling him. Or maybe the girl she had always seen as a daughter was becoming a woman and falling for the one man in the world that scared the living daylights out of her.

She walked over to the counter and picked up a platter of poached eggs, ham, and corn biscuits. Taking a deep breath, she walked back into the dining room.

Serra and Dretho sat staring at her, each with their thoughts whirring.

Frelia sat the platter down in front of them and turned back to the kitchens.

"She knows," he said as the maid departed.

Serra thought for a moment and looked at him.

"So? Is there anything we should be hiding?" she asked, watching his expression.

Dretho relaxed in his chair and smiled.

"I leave that to you, Lady Serra, as this is your home. If you wish for my love for you to be a secret, then all you need do is ask. But if you feel everyone should know, so be it," he said, taking her hand again.

Frelia entered the dining room with a pitcher of pear juice and two goblets. Her eyes grew to the size of galleons as she noticed their hands touching again. But she said nothing. She only placed the items on the table and turned back to the kitchen, biting her tongue along the way.

Chapter Twenty
Intrigue and Awakening

The chamber was well lit by a golden glow that seemed to emanate from the very walls. The room was actually a small chamber of a large complex of caves under the sands of the Yulia Dasana Desert.

The walls of stone were polished and appeared to have been worn smooth by an underground river that had long ago dwindled to a small brook. Only about a foot wide, the clear, pebbled brook traveled the entire complex.

The floor of the chamber was not stone, but was covered by a thick layer of dry moss. Fungi could be found sprouting here and there, their heads varying from bright orange to dark purple.

Kendrasha Lithalicandion lazed on the spongy moss, idly dipping her lion's tail into the water and out again. She absently cleaned the dirt from a fingernail on her human right hand with a sharp claw on her left forepaw.

Her human torso was naked to the waist, where her golden fur began. The muscles on her flanks were trim and muscular, promising power of spring and fleetness of foot.

She looked up as her younger sister ambled into the room, carrying an ancient lute made of ash.

"Vlasisith wishes to see you, in his chamber anew," Sashaleona said, lying down next to the brook and resting her head on a red mushroom.

Kendrasha rolled her eyes and stood slowly.

"What does he want now? His endless mind games tire me," she asked, not expecting an answer. She plodded out of the chamber, without a second glance to Sashaleona.

Serra knocked lightly on Gnarl's worn office door. She waited for a few seconds and then turned the brass handle.

The dwarf lay with his head on his desk, several parchments wet with drool underneath him.

She cleared her throat and the dwarf jumped up, one parchment stuck fast to his face.

It took several moments for Gnarl to gain his bearings, his eyes widened at Serra, and he quickly brushed the parchment away.

"My Lady, I was err... I was takin' a nap," he stumbled. Some of the ink had bled through. Words written in the dwarven script were imprinted backwards on his cheek.

"I can see that," she replied with amusement, "I was just going to tell you that Dretho and I are about to leave to meet with the Feral Five," she said calmly.

The dwarf slumped a little and sat down on the edge of his desk.

"I hope yer trip will be a good one. I hate that I can no' go with ye. I bugged the elf, but he wouldn' give," he offered solemnly.

Gnarl had indeed bothered Dretho about the impending meeting. But the elf had outright refused to let him or any of the brigade accompany them. After nearly an hour of bickering, Dretho had turned to the dwarf and shouted, "Do you not think that I can protect her!" The elf's face had been wrought of frustration by this point. The emotional outburst from the elf had been so uncharacteristic that Gnarl had finally given in.

Serra walked over to the dwarf and placed her hand on his shoulder.

"I will be back before you know it," she said soothingly.

He looked to the floor and bobbed his head lightly in acceptance. He looked extremely sad and broken.

"Gnarl, something else is bothering you, what is it?" she asked in concern, putting her hand to his hairy chin and turning his head.

He looked her in the eye a few moments and then sighed deeply.

"Bern Hilda was me kin. She was a fine lass, ter be sure. I suppose it's botherin' me a little more than it should," he said finally.

She looked at him in pity as he sniffed and stood a little taller.

"We've all experienced loss at the hand of Truth in one form or another. He will meet his day soon, I promise you that."

Serra leaned down and hugged the short man.

"I will not be in contact for a day or two. I trust you with my territory, Gnarl Knottytrunk. Are you up to the task?" she asked, pulling away and punching him in the arm.

Gnarl smiled at the gesture and punched her back.

"Ye bet yer arse... I mean, yes, me Lady," he agreed with a chuckle.

Dretho waited in the foyer for Serra, trying his best to avoid the odd looks coming from the castle staff.

Their travel gear lay at his feet. He glanced out one of the many windows and saw that it was a fine day with not a cloud in the sky.

The elf was dressed in his black robes once again. He tried his best to keep his thoughts of Serra at arms length, but she kept entering his mind. He knew this meeting with the Feral Five would be difficult, more so than he had let on to anyone else.

King Flamarien had left for Sengar Valley that same morning, before Dretho's abrupt arrival, and he was glad he would not have to face his anger at the Feral Five again before their departure. He had tried to talk sense into Flamarien for years about the matter, always to no avail. The King was stubborn and could not realize his wife had chosen her own fate that day. He only hoped that Serra would prove more resistant to the taunts he knew she would receive.

Serra walked through the crowded southern garden to the barracks at the western wall. She had not seen Hildvar around the grounds and figured he might be in the brigade common room with the other warriors.

The Bloodmoon Brigade had worked tirelessly throughout the night and day to bring all the people of Moondale into the safety of the castle walls. She saw families sitting around in groups, talking excitedly about the impending attack. Nearly everyone she passed rose to greet her and pay his or her respect. She smiled and waved at every opportunity, trying hard not to show her nervousness to her people.

She arrived at the long, stone building and walked in. Chairs scraped and hit the floor as the warriors quickly dropped what they were doing and stood to attention.

Glancing around the room, she noticed the tall barbarian standing near the back wall next to Castille Thornberry. She walked up to them and waved for everyone to sit.

"Me Lady," Castille greeted with a bow.

Hildvar bowed as well and they took their seats on rickety, wooden stools. Serra sat opposite them at the small table and noticed a small map of Moondale lying there.

"Hildvar, I need you to make sure that Lorna does not speak with our prisoner while I am gone. I do not want him deceiving her into releasing him. I know that as soon as I leave these grounds, she will try. You are relieved of your rounds and I ask that you stay at his door only to be relieved by you, Castille. I realize a twelve hour shift is a lot to ask with everything that is going on, but I do not trust him," she requested simply.

"Yes, my Lady," Hildvar agreed with a nod.

"Are ye goin' somewheres, me Lady?" Castille asked with a concerned expression.

She had forgotten that her trip was a secret to most everyone. She took a deep breath and chose her words wisely.

"Castille, I am going on a short trip and I will be back before you know it. Please do not mention this to anyone, as only few know. I do not want my whereabouts spread across the land. If anyone asks, I am in the castle planning, not to be disturbed. Do you understand?"

"Aye," he answered simply.

"I trust both of you with the safety of my sister, do me proud in this," she said, rising from the table to again be greeted by the sounds of chairs scraping the floor.

"As you were," she said, leaving the barracks.

She weaved her way through more tents to the courtyard and into the castle foyer to see Dretho standing alone, deep in thought. He turned in her direction and his face lit up visibly.

"Hello," he said with a smile.

"Hello, are we ready?" she asked, smiling back.

"I believe so," he said, shifting on his feet.

He reached down and picked up his two backpacks and their rations bag and Serra grabbed her own backpack.

"We will not be able to teleport directly into their lair, we will have some traveling to do for half a day, but I fear we can not bring horses, as water is scarce," he said, adjusting the straps to the bags, so that his hands were free.

She nodded and waited.

"Take my hand," he said, reaching for her.

He gave her hand a firm squeeze and chanted, "*Arcanus Traveelus Duoti.*"

Vlasisith sat before his small, natural waterfall with his eyes closed. Kendrasha scraped a claw against the stone at the entrance to his chamber, making a loud, screeching noise.

The male wemic looked up to her in disgust and made a low growling sound from deep within his throat.

"What did you need, Vlasisith, I was busy," she asked impatiently, padding into the chamber to stand before him.

"Busy? You have not been busy for two hundred years Kendra, though I feel we all soon will be," he said disapprovingly.

Kendrasha's golden cat-like eyes flashed at the nickname she hated, but she was obviously intrigued with his statement.

"Go on," she said simply.

"Do you remember Dretholzar from the north?" he asked, rising from his crouch. He began pacing the chamber in front of her with a look of superiority across his face.

Kendrasha stood tall and nodded. "The elfling," she answered simply.

"It seems he is coming here with a most unusual companion," he said, making another pass in front of her.

"Most unusual, as in?" she asked, growing frustrated with his attempt to fuel anticipation.

"A human," he said, settling on his hindquarters in front of her.

Kendrasha smiled a sharp, toothy grin and her mouth began to water.

"But not for a meal," he said with a wry smile.

She frowned at him and wiped the spittle from the corner of her mouth with her human hand.

"Enough of your games, why is he bringing a human here?" she threatened, her claws lengthening slowly in irritation.

"You will see," he said simply, padding from the room.

Kendrasha did not follow. She made another screeching pass across the entrance before going back to her own cave, to laze next to the brook again.

Dretho and Serra arrived at their destination moments after they left Moondale. As Serra looked around, she could not believe her eyes. They were standing in a desert, with nothing but sandy wasteland in every direction. It was hot, sweltering hot.

Dretho noted Serra's crestfallen expression and asked, "Not what you expected?"

Serra looked at him in disbelief. "Where are we?"

"We are in the Yulia Dasana Desert, south of the city of Everklent," he stated simply.

He began to disrobe and Serra turned around in embarrassment. He laughed wholeheartedly.

"Do not be alarmed, I have another suit of clothing on under my robe. I prepared for the trip, but did not want to give any indications of our destination to the people of the castle," he said with mirth.

She turned around and her eyes widened at what she saw.

A fine elven chain mail hauberk hugged his trim form, glittering in the morning suns. It had no sleeves and was cut into a V at the neckline. Around his waist, he wore a sash made of some type of reptilian hide she did not recognize. His legs were covered in mithril platemail, complete with greaves and boots. But most remarkable of all, was the sword at his side, a scimitar identical to her own.

Realizing she was staring, she looked up into his eyes and noticed the humor there.

"I took the liberty of having Florianna pack you some suitable armor. You will cook alive in that studded leather," he offered, grabbing his extra backpack and tossing it to her.

As the backpack fell into her hands, she heard the telltale chink of chain mail. She opened the pack quickly and drew out a sleeveless chain mail tunic, not unlike his own. But the tunic was the only contents of the backpack.

"Dretho, this is wonderful, but don't you think that metal will be warmer in the suns than leather hide?" she asked regretfully.

Dretho smiled.

"Few people have ever encountered this type of chain mail. It is imbued to remain at normal temperature in the coldest or hottest environments."

She looked up at him and then around the landscape.

Dretho understood immediately and turned his back.

Serra unclasped her jerkin and donned the tunic. It fit like a glove and was tremendously light, lighter than her leather even. The tunic came to her knees and she noticed it hugged her curves, but thankfully did not expose her flesh underneath. The links were so small that a pin would be hard pressed to pass through.

Folding her jerkin, she said, "You can turn around."

Smiling at her obvious pleasure in the armor, he reached for his small belt pouch, and untied the string.

"And now for the rest of your armor," he said, putting two fingers into the pouch.

Serra laughed, "Do you have a scarf for me to wear, as well?"

Dretho smiled all the wider as he pulled a mithril greave out of the pouch. Her mouth dropped as he continued to reach into the tiny pouch until half a set of mithril plate lay in the sand at his feet.

"You never cease to amaze me, Dretho," she admitted as he turned his back once again.

After she was dressed fully in her new armor, Dretho put her studded leather into his pouch with ease.

Serra shook her head in disbelief and they began their trek to the south.

When Kendrasha padded back to her chamber, Sashaleona was not there. But she heard a haunting melody begin to play from the common cavern. She sprawled out on the moss floor and resumed dipping her tail in the brook.

She tried not to think too much about Vlasisith's vague news. Dretholzar had visited before with two other elves. He and his two companions were the only beings who were not of wemic birth that had ever passed through the puzzle door and survived. Of course, one of his companions, the female, had left torn to shreds, but the fact that two had left alive was rather remarkable.

Her eyes grew heavy as Sashaleona's melody relaxed her nerves. Vlasisith had been grading on her nerves for a millennia now, always playing games. Psionisists were unheard of in today's world, but Vlasisith had not changed with the times. Even in casual conversation, his mind games were exhausting.

Thinking of various ways to rip his mane from his head, she fell into a peaceful slumber.

Vlasisith weaved his way through the rough, stone corridor and paused at Nefarius's chamber door. The older wemic sat on his haunches staring at the cavern wall, which was amassed with brilliant lights. Luminous shapes in various colors of red and yellow whirled around each other, as if performing a dance.

"Fear not, your boredom is about to come to an end, my King," Vlasisith said with a throaty chuckle, settling on his haunches and grinning a sharp, toothy smile.

The lights faded to nothingness the moment he had spoken and Nefarius turned around snarling, his reddish-brown mane whipping with the movement.

"How dare you interrupt me!" the King of the Feral Five Pride exclaimed, padding up to Vlasisith intending upon scolding. But as he raised his front paw to slash at his second, the psionisist's words sunk in.

"What do you mean my boredom is coming to an end, what do you know?" he asked, halting his paw in mid-air, but not lowering it all together.

"Dretholzar from the north is on his way with a human to visit. I expect they should arrive within a few hours," Vlasisith said with pride. It was not a custom of his to toy around with his King. He simply enjoyed distressing Kendrasha for sport.

"Why would he bring a human here?" Nefarius asked. He was not daft enough to believe the elf had come all this way for an offering. This human must be different in some way... remarkably different.

Reading his thoughts, Vlasisith answered Nefarius's unasked question.

"She is most extraordinary. She is the Ruler of Moondale, a twenty-year-old human warrior. It seems they are on their way to ask our assistance in their impending attack from the horde of monsters the sorcerer Jarmassad Truth has amassed in Clandestine."

Nefarius lowered his golden paw to the mossy floor and was pensive for several moments.

"I believe we should go with them, it seems a most intriguing adventure prospect. We have been locked up in this hole for far too long," Vlasisith stated, reading his King's thoughts again.

Nefarius nodded.

"Gather the pride in the common chamber, we must discuss this before they arrive," the King ordered.

He turned and conjured an illusionary wall in front of Vlasisith, to block him from peering inside. Vlasisith casually walked away, swinging his lion tail in excitement.

Serra was more impressed with her armor with every step. It was so light and airy. She felt as if she were wearing a nightgown on a cool evening, despite the pounding heat from Belos and Halos overhead. Everywhere she looked, she could see the air distort with the heat coming off of the sand below their feet.

For the first time, she saw Dretho as a warrior. She could not believe that he wielded a scimitar as well. In fact, she didn't know that mages were able to wield weapons besides staves and wands.

"How long have you had that sword?" she asked as they crossed one particularly deep sand dune.

"Nine years I believe. I had it fashioned after your father's the year after he saved my life," he answered, shifting his backpack to begin the climb up the other side.

Serra was a bit disappointed. It was a copy, not a brother. "Do you know how to use it?" she asked hesitantly.

He had been bent over, climbing up the steep side, but then he stopped and turned to regard her. His look was not one of malice, but of amusement.

"Aye," he said with a wry smile.

Serra nodded and began to climb as well.

Despite their light armor, their feet sunk deep into the sand as they climbed, and it was very difficult to find a handhold when the sand filtered through their hands. It was a matter of continually shifting your weight, but neither complained.

As they crested the top of the dune, Dretho sat down and grabbed his water skin, offering it to Serra first. She took it and drank deeply. As she handed it back to him, their fingers brushed, and Dretho paused before taking it from her.

"All elves are trained in the art of fighting at a young age. I am a mage, Serra, but I have not always been. My father trained me as a warrior before I began my studies in the ways of magic. The scimitar was my choice of weapon. I have not had to use one in more than two-hundred years, but I still remember how," he said before taking a drink.

She nodded her understanding. "I thought our swords might have been crafted together."

Dretho shook his head. "They are brothers by appearance only. Mine is imbued by magic also, but has different abilities than your own."

The got back up and as they crested the hill, Serra forgot about the sword, the sight before her took her breath away.

In the hours they had been traveling in the Yulia Dasana Desert, they had seen nothing but sand in every direction. Now, as they climbed over the rise of a sand dune, they were faced with an oasis. A small pond of crystal-blue water lay in a valley below them. A small herd of gazelle leaned over the water for a drink while peering nervously at a pack of jackals across the way. Several large lizards lazed in the morning suns on large flat rocks. Birds of every color flew about; some landing in trees close to the bank. The trees were small and nearly barren of leaves, but many nests graced their branches.

As if this wasn't enough to amaze Serra, there was a cave just across the pond in the wall of another great sand dune. On either side of the entrance were large statues of creatures with the head and torso of a human and the body of a lion. They were the same color as the sand, but stood as sentinels to the dark hole.

It seemed odd to Serra that the statue with bare breasts had only short fur upon her head, but the one without had a long mane that wrapped completely around his head, just like a lion.

Dretho watched Serra's amazed expression and felt a pang of guilt flow through him. *What if they hurt her? he* asked himself. But as soon as these worries began, they fled. This was the only way they could defeat the horde about to attack Moondale, and he had to bring her, for she was the one needing the help.

"Shall we go?" he asked, offering his hand.

She looked to him and nodded, taking his hand. They began walking at an angle into the valley. As soon as the animals saw them, they fled in the opposite direction.

They refilled their water skins, made their way around the pond, and moved toward the cave. As they drew closer to the wemic sentinels, Serra felt a sudden urge to flee. Panic welled within her and she turned to run away. Dretho had been standing behind her, ready for this.

He caught her after she had only taken three hasty steps. She began to struggle, a look of fright visible on her face.

"Look at me, Serra," he said, struggling to hold onto her.

Serra continued to squirm, but did as he asked. The moment she met his gaze, she calmed.

"It is a spell, my love. You are safe," he said softly, brushing his hand across her soft cheek.

She took a deep breath and stood straight.

"Do not turn around," he said anxiously, "You must walk backwards into the entrance or you will not be able to bare it."

Nodding her head in understanding, she began to walk backwards, Dretho holding her hands to lead her way.

"Why is it not affecting you?" she asked in puzzlement.

Dretho smiled, but did not answer.

Jareth and Jarmassad Truth stood on the terrace above their monstrous army. Nine thousand and thirty creatures had finally made their way to Clandestine, but only seven thousand five hundred and twenty were still drawing breath. Corpses littered the ground, their eyes and flesh sunken from the lack of food and water.

"Are you sure you are up to this task, son?" Jarmassad asked skeptically. He knew his hold on the horde was tentative, but to transfer the dominating hand would be extremely dangerous.

After a long conversation with his son, Jarmassad had realized his debilitated body would not likely make the trek to Moondale. But he was confident now that Jareth's hatred for the Bloodmoon line had finally peaked. Now was the time to teach his son his final magic lesson.

"Yes, father. I am ready," he replied with a stern expression.

He held the book of Gyndless the Almighty and felt its sentient pull. This was the moment of truth. There would be no turning back after he called the ruins of the marked page.

Serra had played him for a fool. She had led him to believe that she loved him, and she was now in the arms of another. He gritted his teeth at the burst of anger that welled in his chest and opened the book to the marked page.

After a quick nod to his father, he looked down to the page.

"*Wasinasticashian estinar bushastica tomen zuchaulos forminsatha*," he chanted.

The five runes written on the page nearly burst with crimson light. As each rune lit up fully, the light left the book to cover Jareth's standing form. His black sorcerer robes turned the color of blood and the light continued until the entire terrace was bathed in its glow.

In mere seconds, Fortin Manor's walls of stone were the color of blood. As the light touched the first row of creatures, they burst into action, finding the closest corpse and feeding with rabid, gnashing teeth.

Though the corpses were not near as numerous as the living horde, turmoil did not break between the ranks. When a creature descended on a corpse, the next in line would wait patiently until its predecessor was done.

The creatures ate until their bellies were full and then lined up side by side, as they had before. Only now, the horde looked even more intimidating. Goblin and giant alike were bathed in the bloody glow and their mouths were smeared with the blood of their kin.

"Very good, son," Jarmassad congratulated. He had known for many years that his son's powers were strong in the black arts, but this had been the first time the boy had agreed to use them of his own free will.

Jareth hid his disgust and handed the book back to his father, but the bloody glow continued to shroud the masses. He felt like his soul had turned to rotten meat with that spell and now he wished only to go to his room and be alone.

"We will depart in two days to overrun Moondale, have Fenlin prepare your things," the young sorcerer ordered, leaving his fanatical father behind.

Fenlin Karling, who had been watching the horrendous display from the kitchen window, picked up his cup of wine laced with poison.

"Oransta, forgive me," he prayed before drinking deeply.

He stood at the window for two full minutes before he fell to the floor dead. The last sight he would ever see was Horace Hangoon's olive-green face covered in the blood of his wife, whose clean bones lay beside the giant's feet.

Hildvar and Florianna stood on the parapet overlooking the Moondale city proper. The town was completely deserted. Every occupant of the territory, down to the last elderly crone, had been brought in by wagon to the packed grounds of the castle.

Florianna looked up at the clouds and wondered how her people faired. She knew the elves of Sengar Valley could defend themselves, but she also knew that the horde would most likely travel through the valley on their march to Moondale.

"What are you thinking," Hildvar asked, noticing her pensive expression.

"I was wondering how Dretholzar and Lady Serra were doing," she lied.

Hildvar nodded his acceptance. He had been wondering that himself, though he did not wish to dwell on it.

"I must go relieve Castille. I shall be in the dungeon if you have need of me," he said with a short bow.

Florianna nodded, but said nothing. She continued to look at the clouds in wonder.

When Hildvar entered the door to the dungeon, he heard a commotion.

"Ye'll get ye back ter yer room right now!" he heard Castille Thornberry yell.

"I am heir to this territory and I demand to speak with him!"

He rounded the corner to see Lady Lorna standing only two cells away from Spike's. Castille had the girl held tight, pinning her arms at her sides and half-carrying her toward the door.

Hildvar ran toward the two, stooping low so he would not hit his head on the low ceiling.

"Lady Lorna, you know you have orders not to be here!" he bellowed, grabbing her by the waist and tossing her diminutive figure over his shoulder.

Lorna screamed in rage and began pounding on Hildvar's back as he carried her out of the dungeon. She continued to bellow up the stairs, through the back hallway, and up the main staircase to her room.

The barbarian unceremoniously threw her on her bed and pointed an enormous finger an inch from her nose.

"You are acting like a child!" he yelled, his hand shaking in frustration.

Lorna scowled and tried futilely to slap his hand away.

"Do you not understand the gravity of this situation?" he asked, planting his massive hands on her shoulders and giving her a firm shake.

"Unhand me, you heathen!" she yelled back. "Get out of my room!"

Hildvar did not back down an inch.

"I will not be going anywhere until you understand! This Forsiad worked for our enemy! Our enemy who could very well be marching to our door this instant!"

Lorna's scowl disappeared, but she turned her head in defiance.

"Have you ever met a giant? A goblin? An orc?" he asked, shaking her again.

She gritted her teeth and did not answer. She merely fixed her gaze on her bed canopy as if he didn't exist.

"Answer me!" he screamed, grabbing her chin and making her look at him.

"No," she replied with venom.

"Then I'm sure you can't imagine eight-thousand of the creatures overrunning the town and killing everyone in this castle, including you," he yelled, spittle flying in her face.

"What does that have to do with Spike?" she shouted defiantly.

Hildvar threw his hands up in frustration.

"If you would open your damned ears you would know! Serra is trying to protect you. She is not doing this out of some petty sibling rivalry. For all we know, Spike could be Jarmassad Truth in sheep's clothing. We are about to be attacked by a horde of monsters, none of which will give a horse's arse if you are a Lady or not. They will kill you regardless. This man you so wish to speak to is directly linked to those that are sending this horde to Moondale. If you think I am lying look out the window. The entire territory is packed into our walls, fearing for their very lives, while you play this petty game of defy my sister!" he shouted incredulously.

Lorna still said nothing, but a look of shame briefly crossed her face.

Hildvar walked over to the bed and knelt before her, looking into her eyes that were so like her sister's. "Lorna, I am not talking to you like a child. I am talking to you adult to adult. Will you push past this petty drama and stay away from that man?"

She wiped the welling tears from her eyes and nodded. "I'm sorry," she muttered.

The barbarian stood up and walked to her door. He did not turn, but said, "Lorna, if you try to see him again I will be forced to lock you in here day and night. Please do not force me to treat you like a prisoner in your own home."

Lorna began crying, as Hildvar left the room, not bothering to shut the door behind him.

Jasin Roostercrowe stoked his small campfire. He looked around at his fellow townsfolk and felt guilty. As the people of Clandestine had fled, he had gathered most and brought them to this mountain mesa facing the town.

"What are you thinking, my love?" his wife, Angora asked.

He looked up into her dark brown eyes and then at their sleeping infant in her lap.

"I'm wondering if I did the right thing," he admitted with a weak smile.

Angora reached over and took her husband's hand, giving it a reassuring squeeze.

"Of course you did. We had to leave the city. It is better we stay together as a group than to run around the wilderness in madness. You are the only councilman that didn't flea when the monsters came, and the people know that, and respect you for it. You're our leader now, as you always were," she said with a smile.

Her words were true. The other seven councilmen had fled on horseback shortly after the first arrival of the entranced horde. He had been on the council for three years and he was the only one that wasn't influenced by Jarmassad Truth's puppet strings. He had always kept the people of Clandestine in mind during the weekly meetings, when the other men had merely done whatever Truth had ordered.

He ran his hand through his thinning, brown hair and sighed. All but a hundred and fifty of the townsfolk had followed him willingly up the steep mountainside to camp on the large outcropping called Denbar's Rise. The other folk had fled in every direction, his twin brother Jafin along with them.

Hubert Elmfodder tentatively approached the small family and cleared his throat.

"Jasin, there's an elf just over the ridge asking for our leader," the young man stated, shifting on his feet. "I thought since you were the one who led us here, you might talk to him."

Jasin hung his head and nodded. He leaned over and kissed his wife's cheek and gave their son's head a soft rub. "I'll be back soon."

Angora nodded and continued to rock young Baine in her lap.

Jasin dusted off his breeches and followed Hubert through a short expanse of forest. They climbed slowly down the short drop-off and walked out onto the next ridge.

An elf with black hair, wearing a golden circlet, stood in the center of a circle of eight elven archers, bows at the ready.

"Are you the leader of this encampment?" the elf asked, gesturing for his guards to put down their bows.

"Aye, if we had a leader, I guess that would be me. The name's Jasin, Jasin Roostercrowe," he replied, walking up to stand before the elf. He stood nearly a foot taller, but the elf's penetrating gaze made him feel weak and small.

"I am King Flamarien, King of the Elves of Sengar Valley."

Jasin's eyes widened," I beg your pardon, we did not know your people occupied this mountain," he said quickly, misreading Flamarien's intent.

"Calm yourself, we are not here to reprimand you."

This took Jasin aback. He knew elves were very protective of their land. Stray off the road through Sengar Valley and one would confront you. Why else would the elf be here, if not to protect his people?

"Why are you here, if I may be so bold to ask?" he asked, feeling very confused and intimidated by the King's presence.

"That remains to be seen. Have you all the townsfolk of Clandestine upon that mesa, or are their others about?" The King hoped this was the majority, he wished to be back in Moondale as soon as possible.

"Aye, I think all but just over a hundred. There are four hundred twenty of us total. Though I don't know how much longer we'll be able to stay here. We're running out of food and fresh water," Jasin replied solemnly.

"Good. Gather your people. We are here by personal request of Lady Serra Bloodmoon of Moondale. She wishes us to move you to a safer and more defensible location. We leave at sunsrise," the King said.

Jasin's eyes widened. It had been years since he had ventured into Moondale. He couldn't believe why she would go to such feats as this to summon them, but he held his tongue. He had learned long ago not to question good fortune.

Chapter Twenty-One
Confession and Passion

Serra turned around as they crested the entrance to the cave. She was amazed to see that the walls were smooth stone and not sand. Spongy moss covered the floor and there was a small brook that meandered through, filtering into the pond outside.

Dretho looked at his feet and sighed.

She looked up at him in alarm and asked, "Are you all right? What is wrong?"

He looked into her eyes and wrapped her in a loving embrace.

"I love you, Serra. If we do not live this day through, know that. And thank you for showing me that emotions are not something to be pushed aside," he said softly in her ear.

He turned his head and pressed his lips to hers. She did not pull back, but kissed him passionately.

"Thank you for that," she said with a smile, her full lips glistening from their kiss.

Taking her hand, they walked down the short stone corridor into a wide cavern with a glittering symbol across the way. The stone had been cut into a large circle, with runes glowing amber in the center.

"What is that?" she asked in wonderment.

"That, my love, is the puzzle door," he replied softly, squeezing her hand.

As they drew closer an eerie melody began to play. She could not discern from whence it came. It seemed to emanate from the very stone. When they were but three paces from the glowing symbol, it transformed into the face of a lion with its mouth opened wide to show its sharp teeth.

Serra's mouth gaped open as a female voice began to sing:

For those of you who are brave of heart, Know this is not your place, before you start. The likes of you are not welcome here, So think and pray before you come near. A riddle you must answer before you may pass, And please notice the bones of fools of the past. Tell the lion's mouth why you wish to meet, The Feral Five who remain discrete. Your answer may grant you what you desire, Or it may not, by consuming fire. So tell us now before it is too late, Answer the question and decide your fate.

Serra glanced at the ground and noticed the charred bones littered here and there. But Dretho looked up at her expectantly and nodded his head in encouragement.

She took a deep breath and said clearly and confidently, "I wish to meet with the Feral Five to prevent a second coming of the *Letuminus Munduni.* I seek their help and offer them an escape from their eternal hiding. Please grant us passage, so that we may discuss our options."

Dretho held his breath as smoke began to billow out of the lion's mouth filling the entire chamber. But to his surprise, the puzzle door disappeared and the smoke dissipated, revealing an unremarkable cave beyond.

He breathed a sign of relief and smiled at Serra in glee. "Well done," he said, taking her hand again and leading her into the cave.

The eerie melody became louder as they turned a sharp bend in the passage. They saw a golden light ahead and followed the brook into a chamber larger than the one before.

Serra took in a deep breath as she saw five wemics lazing beside the brook. Two females lay side by side, one of them absently dipping her tail in the water and the other playing what could only be described as a lute. Three males sat not far away, one sitting upright with the others kneeling in front of him.

"Welcome to our lair Lady Serra Bloodmoon and you also, Dretholzar Derathliona," the upright wemic boomed.

Serra was not surprised that he knew her name. Dretho had told her they could enter her mind. She noted that his reddish-brown mane was much longer than the other two males and he wore a golden breastplate embossed with the same symbol that had been on the puzzle door before the lion had appeared. The two females were nearly identical to the statues outside. They were bare-breasted and had short golden fur on their scalps instead of manes.

"Great King Nefarius, we thank you for allowing us the gift of your gracious presence," Dretho said regally, with a very, low bow.

Serra followed suit and bowed equally low.

"And why have you come to us this day, young woman?" he asked, padding over to stand before her.

She looked up and noted he was nearly two feet taller than her, and much larger in girth.

"Forgive my speechlessness, Great King, for I have never laid eyes upon such magnificence," she admitted in a quiet voice.

King Nefarius laughed with a great, toothy smile.

"Come sit with us young human and elfling."

He turned and walked toward the four others, who were acting genuinely bored.

"This is my mate, Kendrasha, and her sister, Sashaleona. This is my son, Lucadesiad, and my second, Vlasisith," he said, gesturing to each in turn.

Sashaleona stopped playing her lute and bowed her head lightly. "The pleasure is mine, to meet one so fine," she said.

Serra smiled genuinely, "Your mastery of your instrument is astounding, my Lady."

Sashaleona beamed at the proclamation.

Serra looked to Kendrasha who eyed her warily.

"So, why are you really here, human?" she asked bluntly.

She took a deep and steadying breath and began, "If you are to understand, I should start from the beginning."

The wemics came a little closer and lay by the brook, staring at her in anticipation. It was not often that they were granted a story of the outside world. Even Kendrasha seemed slightly interested.

"Nearly three weeks ago, my sister was kidnapped by Jarmassad Truth. He is an evil, tyrant sorcerer who had lived on the island of Hoff's Cove. On the way to find her, I met a man named Jareth the Wanderer, who claimed no parentage. Jareth turned out to be a mage and with his assistance, we were able to break into Truth's fortress and retrieve her, but not before Jareth did battle with Truth by means of magic."

"Jareth was Truth's son!" Vlasisith exclaimed delightedly.

Serra's eyes widened and she looked to Dretho.

"Vlasisith, would you please refrain from ruining her story and enjoy it like a normal wemic for once?" Kendrasha told him venomously.

Nefarius slapped Vlasisith on the back of his head, nearly knocking the wemic completely to the ground.

"Fine," he answered in disgust.

"Please, continue," Kendrasha said to Serra, stealing gazes at Vlasisith who looked at her distastefully.

Serra cleared her throat and began again.

"As Vlasisith said, Jareth turned out to be Truth's son. However, he battled the evil sorcerer while Dretho teleported us back to the safety of Moondale, my territory. I had been injured in the escape, and after many days of recuperation, my Captain notified me of odd goblin activity in the fields of one of my people," she paused to catch her breath, but noted the wemics stared hungrily at her for more.

"We rode out to the field and noticed goblins all walking in one direction, staring straight ahead, and not acknowledging our presence. It was then that Jareth admitted that he thought his father had once again gained the spell book of Gyndless the Almighty. I trust you are familiar with this book?" she asked.

Each wemic nodded, but said nothing. They only stared at her in anticipation.

"We then returned to the castle to find Dretho and King Flamarien, the Elf King, in my courtyard waiting. They had also discovered odd activity and feared the same. After the mages scryed for any information that might prove valuable, we discovered that they were all amassing in Clandestine, where Jarmassad had fled, planning to invade my lands. This army of thousands of monsters could arrive at any moment. I have come today upon the suggestion of Dretho, that you would be the only hope in saving my lands from this impending horde."

Nefarius turned up an eyebrow at Dretho.

"How many have you told of our existence, elfling?" he asked, standing to his feet.

Dretho tried his best to not take the bait, "Six in total; however, two are involved that already knew about your pride, including myself. What Serra says is true, though she has given you only a summary."

This time it was Serra who received Nefarius' upturned eyebrow.

"What have you left out?" he asked.

"She..." Vlasisith began, only to be stopped abruptly by a fierce kick from Nefarius' hind paw that threw him across the cavern.

"I told you to keep quiet. If you can not control yourself, go back to your cavern and wait," Nefarius shouted indignantly.

Vlasisith had hung his head and lay where he landed, cowering next to the cavern wall.

When Serra glanced at Kendrasha, she noticed a toothy smile appear for a few seconds at Vlasisith's punishment.

"Well?" Nefarius asked expectantly.

Serra cleared her throat again and gestured toward the spongy moss.

"May we sit? If you want more than a summary, I fear it will take a while," she requested.

Nefarius nodded and Serra and Dretho sat across the brook from the other wemics.

"What I have left out is that Jareth ended up falling in love with me, although his persistent jealousy pushed me farther away every day. When last I saw him, he was adamant that Dretho and I were lovers behind his back and that I was betraying him. At that time, Dretho and I were only friends and he would not believe me," she admitted.

"At that time?" Kendrasha asked with a knowing smile.

Serra glanced at Dretho uncomfortably and cleared her throat again.

"Dretho has confessed his love for me and we are beginning a relationship," she said softly, smiling at the elf.

"So, this Jareth had a valid claim?" the female wemic asked, enjoying how this line of questioning was making the human squirm.

"As I said, at the time Dretho and I were only friends and I was not aware of his feelings for me. So no, he did not have a valid claim, as I was not aware of the situation, nor had I taken any action to insinuate it," she replied, sitting up straight.

"Interesting, please, continue," Kendrasha said, settling deeper into the spongy moss, her tail dipping long forgotten.

"Jareth would not believe me that night and he teleported away. I have not seen him since. I only hope that he is not helping his father come against us. Shortly after his departure, one of Truth's men, Spike Forsiad, arrived at the castle and informed us that Moondale was the horde's destination. Forsiad was the very man who fed my sister in Hoff's Cove while she was held prisoner there."

"What made you believe him?" Nefarius asked, wringing his hands in anticipation.

"Dretho cast a spell..."

"I cast the truth spell upon the man and asked him a few simple questions. He was completely honest." Dretho interrupted.

"After this admission, I had him taken to our dungeon and that was when Dretho suggested that you would be the only ones strong enough to fend the horde away. However, the part that most drives me to defeat this man and his monstrous army is that he killed my parents a year ago and my brother right before he kidnapped my sister. He has wiped my family from this plane because of a senseless grudge he has had against my grandfather for all these years," she said with tears in her eyes.

"You see, King Nefarius, Serra's grandfather, Harper, was the human responsible for ending the first *Letuminus Munduni*," Dretho offered, taking the attention away from Serra for a moment so she could gather her thoughts.

The wemics looked at each other with wide eyes.

"It seems you come from a long line of warriors, Lady Bloodmoon," Lucadesiad stated with a smile.

Serra noted he seemed a lot younger and softer spoken than the others.

"Yes, that is true," she admitted, smiling back.

"We thank you for your story this day. It is not often we hear the dealings of above," Lucadesiad said. He then looked at Nefarius who nodded.

"If we are to make this decision, we must be alone. I trust you are tired from your trek across the desert sands. Luca will escort you to a chamber in which you both may clean up and rest, while we discuss the situation," Nefarius said firmly.

"We thank you for your graciousness, my King," Dretho said with a firm nod.

Lucadesiad rose to his lion paws and padded across the room to another cave. They followed him in silence through another narrow, winding passageway, through another large cavern, and into the next.

The previous cavern had been barren, but this one was decorated with a large bed of furs that could fit three wemics comfortably. The small brook pooled in one corner of the cavern to form a very small pond.

"We prepared some food before your arrival," he said, gesturing to a large stone bowl filled with various colored mushrooms. "Feel free to sleep or bathe if you need to, it may be the morrow before we reach our decision. But I ask of you not to wander the complex unescorted."

Serra tried her best not to look crestfallen at the admission that more time would pass before she could return to her home. She had come here asking these eternal creatures for help, when they did not know her from a stone. She took a deep breath and nodded.

Lucadesiad left without another word.

Gillianthesp and Fillianthesp Hiralderon approached King Flamarien just after sunsdown.

"The second group has been located, my King," the elven twins said in unison.

"Where were they hiding?" the King asked. He was sitting on a tree stump just outside of Clandestine in full view of the horde.

"They were entering the valley. There were forty-five I believe. They had no leader like the first group, but readily agreed to move in the morning," Gillianthesp replied.

"Good. Has the tree copse been prepared?" he asked, removing his boot to shake out a rock.

"Yes, my King. Food and water have been brought in and elves are already in the trees prepared to protect them," Fillianthesp answered.

"Keep searching for the rest of the refugees. They have to be found. I have given Lady Serra my word."

"Yes, my King," they both replied.

"Dismissed."

As King Flamarien watched his personal guard leave, he sighed. This part of the plan had been all too easy.

As he looked upon the crimson mass of monsters, he was glad that Dretholzar had left to call upon the Feral Five. He did not want to lose any of his people unless he absolutely had to. And if one or all of the wemics died, then so be it.

Hildvar knocked lightly on Lorna's door.

She opened the door a crack and looked at the floor when she saw who had knocked.

"Dinner is prepared, Lady Lorna. It will only be you, Gnarl and I tonight as everyone else is busy with the people outside," he said softly.

"I'm not hungry," she said in a mousy voice.

Hildvar pushed the door forward and stood before the small girl.

"I am sorry if I offended you earlier today, Lorna. I only spoke to you as I did so that you would understand," he said, placing one hand on her shoulder.

She leaned into him and gave him a hug.

"I am sorry I acted the way I did. I was being selfish. I realize that now. Can you forgive me?" she asked, looking up at him with tears in her eyes.

"Of course," he said with a smile. "Let us go down stairs. You do not have to eat, but it would do you good to get out of your room."

She smiled and followed him down the stairs to the dining room.

"Hildvar?" she asked as they entered the room.

"Yes, my Lady?"

"Will you do one thing for me, please?" she asked, shifting on her feet.

"I will try," he answered, dreading the request she was about to make.

"Will you make sure Spike is sent honey mead and jerky?" she asked in just above a whisper.

Hildvar relaxed visibly.

"Of course," he said with a smile as they sat down for their meal.

Serra removed her sword belt and placed it on the large bed. She sat on the edge and removed her boots, emptying a few handfuls of sand from its depths.

"My feet feel skinned," she said, rubbing the sole of her right foot.

Dretho tossed his sword belt next to hers and kneeled before her. "I can make it better if you will allow it."

She smiled and took off her other boot. She wiggled her toes and said, "I would be honored."

He smiled, took her foot in his hands, and began massaging her sole.

Serra closed her eyes, enjoying the soothing motions of his hands.

"Where did you learn how to do that?"

Dretho smiled and began working on her other foot.

"When I studied in Everklent, some of the clerics taught me healing massage. It doesn't require magic, only knowledge of pressure points and nerves," he replied.

She opened her eyes to regard him.

"Was that when you came upon the Feral Five?" she asked in genuine curiosity.

He stood and sat next to her, dusting the sand from his hands.

"When I first came to Everklent, most of the people there had never seen an elf before. So naturally, they told me anything I wished simply so they could gaze at my ears," he said smiling, twitching his long, pointed ears up and down. "I befriended a shaman, that is what they call clerics in this land, and he told me of an altar that I had to see. He was speaking, of course, of the puzzle door at the entrance to the Feral Five's lair. The people of the desert go there to pray. I don't think he knew of their existence. But I was intrigued and came on my own, following his directions."

"Directions? It must have taken you days? Or did you teleport?" she asked.

"Mages can only teleport to places they have been before. It took me a week of plodding through sand dunes until I finally found the place. When I came upon the oasis I was happier to see the water than the statues that grace the entrance to the lair.

The shaman had not told me of the statues so I thought they were gods at first. After coming upon the puzzle door, I was most intrigued. I knew that it wasn't an altar right off. I simply asked, "Who would make such a magnificent wall bust?"

That was when the door turned into the lion's head and Sashaleona sang the same verses we heard earlier this night. Her voice enthralled me. It was the most magical thing I had encountered my entire stay in the southern territory. But I answered this way, "I wish to meet the Feral Five, if only to congratulate them for such a magical place in such a desolate land." I apparently said the right thing. I've told you before that wemics are proud creatures. I believe that is why Nefarius took a liking to you right off, because you made the magnificence comment to him."

"I was being honest," she replied with wide eyes. "This race is so magical in how different it is. Wemic's are beautiful creatures."

Dretho smiled and brushed a lock of hair out of her face.

"You are a beautiful creature as well, Serra Bloodmoon," he said, gazing into her eyes.

She smiled and laid her head upon his shoulder.

"What are your thoughts?" Nefarius asked Kendrasha, lying on his side next to her.

"I believe this human is sincere in her request. I do not believe she will betray us. Though I do not like her," she replied, brushing his mane with the claws of her right forepaw.

"Why do you not like her?" he asked inquisitively.

Kendrasha stopped her brushing and looked at him indignantly. "I saw the way you looked at her. You should be ashamed of yourself Nefarius Lithalicandion. She is not even your race!" she exclaimed.

Nefarius chuckled. "You have been locked up in this hole for far too long, my love. I looked upon her in the same manner as the others. You know as well as I that she is the first human we have seen alive for a millennia."

She pouted shyly and looked at him, batting her cat-like, golden eyes.

"Prove it," she said seductively.

As they made love in their cavern for the first time in seven-hundred and sixty-three years, Kendrasha thanked Serra silently for putting a spark back into her boring life, and most of all, back in Nefarius's life.

Serra yawned widely, covering her mouth with her hand.

Dretho smiled at her and asked, "Are you ready for sleep?"

She squirmed a little at the question and nodded her head.

"I suppose we should discuss that," she said, eyeing the enormous bed. "Though I don't know how I am going to sleep in this armor. I did not bring anything to sleep in." Then she remembered that day at his tower that seemed so long ago. "Do you remember when I came to your tower and I was about to sleep in your bed, so that you could find the source of my nightmares?"

He nodded, already knowing what she would ask.

"Can you summon a nightgown for me like you did that day?"

Dretho muttered under his breath, snapped his fingers, and a red nightgown appeared in his hand like it had those weeks before.

She grinned widely, stood up, and took the gown from him. She looked at her dirty armor and then longingly at the small pond.

"They told us not to leave the cavern, but I so wish to bathe before putting this on," she admitted sadly.

He stood up as well. "I suppose I could wait in the passage. Surely that would be allowed," he said, walking to the entrance.

As soon as his foot reached the threshold it thumped into something hard. He looked questioningly at Serra and then at the open entrance. He extended his arm and again, as his fingers reached the threshold, they touched a solid, invisible wall.

"They've locked us in, it seems," he said, feeling along the clear wall, trying his best to find a weakness.

She hung her head and sighed.

"I will gladly turn away while you bathe and dress," he said, trying his best to keep her as comfortable with the situation as possible. In truth, he longed to see her slender body, but he would not do so without her consent.

She smiled and nodded.

Dretho walked back over to the bed and lay down with his back to the pond. His chain mail and mithril plate were very uncomfortable to lie in, but he would deal with his own needs after hers were met.

Serra removed her greaves, boots, and bracers, placing them in a pile on the floor next to the wall. She then removed her chain mail tunic and her mithril leggings, retrieved her bar of soap from her backpack, and walked over to the pond.

Taking one last glance at Dretho's back, she stuck one foot into the water. It was very warm, almost like bath water, but there was no steam. She sat down on the cold stone, goose pimples covering her body at its touch, and eased herself into the water. It was about three feet deep, just deep enough for her to sit comfortably.

Dretho heard her splashing and fought hard not to glance over his shoulder. He could smell a flowery fragrance and he breathed deeply.

"What is that smell?" he asked, propping his head on his hand.

"Soap. Frelia dries flowers in the kitchen window in the summer and collects their oils in a tin. When she makes up a batch of soap, she puts the oil in to make it smell nice," she said. After a few moments she giggled.

"What?" he asked, intrigued by her little laugh.

"I remember Gnarl got the wrong soap out of the storage closet once. The brigade called him Pansy for a week," she answered with a renewed amount of giggling.

Dretho laughed aloud. It felt good. He had never been alone with Serra long enough to talk about such things. He felt almost relaxed when he was in her presence, as if nothing else in the world mattered.

"I shall have to make a point to ask him about that one day," he said, laughing again.

Serra laughed wholeheartedly and sunk under the water to rinse her hair. She laughed while under and came up gagging and choking.

Dretho turned around instinctively and then turned back with wide eyes. His breath caught in his chest and his heart began to race.

"Are you all right?" he asked a little too loudly.

"Yes," she answered, clearing the water from her eyes. "Rule number two, never laugh while under water."

"What's rule number one?" he asked, trying his best to push away the images of her bare breasts from his mind.

"I may tell you one day," she said as she pulled herself from the pool. "But not today."

She stood there dripping for a few seconds and walked slowly over to the bed and snatched one of the little furs from the bed.

"Don't turn around," she warned, drying her body with the fur.

After her flesh was dry, she put on the red nightgown Dretho had conjured for her. It fit like a glove and hugged her hips and waist.

"All right."

He rolled over and smiled wryly, propping his head on his hand again.

There she stood, the woman he loved, wearing a nightgown of his own design with her hair dripping all over the floor.

"What are you smiling at?" she asked, smiling back.

"You look like a beautiful, drowned strawberry," he said, laughing.

She scrunched up her nose playfully and threw the wet fur at him, getting him right in the face.

He grinned evilly, picked up the wet fur, and jumped into a crouch atop the bed, eyeing her warily.

Serra giggled again and moved hastily to the wall.

"No, I've just had a bath!" she shouted in delight.

He jumped off the bed and ran at her, pinning her against the wall, and giving her face a good wipe with the fur.

She had her mouth open when he made his pass and as he removed it, she began spitting out small hairs and wiping her mouth. After her mouth was clean, she grinned and then noticed Dretho still had her pinned against the wall.

He leaned over and kissed her deeply, wrapping his arms around her slender waist, the fur on the floor, long forgotten.

Serra returned his kiss and felt a fluttering in her chest as desire arced through her body.

Their kisses grew more passionate by the second and Dretho ran his hand up her back to the back of her head. He pushed her chin up and began kissing her neck.

She moaned deeply and Dretho continued, spurred on by her obvious pleasure. He kissed up her neck and whispered in her ear, "Do you want me to stop?"

After a brief moment of deep breaths, she said, "No."

He plunged his tongue deep into her ear and she shivered all over.

She reached for his hauberk and tugged it over his head. He stopped only long enough for her to clear it and renewed kissing hungrily over her mouth. She dropped the chain mail to the floor with a loud chink and ran her fingers over his chest, feeling every muscle tense with her touch.

He pressed harder up against her and she could feel his desire against her belly. She pressed back, wanting to feel her whole body against his. He walked backward and she followed, unable to bear breaking their kiss. He fell on the bed of furs and she fell on top of him.

She reached up and ran her fingers through his long, black hair, tracing her finger along the point of his ears.

Moaning with desire, he brought his hand to her breast and squeezed ever so lightly.

She gasped and pressed her hand against his, wanting more of this excitement she had never felt before.

Rolling her over onto the bed, he continued to kiss her as he unstrapped his greaves and threw them to the floor. He kicked off his boots and pulled back to look into her eyes.

Her breathing was raspy and heavy. She opened her eyes and gazed at him with pure lust.

"Are you sure this is what you want? Here? Now?" he asked. He knew he was breaking the mood, but he did not want her to regret this later.

"Yes," she answered without hesitation.

She reached down and unbuckled the belt on his mithril leggings. Taking the hint, he removed them to be completely naked. She looked down, admiring his form. He was absolutely gorgeous in every way. She looked back up into his eyes and began struggling to get out of her nightgown.

Dretho pulled on the sleeve, exposing one of her breasts. He pressed his mouth against it, taking her nipple into his mouth, biting lightly, drawing a pure moan of passion from deep within her chest.

Serra rolled him over and sat straight up, pulling the gown over her head.

He marveled at her beauty. Her pale skin was unmarred and perfect. Her breasts were perfectly curved and heavy.

She leaned down over him and kissed him again. He rolled on top of her and kissed her neck. He slowly kissed her chest until he took her nipple into his mouth again, biting harder this time. Her back arched in desire and he continued down to her belly.

Her stomach was taught and muscular, perfectly honed like a warrior. He kissed and licked each muscle, drawing more moans and gasps from her every second.

He continued down to her hairline, noting it was as red as the hair on top of her head. He ran his hand softly over her thighs, parting them ever so lightly.

Serra looked down just as Dretho plunged his tongue into her and she felt her whole body explode with release. She cried out and pressed hard against the back of his head until her whole body quivered from her orgasm.

Dretho climbed back up beside her and kissed her again, still tasting her in his mouth.

"I can't believe it," she said breathlessly.

He smiled and ran his fingers lightly over her stomach. She looked up into his eyes and saw his lust splayed across his face. She put her hands on his shoulders and pulled him on top of her, feeling his hardness on her leg.

He stopped to ask her again for confirmation, but before he could, she raised her hips and thrust against him. He moaned as her warmth spread around him.

She cried out for just a moment at the pain, but then as he thrust within her, she began kissing him again, marveling at the feel of him.

He made sweet, caring love to her for an hour, taking his time and making sure he did not go too fast.

He took great pleasure in exploring every contour of her smooth skin. She was perfectly formed and he positively worshipped her.

As he felt his release coming closer, she moaned loudly and thrust faster, wanting her own release. He saw stars before his eyes when he came and she screamed in ecstasy at the same moment. They pressed against each other for what seemed like minutes, not wanting the feeling to end.

Dretho collapsed on top of her and she went limp, closing her eyes.

He raised his head and brushed her soaked hair from her eyes. "Are you all right?" he asked.

She smiled and looked up at him, totally relaxed.

"That was amazing," she said softly, reaching up to brush her finger across his lips.

"Yes. You are amazing," he replied.

Her face turned from one of relaxation to one of seriousness. "Dretho, I do love you. And I'm not saying that because we just made love. I am saying it because it is true."

His heart nearly leapt from his chest at her words. "Oh, how I have longed for you, Serra Bloodmoon. I have searched my entire life for someone who could make me feel again," he said, kissing her forehead.

He looked at her in seriousness, his golden eyes boring into hers.

"Will you be my bride, Serra?" he asked in all seriousness. "Will you spend the rest of your life with me?"

The question did not shock her this time as it had so many times before. She had found her soul mate in this elf. The only man she had ever given herself to in heart, body, and in mind.

"Yes," she replied as a single tear dripped from her eye.

Dretho smiled and kissed her again. "Thank you."

Chapter Twenty-Two
The Feral Five

The Feral Five gathered in the common cavern just before sunsrise. Nefarius and Kendrasha lay together by the brook in a loving embrace while Lucadesiad passed around bowls of mushrooms. Sashaleona, quill in hand, scribbled furiously on a roll of parchment. Vlasisith stared blankly at the water, deep in thought.

"We should make our decision before they wake. Last night we discussed our terms to offer, but we never fully agreed to the quest," Nefarius said, stroking Kendrasha's coat.

"I believe we should accompany them," Kendrasha stated, drawing surprised looks from everyone. "Although, I would like to speak with this human alone before we leave."

Nefarius nodded.

"I realize that it is not our way to interfere with the happenings of the outside world, but after all these years I have begun to wonder if it has been worth it to stay hidden," he said solemnly.

Sashaleona looked up from her parchment and sighed.

"Oh, how I would love to travel the world abroad, to see the humans smile and nod. Oh, how I would love to feel the grass beneath my paws, and write poems and ballads about it all," she replied in a singsong voice.

Nefarius smiled at his sister-in-law's small poem. It was nice to see her writing again. He had heard her scribbling throughout the entire night.

"Perhaps I should show Dretho around the complex. He wasn't allowed last time he was here. That would give you an opportunity to be with the Lady for a while," he said, stroking Kendrasha's coat again.

"They are waking," Vlasisith said in a far-off voice.

Kendrasha and Nefarius rose to all fours and padded out of the cavern side by side.

Dretho opened his eyes to see Serra resting in the crook of his arm. A small smile graced her face and she looked more content than he had ever seen her.

Seeming to sense his thoughts, she opened her eyes and noticed him looking at her.

"Good morning," she said softly.

He smiled and brushed his hand across her face.

"Good morning. How are you feeling?" he asked, pulling her naked form closer to him.

She nestled closer to him under the furs and sighed.

"I feel wonderful and guilty at the same time," she replied, closing her eyes again.

Dretho looked at her with concern, but noted she was still smiling.

"Guilty?" he asked.

She opened her eyes once again and propped her head upon her hand.

"I feel wonderful waking up next to you and feeling better than I have my whole life. I feel completely relaxed and satisfied. And I feel guilty because I should be worrying about my lands, and I am, though I have pushed my worries to the side for a time," she admitted, brushing her fingers across his bare chest.

He relaxed visibly and sighed. She had given her virginity to him the night before. He did not want her to feel guilty or regretful about that.

"I feel the same, my love. Though, is it selfish that we take a night for ourselves?" he asked, entwining his fingers with hers.

"I don't believe so. But I can't help but wish it would not end," she replied sadly.

"It does not have to, Serra. We are about to face possibly the hardest trials of our lives, but there is a difference between today and yesterday," he offered, squeezing her hand reassuringly.

"What is that?"

"Yesterday, we were two different people leading two different lives, going through two different sets of troubles. Now we are together as one. I will be there for you, and you for me, when times are bad and good. That is the core of love, Serra," he said, leaning over to kiss her lightly.

Serra lay her head back down on his shoulder and looked into his golden eyes. He was right, today and yesterday were as different as night and day. Yesterday she had been but a girl, running a territory haphazardly, alone. Now that she had come to realize her love for Dretho, she felt whole. She knew now that she had grown to love him unconsciously for these past weeks, but her incessant denial of domination had shadowed her true feelings from her. Dretho was a man... a true man. He did not covet her for her station or for what she had to offer him. He loved her for who she was. She had given herself to no man before the night before, but had not hesitated with Dretho. She had wanted him to touch her, to explore her, and to feel as she felt.

"I love you," she said simply, tears welling at the corner of her eyes.

"And I you," he replied, caressing her face with his hands and giving her a long, soft kiss.

"Excuse us," they heard from the doorway.

Serra quickly pulled the furs more tightly about her and they both looked up to see Kendrasha and Nefarius standing in the doorway.

"We did not wish to interrupt, but time is of the essence," Nefarius said, entering the room.

"All is well, great King," Dretho replied. "If you would only grant us a few minutes, we will be clothed and ready to proceed to your liking."

Nefarius nodded and walked from the room, Kendrasha following closely behind.

They gathered their armor and got dressed. As they walked toward the threshold, they both paused unconsciously before stepping through. Kendrasha and Nefarius were waiting down the passage patiently.

"You will come with me, Serra Bloodmoon. Dretholzar, you shall go with Nefarius," Kendrasha ordered.

Serra looked to Dretho with concern, but he nodded encouragingly. Dretho walked down the passage with Nefarius and Kendrasha stood idly, watching Serra.

"How my I serve you, Kendrasha?" she asked regally.

Kendrasha did not answer, but padded in the opposite direction.

"Tell me of the horde," she demanded simply.

She took a deep breath and walked closer to Kendrasha's side, trying to keep pace with her four long legs.

"They are of four races from what I understand; giant, goblin, orc, and ogre. They have walked from as far as Glendale and Everklent to gather on the streets of Clandestine. All seem entranced by Truth, though I do not understand how one man can control such a number," she explained as they wound their way into a large cavern. Serra noticed immediately that it was an alchemy chamber.

"Do you know the number of this horde?" Kendrasha asked, padding up to a long table with various bottles and bowls.

"At last estimate it was eight thousand, but that was days ago," Serra replied hesitantly.

Kendrasha turned to regard Serra with an odd expression.

"And you believe that we will be able to help you with such odds?" she asked.

Serra stood straight and nodded.

"If Dretho is confident in your abilities, then so am I. I fear I do not know your ways or what you can do, but I have faith in you regardless," she answered diplomatically.

"You assume much, Serra Bloodmoon," Kendrasha replied. She then paused for a long moment, "But this should not be so difficult a task."

Serra relaxed, despite the wemic's intimidating demeanor.

Dretho followed Nefarius closely throughout the passageway, stopping to a wall of stone. Nefarius waved his hand and the stone dissipated in a cloud of smoke to reveal an entrance to a small cavern.

"Come," the wemic beckoned, gesturing for Dretho to walk ahead of him.

The elf walked into the room and noted the many crystals lying about, ranging from the size of a pea to the size of a human head.

"I see you like my collection," the wemic observed, walking over to rest on a large cushion of furs next to one wall.

"Amazing, I have never seen crystals so varying in cut and size."

"Rest Dretho, Vlasisith tells me you had a long night last night," the Wemic King said with a wry, toothy smile.

Dretho pushed back his offense at the comment and sat down on another pile of furs.

"She is a most remarkable human. And beautiful, for sure. I envy you," he said, trying to draw the elf into conversation.

"I mean no disrespect, Great Nefarius, but I would rather speak of the task at hand," he replied politely.

The wemic leaned forward slightly, "And I would like to speak about your betrothed."

Dretho nodded despite himself.

"What is it you would like to know?" he asked in resignation.

"How did you meet this beauty?" the wemic said, leaning back in satisfaction.

"Her father saved my life ten years ago. Up until a few weeks ago I had not seen her in that span of time. She came to see me and I turned expecting to see a young girl, but as you know, she is a woman now," he replied.

Nefarius nodded.

"That she is. I believe you have made a wise choice, elfling. And now, we will speak of this quest you desire us to embark upon."

Dretho waited with baited breath.

"I believe you had already formulated a plan to gather the horde into one large mass, surrounded by elven and Moondale warriors alike."

The elf nodded.

"That plan will not be altered. We will require your full cooperation and magical abilities, as well as Serra's hold over her men."

He nodded again.

"And then there is the matter of compensation. But that will be discussed later on this day. For the time being, tell me of this marvelous tower of yours that I have heard about."

Jareth wandered into the kitchen to find Fenlin dead on the floor. He had been wandering the manor looking for the man, as his father had demanded his breakfast.

He cursed aloud and noticed the cup on the floor. Stooping down, he dipped his finger into the drying liquid and sniffed. It was wine, but there was an odd herbal scent to it.

"Poison," he said to no one in particular.

He looked down at Fenlin's body and into the man's open, vacant eyes.

"Lucky bastard," he said, standing back up.

The crimson glow out the window caught his eye. His monstrous army still stood perfectly still, awaiting his demands.

Gathering a few pieces of fruit from the cupboard, he left the corpse in the floor and went back upstairs.

His father was lying in bed with a disgruntle expression splayed over his face.

"Where is that damned servant?" he asked indignantly.

Jareth tossed the fruit unceremoniously on the bed and scowled.

"He is rotting on the kitchen floor," he replied, stepping up to the terrace doors.

Jarmassad Truth grabbed a pear and bit into it with difficulty. One side of his mouth hung slack while he chewed, pieces of fruit falling from it onto the blankets.

"Good. He was worthless anyway," he muttered through a mouthful.

Jareth looked at him in disgust and opened the terrace doors, walking out into the morning air. Despite the beautiful day, the crimson shroud over the city dulled Halos and Belos so they looked like bloodshot eyes peering down at him.

He had tried scrying for Serra that morning, but was unable to locate her. It was as if she had dropped completely off the map. He could only assume that her elven savior had found some way to block his attempts.

He slammed his fist down on the railing in anger, feeling a sharp pain. Looking down at the rail, he noticed his blood on a small bur in the metal. He looked at the cut and squeezed his fist, reveling in the pain. Vitality was all he had left, for his soul was now damned.

King Flamarien sat in a tree with his twin guards watching the procession of refugees from Clandestine. They had been able to locate nearly every person. Flamarien thought they had been lucky that the people had been smart enough to stay in large groups.

"I will be going back to Moondale tonight," he muttered.

Gillianthesp and Fillianthesp regarded their King and nodded.

"Do you wish for us to accompany you, my King?" Fillianthesp asked.

The Elf King thought for a long moment and shook his head.

"I will leave you in charge here with the forty-five elves guarding the perimeter. The rest will be leaving for Moondale with me," he replied. He had alerted four thousand of his elven warriors the day before, leaving just under a thousand in Sengar Valley. He hoped that they would be able to defend themselves and the valley with so few.

"Make sure these people are fed and watered. I shall return after the battle is won," he said, nodding to his personal attendants.

"Yes, my King," they replied as Flamarien jumped from the tree to meet with his commanders.

Dretho and Nefarius made their way to the common cavern to see the other wemics sitting with Serra. He smiled in greeting and she smiled back.

"Sit with your mate, we will tell you our terms and plans," Nefarius said, gesturing toward Serra.

Dretho sat down and took Serra's hand. They both waited anxiously to hear what the wemic had to say.

But oddly, it was Sashaleona who began.

The Feral Five will accompany you to your destination,
Despite our low number and lack of reputation.
The Bloodmoon Brigade and their elven friends,
Will be strong and brave as the battle begins.
They will gather the horde in one certain place,
And soon the Feral Five, the horde will face.
Vlasisith will then dominate their wills,
And cease their thirst to mangle and kill.
Nefarius the King will cast an incantation.
Of Sashleona the Bard, a clever illusion,
She will sing her song and entrance the horde,
Drawing them closer with every word.
Dretholzar and Kendrasha will then combine their power,
To surround the horde before they cower.
As the spell is complete, our friends will step away,
While none of the monsters may fight or stray.
Serra Bloodmoon will then kill the sorcering one,
Ending his hold over the horde, the battle almost won.
Lucadesiad will then pray to the divine,
Sending strength to the mages as they are next in line.

As the Feral Five teleport to the desolate island,
The foes will be vanquished and the battlefield silenced.
And now comes the hardest work of it all,
Sending the creatures back to their dwelling halls.
Vlasisith will dominate their simple minds,
With Kendrasha's spellwork not far behind.
Each creature will swim across the Neverlear,
To go home without bothering the goodly folk they come near.
As the creatures cross their long-forgotten threshold,
They will forget at once the evil sorcerer's hold.
And after the work is all said and done,
The Feral Five will come out of hiding and live under the suns.
In payment for our work, we ask the black monolith tower,
To live and prosper for the rest of our hours.

As she finished her poem, she stood and took a great bow. Everyone clapped thunderously.

"What do you think of our plan, Lady Bloodmoon?" Nefarius asked in triumph.

She looked up to the King and sighed. "It is brilliant. Absolutely brilliant." She then looked to Dretho with a questioning expression. "Will you give up your magical tower for this cause?"

Dretho looked at her with a loving expression, "For you, my love, I would do anything."

It was nearly midday when the Feral Five were prepared to travel. The females, to Serra's relief, had donned breastplates, not unlike Nefarius's, embossed with the same symbol.

"I do not think it would be a good idea to teleport into Moondale," Serra offered nervously.

"I've already thought of that," Kendrasha replied, padding over to her with two amulets in hand. "These amulets are akin to our armor and will keep you telepathically linked to all of us. Not unlike that red stone you keep in your belt pouch," she said, handing Serra one of the amulets.

Serra reached into her pouch and brought out the bloodstone that Dretho had given her.

"He told me this would bring me to him if I would only hold it to my heart and say his name," she muttered fondly, rubbing her finger over the smooth stone. It was black in color with many flecks of crimson red. Serra thought it the most fitting gift she had ever received.

"If you wear that amulet around your neck, you need only think of whom of us you wish to speak. When Dretho wears this one," she said, holding up the other amulet. "You will be able to speak with him telepathically as well. But I must warn you. All your thoughts will be heard if you are not wary."

Serra nodded her head and put the amulet around her neck.

"Hello, Lady Serra, welcome to our pride," she heard Lucadesiad's voice clearly in her head.

She smiled and nodded to him in thanks.

Dretho took the other amulet and put it around his neck.

"Dretholzar, I will teleport us to your tower. There we will remain until needed. We will be able to speak with you through these amulets, but we will not be able to hear or see what is going on, save Vlasisith. We will leave it up to you to decide when to expose our pride," Kendrasha continued.

He nodded, "I have an extensive library and alchemy chamber that you are welcome to if you need anything."

Kendrasha smiled. This elf had always amazed her in his demeanor and did again now. In the days when wemic's were many, they guarded their magic to the death. It made her think again of how much the world had changed. Yes, it was time for them to enter into its fold again.

Hildvar opened the door to the dungeon with a pouch and pitcher in his hand. He nodded to Castille, who left promptly, and walked up to Forsiad's cell and saw that the man was writing.

The barbarian cleared his throat and Spike turned to regard him.

"Hello, great man," he said in greeting, rising from his table and walking over to the cell bars.

"And you, Forsiad. I have brought you something at Lady Lorna's request," he said, unlocking the door and handing the items to the man. "I thought it rather odd that she would want to send you jerky and honey mead, but I do as I am told."

Spike smiled and chuckled.

"When she was locked up in her cell in Hoff's Cove, I would bring her black bread and water each day. One day, risking my own mortal peril, I slipped honey mead into her water and squished jerky in her bites of bread. It is a symbolic gesture, Hildvar."

The barbarian smiled and nodded.

Spike put on a serious expression and walked back over to his desk. "I know that I do not have any right to ask this of you, though I feel I must."

He picked up his parchment and handed it unrolled to the large man.

"I realize I am not to see Lorna, but I would like for you to give her this letter. I give it to you open so that you may read it and approve it."

Hildvar looked down at the parchment.

Dearest Lady Lorna,

I wish to extend my thanks to you and yours for allowing me to keep my life. My days here in this castle have been more pleasant than any I ever spent working for Jarmassad Truth. Your people have been kind to me and for that I am forever grateful.

I know you came to see me and were unable to do so, but I ask of you not to try again before Lady Serra allows it. It was nice to hear your voice once again and to know that you are well, but I do not wish for you to risk persecution because of me.

We will see each other soon. I have no doubt in my mind that Moondale will overcome this foe. I know now that my years spent working for Jarmassad Truth were empty and in vain. I have you to thank for knocking sense into me.

Thank you for understanding,
Spike Forsiad

Hildvar finished the letter and rolled the parchment up tight. He looked at the young man before him and gave him a curt nod.

"You seem to be an honorable man, Spike Forsiad. I will deliver your letter," he said politely.

Spike turned back to his desk as Hildvar relocked the cell and walked down the hall to his chair. He wanted to see Lorna, but knew that it would cost her too much. The letter was the least he could do and he hoped she would listen.

They teleported into the foyer of Dretho's tower, the wemics landing gracefully with their feline reflexes. The Feral Five marveled at the high ceiling and the grand staircase circling the walls.

"This is astounding craftsmanship," Nefarius commented, padding up to the staircase and putting a tentative paw on the bottom step.

"Have you placed any offensive wards about the place?" Kendrasha asked, noting the magical emanations coming from every crevice.

Dretho nodded, "You must mutter, *Derathliona*, in order for the staircase to actually take you to a room. Otherwise it continues into oblivion."

Kendrasha regarded him with wide eyes.

"Also, if you do enter my altar chamber, you must mutter, *Derathliona Inaeena*, for my bookcase to open the portal to my alchemy chamber or, *Derathliona Inbeena*, for my bedroom. The other rooms will reveal themselves with simply, *Derathliona Inseena*, including the kitchen, which should still be stocked with food. There is a well just outside, but be wary of who sees you."

"We will be ready at every moment to leave. Merely contact us with your amulets and we will find you," Nefarius informed with a nod.

Serra turned to Dretho expectantly.

"We will leave you now, make yourselves at home," he said, taking her hand.

"*Arcanus Traveelus Duoti,*" he muttered and they left the tower behind, landing softly in the courtyard of Bloodmoon Castle.

A shriek greeted them as Frelia ran up to them, skirts flying wildly. She skidded to a halt, noticing their hands clasped.

"Hello Frelia," Serra said with a warm smile. Her heart nearly skipped a beat as she wondered how she would break the news of her engagement to the woman. But she thought it best to leave it to the side for now.

"Missus, and ye, Master Dretho. I didn' know ye had left. They tol' me ye were in the plannin' room not ter be disturbed," she muttered, finding it very hard to keep her gaze from their hands.

"Will you fetch Hildvar, Florianna, and Gnarl to the planning room? And is the King back yet?" she asked, avoiding the question in the maid's eyes.

"Hildvar's guardin' that man from Clandestine, do ye wish fer me ter gather Castille ter take his place?"

Serra's nodded.

"I don' think the King is back yet, if he be, I hadn' heared of it."

"Good, ask them to meet us as soon as possible," Serra said, walking toward the great double-doors of the castle, still hand in hand with her love.

When Hildvar, Florianna, and Gnarl entered the room, Gnarl and Hildvar stopped in their tracks as Florianna walked on to her seat. There Dretho sat, to the right of Lady Serra, in the seat of a suitor, not to mention they were wearing armor they had never seen before.

Gnarl shook it off and nudged the barbarian roughly in the side and they took their seats across from the elf.

"It's good ter see ye," the dwarf said, noticing immediately how relaxed the normally stiff elf appeared.

"And you, Captain," Serra replied with a grand smile.

"Were ye successful in gettin' them things ter help us?" he asked roughly.

"Take care that you do not call them that to their faces, dwarf. They are powerfully proud creatures. And yes, we were successful, they are waiting in my tower for the proper time," Dretho replied.

"What are those necklaces, if I may ask?" Hildvar asked, noticing that Serra and Dretho wore identical ones.

Serra looked to Dretho, "They keep us in contact with each other," she said vaguely.

Hildvar nodded, but it was obvious she was leaving something out.

"I believe tonight we should bring Nefarius here, if not the rest, to lay out our plans. I hope that King Flamarien arrives, but I am more than sure that Florianna will be able to inform him of the arrangements," Serra said, nodding to the elven woman.

"You may call me Quisp, Lady Serra. Everyone else does," she replied. She had a nagging feeling in the pit of her stomach at the mention of the Feral Five, but she would push her feelings to the side for the cause. She would deal with them later.

Serra nodded and smiled.

"Have ye heard from yer dad, Quisp?" Gnarl asked.

"No, not since his departure. I imagine he is busy gathering the refugees," she replied.

Serra tried to keep a straight look on her face as she thought of Nefarius.

"Nefarius, I will be summoning you this evening to my castle to meet with our commanders. They need to know of our plans," she thought telepathically.

To her surprise, his voice came clearly into her thoughts. "That will be fine. Dretholzar can teleport me there if you do not wish Kendrasha to accompany me."

"I think that would be best," she thought.

Dretho looked at her and smiled.

Gnarl and Hildvar both noticed the smile and glanced at one another curiously.

"Is there somethin' we need ter know?" Gnarl asked, eyeing the two warily.

Serra looked at the dwarf and felt nervous. She did not feel ashamed for her actions the night before or for her acceptance of Dretho's proposal, but her friends did not know Dretho as she did.

"I leave it to you to tell them," Dretho's voice offered in Serra's mind.

"Yes, I suppose there is, though I was thinking of waiting until a better time to tell you," she replied with a deep breath.

Gnarl raised an eyebrow at her and asked, "And tha' would be, me Lady?"

"Dretho and I are betrothed," she said with a grand smile.

Hildvar and Gnarl could not have been more surprised. They both looked at Serra then to Dretho and back to Serra again.

Gnarl cleared his throat and replied with wide eyes, "Well. I don't know how ye did it elf, but congratulations."

Dretho smiled and nodded.

As the others left the planning room, Hildvar and Gnarl stayed behind.

"I wonder if Frelia knows," the barbarian asked with concern.

Gnarl laughed and shook his head, "If she don', ye best be standin' behind her when she finds out."

Serra walked to Lorna's door and knocked lightly.

The door cracked and Lorna rolled her eyes and walked away.

She walked into the room and closed the door, "Lorna, may I speak with you?" she asked pleadingly.

"You are speaking, aren't you?" Lorna answered scornfully. She plopped down on her large, canopied bed and picked up a small book and began reading.

"I have something to tell you," she said, sitting on the bed next to her. "And I would appreciate it if you would look at me when I tell you."

Lorna looked up from her book in exasperation and crossed her arms over her chest.

"I was planning to formally announce this at dinner tonight, but I thought you should know first," she said hesitantly.

"Well?" the girl asked huffily.

"Dretho and I are to be married," she said softly.

Lorna's eyes widened, but she said nothing.

"I was wondering if you would be my maid of honor," she added as an afterthought. She always knew she would be if she ever married, but she hoped the request would lighten her sister's mood.

But it didn't.

"When did this happen?" she asked with a raised eyebrow.

"He asked me yesterday and I accepted," Serra admitted, crestfallen that her ploy had not worked.

"Don't you think it's a little sudden, after Jareth?" the girl asked defiantly.

Serra's lips turned to a thin line and she shook her head.

"I never formally announced a relationship with Jareth. He was a controlling, jealous man like all the others before him, Lorna."

Lorna snorted and picked up her book.

Serra put her hand on the pages and said, "You and I are the only Bloodmoon's left Lorna. I don't want our relationship to be like this. And to show you, I have asked that Spike join us for dinner tonight to be seated beside you."

The girl's eyes lit up like the suns.

"I love you, Lorna. I don't mean to be rash or scornful to you. I only wish to protect you. I have been told by Castille and Hildvar that he has been a very worthy guest and that he even wrote you a letter asking you not to attempt to see him until I granted you permission."

Lorna looked up to Serra with tears in her yes.

"I am sorry I acted the way that I did," she admitted and added softly, "I would love to be your maid of honor."

Serra pulled her close and gave her a quick hug. She waited a few moments before putting on a serious expression and saying, "I do not mind if he takes his meals with you as long as Hildvar sits next to him. I will not take any chances on your life, but I am willing to give you that much."

She nodded. It wasn't often that her sister gave in to her and she knew it was no small thing for her to offer this. Her heart leapt at the thought of seeing Spike again. She only hoped that Hildvar would not be mean to him if he talked with her.

The evening meal began with everyone in good spirits, though the folk of the castle couldn't stop glancing at Dretho and Spike.

Dretho stood during the middle of the meal and tapped his spoon on the side of his crystal goblet.

A collective hush fell across the table, many people even looked fearful.

"I have an announcement that I would like to make," he said, smoothing his black hair behind his ear and trying very hard to ignore the distaste emanating from the people at the table. "I have asked for Lady Serra's hand in marriage and she has accepted."

Most were silent with wide eyes, some gasped in denial, and Frelia fainted in her plate of potatoes. Hildvar stood from his seat, slung the woman over his shoulder and left for the kitchen.

Serra cleared her throat and stood after they had left, taking Dretho's hand.

"I realize that most of you do not know Dretho very well, but I hope that you take the time to try. He is a wonderful man and I am very happy with our decision. The wedding will be postponed for a time, though Dretho will stay on at the castle from now on if he so chooses."

She looked to Lorna and Spike, who were smiling up at her.

"I would also like to formally introduce you all to Spike Forsiad... a friend of Lady Lorna's. I ask you each to make him feel at home, as he will be staying in the barracks with the Bloodmoon Brigade from this point forward if he so chooses."

Lorna grinned from ear to ear and took Spike's hand, as he nodded his thanks.

Serra was surprised at her audacity in her last minute decision, but she had watched Spike closely throughout the meal. He and Lorna had laughed together and had talked right up to the point when Dretho stood. She had rarely seen her sister smile so much. She glanced at Gnarl who looked at her in question, but she knew he would abide by her wishes. If the Bloodmoon Brigade couldn't keep him in line, no dungeon cell ever could.

Florianna, Serra, Gnarl, and Hildvar waited patiently for Dretho's return from the tower. Gnarl and Hildvar were clearly nervous, but to Serra's surprise Florianna seemed calm.

"Please remember to be wary of your words, Gnarl. Wemic's take offense easily I am told," Serra reminded.

"I'll do me best, me Lady," Gnarl replied.

The air shimmered before the table and after only a few seconds Dretho and Nefarius appeared before them.

Gnarl and Hildvar did well in hiding their surprise and Florianna remained as calm as ever.

"Good evening, Nefarius," Serra greeted, rising from her seat and giving a short bow.

Nefarius bowed back and Dretho gestured toward the table. The wemic padded over slowly and looked strangely at one of the chairs and then picked it up, moving it a few feet away, and sat on his haunches on the floor, eye-level with the rest.

"Nefarius, I would like to introduce you to Captain Gnarl Knottytrunk and Lieutenant Hildvar of the Elkhorn Tribe. And this is Florianna Flamarien, King Flamarien's daughter, more commonly known as Quisp."

Nefarius seemed unsurprised until Serra announced Florianna. He looked to her with a kind face. "I have met your father before, he is a great man, and your mother was equally great, before her death," he said nobly.

Florianna found it hard to bite back the thoughts running through her mind, she merely nodded and looked to Serra again.

"Nefarius is the King of the Feral Five pride, he has most graciously accepted our invitation tonight to plan our offense," Dretho offered, trying his best to move the conversation from Lelorianna, Florianna's mother.

"What will ye need o' the Bloodmoon Brigade, King?" Gnarl asked, wanting to move along so he would stop feeling compelled to stare at the creature.

Nefarius looked at the dwarf long and hard before saying anything.

"You are a dwarf?" he asked plainly.

Gnarl raised an eyebrow and nodded.

"Where does your clan reside?" he asked, not bothering to answer Gnarl's question.

Gnarl cleared his throat and said, "The mines under Sengar Valley were me home, til I comed ter Moondale."

"Interesting, does your clan still live there?" the King asked, resting his elbows on the table and propping his chin in his hands.

"I reckon," he answered with a short glance to Serra, "I hadn' been there in ages."

Nefarius looked to Hildvar next, "And you, you are of a tribe. Are you a barbarian?" he asked.

"Yes, sir, I am," Hildvar answered calmly.

"Do you still hunt the elk in the northern countryside?" the wemic asked with a gleam in his eyes.

"I have not been with my clan for over a year now, but yes, we did hunt the elk," the barbarian answered.

"Did you kill them with your bare hands or do you use weapons?" Nefarius asked.

Serra tried her best to remain patient, but she couldn't help but feel sorry for Gnarl and Hildvar.

"I am only trying to get to know your people, Lady Serra," Nefarius stated in her thoughts.

"I only hope they do not upset you, my King," she thought back.

"Not at all," he thought back with mirth.

"I use a battleaxe," Hildvar replied, drawing the weapon from its sheath on his back.

Nefarius reached across the table and stood on all fours, feeling the weapons balance, swinging it this way and that.

"A well-built weapon," the wemic offered, handing the axe back and settling on his haunches again.

"Thank you," Hildvar replied, resheathing his axe.

"Now, down to business," he said, pointing at the map on the table. "My mate took the liberty of scrying Clandestine before our departure. The horde is still in Clandestine, but after viewing the occupants of the Manor, we are now aware that Truth's son is now in control of the horde."

Serra gasped unconsciously.

"That miserable piece of..." Gnarl muttered, slamming his fist on the table.

Hildvar looked over to her, but said nothing.

"She eavesdropped on them as they were talking, and we know they plan to march on the morrow," Nefarius continued, monitoring Serra's thoughts through the amulet.

Serra rubbed her temples and closed her eyes tightly. How could he do it? How could he go from one extreme to the other in so quick a time?

"Men do mysterious things when love is involved, Lady Serra," she heard Nefarius's voice in her head.

She did not reply, but looked up at Nefarius and nodded to him to continue.

"I suggest we meet them halfway instead of allowing them to march to Moondale. The elves are already in Sengar Valley coming this way, but I suggest you go to Flamarien and ask him to wait. If we leave first thing in the morning, we should meet them with our forces."

"Are you suggesting we attack this horde in the sacred valley?" Florianna asked incredulously.

Nefarius turned to regard the woman and nodded, "Yes, that is exactly what I am suggesting."

Florianna gritted her teeth and said nothing.

"Young elfling, do you not realize the horde would march through your valley to reach Moondale?" the wemic asked skeptically.

She sat for a moment and realized that his words made sense. Why would the horde move through the mountains, when the valley was flat and easily passable?

"You are right," she answered.

"There we will execute the Bloodmoon Brigade Vice I have been told about, while the mages prepare. The battle will rage, but we must keep them all in one area in order for our plans to succeed. The rest will be handled by the Feral Five."

He looked over each of them as he said, "I ask only when the warriors notice the horde standing perfectly still, that they step away immediately," Nefarius explained matter-of-factly. He said it with such a cool and calm demeanor that everyone at the table felt confident the plan would work, even against such odds.

Chapter Twenty-Three
The Calm Before the Storm

Jareth sat on a terrace bench with his feet propped up on the railing, staring down at his army. His father dozed next to him on a low bench, drool escaping the corners of his mouth with every snore.

He shook his head in disgust and thought about the day to come. They had decided to leave at first light. Jareth had already packed for the road. There wasn't a servant left in the manor, Spike had fled as well. So he had been the only one to clean his debilitated father and look after him, as well as control the horde outside.

Glancing at the wagon right before the front door, he thought of Gallant, who he had left in Moondale. He knew that the stable master of Bloodmoon Castle would take care of his beloved horse, but he felt guilty for not retrieving the steed in his hasty departure.

"I will get you back tomorrow, my friend," he muttered.

He glanced to his scrying bowl sitting on the bench next to him. After many attempts to scry for Serra that evening, he had finally given up. Apparently her elven lover had found a way to block his eye. He scowled at the thought of Dretho. The last he had seen of the two, the elf had been confessing his love to her and she had kissed him. Anger nearly overcame him as he stood and grabbed the railing with clenched fists.

"You'll die first, you mettlesome elf. Then I will kill Serra and Lorna as they beg for my mercy," he ranted, gripping the railing more tightly.

But oddly, his anger turned to guilt as he thought of Hildvar and Gnarl. They had been kind to him and had accepted him. He had even taken part in Olegareten with Hildvar to prove his honor.

Honor. He laughed. Jarmassad stirred for a moment at the noise, but went right back to his drooling snores.

Then a memory came to him in the blink of an eye. Serra lying, dying in his arms, "A man without honor is no man at all. You are honorable," she had said.

Tears came to his eyes at the memory, but he wiped them away quickly, scooped up his sleeping, debilitated father in his arms, and walked into the manor to feel sorry for himself.

Dretho returned Nefarius to his foyer and disappeared before his eyes. The wemic padded up the stairs and muttered, "*Derathliona Inbeena*," and walked to the ornate door to Dretho's bedchamber. He looked at the door closely and noticed a wemic carved in amidst the scene of creatures and runes.

He smiled at the gesture; though he was quite sure Dretho had never expected one of the Feral Five to look upon the door. Apparently they had made an impression upon him, as he had upon them, those years ago.

After opening the door, he noticed Kendrasha lazing on a few cushions, reading carefully.

"Did you see the carvings on the door?" he asked, walking up to lie beside her.

She did not look up from her book, but nodded. "I believe it is a very close likeness to Lucadesiad, don't you think?" she asked.

"Yes. What are you reading?" he asked, glancing at the open page.

She jerked the book away unconsciously.

"Ah ah ah, the elfling said I... could look in his library, not you," she said in mock defiance.

Nefarius rolled his eyes.

"How did the meeting go with the humans?" she asked, looking at the book again.

"This Serra Bloodmoon is definitely no stranger to adversity," he mused.

Kendrasha looked up to him with an odd expression. "What do you mean?"

"Her Captain is a dwarf. One of her Lieutenants is a barbarian from the north. And Flamarien's daughter was there as well," he explained.

Kendrasha's eyes widened at the mention of Florianna.

"Does she know it was you that killed her mother?" she asked.

Nefarius shook his head, "I don't believe so."

King Flamarien rode on horseback in front of his elven army with ten commanders and his personal attendants leading with torches. He was absentmindedly basking in the beauty of the Faeslarne Mountains in the moonlight when his horse reared. Luckily, Flamarien had learned to stay atop a horse in any situation, and was able to calm the beast quickly.

He looked over his horse's head to see Dretho standing before him with a nervous look upon his face in the firelight.

"What are you doing here, Dretholzar?" he asked sternly, dismounting to stand before the mage.

"My King, I need to speak with you in private," he requested, noticing the odd looks coming his way from Flamarien's commanders who had been riding at the King's side.

Flamarien held his hand up to halt the procession, took a torch from Gillianthesp, and walked ahead of Dretho to stand behind a small copse of trees. He stopped to regard the elven mage as he joined him, out of sight of the army.

"We are marching to Moondale, what has happened?" he asked fiercely.

"The horde will be leaving Clandestine in the morn. Jareth the Wanderer is leading them now. The Bloodmoon Brigade will be leaving at sunsrise to join you here, where we will make our stand," Dretho replied calmly.

"Here? In the valley?" the Elf King asked incredulously.

"Yes, we believe the horde will move through the valley on their way to Moondale. In order to amass the horde in one place, this would be the most beneficial battleground," he replied, ignoring Flamarien's penetrating stare.

"This is our home, Dretholzar. Do you not understand how such a mass will ruin what we've worked so hard these years to preserve?"

"My King, look around you. The valley is shielded on the eastern and western sides by mountains. The horde will come from the south right through the valley. We will be able to flank them as they march, encircle them fully, and execute the vice. After the horde is trapped together, the Feral Five will then use their mighty magic to teleport the whole of them to Hoff's Cove. The battle should not rage very long, we only need to keep them together in a tight circle," Dretho offered.

King Flamarien turned his back to him, deep in thought. His army had already traveled to the middle of the long valley. As he thought more about Dretho's words, they seemed to make sense. But he still had his doubts.

"We will remain here," he said, turning back to Dretho. "If your words are true, the Bloodmoon Brigade should join us just before the battle begins. I have discussed our plans fully for the vice with my army and they are prepared to stand beside them."

Dretho nodded and said, "There has been one alteration to our plan."

The King looked to him expectantly.

"After you see the horde stand perfectly still, you are to step away at a considerable distance. This is when the Feral Five will put the final plans in motion," he explained, relieved the King had not berated him for changing their plans so close to time for the battle.

"Agreed," Flamarien answered, turning to walk back to his army and his nervous horse. When he glanced back, Dretho was gone.

His other commanders looked to him in question, but did not say a word.

"We will stay here for the duration," he announced, remounting his steed.

The commanders nodded and did not question his orders.

"Camp out of sight, along the mountain bases with an equal number on either side, and be ready to move at a moments notice. We will setup the command camp in this very spot to await the arrival of the Moondale forces. Have the archers camp in the trees flanking the road. Pass the word that after the vice is executed, when you note the creatures standing perfectly still, move back, and stand down."

With a firm nod from their King, the commanders rode to their various groups to execute his orders.

Serra entered the water room to find Frelia pouring a bucket of steaming water into the bath basin.

"Good evening, Frelia," she said softly. She had not spoken to the woman since the announcement at dinner. She found herself extremely nervous speaking to her now.

Frelia glanced up at her tentatively.

"Missus," she greeted softly and then immediately turned back to the basin.

She took a deep breath and walked over to the maid, placing her hand on the woman's shoulder.

"Please, do not bear me ill will, Frelia," she said with tears in her eyes.

Frelia sniffled and stood straight.

"I don' bear ye ill will, missus. I jest wish ye woulda tol' me ye were goin' ter court the elf."

"I did not keep it from you on purpose. I realize it is sudden, but there are things people do not understand about Dretho," Serra said quickly, pulling the woman into a hug.

"I jest 'ope he ain' mean ter ye," the maid sobbed.

Serra pushed her back to arms length and stooped a little to look at her face to face.

"He is not what people say, Frelia. He has an undeserving reputation. When his servant was killed, do you know what he did?" she asked, wiping the tears from her eyes.

"No, missus."

"He came here and cried on my shoulder because he had no one else in the world that understood him."

Frelia looked at her in disbelief.

"That elf cried?" she asked, wiping her nose with her apron.

Serra nodded.

"Well, I'll be," the maid muttered with a chuckle.

"Do you think he would have done such a thing if he were the unfeeling tyrant everyone claims him to be?" Serra asked with a smile.

"No, yer right, missus. I shou' tell him I'm sorry fer the way I been actin'," Frelia answered with a guilty expression.

"I'm sure he would like that very much," she admitted, smiling at the maid.

"Get yer bath and I'll go talk ter him."

Frelia left the room without another word.

Serra thought of contacting Dretho through the amulet to warn him, but then decided against it. This was something only Frelia and Dretho could work out.

Spike Forsiad sat in a chair in the nearly deserted Bloodmoon Brigade common room drinking a mug of honey mead.

Castille Thornberry paced the floor in a huff. He wanted to be outside preparing to leave in the morning with the other brigade, not babysitting this human.

"Castille, I assure you that I will not leave the barracks if you wish to help," he offered, drawing a snort from the surly dwarf who merely continued his pacing.

"Ye'll be sittin' righ' there til I sa' otherwi'," Castille mused, walking up to a small window.

The brigade was hard at work lining up wagons and war engines with the main portcullis. He glanced at the many tents around the grounds, noting the horrified expressions of the people of Moondale. Most of them were relieved that the battle would not reach their city, but the rest were scared that nearly the entire Bloodmoon Brigade would be leaving the next morning.

He turned to the young human and grunted, "Come on, bo', we goin' ter 'elp," he muttered gruffly.

Spike smiled and jumped from his seat, but was stopped by Castille's pointed finger.

"If ye step outer me sigh' for one minut', I'll hang ye up by yer toes and beat ye with a cat-o-nine-tails," the dwarf warned.

Spike gulped, but nodded his agreement.

They walked out of the barracks door and moved to a wagon being loaded with water barrels.

"Howlstinger, ye keep an eye on this 'ere bo' wi' me. If 'e moves outer sight, kill 'im," Castille informed a female dwarf as he grabbed a barrel and handed it to Spike.

She smiled and scratched her beard.

"I'll be happy to."

Dretho sat in the study with his feet propped up on the long couch. He sipped his glass of wine and mused over the last few weeks. If a month before he had envisioned his current situation, he would have thought himself insane.

Who would have thought that the reclusive elf would now be betrothed to the most beautiful lady in the land? Who would have thought that the Feral Five would be out in the world once again? And lastly, who would've thought that the book of Gyndless the Almighty would be put to use once again?

He heard a soft rapping at the door and answered, "You may enter."

Frelia tentatively walked into the room and shut the door behind her.

Dretho sat upright on the couch. "May I help you?" he asked curiously.

Frelia looked at the man for a long moment before saying anything. She noticed that the perpetual scowl was gone from his face and though he was sitting upright, he seemed relaxed.

"May I speak candidly with ye, Master Dretho?" she asked hesitantly.

The elf nodded and gestured toward the seat beside him.

She sat down tentatively and looked into his eyes.

"I know ye have a bad repute, but I jest wanted ye ter know I feel ye'll be kind ter the missus," she said, watching him closely.

Dretho smiled and nodded.

Frelia grinned back at him, glad that his scowl had not returned.

"I think yer jest misunderstoo' like most o' us. And I'm sorry if ye ever thought I didn' like ye," she admitted.

"I suppose I could be viewed as a vile man fairly easily. But I thank you for your kind words, Frelia."

The maid's eyes widened, she had not known he had bothered to learn her name.

"I heared yer ter march in the morn. Take care o' the missus fer me?" she asked emotionally.

Dretho nodded.

"I will guard her with my very life."

"Stonewall, get that catapult bucket emptied before ye lower it down, ye idiot," Gnarl yelled from the eastern wall.

Stonewall had been heaving on the rope with the other men, his red hair matted to his forehead with sweat, trying futilely to lift it with the five-hundred pound boulder in place.

Gnarl shook his head and sighed while he walked over to Florianna who was standing with Hildvar on the parapet.

"Well, that'll be the last o' the war engines.. Now we just got ter get the wagons loaded and we'll be ready ter leave in the morn and Howlstinger is in charge o' that," Gnarl said, pointing to a blonde dwarven female loading water barrels into a wagon with Castille. The dwarf smiled when he noticed Spike lending a hand as well.

"Looks like that boy's finally doing some good," he muttered.

Hildvar smiled as he saw Spike tirelessly loading the wagon.

"I believe his intentions are good. He has never led me to believe otherwise," the barbarian replied.

But Gnarl wasn't listening. He sighed and then said, "I sure hope this Nefarius knows what he's doin'."

"Let us go to Bloodmoon's Brew and have a good drink before we turn in," Hildvar offered, trying to relax the obviously nervous dwarf.

"Best idea ye had all day," Gnarl said, punching the barbarian in his right arm.

Gnarl favored his sore hand as they made their way down the stairs and out the main portcullis to the deserted city of Moondale. They hoped Waylin hadn't locked the tavern door when he had taken shelter behind the castle walls.

After her bath, Serra sought Dretho in the study, but found it empty. She walked down the hall to his new quarters and knocked on the door. There was no answer.

She envisioned his face and thought, "Where are you, my love?"

"I am in the courtyard," he thought back.

Serra walked down the stairs and out the double-doors to find him watching the Bloodmoon Brigade packing their supplies.

She took his arm and he turned to her and smiled.

"Frelia came to see me."

"I know," she admitted slyly.

"She seems to like me now. What did you say to her?" he asked.

"I told her of that day in the water room," she replied softly.

He looked at her with wide eyes, but relaxed almost immediately.

"So now she thinks I am soft?" he asked with a laugh.

"Oh no, never that."

They laughed together and continued to watch the brigade until well after midnight.

They ascended the stairs together and paused at the landing. Their rooms were on opposite ends of the corridor.

Serra knew she should sleep alone this night, despite her wishes otherwise. Dretho thought the same.

"I will see you in the morning," he said, kissing her softly on her lips.

She was relieved that he had made the decision and she walked to her room.

Chapter Twenty-Four
The Battle

As Halos and Belos crested the horizon, Jareth stood next to a wagon in front of Fortin Manor. His father was sitting comfortably on a bed of blankets in the back, with their provisions.

Jareth looked down to the book of Gyndless the Almighty in his hands, feeling its never-ending pull. He opened it and sighed deeply before reading the runes on the page.

"*Wasinasticashian estinar bushastica tomen zuchaulos forminsatha*," he chanted and the crimson shield over the horde pulsed in response, renewing its connection to the sorcerer.

He thought of Serra as he turned to the next page of runes. Did he really want to do this? Had she really betrayed him as he had thought all this time? Had he not merely pushed her away with his actions?

The young sorcerer took a knife from a pocket of his black robes. Holding the knife in his right hand and holding the book with his left, he jabbed the point into his left wrist and watched as his life-blood fell upon the page.

It was too late now.

"*Wasinasticashian estinar giefenstata tomen ferrina vehereab Moondale,*" he chanted, watching his blood sink into the page with every word. After he muttered Moondale, a large, fiery globe rose from the book. Jareth watched as it lifted into the sky. He could see swirls of his blood in its depths and could not bear to watch any longer.

Every creature of the monstrous army looked up at the globe and watched as it began slowly traveling north, transfixed by its fiery dominance. The horde began their trek anew, walking slowly toward Sengar Valley, the crimson shroud following them with every step.

The Bloodmoon Brigade left the castle at the same time. Serra Bloodmoon, atop Gypsy, rode in front with Gnarl, Hildvar, and Florianna.

The beginning procession was slow, but after they were on the road to Sengar Valley they gained speed, each wagon falling in behind the next. The war engines took up the rear, as Serra was still unsure if they would be needed. If the Bloodmoon Brigade Vice worked according to plan, it would be too dangerous to fire into the mix, as the warriors on the opposite side of the circle would be too easy to hit accidentally.

"Where's the elf, me Lady?" Gnarl asked, reigning his pony to move closer to Serra.

"He's with the Feral Five awaiting our word and discussing final preparations of their magical assault," she replied. She looked down at her new armor and thought of Dretho. She wished that he could have accompanied her on the road, but she knew he had things he had to do.

Gnarl nodded, "Where they been hidin' all these years?"

Serra looked at the dwarf and shook her head, "I'm sorry, Gnarl, I can't tell you that. I have sworn to keep it a secret."

Gnarl snorted, "Ye sure they're trustworthy?"

"Yes, without a doubt," she replied with a nod.

"I 'spect we'll arrive in the valley before sunsdown," he announced, changing the subject,

"Good, the sooner this is over with the better," she replied.

A knot had formed in the pit of her stomach that morning and had failed to dislodge itself. She had seen many battles in her time, but none such as she expected to encounter today. Never before had a Bloodmoon battle been so dependent upon magic.

She reached up to the amulet on her chest and thought of Dretho again.

"Try not to worry, Serra. We have planned as much as we can without knowing what Jareth plans to do," she heard his voice in her thoughts. Her worries had been broadcasted to him and she figured the Feral Five as well, without her realizing it.

She grimaced at the thought of Jareth.

"I can't believe he has turned so quickly. He went from one extreme to the next in just a few days time. I was a fool to trust him to begin with," she thought bitterly.

"I wish there was something that I could say to ease your frustration, my love," he thought back after a few moments of silence.

"Would you like for me to enter his mind, Lady Serra?" Vlasisith asked, intruding on their mental conversation.

Serra mused for a moment and then thought, "Yes. Use your abilities to see if you can divulge any information of his plans."

"I would be honored," he replied.

The foyer was dark, despite the bright day. Vlasisith sat on the wooden floor with a calculating smile displayed across his face. He fixed his gaze on the banister of the great staircase and focused his thoughts.

He sought out the horde. He was not surprised to see that they were already marching toward the valley. But he was surprised to find that the only thought on their feeble minds was *Follow the orb.*

Searching across the expanse of the army, he finally found a more thinking creature. Jarmassad Truth had been napping in the back of the wagon, but sat upright when he felt the intrusion of his thoughts. Vlasisith recoiled immediately though, and after a few minutes the sorcerer returned to his nap.

Vlasisith smiled, knowing he was close to the other. But he would have to be more careful this time.

The wemic focused just outside of Jareth's consciousness.

The sorcerer cursed to himself as the pitiful giant pulled the wagon with a horse harness over its head. All the horses had fled, and there was not one to be found in the entire city, not even a mule or a pony. He had thrown the harness over the giant before conjuring the leader globe, knowing the creature would follow it no matter what he was hooked to.

Vlasisith ever so carefully flashed an image of Serra into the man's mind, but only for a second. He was rewarded immediately as Jareth began regretting being so harsh to her. It was obvious that he still loved the Lady of Moondale.

He searched his mind for a while, trying to pull his thoughts back to the road ahead, but the sorcerer would not quit thinking of Serra.

The wemic sighed in frustration and pulled his thoughts back to the tower and then to Serra.

"Lady Serra, he regrets what he is doing, but I could not learn any of his plans," he thought to her.

"He regrets it? Then why is he doing this?" she thought back, growing frustrated.

"I know not. I could not draw his thoughts in that direction. He was... preoccupied," Vlasisith answered.

"The elves are prepared for the vice and our scouts have reported dust clouds from the north and the crimson glow from the horde to the south," Darnesian Espanderline reported to King Flamarien that afternoon.

The Elf King sighed, "I only hope that the Bloodmoon Brigade will arrive first."

The Bloodmoon Brigade rode up to the elves just before the horde crested the hill.

Serra Bloodmoon and her commanders rode to the elven command camp while the rest of the brigade split into a V and marched to each side of the valley to hide in the trees with the elves as planned.

"Flamarien," Serra nodded in greeting to the Elf King.

"I hope this works, Lady Serra," he replied, looking uncertainly at the crimson shroud that was edging its way closer.

"Form the top," Serra said to Gnarl.

The dwarf took a horn from his belt and blew one short burst. The warriors standing on the northernmost sides of the valley folded in to form a solid, living wall, five deep, blocking the pass in front of the commanding group.

"They are close," Serra thought through the amulet.

In moments, Dretho and the Feral Five were standing by her side. Serra was amazed that the warriors who noticed did not flee at the sight. They only looked to each other in surprise and stood their ground, contributing even more to their disciplined training.

As the first monsters came over the hill, the crimson light turned the grass a sickly yellow, making it appear that the life was being drained from it.

The mob filed into the valley, oblivious to the army at their sides, and headed straight for the group standing at the end of the pass. The red globe of light leading the creatures looked very familiar to Serra, though she could not place where she had seen it before.

The noise was amazing, the creatures did not snarl or shout, but just the sound of their stomping feet was amplified many times as it reverberated off the mountains. She even noted some of the elves plugging their sensitive ears with small pieces of cloth.

Vlasisith noted the red globe too and knew at once that this was the orb that dominated their minds. He smiled and nearly laughed at the plainness of this feeble human's domination.

Jareth let go of his reins, allowing the behemoth to walk with the rest of his army with the harness still around its thick neck. He grinned as he noted the solid line blocking the valley from Moondale. Did they actually think so few would stop his massive army?

The Lady of Moondale saw the wagon break from the army and grinned as the horde marched on without it. She waited until they were separated by at least thirty yards and yelled, "Form the bottom!"

Gnarl blew four short bursts from his horn and the warriors hidden at the southernmost end of the valley abandoned their hiding places and formed another solid line across the valley, blocking Jareth's wagon from his army.

He cursed and disenchanted the fiery globe with a thought.

He grabbed the book of Gyndless the Almighty and chanted the last page of runes as quickly as he could. "*Wasinasticashian estinar accacio tomen cominaloda oppugnozee!*"

At once, the crimson shroud dissipated and the horde ran toward the northern line. Gnarl gritted his teeth as the mob advanced, but was pleased to see that none of the Brigade or elves moved an inch.

The mob clashed with the warriors like a thunderous wave breaking onto the sand. Giants stumbled on goblins and orcs alike, trying to get to their enemies to rip them apart.

But the line held. The warriors put their blades to deadly use, dispatching the first wave of creatures in minutes. But more took their place in the blink of an eye.

Serra tried to yell over the noise, but no one could hear anything but the sounds of battle.

Thankfully, Gnarl had been watching her closely and blew his horn once more in two long bursts. The warriors that had been hiding along the mountain bases, ran from their shelters, and clashed with the horde from either side.

Elven archers in the trees began their barrage, picking goblins off one by one, as Flamarien had ordered them to do days before. After a few minutes of the pelting, the little creatures realized they had been targeted and ran between giant legs as they waited patiently for their comrades to reach a line of enemies.

The majority of the monsters fought with their bare hands, as they had long ago dropped their weapons during their trek to Clandestine. They fell by the score on all sides, but to their credit many warriors were lost as well.

The warriors pushed and had to step over their fallen friends, knowing they must hold the line at all costs.

Jareth gnashed his teeth in rage as he saw his monstrous army falling back from the pitiful circle of warriors. "This should make things interesting," he said aloud, reaching to his belt pouch.

"*Insenata Enflamaray Forcitha,*" he chanted and an enormous fireball emitted from his outstretched hand, heading straight for the front line.

Kendrasha saw the danger immediately and raised her hands into the air, "*Insenata Aqualiar Forcitha!*" she yelled and a long line of water flew from her hands to pool in mid-air, right in line with the flaming orb. The elements collided with a deafening hiss and burning mist fell like rain to the horde below to add new shrieks of pain to the already deafening sounds of battle.

"We must get rid of that fool now!" she bellowed over the noise. "*Insenata Wistilia Forcita,*" she muttered. Her lion paws left the ground and her body rose into the air twenty feet.

"Do not!" she heard Nefarius scream into her mind. "You must save your strength for the task ahead. Serra Bloodmoon is to kill the sorcerer, not you."

Kendrasha gritted her teeth and lowered back to the ground beside him. Though she generally rebelled against Nefarius, she knew this was not the time or the place. She also knew he was right.

"Take your positions," Nefarius ordered through the amulets and breastplates of the Feral Five.

Vlasisith bounded away from the command camp, climbing the mountainside to get a better vantage point. Using his lion claws, he dug in on a steep slope and turned to see the battle in full. He was surprised to see the plan working so well. The warriors were pushing the mob into a tight vice as they had promised they would, and their lines were holding.

Elven and human clerics scrambled behind the seething, living circle, dispatching fallen creatures and rallying the injured warriors, taking them on makeshift stretchers to the safe end of the valley.

He saw Nefarius and Sashaleona moving back away from the battle, just north of the command camp.

Dretho walked over to Serra and squeezed her hand, drawing her attention away from the battle. She looked at him with fear, but smiled none-the-less.

"I love you," he said so softly that she did not hear, but his expression explained it all.

"I love you too," she replied, leaning down to kiss him for luck.

With that, he followed Kendrasha and Lucadesiad, to climb the mountainside opposite of where Vlasisith was perched. They found a small ridge and stood there watching the battle and waiting for the right time.

Serra turned to Gnarl and motioned for him to join her.

"Me Lady?" he asked loudly over the horrendous noise of the battle.

"I must make my way now! Remember, you must step away when the monsters stop moving!" she responded.

Gnarl visibly gulped and fear flashed in his eyes for her safety.

"Are ye sure ye got ter do this alone?" he asked, grabbing her elbow and giving it a firm squeeze.

Serra nodded.

"You are in charge now. If anything happens to me, take care of Lorna," she said, fighting to keep a determined look upon her face.

Gnarl nodded and Serra kicked Gypsy into a run.

Dretho watched as his love rode around the mountain base just below him, unhindered as the horde was continuously being pushed toward the center of the valley. His heart ached to go to her, to help her, but he knew what he must do.

"She will be fine," Lucadesiad offered, placing his large hand on the elf's shoulder.

Dretho nodded and watched as she made her way toward the end of the valley, where Jareth waited.

Horace Hangoon reached the front line and jumped clear over four elves to run up to a barbarian on horseback. He reached down to the ground and picked up a large rock, raising it high over his head, ready to throw.

Hildvar saw the giant coming and raised his battle-axe over his head. He let fly just as the giant threw his rock. The battle-axe buried itself through the giant's forehead and split his head in two just as the large rock glanced off Hildvar's temple, throwing him from his horse. Gnarl looked down in surprise and saw the barbarian lying motionless on the ground.

Luckily, the giant was the only monster that broke through the Bloodmoon Brigade Vice and after only half an hour, the mob was pushed into a tight circle. The creatures shifted from side to side, trying to gain some ground to go at the enemy. But the warriors pushed in at their own mortal peril, unwilling to give them any room. In the moments before Vlasisith began his mind magic, eighty-three warriors lost their lives.

The wemic closed his eyes tightly and touched the mind of every creature on the field, even the dying.

"Stop your fighting and be still," he imparted to them, using every ounce of his concentration to send his message to so many.

The fighting stopped. The creatures stood motionless and it took a few seconds for the warriors of the vice to realize that the horde they had been fighting were not fighting back.

Each warrior stepped back ten paces and were amazed to see that the horde did not follow. They merely stood mesmerized, staring into nothingness.

Lucadesiad turned to Kendrasha and Dretho and took a small vial from his saddlebags draped over his lion back. He uncorked the vial and poured half the clear liquid into his hand.

"*Eloakisaaaa Fetarakenzisoooo Hisstanlipana Pazzitooo,*" he prayed and flicked his fingers so that the liquid sprinkled over Kendrasha's face. He said the same prayer again, sprinkling Dretho this time.

Dretho felt a calming confidence come over him at once. Kendrasha actually smiled at him and nodded.

The wemic cleric pulled two larger vials out of his saddlebag and gave one to each of them.

They drank without hesitation and felt their minds become perfectly clear. As if they had gained all the knowledge there was to know, and that they could apply it at a moments notice.

Jareth noticed the lack of noise immediately and stood on the seat of his wagon to overlook his massive army.

"What the bloody hell has happened!" Jarmassad Truth screamed, stumbling out of the back of the wagon to fall to the ground.

The young sorcerer turned to see his father trying futilely to stand on his one good leg.

"Why aren't they fighting, you whelp?" the old man shouted when he didn't answer.

"I don't know, you old bastard," Jareth shouted back, jumping from the wagon.

"This is your fault, you let them go! You always were a worthless piece of dung! You can't even maintain a spell once it is cast!"

He snarled at his father struggling on the ground. His blue eyes were flooded with anger. He raised his hand and pointed a finger at him. "Watch your words, old man. This is not even my fight!"

"You should watch your words, fool. I brought you into this world, and by Justar, I can take you out. Help me!" he shouted. "If you want something done right, you have to do it yourself. You're still in love with that red-headed bitch and it's clouding your mind!"

Jareth's anger mounted to rage and he spat on the man and walked away.

"You better help me or I'll..."

"You'll what?" Jareth shouted, walking back over. "You'll bite my heals? You can't even stand on your own! How would you like it if I left you out here for the army's next meal?"

Jarmassad reached into the pockets of his robes and pulled out a golden wand topped with a blue jewel and pointed it at his son.

"I knew you never would amount to anything, I should have killed you when I killed your blasted mother!" he yelled.

Jareth reached into his pocket and pulled out his levitation dagger and before he could think about what he was doing, he walked over to his father, grabbed the hair on top of his head, and slit his throat from ear to ear.

"No, but I'm very proficient with a blade," he hissed right before the light went out of his father's eyes.

Sashaleona took up her lute and nodded to Nefarius who raised his human hands toward the monstrous army. An image of Sashaleona, ten times as large as the wemic herself, appeared right over the center of the mesmerized horde.

She strummed her lute and began to sing.

For those of you who wish to see,
All the glory that life can be,
Drop your arms and free your foes,
For I can show what your future holds.

Dretho grabbed Kendrasha's hand and chanted, "*Espin Sanctus Tormenus Zee.*"

Both mages were bathed immediately in a blue aura.

Kendrasha closed her cat-like eyes as Dretho felt his energy seep through his hand into her own.

"*Seenafasiad Esparanto Incentra Waveem,*" she chanted.

Dretho nearly fainted as their energy pulsed from their bodies and a silvery, shimmering portal appeared in front of the entranced horde, large enough for a giant to walk easily through.

Free your will from this mortal man,
Reach to me and take my hand,
Riches and land will be yours,
If you only step through the shimmering door.

All that I say to you is true,
Free your will and step through.

Vlasisith bound down the mountainside and ran toward the portal, disappearing into its depths. Nefarius and Sashaleona began walking slowly toward the portal from the opposite side. Sashaleona continued to strum her lute and sing the same three verses over and over while Nefarius projected her image over the horde.

Slowly, the monsters began to walk as Sashaleona's image moved to the portal and loomed just above it. The first creature passed through as she began her song anew.

For those of you who wish to see,
All the glory that life can be,
Drop your arms and free your foes,
For I can show what your future holds.

Free your will from this mortal man,
Reach to me and take my hand,
Riches and land will be yours,
If you only step through the shimmering door.

All that I say to you is true,
Free your will and step through.

Jareth wiped the blood from his dagger on his father's black robe. He looked up to the horde and noticed the wemic bard.

"Who is that?" he asked to no one in particular.

To his surprise, he received an answer.

"That, is Sashaleona."

He knew that voice. His heart skipped a beat when he turned to see Serra standing behind him, her scimitar pointed at his back. Her elven chain mail and mithril plate glittered in the dwindling sunslight and her green eyes bore into his soul with their steely gaze.

"What are you doing here, Serra?" he asked, trying his best to watch her movements.

"You are a treacherous dog, Jareth Truth. You know why I am here," she replied, not lowering her sword an inch.

Jareth looked to the ground and shook his head, pulling another dagger out of his pocket with the motion.

"I loved you and you betrayed me. You forced me to do these things," he replied softly.

Serra hissed and bellowed, "Speak not to me of love, you do not know what love is and you never have. I have not forced you to do anything. I have never asked anything of you. I have given you food and shelter and this is how you repay me. You send a monstrous horde to my back door so that you may continue your father's dream of wiping my family from Remus!"

He gestured toward his father's corpse and said, "As you can see, my father is no longer a part of the equation. I killed him for you!"

"You did no such thing! I know it was you who led the horde here!"

Jareth's face turned from a look of misery to a glower. "I suppose your elven lover told you that so that you would love him instead," he replied condescendingly.

Serra laughed. "Do you think after all that we've been through that I would believe a word that comes from your wicked mouth? I was wrong to trust you and I learn from my mistakes."

"You said you cared about me. You said I was honorable. What has happened to that? Do you think that I would come here to attack you? It was my father! I have only now had the opportunity to kill him and release the horde!" he yelled back, advancing a step, keeping his extra dagger hidden behind his back.

"You are a pitiful excuse for a man, Jareth. You are a liar! I should have listened to Hildvar. He tried to persuade me to send you away. I offered you a home and your pitiful jealousy ruined that!" she hissed back.

He advanced another step, gripping his dagger hilt more tightly.

"If you will not love me, then you will love no one!" he yelled, throwing the dagger toward her chest.

Serra had been expecting this all along. She parried the dagger with her sword and jumped out of the way. The dagger fell away harmlessly to some bushes to the side. She advanced on the sorcerer, ready to run him through, but before she could reach him, he rose in the air.

"You can not kill what you can not hit," he said with mirth.

Dretho gasped from the exertion of holding the portal open. Kendrasha's hands were sweating, but she held on tightly, not daring to break the power share.

Half the horde had filtered into the portal now.

Lucadesiad watched the mages closely and drew another vial from his saddlebag. He splashed more liquid into their faces after another prayer and the strain lessened a bit, but not much.

Kendrasha squeezed her eyes tightly. She had never before attempted a spell so powerful. She silently thanked Lucadesiad for his help. She knew without him, she and Dretho would have died from the exertion of opening the portal, not to mention maintaining the constant teleporting of the creatures to the banks of Hoff's Cove.

Gnarl knelt over Hildvar as Bergeron made his way through the crowd to reach them. The barbarian was not breathing and the left side of his skull was visibly sunken in. Bergeron gasped when he saw the fatal wound.

"Can ye help him?" Gnarl asked, trying to remain hopeful.

The bald cleric looked to him with agony etched his face and replied, "I can try."

Nefarius maintained his illusion until the last of the monsters had walked through the portal. He then disenchanted it and waited with Sashaleona at the entrance.

Kendrasha steeled her breath and muttered, "*Arcanus Traveelus pentagii.*"

Just before four of the Feral Five and Dretho disappeared, the elf looked down the valley and saw Serra standing off against Jareth. The last image he saw was the sorcerer in the rigors of spell casting.

Chapter Twenty-Five
Sunsdown

Vlasisith trembled with the strain of keeping all the creatures in a prone position on the island. Controlling them in the valley had not been hard, but after he had jumped into the portal, the distance had increased the pressure. As each creature had made its way through the silver pool, he had had to renew his hold again and again.

Finally, the creatures stopped pouring through and he was able to stabilize his dominance. He felt the presence of the other wemics and the elven mage, but did not dare look up for fear of losing his control.

Lucadesiad bounded over to the psionisist who was crouching in front of an unusually, ugly orc, with his human hands pressing hard against his temples with his eyes tightly closed. The cleric reached into his saddlebag once more and drew out the last of the small vials and splashed its entire contents into the wemic's face and prayed over him for a full minute.

Kendrasha and Dretho sat side by side in the sand, gasping to catch their breath. The spell had taken all Dretho had to give and the release of the pressure made him dizzy. Kendrasha sat with her eyes closed, sweat pouring down her face.

Nefarius walked over to the mages and put his hands on their shoulders. "It is almost over, now we simply have to send the horde home. I do not think that Vlasisith will be able to hold on for much longer. Gather your strength, but be quick," the King said with a concerned expression.

Dretho looked to Vlasisith and took a deep breath. Kendrasha took his hand and he chanted, "*Espin Sanctus Tormenus Zee.*" Once again his energy was transferred to Kendrasha, wrapping them both in a blue aura.

Kendrasha steeled her gaze at the front lines of monsters.

"We should kill them," she muttered, standing to all fours.

Dretho's eyes widened at her proclamation, but he concentrated to keep the magical connection.

Nefarius turned to her and snarled.

"I'm sure that was what the humans said about us before nearly driving us to extinction. Send them home, now!" There was no compromise in his voice and no gentleness in his stare.

Kendrasha gritted her teeth and nodded.

"Gusshaaaleee Eoireitumussss Dominuss Nullis Secoinimicusss."

After she chanted, the creatures began flocking to the banks, paying no mind to their foes. They swam into the great Neverlear River, on their way back to their homes.

Serra looked up at the levitating sorcerer and pointed her scimitar as he began spell casting.

"You should fear our fire and fury,
For know it will seal your doom,
We are the red and mighty,
Fear the wrath of the Bloodmoon's!"

Jareth's eyes widened as the scimitar zoomed toward his head. He ducked and turned a complete somersault in mid-air and his eyes widened as he saw the scimitar turn in the distance and make another run aimed directly for him.

While Jareth had his attention elsewhere, she reached down to her belt and retrieved a dagger.

She watched as the sorcerer dodged another attack and threw the dagger when he stopped to see where the sword had gone. It sunk deep into his thigh, he cried out, and fell from the air.

As soon as he hit the ground, she jumped on his back and willed her sword back into its sheath.

"You give me no choice in this. You have brought about your own demise. You will pay for the suffering of my people with your life," she said, reaching for another dagger.

Jareth gasped as she pressed her armored knee into the small of his back.

"It is you who will pay!" he yelled as he put all his energy into the levitation jewel of the dagger still clutched in his hand.

They soared into the air and Serra tumbled to the ground, twisting her ankle in the process.

The sorcerer grinned evilly at her and Serra could not help but see his father's likeness in the gaze.

He raised his hands to cast a spell and Serra closed her eyes, accepting her fate.

Before Jareth could utter a word, he was propelled back ten feet in the air, an arrow protruding from his chest, right through his heart.

Serra opened her eyes and regarded the sorcerer curiously and then turned to see the archer.

King Flamarien crouched by a bush a few feet away. Neither of the humans had noticed his approach.

Jareth fell to the ground again and tried futilely to pull out the arrow.

She ran over to him and pressed a dagger to his throat.

"I loved you," he whispered in agony, and then ever so softly he chanted, *"Arcanus traveelus."*

Serra's eyes widened and she thrust the dagger quickly toward his throat, but he disappeared before the blade could penetrate his skin.

The dagger fell to the ground as Serra began trembling. She covered her face with her hands and began to sob.

She turned when a warm hand squeezed her shoulder.

"You did well," Flamarien said with a slight smile.

As the suns descended the horizon, people scrambled across the battlefield collecting the injured and dispatching the dying monsters. The Feral Five and Dretho returned just as they lit the funeral pyre for the dead monsters in the center of the valley.

Dretho ran to the command camp, distraught that he did not see Serra anywhere on the field. He was about to collapse with fear when he saw Gnarl exiting a makeshift tent. He ran toward the dwarf, but stopped short when he noticed the crestfallen look on his face. Dretho found it difficult to breathe, but found the strength to walk up to the dwarf.

Gnarl was staring blankly at his feet, looking much older than he should. He looked up at the elf and gave a half-hearted nod in greeting.

"Is she dead?" Dretho asked in a voice cracking with emotion. He was relieved when the dwarf shook his head. Gnarl pointed to the entrance flap of the tent and merely walked away.

He walked slowly over to the tent and felt a tear slide from his right golden eye at the sight before him. Serra crouched on the floor next to a large body covered with a blanket. Her dusty face was streaked with tears and she visibly shook with every breath.

She looked up when Dretho sat down beside her. Her emerald eyes were bloodshot and blank.

"They couldn't save him," she said in a whisper. "Gnarl saw a giant throw a boulder right to the side of his head. There was too much damage."

Dretho looked down to the silhouette of Hildvar under the blanket. The fabric lying across the barbarian's face was soaked with blood.

He put his arm around Serra's shoulders and pulled her close, allowing her the comfort and quiet he knew she needed.

Nefarius, Sashaleona, and Kendrasha began helping carry the dead on their lion backs, hauling two at a time. Many people looked at them curiously, but they knew that these creatures had been the primary reason the battle had been won so fast.

Florianna Flamarien passed by Nefarius on his way to gather more bodies and stopped him with an upraised hand.

"Can I help you, Princess?" he asked, stopping to sit on his haunches before her.

"I must speak with you here and now, before I change my mind," she said, crossing her arms over her chest.

Nefarius merely stared at her in expectation.

"Your people killed my mother. In elven custom that would mean that I should kill the lot of you to sate her death," she began, standing tall and proud, though she was over two feet shorter than the large Wemic King.

Nefarius continued to stare and said nothing.

"However, because of your actions this day, I can not bring myself to do any such thing. And I would like to give you my thanks for your help."

The Wemic King grinned and nodded.

"Your mother was a good warrior, but in wemic custom when a challenge is issued, you must fight or die trying to protect your position in the pride as well as protect your honor. I did not enjoy killing your mother in the least, but it was not something that could have been avoided due to her challenge of my abilities. I hope that some day you will understand that."

Florianna pushed a strand of blonde hair from her eyes and nodded.

"I understand honor, Nefarius. But know this. If you are to live in Dretholzar's tower, you must understand that you are in elven territory and the rules are different here. Sometimes people have to change to live for the better," she said simply.

Nefarius nodded, "Indeed."

Vlasisith padded over to where Lucadesiad was speaking with a bald human man. He thought it odd that the man was not fearful, but actually speaking comfortably in the firelight with the young wemic.

"I did everything I could, his brain was damaged and he was dead when he hit the ground. Lady Serra is in the tent with him now."

Lucadesiad placed a large human hand on the man's shoulder and nodded, "I will see if there is anything I can do."

Vlasisith looked curiously at Lucadesiad as he walked toward the tent, but the wemic cleric kept going, not providing any explanation.

The bald man looked up to the psionisist and smiled.

"I am Bergearon, High Cleric of Bloodmoon Castle," the man said, offering his hand.

Vlasisith thought the custom odd, but had seen a hand shake many times in the years before they had gone into hiding. He offered his hand and gave the man a firm shake, nearly knocking him off his feet.

"Where is Lucadesiad going?" he asked, looking back toward the tent.

Bergearon looked after the wemic cleric with reverence, "To work a miracle, I hope."

After the elves guarding the Clandestinian refugees received word that the battle was won, they all packed up their gear and made their way to the battle site. As they crested the hill and saw the carnage and the high funeral pyre, some trembled in fear and others felt relieved that their bodies weren't a part of it.

Jasin Roostercrowe sought out King Flamarien as soon as Angora and Baine were settled at the base of the mountain under an ash tree. Finding the elf turned into a difficult task, as all elves looked alike to him, especially in the low light, and Flamarien dressed the same as the rest.

The tents on the north end of the valley drew his attention and he spotted Flamarien speaking to a tall, redheaded, young woman. He weaved his way through the mass of warriors clearing the battlefield of monsters and tossing them on the fire and stepped up to the elf and woman.

They turned to regard him and the Elf King grinned.

"How did you fare, Roostercrowe?" he asked with a nod of greeting.

"We fared fine indeed thanks to you and Lady Bloodmoon. I would like to thank her myself one day for sending your elves to protect us."

The elf turned to regard the young woman and smiled even wider.

"Lady Serra Bloodmoon, I give to you Jasin Roostercrowe, last remaining Councilman of Clandestine," the Elven King announced.

Jasin's eyes widened as he looked at this young woman before him.

"I am glad your people are safe, Councilman Roostercrowe," she said solemnly.

"We're here to offer our help, Lady Bloodmoon. Anything we can do, just ask," he said. He knew that the sadness on her features was for the warriors lost in battle. Offering to help was the least he could do when she had went out of her way to provide safety to his townsfolk.

"That would be greatly appreciated, speak with Captain Gnarl Knottytrunk. He was near the fire when last I saw him, with Dretho the Mage. I'm sure they'll need strong backs to load the injured and dead onto wagons to take back to Moondale," she said, gesturing to the fire.

Jasin nodded and turned to go gather as many as he could to help.

"I don't believe you will ever get used to the reaction people have at the discovery that you are the leader of Moondale," Flamarien offered, watching the man go.

"I don't believe I will ever get used to being the leader of Moondale. I have failed today."

"You have not failed. I know you feel like that now, but had you and Dretholzar not ventured to gather the Feral Five, many more lives would have been lost this day. I have long had a grudge against Nefarius for the death of my wife those years ago, but I realize now that it was her actions that were foolhardy, not his. Jareth's wound was a mortal one, of this I assure you. And if he does live, he will never be able to show his face again. We will make sure of that."

"Let us go gather Jarmassad Truth's body. So that we may give it a proper burial on top of the funeral pyre," Flamarien said, offering her his arm.

She took his arm and they walked slowly to the wagon. No one else had bothered with it considering how many it was taking to clear the field. As they walked toward the sorcerer, she noticed a book lying next to where she had last seen Jareth's face.

She squeezed Flamarien's arm at the sight and he turned to regard what had caused the reaction.

"It's the book of Gyndless the Almighty," he gasped, pushing Serra behind him as if the book would attack.

She pulled out her scimitar and walked over to the book, to Flamarien's distress.

"This book is responsible for the murder of my brother and my parents. It's time it was murdered as well," she said.

With grim determination set upon her face, she grabbed her sword hilt with both hands and lifted them high over her head. She stabbed down with all her strength and the scimitar sliced through the center of the book and into the ground below it.

Crimson light began billowing out of the tear, beams reaching the clouds and beyond. She turned to shield her eyes and felt a rush of heat as the book exploded, knocking her twenty feet into the air.

Flamarien ran over to her prone form. She was covered in soot, but was breathing normally. He looked over his shoulder to where the book had been and noticed it had disintegrated, leaving her scimitar behind.

Serra opened her eyes and sat up, wiping the soot from her arms.

"That was not what I was expecting," she said simply.

Flamarien turned to her with a huge smile.

"If you had any doubts as to your performance this day, Lady Bloodmoon, know that you have achieved what no other has ever been able to do."

Epilogue

A month later the grounds of Bloodmoon Castle were teaming with patrons and visitors. Even the Feral Five had made the magical journey to be with their newfound friends on this special day. The torch poles were decorated with white, flowered garlands and each person wore their best clothing. The fountain in the courtyard had been filled with several white geese and the summer day was as glorious as the décor.

Serra stood before her chamber mirror in a gown of the whitest silk. Frelia fluffed her long train for perhaps the fiftieth time. The woman, who was dressed in a pretty, blue cotton dress, could not stem the tears that fell from her eyes.

"I can no' believe ye're gettin' married. Yer all grown up now. Yer ma would be so proud."

A knock on the door drew Serra from her contemplations and she watched as Frelia flocked to the door with a spring in her step.

Gnarl Knottytrunk, dressed in brilliant new mithril armor, walked in carrying a handful of white daisies. He stopped in his tracks when he saw the beauty before him.

"Ye look lovely," he whispered, his voice cracking.

Serra smiled and punched him in the arm.

"I came ter bring ye yer flowers, but I also wanted ter ask ye a question," he announced, shifting on his feet.

"What is it?" she asked, worried something was wrong.

The dwarf's cheeks turned the shade of his red hair and he grinned sheepishly.

"I was wonderin'... if ye'd let me give ye away."

Serra smiled and wiped a tear from her eye.

"I would be honored."

Dretho stood at the fountain under a trellis that had been built specially for the occasion. He had abandoned his black robes and was wearing a white tunic with a red silk sash and black breeches. Nefarius and Vlasisith stood next to him, dressed in their breastplates embossed with their wemic crest. Lorna, Sashaleona, and Kendrasha stood on the other side of the trellis dressed in red gowns. Lucadesiad stood under the trellis, waiting for his moment to arrive.

The great double doors of the castle opened and Sashaleona began to play her lute very softly.

Gnarl and Serra walked out of the castle and the people gathered in the courtyard stood from their wooden benches to honor the bride.

The elven mage's heart swelled at the sight of the one woman in the world that understood him. The one woman who loved him unconditionally.

As they stopped before the trellis, the people sat down and Sashaleona stopped playing.

"We are here on this glorious day to witness the vows of Lady Serra Bloodmoon and Dretholzar Derathliona. No other two people on Remus are more deserving of this moment than they. They have taught us many things these last days. One being that with friendship and cooperation, no battle is too great. Another being that no matter what race you are, you are equally welcome into their fold. And lastly, that no occurrence can break the bond of love that these two share," Lucadesiad began.

"Who gives this woman to be wed?"

"I do," Gnarl answered, emotion clearly etched in his voice and on his features.

Gnarl took Serra's hand and led her to Dretho's side. He then stepped back to stand beside Nefarius.

"You may now exchange your vows," Lucadesiad said, gesturing toward Dretho and Serra.

Dretho looked into her emerald eyes and smiled.

"Serra Bloodmoon, my love for you has grown complete over these past months. And I know now that I could love no other. You have shown me that I can be a better person and that your love holds no bounds. I promise to love, protect, and cherish you for the rest of my days," he said, taking her hands in his.

"Dretholzar Derathliona, you have shown me that love is not something to push away, but something to grab and take hold of, even at mortal peril. You have shown me that two heads are better than one in any situation and that you are the one person in this world that I can love unconditionally. I promise to love, protect, and cherish you for the rest of my days," she said, feeling her heard swell at her vows.

Lucadesiad nodded to Gnarl, who took two rings out of his pocket and handed them to the wemic cleric.

"Exchange your rings and know that these signify infinity, as your love is complete and never-ending."

Serra took the gold band she had chosen for Dretho and pushed it onto his left ring finger. Dretho took a gold ring, set with a bloodstone, and pushed it onto her left ring finger.

She smiled at the bloodstone. The same type of stone she now wore as a talisman on a silver chain about her neck.

"I now pronounce you, husband and wife. You may kiss the bride," Lucadesiad announced, smiling at Dretho.

Dretho pulled back Serra's thin veil and took her face into his hands. They kissed passionately and the courtyard erupted as patrons stood and cheered.

"I present to you, Dretholzar and Serra Derathliona."

Before they walked down the isle back into the castle, Serra stopped at the front row of seats to her left and stood beside the man standing there.

"I am glad you are here to see this day," she said with a smile.

Hildvar of the Elkhorn Tribe kissed her hand and nodded, with a tear in his eye.

Be sure to stay tuned for the next installment in The Trust Series by L R Barrett-Durham!

Spring 2012

Acknowledgements

There are so many people I am thankful for; it will be hard to list all of them. So, I will start off by thanking my husband, James. He's stood by my side for over eleven years now and never ceases to amaze me. I love you, babydoll.

I would also like to thank my son, Patrick. He's the greatest thing I ever did. I praise God every day for blessing me with such a cool little boy. Life is never dull at our house. I love you so much, punkin'.

Next, I thank Shara Ezelle, who read this book while I was writing it and loved it. She kept me going, even when I wasn't sure if I would finish.

And, of course, I would like to thank my mother, who encouraged me to publish this and is, well, my mom! Love you, mom.

I would also like to thank Melissa Johnson and Matthew Van Ormer. Avid readers who were kind enough to lend me their eyes and tell me what they thought.

And, of course, I thank the Ladies of the Round Table of Listerhill Credit Union. Always ready to lend me their thoughts, even if they make me blush.

And now, big time thanks go out to Wayne Parker, my impromptu editor, who found out I couldn't spell really quickly! And to his fabulous wife, Kristi, who kept on him about it. Thanks so much Wayne, you are a lifesaver!

Last, but certainly not least, I would like to thank God, who holds me in his hands every day and never gives up on me.

About the Author

L R Barrett-Durham lives in Cherokee, Alabama with her husband, son, and their two dogs. She works at a financial institution as a Network Technician. She is an artist at heart and loves all things crafty.

You can find L R Barrett-Durham at:

http://www.facebook.com/LRBarrettDurham

or

Email her at:

SerraBloodmoon@yahoo.com